THE DA...
DATING...

BY
SUE MacKAY

THE DOCTOR, HIS
DAUGHTER AND ME

BY
LEONIE KNIGHT

MILLS &
BOON

THE DANGERS OF
DATING YOUR BOSS

BY
SUE MacKAY

*Behind every author is a great editor. Thank you, Megan Haslam,
for your patience and wonderful encouragement.*

First published in Great Britain 2012
by Mills & Boon, an imprint of Harlequin (UK) Limited.
Harlequin (UK) Limited, Eton House, 18-24 Paradise Road,
Richmond, Surrey TW9 1SR

© Sue MacKay 2012

ISBN: 978 0 263 89788 3

Harlequin (UK) policy is to use papers that are natural, renewable
and recyclable products and made from wood grown in sustainable
forests. The logging and manufacturing process conform to the
legal environmental regulations of the country of origin.

Printed and bound in Spain
by Blackprint CPI, Barcelona

Jack's hands slid over her back—a caressing movement that stole the air out of her lungs, nullified the common sense trying to take hold of her mind.

When he wrapped his hands over her shoulders and tipped her slightly backwards she knew he was going to kiss her and she was powerless to stop him. She wanted it. Forget right or wrong. This was Jack and she was finally kissing him. Common sense was highly overrated.

His mouth touched hers: softly, tentatively. Seeking what? A connection from the past? A new beginning? She thrilled as his lips moulded with hers. And when she opened her mouth under his her tongue tasted him. Jack went from slow and quiet to fast and hot in an instant. His kiss deepened so quickly Ruby was spinning through space. Her arms gripped him tighter for support, trying to keep herself firmly in the here and now as she tilted further back to allow Jack better access to her mouth.

At last. She was kissing Jack Forbes again. Memories of other kisses flooded her senses. Nothing over those years had changed. They fitted together. They were two halves that needed their matching piece to be complete. And yet this kiss felt different from every other kiss she'd shared with Jack. Filled with need so long held in abeyance. Filled with the promise of new beginnings...

Dear Reader

Welcome to Wellington, New Zealand's capital city. Affectionately known as Windy Wellington, the city sits on the edge of a large harbour where ferries regularly ply back and forth across the wild Cook Strait to the South Island.

I haven't set a story in a large city before, and have only touched on a very small piece of this one. I love using real settings that I know, because the moment I sit down to write I'm transported to that place. I can share the memories of wandering along a certain beach or walking through a busy street or cycling in the hills.

Ruby and Jack both love Wellington. It's just taken Ruby a long time and some life-changing experiences to realise that. Coming home to settle down is exciting for her, while Jack's finally decided there's got to be more to life and it's probably not in his home town.

I hope you enjoy the journey these two take to overcome their previous broken relationship and to find common ground for starting over…together.

Cheers!

Sue MacKay

CHAPTER ONE

'IF I DON'T eat in the next five minutes I'm going to slip into a coma,' Ruby Smith told her boss and crew partner, Dave.

'Yeah, yeah. Heard it all before. Didn't you have breakfast?' Dave stacked the two medical packs at the helicopter door, ready to be taken into the storeroom and replenished.

'That was hours ago.' She glanced at her watch. 'Six hours ago, to be precise.' A call had come through as she'd been about to sit down to a hot steak pie from the local bakery. Now they'd just returned from an MVA on State Highway One. They'd airlifted a young man with both femurs broken and one femoral artery torn to Hutt Hospital.

'Hey, Red, is that you?' A deep, male voice with a slight rasp called from down on the tarmac.

Ruby's heart leapt into her throat. Jack? Even after years apart, that voice was as familiar to her as her own. And it still had the power to unravel her carefully put-together resolve to keep him at arm's length. That voice had been what had first attracted her to Jack, the only man she'd ever loved. The man she'd walked away from. For the dumbest of reasons.

But what was Jack doing here? Today? He wasn't due to start until Monday, when she'd have been prepared. Right now she was still getting her head around all the ramifications of working with him. Would it be like old times? Jack the consummate professional watching her like a hawk, always teaching her, helping her improve her nursing skills? And would she be listening impatiently, wanting to touch him every time no one was looking? A sigh tickled over her lip. Want to or not, she had to keep her hands to herself. She'd go around with them jammed in her pockets if necessary. She'd moved on, grown up, knew her worth. So if there were a few blips between them as they got used to working together again, she'd survive.

There was no choice. Wellington was home now. Never again would she toss her few possessions into her pack and head away. She'd even burnt that pack against the day wanderlust struck again. She'd done her searching, found what she'd been looking for and sucked up the pain from knowing she'd wasted years of her life because of it. To let Jack back under her skin would risk her newfound and fragile contentment.

She peered out into the glittering winter sun, gripping the doorframe, her knuckles white. Jack, tall and slim, emanated strength in his stance as he stared up at her. Her mouth dried. Solid need sliced through her, heating and freezing her all at once. Need she believed she'd finally wrestled into submission. Jack Forbes. Her new boss and crew partner. Her old lover.

She couldn't do this. She had to do this. 'Hi, Jack,' she managed feebly. *Hi, gorgeous,* her brain mocked her.

He grinned his well-practised, impish grin that had always got him everything he wanted, including her. 'Get your butt out of that flying machine and come say hello to an old mate.'

So that was how he was going to play it. Mates. She could work with that, and it was a better start than she'd hoped for. Ruby jumped down onto the tarmac, grimacing as she jarred her bung knee. Tugging her shoulders back tight, she strode towards the moment she'd been both look-ing forward to and dreading since returning home to New Zealand. She strode towards Jack, apparently her friend. She hadn't been sure if she was as over this man as she should be. And now? The jury was out.

'Jack, it's great to see you.' Talk about the understate-ment of the year. Of her life.

'Great to see ya, ruby-red girl.' His old greeting. The one he'd shouted out as he'd come in the door at night, when he'd rolled over in bed in the morning.

Ruby's heart tripped. Ruby-red girl. Did he even realise what he'd said? She blinked up at him, saw his Adam's apple bob and shoved down the sense of drowning brought on by that greeting. Fixing a tight smile on her face, she desperately hoped she'd managed to hide the shock blow-ing through her at the close-up sight of him. Jack had al-ways been a handsome dude, but three years on and wow. Her fingers tingled. Her stomach crunched. Lust, pure and simple, hot and complex, bubbled through her. Oh, boy, this reunion wasn't supposed to be filled with desire and temptation. Mates, remember? 'To think you're going to be working on the helicopters.'

'Why wouldn't I?' His grin faded. 'I was blown away when I saw *your* name on the staff list. I didn't know you were back in the country, let alone Wellington.' His eyes narrowed as he looked her over with a familiar slow slide down her body that made her blood race and lifted goose-bumps on her skin. Made her want him. Badly.

The whole thing about having to work with Jack had just got monumentally harder. She fought the flare of an-noyance that he could make her feel like this so easily after such a long time. 'I know what you mean. To think you'd even consider leaving the emergency department came as a bombshell.' That was the truth.

'I'm full of surprises.' Was that a hint of sarcasm in his tone?

'Maybe I've got a few of my own,' she retorted. Like the house she'd bought and the renovations she was doing to it, like her cute little friend sharing the place with her. If those things didn't astonish Jack then he must have turned to stone over the years she'd been away.

Then a memory swamped her, flattening her with shame.

Three years ago Jack's face had registered shock and disbelief over her biggest surprise ever. 'You're really going? Leaving Wellington? Leaving me?'

'I have to. I'm never going to find my father by staying here, and since I've learned he's American it makes sense to go over to the States. Come on, Jack, try to understand. For the first time ever I've got a starting point. How could I not go?' Her hands had trembled so much she'd dropped her dinner plate and splattered her meal all over the floor. 'You could come with me,' she'd whispered in desperation.

'Sure, Red, just drop everything and leave. Like it's that easy. I've got nearly a year to go before I qualify as an emergency specialist. Stopping in midstream just isn't possible.' He'd taken her cold hands in his. 'You could wait for me.'

She'd shaken her head, beating down the urge to fling herself in his arms and hold on for ever. 'I can't. I've waited all my life to meet my dad and this is the closest I've ever got to finding him. This is so important to me. I have to go.' Jack had been just as important, maybe more, but she'd foolishly believed finding her parent had been paramount.

Jack's face had been bleak, his eyes dark with sadness.

'*Until you do this you're never going to be completely happy, are you? Not even with me?*'

She hadn't been able to answer him for the lump in her throat.

That was when the arguments had begun, almost as a defence mechanism to protect their shattering hearts. They'd agreed they had to make a clean break but the days before she'd flown out had been intense as they'd crammed as much loving as possible into the little time left.

Now Jack lifted a hand in a stop sign, worry darkening his all-seeing eyes. 'Hey, let's leave the past alone. After all, it isn't called the past for nothing.'

Ouch. 'True. This is a different job; we're probably different people now.' She certainly was. Forcing a smile, she asked, 'So how's life been treating you? You're looking pretty good for an old guy.'

His smoky grey eyes lightened, twinkled, the crinkles at their corners bunching up. That heart-stopping smile lifted his mouth. And cramped her stomach. 'Can't complain. And less of the "old guy" stuff. Turning thirty was an event, not a disaster.'

So why the sudden doubt reflecting back at her? Jack had always been confident, in control. Doubt hadn't even been in his vocabulary. These days she wasn't in a position to ask anything personal. Not that he'd tell her anyway. Talking about the things that bothered him wasn't in his make-up. He took everything life tossed at him and moved on with a nonchalance that hid his true feelings. He was a rock. The person everyone could, and did, rely on in all situations. He didn't ever ask anyone to prop him up.

So she knocked on her head in fun. 'Of course, you've had one of those big birthdays.' She did a quick tap dance on the spot, checked him out. 'I hope that means everything's okay with you, no bits rotting and dropping off your wrinkled old frame.'

'Heck, Red, I've missed your cheek. No one else is ever so damned rude to me.' Suddenly Ruby's feet were off the ground as Jack swung her up against his hard-muscled frame and engulfed her in a bear hug.

'So who's been keeping you in line, then?' she gasped against his chest. His heart pounded under her ear. Strong and steady, like Jack. His arms were muscular and warm around her back. Just like old times. As her bones liquefied with longing, she wriggled to be set free in case she did something dumb like press in against him and hold on for ever.

Jack tightened his grip, but he didn't answer her question. 'You're looking good, girl. Even with that weird spiky hair and the glaring scarlet colour you've dunked it in,' he murmured against her ear, sending thrilling shivers down her spine. 'What happened to that beautiful, sherry-coloured mane?'

It had reminded her of Jack too much. Every time she'd looked in a mirror after they'd broken up her heart had snapped in half all over again. 'It was a nuisance whenever I put my headpiece on in the 'copter.'

'Fair enough.' His disappointed sigh blew against her cheek. His arms tightened further. 'Pity, though.'

She murmured against his jacket, 'You would say that. You didn't have to look after the darned stuff.' But he had spent hours brushing the waist-length hair that had been her one vanity. She quickly added, in case he thought she was stirring up trouble, 'It was a full-time job.'

When his fingers pressed a little harder into her waist Ruby felt a pull of the love they'd once shared. A steady love emanating from Jack's goodness, strength and caring. Added to by her quirky sense of humour and the wonder she'd felt at someone so smart wanting *her*. Not even her beloved mother had made her feel as good, as safe, as Jack had. And just as she'd done with her mother's love, she'd fought that feeling, turned it against herself, shunned Jack's love for her own needs, thereby ruining something very special and worth holding on to at all costs. Hindsight sucked. Big time.

Would she get a second chance?

Ruby breathed Jack in. The scent of pine needles teased her and brought back recollections of long, frenetic afternoons spent making love. So he still wore the same aftershave. What else did he do the same? Was he even the same person? Not if that doubt in his eyes was an indicator.

Then, as suddenly as he'd lifted her into his arms, he plonked her back on the ground. She stumbled as she struggled to maintain her balance. A firm grip on her elbow helped, until a zing of heat spiralled up the inside of her arm, warming the sensitive skin.

'Careful.' His tone was suddenly abrupt.

'Thanks.' Tugging her arm free, she rubbed hard to dissipate the heat he'd so easily generated. Looking up, she found Jack studying her with the same disconcerting expression in those eyes that had haunted her from the moment she'd walked away from him at the airport. The expression that said you didn't know what you had until you lost it. How true that had turned out to be.

Jack jerked his head up, looking beyond them, as though suddenly remembering where he was, who he was talking to. He would soon be in charge of the Wellington Helicopter Rescue base and she was a crew member. 'So you're now a paramedic on the rescue helicopters. That's quite a sideways step from the emergency nurse you desperately wanted to be.'

'Close enough to the same thing. Emergency department, ambulance crew.' Her spread hand flipped left and right. 'No different from what you're doing by taking up this position, I'd have thought.' She strove to avoid what he was really saying: that she never finished anything she started. How could she? She'd always been too busy moving on to stay anywhere long enough to see any project through.

But for the first time in her life she had completed something, something very important to her. A genuine certificate hung on her bedroom wall. Signed by the Chief of Ambulance Services, San Francisco.

Ruby Smith, Advanced Paramedic. Honours. Right alongside the citation for bravery during duty. And on the other side hung the nursing certificate she'd finally obtained in the States.

If only her mother could see those certificates. She'd have been pleased with her daughter for once. The only other person she'd wanted to share her success with at the time now stood in front of her and it was too late. He might know she'd finally qualified at something but he hadn't been there to share in the sheer wonder of achievement. Because of all her stupid mistakes she'd been alone.

From the day she decided to head back here she'd known she'd eventually catch up with Jack. This was the first city she'd ever returned to. She'd come back for Jack, because of Jack. Wellington was Jack. And yet she'd been dragging her heels about calling him. Afraid to find out he'd moved on and barely remembered her.

Ruby closed her eyes briefly. This was way too hard. *Be strong, be tough.* She repeated the mantra that had got her through the last few years, and then diverted the conversation to safe ground. Again.

'I didn't think you were starting with us until next

week.' Ruby huffed out a breath and tipped her head back to stare up at him. 'Did I read the wrong memo?'

He grinned that grin, though his eyes were a little slow in keeping up. 'I've been at the aero club for a couple of hours. Since the club's almost next door I figured I'd cruise over here and meet whoever was on duty.'

'Aero club? Your brother still flying those little things?' She glanced across the tarmac at the tiny planes pegged down outside the clubrooms.

'No, Steve's on jumbos these days. It's me who's flying those Tomahawks you're staring at.' A deep chuckle rumbled through him. Another familiar, heart-warming thing she'd missed, desperately at times when she'd been terribly lonely.

'No way.' She grinned as she swivelled back to gape at him. Jack had never had time for play. 'Really? You're learning to fly?'

'And loving every minute I get in the air.' Another chuckle. But it sounded brittle. Something was wrong with this picture. Was happy Jack not really so happy?

'Can you take me up one day?' Bad question. Mouth on the run.

Taking a backward step, Jack told her firmly, 'Sorry, no passengers allowed until I've got my licence.'

He needn't look so relieved. 'How many hours have you flown?'

'Twenty-seven and I need at least fifty before my flight test.' He looked towards the helicopter. 'Want to introduce me?'

Yikes. She'd totally forgotten Dave waiting for her to help tidy up the aircraft's interior. She spun back to the 'copter looming above her, talking to Jack over her shoulder, trying not to stare at his beloved face. 'I thought you

two would've met already since it's his job you're taking over.'

'When I came out here with the director, Dave was away
on a job.'

'Then you'll both have lots to discuss.' She called up,
'Dave, come out here for a moment. Please.'

Dave poked his head out. 'So how come you didn't kill
this guy for calling you Red?'

Because Jack had always called her that. She hated anyone else using the nickname because it tainted her sweet
memories of him, and played havoc with the sexy ones as
well. 'He's going to be my boss.'

'Didn't stop you reading the Riot Act when I dared to
call you Red.' Dave looked across at Jack, then back at
her, a hint of worry in his eyes. 'So you two already know
each other.' Was he wondering if this would affect the job
situation? If it did then Jack could swap crews.

'We worked together once.' In another, totally different
life. Ruby gritted her teeth. 'I was a trainee nurse, Jack
was a bossy intern.'

Jack grunted. 'Me? Bossy? I'd have given you that hat,
Red.'

'Medicine's a small world.' The older man smiled down
at Jack. 'Well, hi, there, anyway, welcome aboard. You're
in for some adventures for sure.'

'There'll definitely be some interesting days,' Ruby seconded her partner. Like when the weather was atrocious
and any flying became scary. She never admitted to those
fears, just tightened her harness and pretended nothing was
wrong. Now she officially introduced the two men. 'Dave,
this is Jack Forbes.' She watched them size each other up
in a man kind of way as they reached to shake hands.

They must've decided the other was okay because
within moments Dave handed down the packs to Ruby

and invited Jack on board for a cursory rundown on how things worked.

'I'll leave you two to it,' Ruby said as she slung one pack over her shoulders. 'When I've topped these up, I'll put a brew on.' And finally get to eat that pie. It'd be cold and congealed but right now it made her mouth water and her stomach expand with hope.

Jack reached for the second heavy bag. 'I'll take this one in for you.'

Ruby grabbed it out of his hand. The bags were heavy but she never, ever let the men carry them for her, even on the days her damaged knee played up. Hauling them was part of her job. 'I'm fine with it. Dave's got lots to show you.'

'I'm not a greenhorn, Red. I've done the training, know where everything is kept, how to activate the winch, how to use the radio.' Exasperation tinged his voice.

'Still, each 'copter has a slightly different configuration. You might as well take a look with Dave while it's quiet.'

Jack shook his head. 'And I thought I was in charge.'

'Not until tomorrow.' Ruby winked at him. 'And only once you've been out for three retrievals.'

Not entirely true but the crews checked out a newbie on the first few trips before accepting him or her completely. Being an A and E specialist with loads of experience wouldn't save his backside. Working with the limited resources they carried in the helicopter was very different from being in a fully equipped emergency department, not to mention the situations they often found themselves in.

Ruby saw a frown developing on Jack's forehead. He'd hate her telling him to take a back seat, but he'd better get used to it. The other crew members would be tougher.

His eyes narrowed. 'Three? First I've heard of it.'

'Don't tell me that you didn't keep an eye on any new staff in the emergency department?'

'Of course I did. It goes with the territory,' he snapped.

Where had that come from? 'Relax, we're a friendly lot. You'll be a perfect fit in our team.'

Jack blinked, flexed and shook his hands, loosened his shoulders, then pushed a cautious smile across his mouth. 'You're presuming I haven't taken up any edgy hobbies lately.'

'You betcha.' One thing she could be sure of, he didn't do edgy. Except he was now learning to fly. For Jack, that really was putting himself out there, a bit like hanging off a cliff on a dodgy rope. Who was this Jack? She didn't entirely recognise him and yet he looked the same. More mature, more handsome, sexier than ever but still the same. Yet something was different. That flicker of doubt in his eyes, that sudden annoyance with her, for starters.

Maybe she was looking too hard. More likely he was reacting to seeing her again. Not easy for either of them.

Ruby headed for the hangar before she got tangled up in trying to solve the puzzle. The next four months would give her plenty of time to sort Jack out. Not to mention her own mixed-up feelings towards him.

Jack's hands gripped his hips as he watched Red lug those bags across the tarmac. She displayed all the nonchalance of a weightlifter. Her slight, short frame was taut, her boots heavy as they trod the concrete. She'd already got to him. Anger flared quickly, fizzed along his veins. This was supposed to be the start of a whole new life for him, not a revisiting of the old one. He'd broken his heart over her once. That had been bad luck. To let it happen again would be plain careless.

If he had known she was back in town, would he have

quit his Head of Department position? Damn right he would have. Ruby had long given up the right to alter his life decisions. And this job was the result of those decisions.

He tossed caution aside, and called, 'Hey, Red, I'm going to give you a hand.'

She turned slowly, balancing carefully, smiling widely, fixedly. 'Got two perfectly good ones of my own, thanks.'

A familiar 'don't fool with me' look had snapped into her big green eyes. Was it because he dared to question her capabilities? Was she more confident these days? Or better at hiding her insecurities?

Jack tried to grin back. He didn't do so well. 'That was my last offer.'

'No worries.'

Was she favouring her left leg? 'Did you jar your leg when you jumped down? You look like you're limping.'

Her smile tightened further, warning lights switched on in those piercing eyes. 'I'm perfectly fit, thank you.'

'I don't doubt you are but I'm allowed to show an interest in my colleagues.' With a fierce flick of his shoulders he filed her limp in the dossier in his mind. For now. Remain aloof with her. Do not get involved. Was there a textbook on how to behave around ex-girlfriends?

'She's a tough one,' Dave said behind him. 'Doesn't like any of the men singling her out to give her a break with some of the heavy stuff.'

Huh? Since when? 'Ruby wasn't always like that.' Jack clambered inside the gleaming red helicopter. 'Guess I don't know her as well as I used to,' he added as he looked around the compact interior. At last the excitement he was supposed to feel for this job began leaking into him.

'People change,' Dave muttered.

Jack winced. Yeah, that was exactly why he was here

instead of running the emergency department. 'I'm sure we'll get along just fine.'

Dave said, 'Funny thing but Ruby's tough-girl attitude actually makes all of us try to do more for her than you'd normally expect. On and off base. All the crews are close, and we spend a lot of time together, but with Ruby we seem to go those extra miles, if you know what I mean?'

'I'll keep that in mind.' And keep my distance. Going the extra mile might take him a lot closer to Red than was healthy for his future plans. Or for his body if his over-heated reaction when he'd held her minutes ago was any-thing to go by. How would he put distance between them when they were stuffed inside this cramped area?

'Good.' Dave turned back to the stretcher he was clean-ing.

Jack studied the man he'd be relieving. 'You worried I'll have scared her off by the time you come back?' Ruby would go, but not because of him. Moving on was her modus operandi. Ironic that soon he would be heading away too.

'We've got an excellent group of very professional people working here now and I'd hate to see the status quo change. If my wife hadn't gone and bought our tickets and booked our tours, I probably wouldn't be going to Europe this year.' Dave's brow creased. 'Which is why Gail did it, of course. Women are very crafty, aren't they?'

'They can be.' But not Red. She was more like a moth continuously flying at the light, getting nowhere. Always a tight coil of tense muscles with a sharp tongue to match. Jack used to wind her up just so they could kiss and make up later. He'd be wise to remember that in the weeks to come and ignore any outbursts. There'd be no making up now. Forget those heady kisses, the hottest sex he'd ever experienced and a lot of plain old fun and laughter. Forget how she could melt into absolute sweetness at the most unexpected moments.

Start with remembering her name was Ruby. Not Red. And that she wasn't his type of woman. He took another glance outside, his eyes tracking the one woman he'd ever cared about. His gut twisted. Red's sassy butt still swayed saucily. Sex in boots. Hot sex in a jumpsuit. 'It's been a while.'

Since he'd seen her. Since he'd held her in his arms and kissed her senseless. Since— Stop. Tormenting himself would only lead to trouble. But she'd felt wonderful when he'd lifted her up against his chest minutes ago. Warm, lithe, exciting.

'Odd that she didn't mention knowing you.' Dave's words crashed into his brain, slamming him back to reality.

Words that stung. Hard and deep. He shouldn't be surprised. When he and Red agreed to split they'd both made it perfectly clear there'd be no going back on their decision. But surely that hadn't meant they couldn't acknowledge one another. 'It was a few years ago. How long has she been working with you?'

'Two months. Came straight from San Francisco.'

'Two months?' Jack all but shouted. If Ruby had kicked him in the guts it couldn't have hurt any worse. Two months and not a word. Talk about putting him in his place. Sensing Dave's eagle eye on him, he bit down on the oath hovering on the tip of his tongue and tried for casually unconcerned. 'I've got a lot of catching up to do with her.' But not on this shift.

'She certainly has great work experience. Her credentials are superb.'

'It's the first time Ruby's actually stuck at anything long enough to qualify.' Amazing. And as far as he knew it was also the first time she'd returned anywhere. Had she finally tracked down her father and dealt with the past? That was the only explanation for her spending long enough in one place to put in the required hours to become a paramedic. Did that mean her angst had disappeared? Did a dog suddenly grow wool on its back?

Jack asked, 'Is Ruby still taking on everyone head first? Like she has to knock them down before they get to her?' He shouldn't be asking Dave, but he was speaking boss to boss here, needing to know about a member of his crew.

Believe that and he'd believe anything.

Dave studied him thoughtfully. Was he having doubts about leaving his job in Jack's hands? 'Can't say as I've noticed. And working in stressful situations on a daily basis I think I would've. Is that the Ruby you used to know?'

Already regretting his question, Jack nodded. He'd hate for Dave to think differently of Ruby because of him. 'She used to have a few issues that distressed her big time but from what you're saying maybe she's sorted them out.'

'Some relationships don't stand the test of time, do they?' Dave was studying him with a glint in his eye suggesting he'd somehow be watching out for Ruby even from afar, making sure his replacement didn't upset her. Nice to know she had such a good friend. The man hadn't finished. 'But others can.'

Shaking his head, Jack muttered, 'Not this one.'

Dave shrugged. 'That's a shame. I get the feeling Ruby's ready to settle down.'

'Then you really don't know her.' Ruby didn't do settling down. Ever. Not like him. He'd been happy to stay in this place where he'd lived all his life. Until recently. Now he was so restless he itched. He was on the move, done with being the man everyone relied on to be a permanent fixture for them, of always being around when others found their lives going pear-shaped. It was time for his own adventures, and no one, not even a certain scarlet-haired woman, was going to upset this. *Look out, world, Jack Forbes is coming. Yeah, right.*

Jack forced a smile as he continued to watch her disappearing inside. She was as sexy as ever. His body had recognised her instantly. That slow burn starting in the pit of his belly when he'd seen her in the helicopter. And now it had spread out, down and up, engulfing every cell of his body. He wanted her. As strongly as he always had. *Great to see ya, ruby-red girl.*

Enough. Just seeing Red made him reel. Why he'd lifted her into that hug was beyond him, but nothing could've stopped him when she'd dropped to the ground right in front of him. To feel her body along the length of his, to touch that spiky hair with his chin, had brought longing charging through him. He flicked his finger against his thumb. *Dumb ass.*

So much for keeping everything on a boss to crew member basis. Should he hug every member? For a brief moment with Ruby in his arms he'd felt as though they'd never been apart. As if all that pain hadn't happened, hadn't torn him into shreds.

Jack turned and deliberately began studying the interior of the aircraft that would become a big part of his life for the next few months. 'It's a bit of a squeeze.'

Dave grinned. 'Takes some getting used to.'

'And I'm always at the front,' a man drawled from the other side of the bulkhead. 'Along with Slats. He's ducked into the hangar for a minute.'

Dave grinned. 'Chris, get through here and meet Jack.' To Jack he said, 'This guy is one hell of a pilot. You want him with you when the sky's full of bumps.'

Jack shook hands with the man who didn't look old

enough to have left school let alone know how to fly one
of these massive helicopters. 'Good to meet you. How
many hours have you done on this bird?'

Chris laughed. 'More than you'd ever believe. For the
record, I stopped drinking milk thirty years ago.'

The man had to be pulling his leg. The same age as him?
Nah, couldn't be. But Chris looked like he meant it. 'Bet
you have to produce your ID every time you buy a beer.'

'Damned pain at times,' Dave muttered. 'But that innocent face pulls the girls, make no mistake.'

Jack could believe it. What about Ruby? Was she a fan
of the pilot? As in had she been out with him, been to bed
with him? A cold knot formed in Jack's belly. There had
to be a man in her life. A very attractive, sexy woman always had a man, and Red was both. But it wasn't his place
to comment, despite the chill creeping over his skin. Red
was a free agent. Like him. The fact that they were going
to work together again didn't give him any rights over who
she went out with. *So behave, Jacko.*

Jack dragged his hand down his cheek. As her boss, he
had to learn about her situation, as he did boss all the staff.
If anyone's private life was out of sync over anything at
all he'd want to know about it. Happy staff meant a happy
work environment, which in turn meant everyone pulled
together to give an exceptionally good service to the public.

Just remember her name was Ruby, not Red, and he
should be able to keep everything in perspective. Haa!

CHAPTER TWO

JULIE, the part-time office lady, stood in the middle of the hangar, staring over at the helicopter. 'So who's the hottie?'

Ruby grinned at her. 'Jack Forbes.'

'As in Dave's replacement? No way. He's got a body to die for. And that face, that grin…' Julie spluttered to a halt, her eyes enormous.

Ruby shook her head. 'Too hot to handle?'

Flapping her hands at her cheeks, Julie replied, 'Remind me to bring my oven mitts to work tomorrow.'

'Got two pairs?' There was no point denying Jack's good looks. That would only make people question her ability to see.

'Guess you'll need them more than me, since you'll be working alongside him. Wonder what he's like behind those looks?'

'Imperturbable,' she muttered. Gorgeous, funny, trustworthy, lovable Jack.

'You already know him?' Julie's perfectly styled eyebrows rose as she continued to stare in the direction of the helicopter.

'From the days when I was training to be a nurse.' She'd spent seven months in Wellington, on her way from Nelson to somewhere else, which, on the death of her mother, had

turned out to be Seattle. Her training had spread over four
cities, and had to be the most erratic on record.

'You weren't an item? You know, had a doctors-and-
nurses thing going on?'

They'd certainly had something going on, something
very hot. Don't forget the love. There'd been plenty of that
too. But not enough to keep them together. What if she
was incapable of loving someone enough to get through
all the things that got tossed up along the way?

She shuddered, shoved that idea out of the way and said
to Julie, 'If I didn't know how happily married you were,
I'd be arranging a date for you with Jack.' If he wasn't
already in a relationship with the stunning, lithe blonde
Ruby had seen him with in a café four weeks ago. Blondie
had been as close to Jack as sticking plaster, and he hadn't
been objecting. Ruby tripped on an uneven piece of concrete. Her knee jagged. She sucked air through her teeth
and swore to be more careful.

Julie chuckled. 'Looking's fine. It's the touching that
gets people into trouble.'

Ruby winced. Didn't she know it? Touching Jack had always led to a lot of up-close involvement, a conflagration,
so there'd be absolutely no touching this time round. Huge
problems lurked there that she wasn't ready to face. Jack
was her past, no matter how much she suddenly wished
otherwise. She'd hurt him once, she wouldn't do that to
him again. Or to herself. She headed the subject to safer
ground. 'How come you're here on a Sunday?'

Julie told her, 'I'm taking tomorrow morning off so I
can go on a school trip with my girls. There's a pile of reports that need filing with the health department before
Wednesday so here I am.'

'I'd better get these bags sorted.' Ruby reached the storeroom, exhaling the breath she'd been holding while study-

ing Jack. The sight of him made her giddy, while being near him, being held in that embrace, had made her feel somehow complete. As only Jack had ever made her feel. Damn him. If she'd stayed in Wellington way back then she'd have saved herself a lot of anguish with her father. *And* she'd still be in a relationship with Jack.

Or would she? They'd both had a lot of personal issues to sort out that might've strained their relationship to the point it couldn't survive. Could be they'd both needed to grow up. Ruby blinked. Definitely true of her. Not so sure about Jack. Did he still resent his father for leaning too hard on him for support? How strange that set-up had been. Parents were supposed to look out for their kids, not the other way round. But of course Jack had never gone into any detail about his family so she only had half the story.

Grabbing at airway tubes, she quickly topped up the bags, while musing on the past. Staying put in one place had been an alien concept for her. That she'd even considered stopping here three years ago spoke volumes about her feelings for Jack. But in the end the forces that had driven her relentlessly onward all her life had won out. Not even for the love of her life, Jack, could she have given up something that had eaten at her as far back as she could recall.

Julie stood in the doorway. 'You planning on smashing those vials or what?'

Ruby looked at the replacement drugs she'd just rammed into their slots. 'Guess not.'

'Mr Gorgeous has got to you already, hasn't he?'

Unfortunately, yes. 'I'll get over it. You wanted me for something?'

'Can you translate Jason's writing for me?' Julie held a report form out to her. 'Sometimes I wonder if medical staff do a 101 course in Scribble.'

'Doctors say it's because they're always frantically busy.' At least that was what Jack used to tell her.

Jack. Jack. Jack. Suddenly everything came back to him. Already there was no avoiding him. It was so unfair. She'd come here first, this was her job, her sanctuary. There were plenty of places out there for an emergency specialist to work. *Why pick this one, Jack?* Despair crunched inside her. It was hard enough getting her life on track and keeping it there, without the added difficulty of having to spend twelve hours a day with a man who knew the old Ruby. And who was going to struggle to believe the new version she'd made herself into—if he'd even take the time to get to know her again. And suddenly she really, really wanted him to.

Julie laughed. 'That's a cop-out. But, then, most people blame texting for their appalling spelling too. Lazy, I reckon.' She turned for her office. 'I've put the kettle on.'

'Ta. I'll tell the guys.' Ruby cringed. A cop-out. Her father had come up with a million reasons for never coming to New Zealand to meet her, all of them cop-outs. If only she'd believed her mother, whom she'd badgered incessantly all her life for more information about the airman she'd imagined to be a hero. But her mother had only ever said Ruby was better off not knowing him.

As a child Ruby had waited for him to turn up bearing gifts and hugs. He would tell her he was home for good and that they'd have a happy life doing all the things her mother couldn't afford to do. Not until she'd packed up her mother's home after her death did Ruby learn her dad was American and had been in the US Air Force. Her parents had met when her father's plane had stopped in Christchurch for a few days on the way to Antarctica.

Finally it hadn't been too difficult to finally track down the man who'd spawned her. Reality had been harsh. The hero of her childhood had turned out to be a total nightmare. Her humiliation at her father's lifestyle equalled her embarrassment at how badly she'd treated her mother over the years. Then had come the acute disappointment at the realisation she'd given up Jack for that man.

The Greaser—she no longer called him her father—was a good-looking man who'd used his abundant charm to marry into a fortune and produce offspring to keep everyone onside, especially his wealthy father-in-law, while he philandered his way through half his town's women.

Outside, Ruby heaved one of the replenished packs up into the helicopter. 'Kettle's boiled.' At last she'd get to eat that sorry-looking pie. Her stomach rolled over in happy anticipation.

Jack took the pack and strapped it into place. 'We're about done in here.'

She bent down for the other bag, grimacing as she lifted the heavy weight up.

'Here, give me that.' Jack reached down and took the load from her, his fingers brushing hers.

Instant heat sizzled up her arms. Clenching her hands at her sides, she spoke too loudly. 'Thanks. It goes—'

'Over there by the stretcher,' Jack finished with a growl, his eyebrows nearly meeting in the middle of his forehead. His gaze appeared stuck on a spot behind her head while shock flicked through his eyes. So he'd felt the same sparks too. The sparks that made everything so much more difficult.

'Glad you've got it sussed.' It was important. If any equipment got put away in the wrong place, it could delay things in an emergency.

'It's not rocket science.' A glint in his eye warned her he wasn't happy with her telling him anything about the helicopter.

'You didn't used to be so touchy.' But he had touched her often.

Jack dropped down beside her, and unsure of him, she tensed, waiting for him to bawl her out, ready to meet him head on. Instead he stole the breath from her by saying, 'So, a paramedic, eh? Did you ever finish your nursing certificate?'

'Advanced paramedic, actually.'

'Sorry, advanced paramedic.' His eyebrows rose. 'That's fantastic. I'm glad you qualified. You certainly have the smarts.'

She straightened a little at his compliment. 'Yes, I did finish the year on the wards required to finalise my nurse's practising certificate.' She'd worked extremely hard to get all her qualifications. Not being satisfied with a pass, she'd aimed for the highest grades possible. That had been the first good turning point in her life. Jack could raise his eyebrows all he liked but he wouldn't dent her pride in her accomplishments. 'I trained on the ambulances in San Francisco. Then during the last four months there I took a rotation on the rescue helicopters, which stood me in good stead for this job.' She'd found her niche. Nothing, nobody would make her give it up. Not a bung knee. Definitely not Jack.

'San Francisco, eh?' His tone was acid and he stared straight ahead as they walked towards the hangar and the staffrooms.

Beside him she grinned, refusing to be intimidated by his attitude. He might think he still knew her but, boy, oh, boy, he didn't have a clue. She'd returned to Wellington, this time permanently. This was the first city in a long line of cities that she'd come back to. Might as well get some of the details out of the way, let him have his 'I told you so' moment. 'I started in Seattle, then went to Vancouver. I really loved Canada but couldn't get a job without a work permit. Back in the States I headed down to Kansas, LA, San Diego and finally San Francisco.' She wasn't going to enlighten him about her reasons for all that tripping around. Not yet anyway. Not unless they got past being mates. Which, right now, looked doubtful. *Unfortunately.*

'When did you find time to fit in your training?' Strong acid.

'I lived in San Fran for two years, ample time to qualify. My nursing training put me ahead on the course when I started on the ambulance.' And she'd focused entirely on her job, no sexy distractions anywhere in sight.

'Two years in one spot?' The acid sweetened up a little. 'Did you ever come back here for a visit?'

'No. Too busy.' And, because they'd agreed their break-up was final, there'd been nothing, no one, to come back for.

'Where are you living now?'

'I bought a villa on Mount Victoria.' Glancing sideways, she saw his eyebrows lift, his lips tighten, and she braced herself.

His words dripped sarcasm. 'Don't tell me you're set-tling down? Not you. Come on, I bet you've still got that backpack in the corner of your wardrobe, waiting for the day you've had enough of Wellington.'

'Long gone, fallen apart from overuse.' Not a great testament to her reliability. But, 'I'm renovating the house. It's so out of date and colder than an iceberg now that win-ter's here. The electricity and plumbing need completely redoing, not to mention the antiquated kitchen and a bath-room requiring a total refit.' All of which were already guzzling up cash like a thirsty dog.

'You haven't exactly answered my question. How long do you think you'll be around this time?' His mouth was still tight, but his eyebrows were back in place. 'You never showed any interest in owning a house. Too much of a tie, you reckoned, if I recall correctly.'

Which, of course, he did. But that had been aeons ago. And deep down she had wanted a home but fear of not being able to make a success of it had driven her to deny the need. What had she ever known about setting up a permanent home? Continuing to ignore his underlying disbelief, she said, 'The villa's eighty-nine years old, and showing its age. But I love it. There's so much potential.'

'Oh, right. You'll be here until you've done the house up. A quick lick of paint? Some new carpet?' He held the door to the staff kitchen open for her. 'Can't quite picture you as a house renovator.'

'Give me a break. I've never had the opportunity before.' And they both knew that had been her fault.

Behind her Dave piped up. 'Ruby's a dab hand at pulling down walls. You should see her swinging a hammer.'

'That's the best bit,' she agreed, grateful for Dave's support.

Jack peered down at her. 'You do know what you're doing, Ruby? Has a builder looked over your plans? Or are you leaping in feet first and knocking out parts of the house any old how? You could bring the roof down on your head if you take out a load-bearing wall.'

'Tea or coffee?' she asked sweetly, fighting the urge to hit him. Of course she knew what she was doing. 'I have expert help.' Chris had been a builder until he'd decided there had to be more excitement to life and learned to fly helicopters. He'd been more than happy to take a look at the house and tell her what she could and couldn't do to it. He'd also put her in touch with a reliable draughtsman who fully understood her need to keep the house in period while modernising the essentials.

'Coffee, thanks.' Jack dropped onto a chair at the table. Questions still clouded his eyes.

'Dave, Chris?' Outside, the rotors of the second rescue helicopter began slowing down. Ruby got out more mugs for the other crew. 'Where's Slats?'

'Right here.' A short, wiry man sauntered in and handed Dave some paperwork.

Chris sat down and introduced Jack to his offsider before returning to the previous conversation. 'Ruby's got everything under control with the house, Jack. We made sure of that the moment we learned what she was up to. She's one very organised lady. And damned determined when she sets her mind to something.'

'Here you go.' Ruby slid the filled mugs across the table towards the men.

Jack's eyebrows were on the move again. 'Ruby? Organised?' His eyes widened and he turned to her. 'Have you had a total mind make-over since I saw you last?' He certainly didn't have any hang-ups about everyone knowing they used to know each other.

'Sort of.' She shrugged off his criticism. 'I definitely don't rush things like a sprinter out of the starter's block any more.'

Jack told Chris, 'Three years ago, if she'd wanted a wall taken out, she'd have taken it out, regardless of load bearing or any other constraints.'

Chris laughed. 'Sometimes it's hard to slow Ruby down once she gets going with that mallet, but she's very conscious of making the best out of this house. It's going to be well worth all her efforts.'

Jack pressed his lips together. Holding back a retort? Then he headed to the sink, poured the coffee away and began making another one. Without milk.

'Oh, sorry.' She'd made it the way he used to drink it. Silly girl. She should've asked, not presumed, she knew.

'Not a problem.'

Leaning back against the small bench, Ruby folded her arms over her abdomen, holding her mug in one hand. Her pie was heating in the microwave. She put distance between her and Jack, all too aware of the sparks that would fly if they touched. Trying not to watch as he stirred the bottom out of his coffee mug was hard after all those years of wondering about him; yearning for his touch, his kisses, even his understanding. She remembered how those long fingers now holding the teaspoon used to trip lightly over her feverish skin, sensitising her from head to toe.

He glanced over. 'What?'

'Nothing.' Thoughtlessly she laid a hand on his upper arm then snatched it back as his eyebrows rose. Dropping onto a chair, she surreptitiously continued to study him over the rim of her mug. There were a few more crinkles at the corners of his eyes, an occasional grey strand on his head. His tall frame still didn't carry any excess weight, but when he'd held her he'd felt more muscular than before. Had he started working out? In a gym? Not likely. But, then, how was she to know?

On her belt the pager squawked out a message, as it did on Dave's. He said, 'I'll get the details.'

'Damn it, when do I get to eat?' She spun around to empty her coffee into the sink and bumped into Jack. As she snatched the microwave open, she clamped down on the sweet shivers dancing over her skin. 'Lukewarm's better than no pie at all,' she muttered, before sinking her teeth into the gluggy pastry and racing for the helicopter behind Chris and Slats. Would lukewarm Jack be better than no Jack at all? At least she was getting away from him, and he'd have gone by the time they got back.

As Ruby clambered up into the 'copter Dave called out, 'You're picking up a cardiac arrest patient from the inter-island ferry.' He came closer, Jack on his heels. 'Ruby, I'm sending Jack in my place. Show him the ropes, will you?'

'Sure,' she spluttered. Didn't anyone around here listen to her? Couldn't they hear her silent pleas? She did not want to be confined inside the 'copter with Jack until she'd had a few days to get her mixed-up emotions under control. Her heart thudded against her ribs. Would that even be possible?

Toughen up and deal with it. Deal with Jack. He was here. That was all there was to it. Her chin jutted out and her spine clicked as she straightened unnaturally tight and upright. She'd do the job, show him the ropes, and then she was due two days' leave.

Out over Cook Strait, Chris hovered the helicopter above the rolling deck of the inter-islander. The sky was clear and cold, the sea running fast with a big swell. Not ideal but it could've been a whole lot worse.

'Send the stretcher after me,' Ruby instructed Jack as she prepared to be lowered to the deck with a pack and the oxygen bottle on her back.

'Right,' Jack snapped.

So he thought he should go first. Tough. It was her job today. At least he hadn't argued and wasted valuable time. That was the Jack she remembered.

The ship lurched upwards as her feet reached for the deck, jarring her whole body and giving her knee some grief. Mindful of the ship's crew, she swore silently and tried hard not to limp as she crossed to her patient, checking the area for any obstacles that might get in the way of the stretcher being lowered. She waved the crowd of on-lookers further back.

A woman looked up as Ruby crouched uncomfortably beside her. 'I'm a GP. This is Ron Jefferies, fifty years old. Lucky for him I was close by when he fell. I started CPR within sixty seconds. The ferry crew supplied a defibrillator, which I used at maximum joules. We now have a thready heart rhythm.'

Ruby introduced herself as she unzipped the pack and removed an LMA kit. 'Ron, I'm going to insert a tube in your throat and place a mask over your face to give you oxygen.'

'I'll put an IV in.' Jack was down already and knelt opposite.

'Please.' Ruby was already pushing up Ron's sleeve and passing the bag of saline to the GP now standing behind her. Holding the bag aloft helped the fluid flow more easily until they were ready to winch their patient on board the helicopter. She and Jack worked quickly and efficiently together, unfolding the stretcher and snapping the locks into place at the hinges.

She directed Jack and the GP to grip Ron's legs and upper arm, while opposite them she clutched handfuls of his trousers and shirt, ready to pull. 'On the count of three. One. Two. Three.' And their patient was on the stretcher, being belted securely.

'We're ready to transfer.' Ruby spoke to Slats through her mouthpiece as she checked Jack had attached the winch to the stretcher. Within minutes they were all aboard and Chris had headed the machine for Wellington and the hospital.

Jack checked their patient's vitals while Ruby wrote up the patient report form.

'He's one lucky man,' she murmured. 'How often does a GP witness an arrest? Getting the compressions that quickly definitely saved him.'

'He owes her his life for sure.' Jack glanced up at her. 'Did you get her name?'

'No time for that.'

'We didn't learn anything about our man here either, apart from who he is. I wonder if he was travelling with family? Friends?'

She shook her head. 'According to the steward I spoke to while you were being winched up, he'd put it over the loudspeaker for anyone travelling with Ron Jefferies to come forward, but no one appeared. It will be up to the hospital to track down relatives.'

'They'll be able to talk to him when they remove the LMA.'

'Maybe.' The man didn't look very alert. Ruby watched as Jack rechecked all his vitals.

In her headphone Slats said, 'We're here, folks. The team's waiting for your patient.'

Jack glanced up. 'Thank goodness. Ron needs a cardiologist urgently.'

It didn't take long to hand Ron over to the hospital emergency staff, and then the pilots were skimming across the harbour to the airport and back to base.

Usually Ruby would gaze out the window during this short flight, looking at all the city landmarks, enjoying the moods of the harbour, unwinding after an operation. But now her eyes were drawn to Jack as he sat, hunched in the bucket seat, reading the clinical-procedures notebook they all carried.

Had he missed her as much as she had him?

Jack glanced across to her, a wry expression in those eyes. 'Did I pass my first test?'

She held her hand out flat and wiggled it side to side. 'Maybe.'

Annoyance flickered across his face. 'I'm being serious, Ruby. You made it abundantly clear you'd be checking me out, so I've the right to know what you're going to tell Dave when we're back on the ground.'

Whoa. Who was this angry guy? No one she knew. For someone who wanted to be mates he didn't seem to understand when she was teasing him. 'I couldn't fault you. Okay?' It had been a straightforward job but she refrained from pointing that out.

'Thank you.' He studied her for a long moment before returning to reading the notebook in his hand.

Prickly so-and-so. Jack would have to learn everyone on the base teased each other every opportunity they got. It helped ease the stress levels. Pulling the boss card wouldn't keep Jack safe at all, but he could learn that from the others. Right now she wanted out of this confined space so she could breath some Jack-less air, could look in any direction and not have her sight filled with a hunky, mouth-watering vision, could move without fear of bumping into him.

As the helicopter settled gently on the ground and the rotors slowed she stood and ran her hands down her thighs, ready for a quick escape.

'Do we need to take that bag inside to top up or is it all right for me to bring out replacement equipment?' Jack asked.

Peering down at him, Ruby was disconcerted to find him watching her rubbing her thighs. Tucking her hands behind her back, she answered quickly, 'It's fine to bring what's needed out here as long as it's done immediately.' Did he remember smoothing her thighs, running exquisite circles on her skin with his forefinger? Why would he, when she'd only just remembered?

'Then that's what I'll do,' he snapped back. Unlocking

the door, he dropped to the ground and strode towards the hangar.

Ruby lowered herself down, mindful of her now throbbing knee. Sucking in her stomach, she concentrated on walking without limping and trying to force Jack out of her mind.

Except he wouldn't go away. She'd angered him again. Since when had he had such a short fuse? He'd been the one to tell jokes and tease people, and had happily accepted the same in return. Had something happened to him during the time she'd been away? Had someone hurt him? Apart from her? Another woman? Ruby stumbled. He could be married by now—to Blondie. No wedding ring meant nothing. Not all men wore them. He was very desirable and she hadn't been the only nurse to set her sights on him in the A and E department. A smug smile tugged at her mouth. She'd been the one to win him, though. Her smile flicked off. That was then. Now was different. He wouldn't let her close a second time.

The sound of her pager snapped through her thoughts. 'Here we go again.' Reading the details coming through, she turned back to the helicopter and clambered inside.

Jack was right behind her, breathing heavily. He slammed the door shut and dropped onto the seat he'd only moments before vacated. 'What have we got?'

Ruby pushed to the front and read back the details coming through on the electronic screen. '"MTV on the Rumataka Road. Female, thirty years, minor injuries but trapped. Stat two. Female, six years, serious facial injuries, possible brain injury. Stat four."'

'Do we pick them both up? Or just the child?' Jack asked.

'Just the child at this stage. Being a status four, we can't afford to wait until the mother is freed. The mother will be transferred to Hutt Hospital by road.'

'Will we take the child to Hutt Hospital or back to Wellington?'

'It's not our call, but most likely Wellington, where they've got an excellent neurological department. It's only a few minutes' extra flying time.'

'Every minute can count.' Jack's eyes darkened. 'More than anything else, that mother's going to want to be with her daughter.' He twisted around to stare out the window, his hands clenching and unclenching on his thighs, his mouth a white line in his pale face.

'Jack?' Ruby leaned closer, put a hand over his. What was wrong? It couldn't be the flying, he'd been okay on the last trip, and anyway he was training to be a private pilot.

'I'm fine.' He slid his hand out from under hers, and continued staring outside.

If she hadn't been looking so hard she wouldn't have seen the way his bottom lip quivered ever so slightly. 'Sure.' She had no idea how to get him to open up. Once she'd stupidly thought that if Jack had something to say he'd say it, but now she realised he'd never told her anything that involved his feelings.

Minutes ticked by. Then he coughed. 'I always struggle with seeing kids injured.' His fingers flexed, fisted, flexed.

'I think we all do.' Ruby thought back to when she'd worked alongside Jack in A and E. Had they ever worked together with a seriously sick child? Her mind threw up a memory from her first week in A and E with Dr Forbes.

Ruby, for God's sake, hurry up with that suction. This kid's going to choke to death.' Jack whipped the tube out of her hand. 'Turn it on. Now.' He whisked the end of the hard plastic around the little boy's mouth, gentle but firm,

sucking up the blood and mucus that filled the cavity.
'Damn it, kid, don't you die on me now.'

Nurses worked around them, stemming blood loss from
the child's legs and head, cutting away clothes and order-
ing X-rays. Ruby smarted as she tossed the boy's now use-
less trousers into the rubbish bin. She'd reacted instantly
to Jack's command to suction the boy's mouth. What was
his problem? 'I was doing just fine,' she snapped at him.
'I can take over now.'

'Press on that leg wound. It's bleeding again.' Jack
continued suctioning, his fingers unsteady and his mouth
a white line in his pale face. He issued orders to the se-
nior nurse about getting the oxygen mask ready, ignoring
Ruby.

Later that night, when they knocked off work, Jack said,
'You've got to learn not to answer back in those situations.
Whatever I say goes. Understand?'

She'd nodded. 'Sure.' But she'd been shocked at the
way he'd snatched that tube out of her hand.

'Ruby, we can always discuss a case afterwards.' He
turned for the door, spun back. 'You did well in there. If I
seemed a little abrupt I have my reasons.'

He'd never told her what those reasons were. That had
been before they'd got together so she'd put his reticence
down to not knowing her very well. Wrong. It was just
how he was. Had something dreadful happened to Jack as
a trainee? Had he lost a patient in circumstances he blamed
himself for?

In her ear Chris's voice was an abrupt interruption.
'ETA one minute. I'll land on the road above the crash
site.'

'Right.' Ruby prepared to leave the helicopter the instant it was possible.

As they raced towards the squashed car, their packs

banging heavily on their backs, oxygen tank and defib in Jack's hands, Ruby checked him out. She sighed with relief. Whatever had been disturbing him had gone, replaced with a professional, caring expression and the urgent need to help the little girl they were there for.

A policeman lifted the tape protecting the scene from the crowd of onlookers for Ruby and Jack to duck under. 'I think you're wanted at the ambulance.'

Changing direction, they crossed to the paramedics, who were working with a small patient on a stretcher. Ruby's heart ached when she saw the small, blood-soaked child. A quick look at Jack but, apart from a whitening of his face, he was in full control of himself.

They listened carefully to an ambulance officer's report. 'I've given her a second bolus of saline as her BP keeps dropping. GCS is nine. She's got a poor airway and I couldn't intubate.'

A Glasgow coma score of nine. They didn't come worse than that and the patient still be alive.

'Upgrade to stat five.' Jack immediately opened his pack and reached for a small-sized LMA kit. Ruby took the child's head and tipped it back slightly to allow Jack easier access to her throat. Together they quickly had the airway open and oxygen flowing. Jack's expertise was impressive, and Ruby enjoyed working with him. The girl was in excellent hands.

But as Ruby began to relax, the child went into spasms. A seizure was common with her injuries but distressing for everyone observing it. Other than making sure the girl didn't choke, there was nothing Ruby could do but hold the child's bloodied hand in her gloved one until she fell still again.

After a fast but thorough examination they transferred the girl to the helicopter. As Jack began taking her vitals again, she had another seizure. Followed minutes later by another. And another.

'We'll give her a sedative intra-nasally,' he instructed Ruby as the rotors began speeding up.

Ruby held the nasal cannula in place and talked quietly. 'Come on, sweetheart. This will stop those nasty fits.'

'Blood pressure's dropping.' Jack's voice was calm, steady.

'Stay with us, sweetheart.' *Chris, spin those rotors faster, we need a hospital right now.* 'I wonder what your name is. No one back at the accident scene knew. I bet it's something pretty.'

Jack checked the oxygen saturation level, adjusted the flow from the tank. Took blood-pressure readings again, counted the little girl's respiratory rate.

Ruby, uncharacteristically feeling totally helpless, called up Wellington Hospital Emergency Department and gave them the child's medical details and their ETA. They were doing all they could but it was nowhere near enough.

Slats's calm voice sounded in her headset. 'One minute to touchdown.'

A team of paediatric doctors and nurses awaited them, moving towards the helicopter the moment Ruby shoved the door open. The transfer was made with such care that Ruby felt an urge to cry and had to squash it down hard. Everyone knew that this little girl was fighting for her life.

Ruby and Jack stood on the rooftop, watching as the team took charge, their own part in saving the child over. A sense of inadequacy touched Ruby even though she knew she'd done all she could and their patient was better off with the hospital team now. Glancing at Jack, she saw him swallow hard.

'You were awesome with her,' she said.

'Thanks, Red. It's never enough, though, is it?'

'Sometimes it has to be.' Unfortunately. The downside of the job.

Jack looked down into her eyes and for a moment they connected. Really hooked up. Ruby forgot to breathe. Forgot where she was. Forgot about the waiting 'copter. Only Jack mattered. And how good it felt to be with him again. With Jack at her side she could accomplish anything. Even staying in Wellington for ever.

Behind her Chris called out to them, 'Time to hit the sky, you two.'

And Ruby leapt away. Jack wasn't by her side, figuratively or otherwise. And never would be. Racing for the 'copter, she chastised herself for her odd moment of wishful thinking. She wasn't the same person any more, and from what little she'd seen so far, neither was Jack. Getting together again would never work out. They hadn't managed to stay together when they'd been happy and in love. How could they possibly have a workable relationship with all that hurt they'd inflicted on each other?

CHAPTER THREE

As the helicopter settled on the hard back at base, Ruby glanced at her watch. Six forty-five. Yee-ha. She could sign off and go home. Grab some take-aways for her dinner on the way. Feed Zane. Put distance between her and Jack. Take time to absorb her initial impressions, think about the differences she'd already noted in him.

Up front Chris clicked off numerous switches as the whine of the rotors slowed. Then he poked his head around the bulkhead. 'Dave's just come through, says to meet him at the Aero House for beers. Something to do with you, Jack. An unofficial welcome aboard sort of thing.'

The Aero House was the local watering hole, frequented mostly by pilots and the girls hoping to nab them. The rescue staff used it regularly for winding down from bad days, for having a quiet drink with people who understood they didn't always want to talk about work, and occasionally for partying.

Jack said, 'Sounds good to me. Ruby?'

Going home where Jack wasn't in her face all the time, where she could breathe without effort, was her preferred option. But this was the team, her family of sorts and, whatever her feelings, Jack was being made a part of it. 'Sure, a cold one is just what I need.'

One beer and then she could leave guilt-free. Hopefully no one had a mind to start a party. Not on a Sunday night.

'Let's top up the packs and get out of here.' Jack dropped to the ground and reached up for the bags Ruby handed down.

She finished cleaning up inside the 'copter and dropped the dirty laundry bag outside for pick-up in the morning.

'Have a busy night.' Ruby waved goodbye to the night crews a little while later and headed out to the well-lit parking lot. As she tossed her bag into the cab of her truck she heard Jack say, 'What are you driving now?'

She grinned. 'Nothing like my old car, is it?' And her grin widened at the stunned look on his face.

'You haven't borrowed it?' He stared at her shining black pride and joy. 'This truck's yours?'

'Right down to the last wheel nut. Isn't it fabulous?' She ran a hand over the bonnet. It still thrilled her to drive this beast. And she so loved the stares she got whenever she pulled into the yard at the building centre and clambered out.

'It's seen a few kilometres.' Jack nodded at a couple of minor dents.

Hello? A new one cost a fortune, and she certainly didn't have that sort of money lolling around in her bank account to spend on a vehicle. Not when her house was costing a bomb. 'I bought it privately for a bargain. My old neighbour's son was moving to Australia and wanted to get rid of it. He gave me a good deal if I promised to keep an eye out for his mother.' Funny how her luck had started to change from the day she'd decided to put the Greaser into perspective. The moment she'd let go all the anger at his betrayal of her and Mum, her life had begun looking up. A quick glance at Jack had her wondering just how high it could go.

Jack's eyes popped. 'You're kidding me?' But then he shook his head. 'No, not with that smug look on your face. And judging by the gleaming paint work, this is your most prized possession. It's fantastic. Way to go, Red.' Jack strolled around the truck, looking it over with something like envy in those gunmetal eyes.

She couldn't resist showing off her wagon. 'Can I give you a ride to the Aero House?'

'Thanks, but I'll see you there.' He waved the keys he held between thumb and forefinger towards a saloon, and the sound of locks popping was loud in the frosty air. 'I'll take the old dunger.'

'Want me to follow in case you break down?' she quipped.

'Lady, you might have the wheels but I've got the experience.'

'Is that a challenge?' The words were dry on her tongue. He'd always had way more experience than her at almost everything. Especially in bed. He'd been her first lover. The one-off couplings she'd tried in her rebellious teens didn't count.

'It would be if we had somewhere to race, and I had time to put a V8 under the hood.' His hands were light on his slim hips, his gaze thoughtful. Then he shifted his hands to her shoulders and drew her nearer. 'How have you been, Red? Really?'

Swallow. Gulp. 'Um, good, great.' Duh. She shrugged from under his hands, certain she'd have more chance of stringing a sentence together if he wasn't touching her. 'And you?' she croaked.

'Me? A bunch of fluffy ducks.' His eyes didn't lighten up one bit. 'We'd better move it or the others will be wondering what's happened to us.'

And knowing those guys, they'd have no restraints

about asking what she was doing chatting to Jack in the car park at night. She swung up into the cab and turned the motor over. Just one beer and then she'd head home to her little piece of paradise. Paradise without Jack? The picture was starting to look all wrong.

Jack watched in awe as tiny Red settled on cushions and stretched her legs towards the pedals. The big vehicle dwarfed her already short frame. Heck, she almost fell out reaching for the door to slam it shut. But as she pulled away she was sitting up straight, her arms out level as she gripped the steering-wheel, pride pushing her chin forward.

A warm sensation curled around his heart, and an involuntary smile tugged at his lips. She was still a spunky woman. She intrigued him, despite that screaming, bottled-red hair that had shocked him when he'd first seen her again. She seemed more relaxed about life than he'd ever known her. Hell, she even appeared genuinely happy. So unlike the Ruby he'd loved. The Ruby he hadn't been able to help.

Had he tried hard enough? He certainly hadn't fought to keep her by his side. Neither had he tried to come to any arrangement where they went to the States together. It had been downright lousy of him to let her face that trip alone, but he'd been too wrapped up in his own injured pride to look past her brave words and see what it was she'd really wanted. That had only become apparent as she'd slid away from him at the airport. Hunched in on herself, departure card, boarding pass and passport gripped in her white-knuckled hand, she'd ducked out of his life.

And now she was back.

Had things gone well with her father? For her sake he

hoped so. She'd spent so long carrying that particular chip around it had soured her outlook on just about everything.

Gravel spat as she rolled quickly out onto the road. Jack grinned after her and headed for his wreck of a car. Too bad the mortgage hadn't allowed him to buy something bigger and better. The pay cut he'd taken to come here wouldn't help either but, according to his best mate who made truckloads on the fishing trawlers, money wasn't everything. But it sure helped.

The Aero House was quiet when he sat down, a beer in his hand, with his new workmates. Slats was not there, apparently not a very social man. Jack had automatically sought out the chair beside Ruby. Big mistake and too late to change. He wished he could ignore her, forget the past and all the great times they'd had together. He needed to focus on the future, the uncertainty of that still gnawing at his gut, keeping him awake at night wondering why he'd so impetuously walked away from the job he'd spent his adult life aiming for.

'So how did your first two trips go?' Dave asked from across the table.

Grateful for the interruption, Jack replied, 'Fairly good. I think.' He raised an eyebrow at Ruby, belatedly remembering she'd witnessed his moment of confusion before they'd landed at the site of the car accident. The last thing he wanted was for her to rat on him. But, then, he already knew she wouldn't. This reaction was all to do with how confused she made him feel around her. He needed to relax. Like, how?

'For a newbie you weren't bad.' She tipped her bottle to her lips and gave him a wink.

'Thanks a bundle,' he growled in mock seriousness. Then his gaze stuck on her throat as she swallowed. The warmth he'd felt in the car park became a raging inferno in his veins. So much for thinking of her as a teammate. Angry at himself for letting her get to him so easily, he jerked his head around, focused on the others at the table. His chair screeched on the floorboards as he put space between himself and Ruby. 'Yeah,' he drawled, 'I had a good afternoon.'

Except for having to pick up a little girl who might never get to go to school again, or play with her pals or even know what was going on around her. He'd give the hospital a call later on to see if there was any improvement. One of the advantages of having worked there was that someone would tell him what he wanted to know. Heaven help the girl's parents. Jack knew the horror and fear they'd be feeling. He'd seen that expression on his dad's face when he was seven, and even at that age it had been something he'd understood. And never forgotten.

Dave was talking to him. 'You'll soon have the hang of it. Anyway, we've got time to iron out anything you're not sure of.' Dave's leave didn't start until the following week. 'Here comes the other day crew. And Sandra.'

Jack was soon shaking hands all round and putting faces to names he'd read on the staff list. The tension that had niggled him all afternoon relaxed. Ruby, now slightly turned away from him, was talking to Sandra, one of the base's aeronautical engineers and apparently Chris's partner. Was Ruby avoiding him? Why would she? So far she'd treated him the same as the others. As he should be treating her. He was just being super-sensitive. He and Ruby were to be mates, and she was playing the game. What if he took her out for a meal so they could talk over things and definitely cement their new footing? Yeah, he liked that idea. But he'd wait for a quiet moment to ask her. It wouldn't do for the others to think he was favouring one of the team even if he hadn't officially started yet. And if he believed that then he was an even bigger fool than he already thought.

Half an hour later Derek, a paramedic on the second crew, stood up and said, 'Sorry, guys, but I promised the wife I wouldn't be too late tonight.'

Ruby drained her bottle. 'Me too. Not that I promised the wife anything, but Zane will be hanging out for his dinner. Jack, it's great to have you with us. Enjoy your days off, guys.'

'Thanks.' Zane? Who the hell was Zane? Acute disappointment rocked through Jack, tightened his gut. Come on. Even though he'd half expected her to have a boyfriend, finding out for sure didn't make him at all happy. Zane. What sort of moniker was that? Some American name?

Damn it, this is not how friends thought about each other. Jack shuddered. At least he'd saved himself from looking an idiot by asking her out for dinner.

Just then Chris returned from the bar with more beers. 'You still okay for me to take out those cupboards tomorrow morning, Ruby?'

'Looking forward to it.' She grinned, pushing back her chair.

'You don't get to swing that sledgehammer this time. I want the cupboards whole so I can sell them for you.' Chris sat and draped an arm around Sandra's shoulders. 'You okay with me spending a few hours at Ruby's?'

'I'll only be getting in the groceries so go for it,' Sandra replied. Then she nudged him in the ribs with an elbow. 'Gives me some time at home to myself.'

'Like I'm a proper pest.' Chris grinned.

Dave asked, 'Need a hand with those cupboards, Chris? I'm free until after lunch.'

'The more help the sooner we're done. It's not like little Ruby can hold the cupboards while I take them down.'

Chris ducked as Ruby waved her empty bottle threateningly at him. 'Down, girl.'

Jack opened his mouth without thought. 'If it's more help you need, count me in.'

'Aren't you officially starting work tomorrow?' Ruby's eyes widened.

'Since Dave's off until Wednesday, we decided I'd start then,' Jack explained. Then, ignoring that 'don't come near' sign in her eyes, he asked, 'What's your address?'

Noting down her directions, a little devil stomped on his brain: bad move. Bad move. He had four months working with Red before he headed off on his next adventure far away from Wellington. Away from Ruby. He could do it. So why the feeling of standing on a precipice? Why the sudden urge to haul her into his arms and kiss her senseless? The answer blinded him. Because he wanted to go back to where they'd left off three years ago, to pick up their life and live through those missing years, that turmoil, and arrive here, today, together. Happy.

Ruby pushed her gate shut the next morning and unhitched Zane's lead. 'There you go, my boy. That walk should keep you happy for a few hours.'

She glanced up the path, looking to see if any of the guys had arrived yet. 'All quiet, Zany.'

Then she rounded the corner of her house and walked slap bang into someone. A man, if that hard body was anything to go by. 'Oof. Ouch. Sorry.'

Firm hands grabbed her shoulders, steadied her. 'Look where you're going, Red.'

What she looked at was the expanse of jersey-covered chest right in front of her eyes. All she breathed was that pine scent she'd smelt the day before. All her mind had in it was confusion. Heat seared her, pooled in her belly.

Jerking out of his hold, she glared up at him. 'What are you doing back here?'

'Looking for you. I forgot to ask what time the other guys were turning up so thought I'd better get here. Seems I'm early.'

'Chris won't be far away.' She hoped. Time alone with Jack was the last thing she needed. It made keeping the 'mates' thing too difficult. 'Let's have a coffee while we wait.' And she could put some space between them. Through the long, sleepless night she'd begun asking herself why Jack had never quite disappeared out of her heart, still lurked in the corners of her mind at the most unexpected moments. No matter how hard she'd tried to pretend he no longer mattered, it was now blatantly obvious to her that he did. She should send him packing before she got in too deep, before it became impossible to say goodbye again.

Before she hurt him once more. She'd do anything not to hurt Jack. Even leave Wellington? Put her own needs aside? Unlike last time. Maybe this was how she could make it up to him. But to let go of her dream, say goodbye to her roots and go. Go where? There was nowhere else she wanted to be, nowhere else she belonged—with or without Jack.

Peering up into those disturbing grey eyes, she couldn't think of anything to say without spilling her guts. 'Come inside,' she muttered.

'Some house you've got here. Love the land. I'm surprised no one thought to subdivide it. The grounds must keep you busy with mowing, pruning all those fruit trees and keeping that hedge in shape. What's the dark patch over there by the back fence?'

Glad to be on safe ground, she spewed out words. 'Lupin. I'm wintering over the soil and come spring I'll plant my vegetable patch. Just think; fresh tomatoes, peas, lettuces, zucchinis, all at the end of the section.' Even she could manage making salads.

'I didn't think you knew what a spade was for.' Jack's face was neutral as he added in a flat voice, 'This speaks of permanence, Red.'

Red. All over her body her cells danced as his name for her tripped off his tongue. Red was that woman from a long time ago. That woman he'd made love to, tenderly, feverishly, exquisitely, often. Every time he called her Red she wanted to strip down naked and pole dance for him. Which would shock the hell out of her workmates if they arrived midway through.

But to answer his underlying criticism. 'I didn't buy the house on a whim, Jack. I want somewhere I can call home, for ever.' That should knock his socks off.

Those thick, dark eyebrows rose in a disconcerting fashion. 'You've been here how long? Two months?' The sarcasm dripped off his tongue like lemon juice.

'Long enough to know I've bought the perfect property for me. It's where I want to put down roots, and not just the plant kind.' Dredging up a smile, she hooked her shoes off. She would not let him get to her, wouldn't let him undermine her resolve. She could do that all by herself. 'I'll be like that walnut tree out there, here for decades.'

He stared at the gnarled tree she nodded at for a moment, then turned his gaze to the exterior of the house. 'I'd have thought you'd want modern. All these weatherboards need regular upkeep. A lot of commitment goes with a place like this.'

'Commitment I'm learning to make.' She widened her smile especially for Jack, swallowed her despair at his disbelief. 'This is a long-term project. And I love the character that comes with old homes. Far more interesting and less predictable.'

The tone of his voice matched the scepticism darkening his eyes, but he did ask, 'Do I get a guided tour?'

'Later.' They'd start with the kitchen and that drink. Hopefully the others would arrive before she had time to show him anything else. Somewhere deep inside she felt a twist of reluctance, as though by opening up her home to him she'd be exposing her soul and showing him a side of herself he'd never seen. How could he have? She'd not long found it herself. So what was she afraid of? That he'd take fright? Run away? This was all so, so damned hard.

She stepped past him and tripped over her dog. 'Zane, out of the way. Oh, no, naughty boy.' Ruby grabbed Zane's collar and hauled him away from Jack's bootlaces.

Jack blinked, gaping at her black Labrador. 'That's Zane?'

She squinted at Jack, then Zane. Nodding. 'Yes, this is my dog.' Who else could Zane be? He'd thought Zane was her man. She chuckled. It was true. Zane guarded her, protected her, played with her and gave her loads of love. The perfect male, actually.

Jack's face flushed a delicious red. 'How long have you had him?'

'I got him from the SPCA seven weeks ago. He'd been dumped as a six-month-old pup and no one wanted him because he's blind in one eye from being poked with a stick. The moment I saw Zane I had to have him. When I knelt down to pet this guy through the wire of his cage, he licked me and I was a goner.'

'Blimey, you're becoming a right softie, as well as very domesticated.' Jack peered down at her, amusement mixed with confusion colouring those steely eyes. 'House. Dog. Truck. What's next?'

'Nothing I can think of.' Except a hot man to come home to at the end of every shift. Pity the one she was thinking of obviously didn't think she had stickability, so there went that idea. Not that it had had any substance in the first place. They'd done their time together, and now they were meant to have moved on. Great theory. A shame it wasn't ringing true for her. A sigh trickled past her lips and she changed the subject to a safer topic. 'I'm sorry Zane's undone your laces but be glad he hasn't had time to eat them. Laces are his favourite distraction at the moment. Last week it was underwear.' Gulp. Shouldn't have said that.

'Underwear?' His eyes suddenly twinkled wickedly. A crooked grin split his face, and set butterflies flapping in her tummy. 'Yours, I take it.'

She sucked chilly air through clenched teeth. 'Sometimes but not always. Old Mrs Crocombe next door lost a pair of bloomers off her clothes horse last week.' A giggle erupted up her throat as a picture rose in her mind. 'Zane looked hilarious with them draped over his head. Thankfully Mrs Crocombe thought so too.'

'I thought bloomers went out with my great-grandmother.' Jack shook his head as he retied his laces. 'Seriously, does your neighbour really wear them?'

'Big pink ones. With wide elastic around the legs that caught in Zane's eye teeth.' Another giggle broke through. 'She's ninety-two not out.'

'Ahh, the neighbour you're keeping a watch over.' Jack rubbed Zane's ears. 'Where'd your name come from, dog?'

Zane licked Jack's hand as Ruby answered. 'They gave him that at the SPCA. Zane for zany. It suits him.'

'What will you do with him when you leave Wellington again?'

She snapped, 'Zane will long have been resting under

the walnut tree by the time I even consider moving away.'
Ruby crossed her fingers and headed inside. 'Give me a
break, Jack.' Was it that she'd chosen this particular city
that stuck in his craw? Did he think she'd invaded his territory? He only had himself to blame for that. This was the
place she'd been happiest, the one town she'd struggled to
leave. Because of Jack.

Jack straightened up and rubbed his gritty eyes. Sleep
had been elusive last night as his mind had chased images of Ruby. The old Ruby struggling to become a nurse.
Paramedic Ruby performing highly competently yesterday
with her patients. Both versions had tangled and twined in
his brain, giving him a headache. He had to keep reminding himself there was only one Ruby. One he couldn't rely
on for any sort of permanence. Not that he would be going
down that path with her again.

He followed her inside. He'd work on the presumption
that deep down Ruby was still Ruby, and that well within
twelve months she'd be casting around for a new city to try
out. That way he'd survive the turmoil rolling through him
when he was with her, when he thought of her in the middle of the night, when he heard her sweet laughter around
the base. That way he'd remember to keep everything on
a friendship level. That way he wouldn't risk being left
again.

Ever since yesterday that prickly, restless feeling that
had driven him to quit the hospital and take on the rescue job had started begging to be scratched again. He'd
believed he'd doused the itch by getting different, exciting work outside his normal sphere of comfort. He was on
the move himself these days. Rescue helicopters, the deep
south, then who knew where? Yet, in one emotion-packed
moment of reunion, he was wondering what his life was
really all about.

Had he got it wrong leaving the A and E department? He'd loved his job—the work, staff, patients who needed his skills. But something had been missing. Something that had started small and grown bigger with each passing week until he'd snapped. Gone and got a temporary job. Given up his awesome career. For what? He wasn't sure now.

In her cramped kitchen he looked around, trying to keep a space between him and Ruby. Hard to do when the room was the size of a toy box. Sucking in a Ruby-scented breath, he asked, 'Have you got flatmates?'

'Not yet. I thought about it but no one in their right mind would want to live here when I'm busy pulling the house to bits.' Flicking on the tap to fill the kettle, she asked, 'What about you? Are you sharing a place with someone?'

Was she asking if he lived with someone special? 'I bought a four-year-old house in partnership with Steve and Johnny. Neither of them is home much so they've got a base to return to whenever they want. And it makes good financial sense to share the mortgage while we're all doing other things with our incomes.' He chuckled. 'Actually, the house is only about three kilometres from here on the other side of Mount Vic.'

Ruby nibbled her bottom lip. 'Sounds a perfect solution for all of you. So if Steve's flying 747s, is he an international pilot now? He must be stoked. That has always been his goal.'

'He's based in Dubai but heads home for a few days every second month.' His brother needed to keep those family ties alive to stay on an even keel in his chaotic, globetrotting life. Truthfully Jack needed Steve to need him. It was a lifetime habit that had kept him sane and safe and he wasn't about to break it. At a very young age Jack had deliberately made himself the centre of the universe for his dad and Steve. That way they'd never leave him as Mum and Beth had. At seven it had all made perfect sense. At thirty he saw no reason to change.

He continued, 'Johnny works long and hard as a skipper on a fishing trawler, saving every cent for the day when he can buy his own boat.' The perfect flatmates, hardly ever there but when they were they were great for parties and going to the odd rugby match.

'Remember that horrible old flat we shared with Tina and Gerry? Cold and dark in winter, hot and stuffy in summer. And the neighbour was so noisy you used earplugs so you could get some sleep.' Ruby shuddered. 'And yet I loved it at the time.'

'It was very handy for Courtney Place and all the pubs and cafés. If I remember correctly we spent most of our spare time down there playing pool and drinking beer.' Jack looked wistful for a moment. Then he pulled a chair out from the table and straddled it.

'The whole flat wasn't much bigger than this tiny kitchen.' Nostalgia filled Ruby's eyes. 'We were happy there.'

Jack gasped at the intensity in her voice. Red was right. They had been very happy. 'We didn't need much to get by on back then.'

'Just as well. Nowhere to store anything. You ever hear from Tina and Gerry?'

Jack shook his head. More people who'd moved out of his life. 'They're in Dunedin now. Gerry's a GP and Tina's got her own interior design shop.'

'I wonder if Tina ever made up with her sister after that horrendous argument over where to scatter their father's ashes.' Ruby tapped her mouth. 'Families, eh? They certainly put people through a lot.'

And now Ruby didn't have one. At least, not here in

New Zealand. Jack missed his chance to ask about her father when she said, 'At least with Zane I know exactly where I stand. Chief provider of life's essentials in return for complete loyalty and undivided love.' She stared at her mutt with an odd blend of love and sadness in her eyes.

Was that where *he* had failed her? By not providing those things? He had loved her. He had been loyal. To the point where Ruby had come first? No. Definitely not.

'So how do you think we're going to go, working together?' Ruby banged two cups on the stainless-steel bench.

Stunned at the sudden change of subject, he muttered, 'Can't see why it won't be okay.'

She leaned back against the bench. 'It has to be unless you want to change your mind about continuing at Rescue.' She lifted one eyebrow at him. 'Because I have no intention of leaving.'

He swallowed a retort. 'It won't come to that, Red.'

'I'm Ruby. Think you can remember that? Ruby.' Worry flittered through her eyes. She looked uneasy. Because of him? Did he still unnerve her? Male pride puffed out his chest. He liked it that he'd had some effect on her. But his pride quickly deflated. Ruby was right to worry. They were supposed to be mates, not ex-lovers looking for a road back to each other's arms. Damn it, because right now the thought of being held by Red was the most attractive notion he could come up with.

'Believe it or not, I'm trying. But old habits tend to hang around.' He stared at her, her troubled eyes disconcerting him. 'Ruby.'

The sound of a heavy toolbag being dropped onto the back porch saved him from unwisely delving any deeper into whatever was bothering her. He didn't want to know, didn't need to get involved. She was sorting out her life—he had his own to think about.

Chris called out, 'Hey, hope you've got the kettle on. It's frigid out here.'

'Dave with you?' Ruby called back.

'Yep, he's bringing in the crowbars. Jack here already?'

'Yes.' Jack shuffled around to make room for the two men, bumped into Red. Catching his breath, he carefully eased sideways from her soft, pliant body. 'How are we all going to squeeze in here and bring those cupboards down?' Couldn't Ruby go to town or anywhere far away from him?

'We'll manage,' Chris told him.

Ruby spooned coffee granules into two more mugs, shovelled sugar on top. 'Let's drink up and get cracking.'

Jack couldn't agree more. The sooner they started the sooner they'd be done.

But a little while later Chris swore out loud and then said, 'Cupboards aren't coming down as easily as they should. We mightn't be able to save them after all, Ruby.'

Her hands slapped onto her hips as she glared at the offending cupboards. 'If you can't, then you can't.' She craned her neck and peered up into a corner where Chris had prised off some timber. 'What's through that gap? It's like another ceiling.'

Chris slid the ladder across and climbed up, poked a crowbar through where Ruby indicated. 'Great. Fantastic. Just what you don't need. I'd say that's the original ceiling and this one...' he tapped above his head '...is a false one.'

'Another darned complication.' Ruby's brow crinkled as she continued to stare upwards, blinking rapidly.

'I should've expected it. False ceilings are common in older houses where the original ones are very high. People

renovate, putting in new, lower ceilings to help keep rooms
warm.' Chris dropped to the floor. 'Ruby, you'd better put
your kitchen designer on hold until we're done with hauling out these cupboards and I can ascertain just what's up
there. You might want to pull out the false ceiling.'

'That'd mean a lot more cabinetry, wouldn't it? I
couldn't have a gap above the new cupboards. It would look
odd.' Ruby's teeth nibbled her bottom lip, worry clouding
her eyes.

Jack somehow refrained from giving her a hug, those
imminent tears piercing his heart. 'Sounds expensive.'
Ruby wouldn't be able to afford big changes, surely?

Chris picked up the jemmy again. 'You still happy to
carry on, even if I have to wreck them, Ruby?'

Her sigh filled the room. 'Definitely. They've got to go,
they're far too ugly.' She shook her head. 'Nothing's ever
straightforward, is it?'

Not with Red, that was for sure. Jack picked up a second crowbar and joined Chris. 'What do you want me to
do?'

Ruby watched every move the men made. Every screech
as a nail was ripped out underlined her fear of not being
able to complete her plans for her future. Her whole life
plan started here. If this went wrong, so might everything
else, eventually driving her away. Her heart blocked her
throat. Chris had warned her old houses held secrets, secrets that would have an impact on her bank account. She
had a reasonable-sized budget but too many added expenses might jeopardise everything.

It was one o'clock before the walls were clear, and the
false ceiling completely exposed. Ruby turned to Dave.
'Thank you so much. I'll rustle up some lunch for you all.'

Dave chuckled. 'Don't bother for me, Ruby. I'm not hungry.' Then he called to Chris and Jack, who were wrestling

an undamaged cupboard through the back door onto the porch, 'Ruby's keen to make you some lunch. That okay?'

Chris stopped moving, a grin on his face. 'Not for me, thanks. I'm thinking of my stomach.'

Ruby reached for the phone and began punching in a familiar number. 'So I'll order pizza for one, shall I?'

'Ha, ha, very funny.' Chris stepped backwards and Jack at last could put down his end of the cupboard.

'Are these things lead lined, or what?' He straightened his back with a groan. From inside he heard Ruby order three pizzas. 'What's with the lunch?'

'Ruby's not the best cook on the block. Last time she rustled up something we all had a guts ache for hours.'

Had Ruby done much cooking when they'd been together? Nothing came to Jack's mind except two-minute noodles and instant-soup packets. But the four of them sharing the flat had always been too busy to do anything more strenuous than grab 'heat and eat' food. At last, something about her that hadn't changed. He smiled as warmth touched his bones and charged his hormones.

Ruby was back in town.

And in a short while he'd be leaving. He'd finally learned his lessons from those he loved. His sister and mother. Gone. His father and brother. Moved elsewhere. Ruby. Gone. Now back. But not for long. Despite all her assurances. He knew her too well to believe a word of them.

CHAPTER FOUR

'What's next on your list of things to do here?' Dave asked Ruby as they devoured the welcome pizzas.

'I've got to get that old vinyl off the kitchen floor before the new units go in, even if I do change the plans. The floor-sander guy said he'd be here next Monday.' Ruby licked a thread of cheese off her chin and pretended Jack wasn't watching. 'That job should keep me busy for the rest of my days off.' For the next month more like. It was hard work, scraping the well-glued floor-covering off with a spade. But when the kauri boards beneath were sanded and polished the result would be worth every drop of sweat. As long there weren't any nasty surprises beneath the vinyl.

Jack's eyes were still fixed on her chin. 'Want a hand? I'm not doing anything this afternoon.'

Like she was going to turn down an offer like that. Even from Jack. 'I'll order in more pizzas for dinner.'

'I take it that's a yes,' Jack said, with more force than needed. Regretting his offer already?

'You're a sucker for punishment.' Dave punched him lightly on the biceps. 'Ruby's a slave-driver.'

'Thanks, Dave. Go ahead and scare my worker away.' Ruby gathered up empty pizza boxes and slid past Jack, careful not to touch him and yet still her shoulder brushed his chest. She stumbled. Righted herself. Headed out to the rubbish bin and squashed the boxes on top of previous take-out containers.

She could hear Chris saying, 'This house is going to be spectacular when Ruby's done.' Her heart swelled with pride.

'It must be costing a bundle.' Jack's low voice held a question.

He didn't know about the money she'd inherited from her mother. An amount big enough to make this house a tribute to her mum. It was her way of expressing her deep sorrow for all the pain she'd caused while growing up. She shuddered as a chill slid across her skin. If only there was a way to take back the terrible things she'd said whenever they'd talked about the Greaser. Ruby had blamed her mother for wrecking her life by keeping her father's whereabouts a secret when all along her mother had been protecting her.

'That's why I hope to sell those cupboards for Ruby,' Chris, who knew nothing about her inheritance either, told Jack. 'Every dollar counts.'

As Ruby sauntered inside, Chris hoisted his toolbag and strode to the door. 'See you Wednesday, Ruby, Jack. You want a lift somewhere, Dave?'

'Chris makes me sound like a charity case.' Ruby stared through the window, watching her friends tramping down the path.

Jack leaned against the bench. 'You're lucky to have their help.'

'I helped paint the inside of Chris and Sandra's house the first weeks I was here.'

'I'm not criticising, Red. It's wonderful that you all get on so well. And from what I've seen, it reflects in your work at the base. We never had anything like that at A and E.' Without the cupboards to absorb sound his words echoed quietly around them, creating a cosy feeling.

'Why did you change jobs? I thought you'd be there for a few years once you were made Head of Department. That was your plan.' That was why it had been pointless to wait until he qualified before she went to the States. Seems she'd got it wrong.

She moved to fill the kettle. Something to occupy her hands. From somewhere deep inside her soul came a fierce urge to reach out to Jack, to slip her arms around his waist and touch those full lips with hers. The kettle overflowed. Snapping the tap off, she thumped the jug on the bench.

Despite the increased kitchen space with the cupboards gone, the room was far too small for both of them. Goosebumps rose on her arms when Jack looked at her.

'You knew I'd made HOD?'

Huh? What did that have to do with anything? Concentrate. 'I'm sorry, I only found out when you got the job working with us. I knew how much you'd wanted it so it surprised me to find you'd given it up.' Regret singed her. She'd deliberately not kept up to date with what Jack had been doing. It would've only made her even more unhappy. Now a trillion questions flicked up in her mind about what he'd been doing since she'd left town.

His lips flattened as he stared thoughtfully at his feet for a few minutes. Finally he said, 'It was the job I'd wanted since the day I decided to specialise in emergency medicine, and when I was offered the position I felt everything I'd worked so hard for had come together.'

'So why the sadness?' The question was out before she thought about the sanity of getting involved in something so personal with him.

'Sad? Me? I don't think so.'

Ruby did, but she refrained from pressing further. 'So why leave?'

'I wanted to try other jobs that my qualifications lend themselves to.'

Ruby jerked her chin up. 'So what have you got planned after the Rescue job?'

'I've applied to go to Scott Base for the summer.'

Ruby felt her jaw drop. 'What?' This was so unlike Jack. Changing careers in midstream was surprising enough, but going to Antarctica? Growing a tail would seem more feasible. What had happened to make him seek a different career? Jack had had to struggle to pay his way through med school so he probably still required the fat pay packet that came with being Head of Department.

'There's more to life than being tied up running a busy emergency department.'

Ruby's jaw cracked as it dropped further. 'So you're looking for some excitement?'

Jack grinned that heart-stopping grin. 'What's wrong with that? Wanting some fun? It's not as though I've spent a lot of time doing anything other than studying and working. Didn't you join for the exhilaration of jumping out of helicopters?'

She shuddered exaggeratedly. 'Hardly. I loved the pace of ambulance work and hadn't intended giving it up. Being on the trucks, out there amongst it, looking out for people made me feel I was doing some good.'

'Sounds like excitement to me. And it's not as though having fun while doing your job brings the standard of care down.'

'I guess, but I never looked at it like that. I turned down my first opportunity to work on the helicopters in San Francisco. Me leap out of a flying machine? That wasn't exciting, that was downright scary.' Ruby sighed, dredged up a smile. 'I got conned into going for a ride, and from then on I was hooked. Literally. The guys had me strapped and latched and swinging over a field in no time at all. I loved it.'

'I know what you mean. But it's still emergency medicine, right at the edge.'

'It is, but mostly it's about helping people when they're facing their worst nightmare.' About caring, about saving lives. This was getting too deep with a man she didn't want to do deep with yet. Liar. Wasn't that what she really wanted? To get to know Jack all over again?

Again? They hadn't known each other very well last time. Now she was beginning to understand that they'd shared only the fun times. There'd been no discussions about what they'd wanted for the future. They hadn't even known each other's tastes in houses. She loved old, he obviously liked modern. On the other hand, they were both dedicated to helping people. She waved a teaspoon at him. 'You want another coffee before we start on this floor?'

'Please. I'll just make a call.'

Ruby stirred the coffee then headed out into the chilly air, Zane at her heels. She rubbed his ears. 'It's not walk time yet. Give me a couple of hours attacking that damned vinyl and then we'll negotiate terms.'

Zane ran past her to the base of a tree and snapped up a tennis ball, racing back to drop it at Ruby's feet.

'Didn't you hear a word I said?' She tossed the ball at the solid wooden fence. Zane sped across the wet, slippery lawn, snatching at his toy and missing, finally picking it up and returning to her.

After the fifth toss Ruby laughed. 'That's it for now. I've got work to do.'

'He's full of energy, isn't he?' Jack said from behind

her, causing her to nearly leap out of her skin. 'Here, Zane, I'll throw that for you.'

Zane obliged, not at all fazed over who played with him, just so long as someone did.

'He's getting better at retrieving the ball. Sometimes I think he uses his blind eye.' Ruby went to collect the spades and some cartons to put the vinyl in and headed back to the house, Jack and Zane following.

Jack told her, 'I checked with the hospital. There's no change with Lily Byrne. She's still in an induced coma.'

The little girl they'd lifted from the car crash yesterday. The downside to their job. A long, slow breath slid out of one corner of Ruby's mouth. 'Those poor parents. They must be going through hell. I really hope Lily comes right. She's so young.'

'Unimaginable what her folks must be feeling.'

Something in Jack's voice made her study him closely. 'You had a moment there yesterday when we first heard about Lily.'

'Yeah, I did.' He lifted one of the spades and began scraping at the floor. Immediately the spade edge snagged and skidded across the vinyl. 'Our sister died of head injuries when she was four. Every time I have to attend a child with those types of injuries I have a moment, as you call it.'

'You had a sister?' She reached a hand to him. 'Jack, I didn't know.' *You never told me. What other important things did you avoid mentioning?*

He twisted away, putting space between them. 'I don't talk about her.'

'Obviously.' He couldn't have hurt her more if he'd tried, turning from her like that. Swallowing hard, she focused on her coffee. Ready with a hug if he needed one. Would he tell her more?

Finally he continued, 'I remember the expression on Dad's face as if it was yesterday. That look of terror has stayed with me all my life. The awful fear, the complete helplessness of the situation, waiting for someone to fix his child. When they couldn't, when she died, Dad just— just crumbled.'

Ruby couldn't wait any longer to be asked. He might never get around to it. She tried not to think how he'd just revealed more about his past than he'd done in all the time they'd been together before. Instead, she stepped close and wrapped her arms around him. Held him tight. Giving him the only thing she had to offer. Felt free to offer. In any capacity he chose to accept.

Jack froze, his back rigid under her hands. Ruby held him, saying nothing, her fingers making soothing circles, her palms pressing into him. Slowly, slowly, he began relaxing. His arms slid around her back. Did he even know he was pulling her ever so slightly closer? Time to shift away, before this got too involved, too awkward. But her legs wouldn't move, had turned boneless. Instead, her arms tightened further. Here in Jack's embrace was where she belonged. This was what she'd been hankering after for three long, lonely years. Why she'd come home.

That didn't make any of this right. If they were to get back together there was a lot to discuss first, issues to clear up. She began to tug back, common sense starting to prevail. She couldn't, shouldn't, revisit the past. She'd hurt Jack, and herself, by leaving. She didn't deserve a second chance.

Jack's hands slid over her back, a caressing movement that stole the air out of her lungs, nullified the common sense trying to take hold of her mind. When he wrapped his hands over her shoulders and tipped her slightly backwards she knew he was going to kiss her and she was powerless to stop him. She wanted it. Forget right or wrong. This was Jack and she was finally kissing him. Common sense was highly overrated.

His mouth touched hers; softly, tentatively. Seeking what? A connection from the past? A new beginning? She thrilled as his lips moulded with hers. And when she opened her mouth under his, her tongue tasted him. And Jack went from slow and quiet to fast and hot in an instant. His kiss deepened so quickly Ruby was spinning through space. Her arms gripped him tighter for support, trying to keep her firmly in the here and now as she tilted further back to allow Jack better access to her mouth.

At last. She was kissing Jack Forbes again. Memories of other kisses flooded her senses. Nothing over those years had changed. They fitted together. They were two halves that needed their matching piece to be complete. And yet this kiss felt different from every other kiss she'd shared with Jack. Filled with need so long held in abeyance. Filled with promise of new beginnings.

Heat zinged along her veins, dipped through her body, lit the dampened fires of desire she'd been denying since setting eyes on Jack close up yesterday. No other man had ever made her feel so weak, so tight, so warm, so needy, all in an instant. Just by kissing her, Jack turned on every switch her body had.

He walked her backwards up to the wall, his mouth not breaking contact with hers for a moment. Pressed against the wall, Ruby wriggled up onto her toes, all the better to continue kissing him. And as she did, she rubbed against his arousal, turning her heat into a conflagration. They were going to make love. The need, the desire, pulsed between them, hummed in her blood, tasted sweet in Jack's mouth.

Then Jack lifted his head and hurriedly stepped back. Ruby stumbled, steadied herself. 'Jack?'

His gaze was dark, deep. Wariness slowly filtered through the desire, cooling it. Caution took over and he stepped further away, taking his warm hands from her shoulders. 'Sorry.'

'You're sorry?' Pain sliced at her. He'd rejected her. Then anger emerged within her, drowning out the hurt he'd inflicted. Because Jack wanted her. He couldn't hide that. Desire had turned his eyes smoky, made his hands warm on her skin. What about his hard need that had pressed against her belly? He wanted her. Why had he broken off?

'Yes, I am.' Dragging a hand over his dark hair he winced. 'Very sorry.'

He sounded like he meant it. The pizza in her belly soured and she swallowed an acid lump in her throat. 'Sorry why, Jack? Because we kissed? Or is there another reason? Another woman?' She paused, remembering the blonde she'd seen him with.

He shook his head, not really an answer. But if there had been someone else, he'd never have kissed her.

She added, 'I'll tell you this for nothing. I don't regret you kissing me. Or that I kissed you back.' But did he have to kiss like the devil and then expect her to be happy when he stopped? At least she knew where she stood with him. They wouldn't be having an affair, not even a brief one. They couldn't even manage the friends thing yet. Her heart rolled over painfully. Talk about stupid. Why had she let him kiss her? Deep down she'd known kissing with Jack had to be avoided at all costs.

She should be grateful one of them had had the strength to haul on the brakes before they'd gone further and headed down the hall to her bedroom. Hadn't she earlier decided to get to know Jack properly this time? Whatever they'd started today had to end now.

Jack spun around and stared out the window. His shoulders dropped as he rammed his hands into his jeans pockets. The silence between them stretched out, growing chillier as the seconds ticked by. Finally, when she couldn't stand it another moment, he turned back.

Anger spat out at her from those steely eyes. 'Why didn't you look me up when you first got back?'

She gasped. 'I did.' Once.

'Yeah, right. Was I asleep? Did I miss something?'

You were out with the blonde sticking plaster, having a lovey-dovey moment in the café at the end of your road. 'No one answered the doorbell so you might've been asleep.'

'You didn't think to come back another time?'

And get to meet Blondie face to face? 'I *have* been busy. I haven't got around to looking up anyone from the old days yet.'

'I deserve better than that. I wasn't just anyone.' He stamped across the room, reached the door and yanked it open. 'Let's stick to professional and friendly. Nothing more. Nothing less. What happened a moment ago will not happen again. Got it?'

'Loud and clear.' She was sorry she'd hurt him, very sorry. But her one attempt to see him had underlined the fact that she couldn't waltz back into his life and pick up where she'd left off. Straightening her spine, tugging her chin up, she locked eyes with him. 'I'll see you at work and not before.'

Then she picked up the spade and began to attack the vinyl with renewed vigour. Slam. A piece the size of a fifty-cent coin flicked through the air and hit the wall. Slam. Another piece spun off.

Jack watched her from the door. Please go, she begged silently. She was starting to feel like an idiot. Cold, hard reality had a certain chill to it. They had made a mistake. She glared at him. 'For the record, you're right. We need to keep our relationship light and friendly.' Not intense and sexual.

His beautiful mouth tightened. 'I'm glad you see things my way.'

His way? 'Don't get me started.' Another piece of vinyl spun across the floor. His way?

Everything had been going perfectly until Jack had stepped back into her life. The plans for her kitchen, her job. Even her lack of a love life hadn't bothered her. Now? Now she had more problems than she knew what to do with.

Jack braked sharply at the bottom of the hill. Fleeing from Ruby. Now, there was a laugh. Hilarious—not. A total role reversal. That mind-blowing kiss stayed with him, making his heated blood race. Pressing his foot harder on the accelerator, he careered out onto the main road. It seemed he couldn't leave the heady taste of Ruby behind. Not even her lack of a real answer about looking him up dampened the fires raging through his body. Another woman? Where did Ruby get such a notion?

There'd been huge disappointment in her jade eyes when he'd stopped kissing her.

What about *his* disappointment? He still didn't know how he'd managed to drag his mouth away from those lips that tasted of nectar. He'd wanted—needed—to take her there and then. The tension had been building all morning. Yet somehow reality had turned a cog, clicked some sense into his brain. At least he wouldn't be leading Ruby on only to desert her in a few months' time. She could be grateful for that.

In self-defence he'd got angry with her. And she'd got angry back. At last the Ruby he recognised. A quick burst of temper had always been her way of getting out of a tight spot.

And sometimes her anger wasn't a quick burst. More like a hard, slow burn that she'd still hold a week from now. And behind that burn was a big glob of hurt. He'd rejected her. And she hated that. She could reject him, but take it in return? Not at all.

Right now relief should be pouring through him that he'd got away before going too far. It was Ruby's fault they'd kissed. She was too attractive. Temptation in a small, neat body that made him forget his hurt at her not calling in to see him since she'd returned. So he should slow down and relax, put out of his head the feeling of her lips on his. His hormones could go back into hibernation instead of overheating his body.

Toot, toot. A car cut him off, the driver waving a fist at him.

'What did I do?' Jack glanced in the rear-view mirror, side mirrors, couldn't see anything out of order. He checked the speedo. 'Yikes. Now I'm crawling along like I've got four flats.'

He indicated to pull over and slipped into a parking space right beside the beach. A brisk walk would help clear his head of all things Ruby.

His cellphone rang. Snatching it up from the passenger seat, he paused to check who was calling. If it was Ruby he'd ignore her. Really? Fortunately he didn't have to make that decision. 'Hey, Tony, how's things?'

His flying instructor replied, 'I've had a cancellation.

You want to go for a buzz around the sky? Practise those engine-failure procedures?'

'Yes.' Jack tapped his fist on the steering-wheel. 'Yes.' An answer from heaven. Concentrating on putting his plane down in a tiny paddock without actually landing would send images of Ruby to Arizona. 'Give me fifteen. I'll drop in at home and grab my logbook.'

Jack didn't think of Ruby for thirty-two minutes, the whole time he was piloting the two-seater airplane.

But as he shoved the plane's door wide to step down onto the strut she reappeared, banging around inside his skull. Those piercing green eyes accused him of letting her down by stopping that kiss. The way she'd attacked the floor like her life had depended on it. The floor he'd offered to help with clearing, and which would take her twice as long to finish now that he'd stormed out. A sneaky feeling of guilt shimmied through him. It was easy to blame Ruby for everything. She'd done the leaving but not once had he offered to put his life on hold to go with her. Impractical for sure, but it might've been the right thing to do. Given the same circumstances, would he go now? He squashed that question firmly into the too-hard basket.

It was Zane who noticed him first. 'Hey, dog, how's your mum? Calmed down a bit?'

'That depends why you've come back.' Ruby stood on the porch, another coffee mug clasped in her hands, Zane's ball at her feet.

He was there because he had to prove their kiss had meant absolutely nothing. 'Figured you still needed a hand with that vinyl despite what went down between us earlier.'

Jack wished he could turn back down the path but he'd

already run away once today. Where Ruby was concerned he had no control over his mouth, his mushy brain or in fact any part of his body. He should never have returned. Having left once this afternoon, he should've stayed gone—from her home, from her private life. For the next four months. Until he left for Antarctica in the summer.

'Want a coffee or a beer?'

A peace offering? 'Beer, thanks. The amount of caffeine you drink you must be wired.' Maybe that was why she had kissed him back so readily.

Believe that and he'd believe pigs really did fly. She'd enjoyed kissing him as much as he'd enjoyed kissing her. Returning here was akin to walking through a pack of hungry lions. The sooner they'd done the job, the better for his sanity. Then he'd go home, turn on the computer and start seriously looking into jobs overseas for next year.

CHAPTER FIVE

THROUGH his office window Jack watched Ruby sliding out of her truck in the parking lot on Wednesday morning. Those short legs looked good in her jumpsuit, her heavy boots cute on her tiny feet. There was a line across her mouth-watering backside, probably made by her tucked-in undershirt. The stubborn set of her shoulders caused his mouth to curve upwards. Woe betide anyone who argued with Ruby today. What had brought that attitude on? Her shocking hair stood upright, no doubt glued into place with a handful of hair gel.

Outrageously gorgeous. That was Red. Ruby. The pen he held spun across the room. Get a grip. They were about to spend the day working together. *Her name is Ruby.*

Despite two days thinking about little else, he was still flummoxed as to why he'd kissed her. Other than being sidetracked by all that gorgeousness, that sexiness, her warmth and compassion. When she'd wrapped her arms around him in a sincere attempt to cheer him up he'd been doomed. He'd known he'd missed her, but that hug had brought need slamming through him. Need for Ruby. Need that would not take a back seat to his professional demands, or to his decision to remain buddies with her. Need that he might've thought had eased off since he'd last seen her but was now screaming around his veins with very little restraint.

On Monday he'd helped her finish the floor and then hightailed it for the pub and a few well-earned beers with Johnny, who had been home for ten days. It hadn't done any good at all. Not even spending most of yesterday at the aero club had doused his ardour for Ruby one iota.

But what had really frightened him was the thing slowly unfurling in his gut. Something that wasn't physical, more a sense of belonging to—with—Red. Like a light at the end of a long, dark corridor. Frighteningly like she was his beacon. As though he needed her for stability in his life. That revelation had come in the early hours of the morning, terrifying him.

He was the strong one around here, the man people came to for support, love and care. His fingers dug into his palms. He didn't need his own personal rock to lean on. Especially one in the form of a tiny, feisty redhead. But slowly it was dawning on him that Ruby was the counterbalance to all the haywire parts of him. She might be able to save him from his crazy schemes, such as chucking in his dream job to go off on a tangent. Or attempting to become a man he didn't recognise. He sure didn't recognise himself as someone about to start wandering the globe.

A slow sigh leaked over his bottom lip. Last night he'd driven past her house, drawn by an invisible thread. When he'd found the place in darkness a rare spurt of loneliness had gripped him, hollowed him out. Then he'd spent the rest of the night wondering where she was. Who she was with.

Ruby disappeared from sight around the corner of the building, and Jack took the moment to collect himself. This had to work, for both of them. Which meant no more hot kisses. Kisses were what had started this whole weird thinking about rocks and beacons, and kept him awake all night.

He heard Chris ask her, 'How was the rest of your time off?'

Ruby chuckled. 'Smashing, thanks.' She was coming closer to the office and Jack braced himself.

Chris asked, 'Oh, great. What did you take your hammer to?'

'That old wood shed. It was already falling down and only taking up space I want for planting spuds in spring.'

Planting spuds in spring? In time for Christmas dinner? When he'd be at Scott Base, freezing. Jack's spare pen snapped in his hand.

Chris continued, 'Did you get all that vinyl up?'

'Every last square inch of the blasted stuff, with Jack's help.' And there she was, standing in his doorway, studying him with a definite caution in those jade eyes. 'Morning, Jack.'

'Hi, there. So what's next to do in the kitchen?'

'The floor's being sanded tomorrow, earlier than I expected, so here's hoping for a fine weekend when I can start bringing those kauri boards to life.' Her eyes sparkled, caution forgotten as she bounced on her toes. 'It's going to look so cool.'

Jack asked, 'When does the builder put in your new cupboards?' Keep the conversation focused on everyday matters and he might make it through the first hour.

'Not sure about that. A week or two, I think. Longer than originally planned, anyway, since we took out that false ceiling.' Ruby shrugged. 'Are you coming with me to do a stocktake of our drugs? We do our bags before team two as the storeroom's too small for all of us at once.'

Anywhere would be too small with Ruby there, but he couldn't avoid the job. It was imperative to complete it efficiently and quickly. Jack pushed back his chair. 'Of course. Dave mentioned that's a priority for our first day on.'

'Dave's here, then?' Ruby asked over her shoulder as she headed for the locked storeroom where their packs were kept when not in use.

'He's over talking to Sandra about a malfunctioning light in number two 'copter.' Jack's gaze encompassed the compact woman he was following. The shapeless jumpsuit shouldn't make her look so delectable, but the way she cinched the waist in with a wide, non-uniform belt caused the fabric to flare softly over her tiny hips. And made his mouth go dry.

Ruby punched in the access code and tugged the door wide. She must've used up all the air in the small room because from the moment he entered Jack couldn't breathe. And when Red hauled their packs out backwards from a low cupboard she bumped up against his legs, causing Jack's heart to thump hard against his ribs. And he was supposed to work with her?

'Sorry,' she muttered, her cheeks flaming.

'Not a problem.' Sure thing, buddy. No problem at all. He reached around her for a pack and swung it up onto the small table.

Glaring at him, no doubt for intervening, she waited, hands on hips, while he unzipped one and spread the two sides out wide.

'Check the expiry dates first, right?' he asked, ignoring her rising irritation and carefully keeping far enough away so as not to inadvertently touch her.

Ruby picked up the stock list and pulled a pen from her pocket. 'You got it. Call them out and I'll sign them off.' She leaned against the furthest wall. Still not far enough away.

The routine quickly settled Jack's oddly whacking heart and solved his breathing problems, but he knew it wouldn't last. Ruby had always rattled him. The only mistake he'd made had been to think he would no longer be affected by her. Oh, and taking a job where he had to work alongside her. Add in kissing her the other day and he had quite a list, considering this was his first official day on duty.

Ruby slipped the stock list back onto its hook, surprised her fingers were steady. Nothing else about her was. Her stomach was doing mini-skips. Her heart rate pattered way too fast. And her tongue kept doing circuits of her mouth.

And whose fault was this? Jack Forbes. That was who. He should've withdrawn from the job when he'd learned she held a position at Rescue Helicopters. How was she supposed to work with him when she couldn't think straight whenever he was within touching distance? When they weren't squeezed into this cupboard of a storeroom they'd be crammed together in the back of the helicopter. Or sitting opposite each other in the tearoom.

'Anything else we need to do right now?' Jack's husky voice broke through her turmoil. The texture of his words had always excited her, especially when it came as a whisper near her ear.

'No.' She blinked. Slid towards the door and bumped slap bang into the man she was trying to avoid.

His hands gripped her shoulders. 'Steady.'

That husky voice sent shivers down her spine. Flipping her head back, she locked eyes with Jack. His mouth so close she only had to rise up on her toes, slide her hands around his neck to tug him closer and they'd be kissing again. He looked good enough to eat. Male, virile, exciting. Her breasts ached sweetly as she imagined his hands caressing them.

'Red?' Her nickname slid slowly off his tongue.

'Nothing.' Ruby jerked back and all but ran from the storeroom, not looking at Jack. Light drizzle had begun falling and as she made her way to the 'copter she shivered. A sharp southerly was rapidly approaching, bringing icy air. The one thing she didn't enjoy about being back home was winter. Wellington was living up to its cold and windy reputation. For a brief moment she missed San Francisco, even the fog-enshrouded days, then dismissed the sensation. Wellington was home, which meant dealing with the good and bad. Which meant dealing with facing the truth about her feelings for Jack. She might be falling in love with him all over again, but it didn't necessarily follow that he wanted her. Apart from in bed, because that had been so obvious back there, crammed together in the storeroom. His eyes had practically told her. But that was sex, not love. If Jack couldn't find it in his heart to love her again then it was just as well he was going away soon.

And then what? Slumping onto the jump seat, she tasted fear in her mouth. Had she made a mistake, coming back here? She'd so wanted to make a home for herself in this city where she had some wonderful memories of her time with Jack. Even of her mother and grandfather. She couldn't run now. She had to stop somewhere and she'd chosen Wellington. Had to stay long enough to see her vegetables grow, to finish her house and live in it. But what if Christmas arrived and loneliness drove her away in search of people to fill her days with? She'd always been hoping Jack would be around then. What if she really couldn't stay in one place, especially without Jack to anchor her?

Be strong, be tough. Her slump straightened a little. She could do this. She had to for her own sake. If she couldn't look out for herself, how could she expect anyone else to help her, love her, share her life with her? Her shoulders dragged back. Be strong, be tough. She had Zane. He'd be ecstatic to share the Christmas ham bone with her.

The clicks of switches up front as Chris and Slats ran through their daily checks reminded Ruby she did have friends here. She'd like to talk to Chris, ask him how long he'd lived here and did he think he'd stay working for the helicopter rescue unit, but she knew better than to talk to him now. The only time she ever saw him get cross was when someone bowled up and started yakking in his ear while he ran through his lists. He'd once told her that checks were a very important part of flying and he pre-ferred total concentration otherwise he'd spend the day worrying he'd missed out something vital to a flight. So no interruptions. Anyway, what could he tell her that would put her at ease? He'd got his life together, had his dream job, a wonderful partner.

Yeah, and, Ruby, you've got your dream job, your house and a wonderful, wacky dog. Don't be greedy. Don't tempt fate to bring it all crashing down on your head because you're afraid to relax and make the most of those things. Get to work and stop daydreaming.

Vigorously scrubbing the stretcher with antibacterial cleaner, Ruby became immersed in the routine of her day, and Jack was finally on the back burner in her mind.

'Quiet day so far.' Chris poked his head around the bulkhead half an hour later, startling her. 'Jack seems an okay guy. You getting on with him?'

Sitting back on her haunches, Ruby considered the real question behind Chris's query. He probably wasn't the only one wondering if her previous relationship with Jack might sour things for everyone else. 'It's a bit early to comment on that. We've only had one afternoon together on the 'copter.' And one hot kiss. 'But having worked with him in A and E, I know he's a dedicated and skilled doctor. He's exacting, and doesn't suffer fools or shoddy work.'

Slats called from beside Chris, 'You'll be okay, then. Everyone says you're a very good paramedic.'

A compliment from Slats was rare. Heat spilled across her cheeks. 'Why, thank you, sir. As long as Jack thinks so.'

'Is that a general wish? Or a personal one?' Chris asked.

Ruby flipped her head up. 'What do you mean by that?' Had he guessed her feelings for their new boss? Not possible when she wasn't overly sure herself. Crikey, did everyone on the station think something was going on between her and Jack? Her hands fisted. Worse, had Jack heard anyone talking about them? That would definitely put him in a tailspin.

'Relax, Red.'

She bared her teeth at the use of that nickname. 'Don't.'

Chris chuckled. 'I rest my case. When Jack uses Red you don't bat an eyelid.' As a scowl began squeezing up her face he winked. 'It's okay, Ruby, your secret's safe. And for the record, I think it's time you had some fun.'

'I'm having heaps of fun. Look at what I'm doing with my house. That's the most amazing and exciting thing I've ever done. And I've got Zane, remember?' And the nights were long and lonely.

'I can't see you letting a dog snuggle up on your bed on a cold night.'

How true. She loved her mutt to bits but there were rules and sleeping in the laundry on his blankets was one. 'Yeah, well, I'm hardly going to let Jack snuggle up with me either.'

'For now.' Chris grinned, and ducked to avoid the plastic airway tube Ruby threw at him. He caught it effortlessly and tossed it back. 'You give yourself away every time.'

'True.' According to other people, she was an easy read. Jack had certainly always known what was on her mind, sometimes before she did. But he hadn't always got it right. He hadn't seen how desperately she'd wanted him to ask her to wait for him to go with her to the States. Unable to put her need into words, she'd relied on him working it out himself. Of course he hadn't. Could he still see through her? This Jack seemed more unsettled than the man she'd once loved. He'd always been very focused on reaching the top in his career as quickly as possible. She'd never doubted he'd make head of department. So why had he quit? What had happened that had pushed him away from that dream and into rescue work? Leaping out of an aircraft didn't seem to match the picture she held of a grounded, dedicated doctor like Jack.

A doctor who nowadays joined in with the crew for tea breaks and after-work socialising. He'd not done that when they'd worked in A and E, preferring to keep work and his private life separate. And he certainly wouldn't have turned up at the home of any staff member to help pull out cupboards.

She'd questioned him once. *'How can you justify having an affair with me when I'm a trainee nurse on your team?'*

'Why wouldn't I? You're my girlfriend. I love you.' That was all there was to it in his eyes. He'd continued to keep that side of their relationship separate from their working one, while she'd often crossed his boundaries and earned his wrath.

The helicopter rocked as a sharp gust of wind buffeted it. Ruby glanced outside. 'Great. The drizzle is now horizontal rain. Should make for interesting flying conditions.'

Chris said, 'That front's coming in a lot faster than

forecast. Hopefully it'll pass through as quickly. But the wind's predicted to get worse first.'

'Just as well we're quiet, then.' Ruby straightened up. 'Guess I'm going to get soaked going back inside. Want a coffee?'

'Might as well. Nothing happening out here.' Chris squeezed his broad shoulders through the narrow gap into the body of his 'copter and slid the door open.

Up front the radio crackled. Slats read out, 'Rescue Helicopter Crew Two, pick up MVA, Hutt highway, south-bound, one POB, stat three.'

Ruby muttered, 'At least some of us have got something to do.' Crew Two usually took the less serious cases, leaving her crew on standby for the stat four or five calls.

'Be grateful. They're not going to have a comfortable flight.' Chris dropped to the ground and dashed to the building.

Ruby raced after him, cursing the numerous puddles. 'Have a rough trip, guys.' She waved as she passed Jason, Kevin and Cody heading out to their 'copter.

'It'll be a picnic,' Cody quipped.

Jack held the door open. Had he been watching out for them? 'Hot savouries and cake in the tearoom. My shout since it's my first proper day on the job.'

'Glad you've studied the rules for new staff.' Ruby shook herself like a wet spaniel, water droplets from her hair flying all around. 'I hate this weather.'

'Toughen up, Red. What's a bit of water?' Jack's smile was full of caution.

'Shut that door, will you?' she retorted. Straightening her shoulders, she turned for the tearoom, shivering as the cold air from the still open outside door swirled around her. 'Winter's the pits.'

And so was denying her attraction for her boss.

* * *

The day dragged. No major emergencies. Not even a minor one for Crew One to attend while Crew Two was busy. Ruby attacked the storeroom, scrubbing the already sparkling shelves, straightening the already straight lines of equipment.

The book she'd begun reading during her days off lay in her locker. Normally she'd have finished her chores and then sat in the staffroom reading that or studying current medical procedures, but today she was avoiding Jack who, with Dave, was working in there. They'd spread files and papers over the table, taking up all the available space. Eager to avoid Jack as much as possible, Ruby struggled to fill in her time elsewhere. When she could not avoid the staffroom any longer, she cranked up the spare computer to go online and order some books.

'What are you smiling about?' Jack asked from across the room.

She started, looked around. Where had Dave gone? 'Nothing.' He'd never believe her if she told him what she'd ordered.

Jack watched her closing down the website. 'Did you finally catch up with your father in the States?' he asked suddenly.

'Yep.' Double click on her email site.

'Not as good as you'd hoped?'

'Nope.' Five new emails.

Jack continued watching her. 'I'd like to know, Ruby. He was like a hovering black cloud that had to pass before our relationship could grow.'

'That's true.' The vet had sent a notice reminding her Zane was due for a check-up. She raised her head, peered at Jack. 'All right,' she muttered. 'The man I tracked down is my biological father, nothing more. He's a two-timing sleazeball that I'm ashamed to have wasted so many years daydreaming about. Mum was well shot of him.'

Click. Reply to the vet. *Please make me an appointment for next Monday.* Click. 'And so am I.'

A warm hand curled around her shoulder. Strong fingers squeezed gently. 'I'm sorry, Red, really sorry. I know how much you needed him to be a great dad.'

Click. Close the program. Log off. 'We don't always get what we want.'

Pushing her chair back, Ruby stood up, forcing Jack to remove his hand. She didn't need sympathy. Especially not from the man she'd hurt in order to find the Greaser.

'Red, remember that black night I came home after A and E had been swamped in casualties from a train and bus accident?'

Ruby's eyes latched on to Jack's. Horror rolled through her as a dreadful scene bowled into her head. Jack crying. Jack shocked. Jack believing he could've saved more lives than he already had. Jack swearing he'd give up medicine the very next day.

'Red?' A feather-light touch on her chin. 'You listened to me for hours that night. You wrapped your arms around me and rocked me like a baby. You refused to let me feel sorry for myself.' Jack's eyes were enormous, and filled with…love?

No, not that. Understanding. That's it. Understanding. 'I remember,' she whispered.

'You saved me that night.'

'Yeah, I guess I did.'

'No one else has ever done something like that for me. Ever.' His finger slid up her chin, over her mouth. 'I'll always be around for you.'

Except you're going away. Gulp. Pain burned in her throat, her stomach. Did he know how much she longed to throw herself at him and tell him of her shame over hurting him for the sake of the Greaser?

Well, she wasn't going to. She couldn't. He might feel sorry for her. Straightening up, she stepped away, refusing to be drawn in by his sympathetic gaze. She couldn't afford to go there. Jack might be offering to help her in the bad times but he wasn't staying around for *all* the times. The good, bad and indifferent times.

'Thanks, Jack. Glad to know I've got good mates.' She'd go and annoy Julie until the shame burning her gut dissipated.

Jack watched her go, hurting for her, hurting for them. They'd had a good thing going in the past. They'd connected in a way, not as close and honest as it should've been but there'd been the basis for it getting better.

What had happened between her and her father? If only she'd talk to him about it.

Huh? Ruby should talk to you? As in the guy who never told her anything more important than where to meet him after work?

Jack shivered. Any right he had to help Red was long gone. He'd made a right pig's breakfast of things back then. And still was.

That was because he didn't know what he was doing with his life any more. This grand plan to get out and see the world was already stuttering to a halt. Working on the helicopters still excited him. He was looking forward to that. And going to Scott Base.

It's the other stuff he couldn't get his head around. Life outside work. Ruby stuff. How could he sort out her problems when he couldn't deal with his own? She didn't need a basket case in her life.

His cellphone vibrated in his pocket. Flipping it open,

he saw the caller was his mate from the paediatric ward at Wellington Hospital. 'Hey, Ian, what've you got for me?'

A few minutes later he found Ruby sitting on the floor of Julie's office, screeds of patient reports lying over and around her legs. 'Hey, what are you doing down there?'

'Making myself useful.' She didn't look up.

'I see.' She was trying to avoid him. Fair enough. He couldn't find fault with that. 'I thought you'd like to know that Lily Byrne regained consciousness this morning.'

Ruby raised her head sharply. 'That's fantastic news. Do the doctors know if she's going to be a hundred per cent all right?'

'Too soon to know. They've got a whole battery of tests lined up to do over the next few days. But at least Lily's situation is improving.'

The reports spilled from Ruby's fingers as she stopped sorting them into alphabetic order. 'Her parents must be feeling more hopeful. How is Lily's mother, do you know?'

'She's well enough to have been transferred from Hutt Hospital into Wellington. She's thrilled to be closer to Lily but until the results of all those tests are known there'll be no relaxing for those parents.' Sadness gripped him as memories of Beth's accident assailed him. Every time he dealt with an accident involving a child he went through this pain of wanting to make everything work out all right for the families involved. Every time it didn't he felt the agony the families were going through.

On his belt his pager vibrated. At last. A job. 'We're on, Ruby. Let's hustle.'

CHAPTER SIX

'DESTINATION Rapara Island.' Ruby looked up as wind rattled the window. 'Ripper stuff. We're about to get slam-dunked all over the sky as we cross Cook Strait.' The island was part of the Marlborough Sounds at the top of the South Island. A beautiful spot in summer, isolated and harsh in winter. 'Let's move.'

Jack read from his pager, '"Forty-one-year-old female. Premature labour at thirty-one weeks, heavy bleeding."'

'Buckle up tight,' Chris told them as they scrambled inside the helicopter.

'What's the forecast for the next two hours?' Jack asked him.

'Wind should be abating by now, so here's hoping it sees fit to do just that. I'm guessing this won't be a quick transfer?'

'Can't answer that until I've examined the woman,' Jack answered, 'but I'll—' He stopped, nodded at Ruby. 'Sorry, we'll be as quick as safely possible.'

Ruby tugged her safety harness tight and leaned her head back, closing her eyes.

'You okay?' Jack asked as his harness buckle clicked into place.

'Yes.' She added in a softer tone, 'Just running through what I know about prem babies and what we can expect.'

'I wish we had a few more details, such as is the mother having regular contractions? Who decided she was even in labour? Is she panicking because of the bleeding?' When Ruby opened her eyes and stared at him, Jack was quick to snap, 'That's not a criticism, merely a concern. I'm guessing living out on Rapara Island would automatically crank up the worry scale for any pregnant woman, and especially one in her forties.'

'The woman probably intended being off the island well before her due date. I wonder if she has other children or if it's a first pregnancy.'

'Let's hope not. She'll at least understand what's happening if she's been through it before.' Jack rested his elbows on his knees, his chin on his tightly interlaced fingers. 'Okay, what steps do we take when we arrive?'

Ruby ran down the list. 'First the usual obs—BP, resp rate, temperature in case of infection, listen for the foetal heartbeat.' She tapped her fist on her thigh. 'Oh, and time any contractions.'

The helicopter lurched and Ruby gripped the sides of her jump seat, calling out to Chris, 'Hey, if I wanted a roller-coaster ride I'd have gone to the theme park.'

'Just saving you the air fare to Auckland,' Chris quipped, before adding, 'So much for the wind dropping. I can see the *Kaitaki* down below. Those passengers will be having the trip from hell.'

'I'd have refused to go,' Ruby called back. 'I'm not keen on the ferry on a flat, calm day.'

Jack's brow creased. 'You get seasick?'

'Prostrate with nausea.'

'You did okay when we lifted that cardiac arrest patient off the other day.'

'Had other things on my mind.' Like saving a patient's life.

'Rapara coming up,' Chris called. 'There's a vehicle with flashing lights below the ridge. Hopefully that means we'll be sheltered as we go in.'

Within minutes Ruby and Jack were squashed into the cab of a four-wheel-drive vehicle with their patient's husband and bouncing across paddocks to the farmhouse. Every bump caused their thighs to rub against each other. Every sway of the truck banged their arms together. Ruby clenched her jaw, hoping they'd reach their destination soon. She heard Jack's sharp intake of breath. So she wasn't the only one suffering.

'Mary got backache late yesterday,' Colin Archer said in response to Jack's brusque questioning. 'She wanted to get off the island and go to Blenheim where our GP is but then her back came right. I had to go over to the other side to muster sheep and she said she'd be fine. Should've known better and taken her out then. It's my fault she's in the state she is.'

Jack sighed. 'We'll soon have Mary on the way to hospital. Don't go blaming yourself for anything, just concentrate on being calm and cheerful for your wife.'

'Just like that, eh?' The other man rolled his eyes at Jack, before leaning over the steering-wheel to peer through the murk. 'There's the house. Mary's probably still pacing the floor. I tried to make her lie down but she got mad at me, said I didn't know a thing about having a baby and to get out of the house. Guess this is a bit more complicated than lambing my ewes.'

Ruby bit down on a sudden smile. 'Is this your first baby, then?'

'We're latecomers. Got married less than a year ago and tried for a family straight away. Took a few goes till we got it right.' Colin winked, then his mouth dropped again. 'I should never have brought Mary out here until after the little blighter was born. But she insisted, even learned to drive the boat in case she had to take herself to town to see the GP.'

Jack asked, 'So when did your wife last see her doctor?'

'Some time in March, I think it was.'

And this was June. Ruby shook her head slightly. The woman should've been seeing her GP regularly. 'Has Mary had other children?'

'No, none at all. She was too busy working on her career as an international journalist to be having kids. Found it hard to stop here at first but she's learned to ride the tractors, dock the sheep. Turning into a right little farmer she is.'

If an international journalist could make a life for herself out here where there was absolutely nothing but animals then surely she could handle Wellington, Ruby mused. And maybe she could find a way back to Jack.

Mary Archer met them at the back door, her hands tucked under her very pregnant belly. Her face was grey, her eyes dull. 'Sorry for all the bother but I think I'm in trouble,' she said after they'd introduced themselves.

Jack didn't waste any time. 'Can we go through to your bedroom so I can examine you? Tell me why you think you're in labour.'

'I'm getting regular pains, Doc. Here.' She stabbed her abdomen. 'My back's been giving me grief since last night. There's been lots of blood. My baby will be all right, won't it?' Her teeth dug into her lower lip.

'Let's take things one step at a time. How far apart are your pains?' Jack helped the woman onto the unmade bed.

'About five minutes, I reckon. I haven't been timing them. Figured there was no point. If it's coming, it's coming.'

Ruby unzipped the pack and pulled out the blood-pressure cuff. Around the other side of the bed she reached for Mary's arm. 'Has your blood pressure been normal throughout your pregnancy?'

'In March the doc said it was fine for a pregnant lady.'

Which told them absolutely nothing. Mary wouldn't have been to antenatal classes either. She could be in for a shock. Did she know how to breathe her way through the contractions? Ruby wrote the BP reading on her glove, too low, and showed it to Jack. 'I'm going to take your temperature, Mary. Then I'll check your glucose level.' Pregnancy diabetes could be a further complication.

Jack made an internal examination. Then he listened for a foetal heartbeat. As Ruby watched him his brow creased. What? No heartbeat? Oh, hell.

'Two beats.' Jack grinned at Ruby. 'Two.' He looked to his patient. 'Mary, have you had a scan since becoming pregnant?'

'No. I've avoided all those things. I guess you're going to tell me off.'

Jack shook his head. 'It's too late for that. But we need to get you to hospital ASAP. I think you're having twins. Which would partially explain the early labour.'

'Twins?' Mary gaped at Jack.

'Twins?' bellowed her husband from the doorway, causing Ruby to jump with shock. She'd forgotten all about the poor man. 'You mean we're having two babies? But we're not geared for two. We've only got one crib, and one set of clothes, and…' His voice dwindled from a roar to a whisper. 'Hell, who'd have thought, eh?'

'You'll have plenty of time to go shopping,' Ruby told him. 'If these two arrive today, they'll be in hospital for a little while.'

Mary groaned as another contraction gripped her.

Ruby wiped Mary's forehead and held her hand. She

was sure that all her metatarsals would be broken in the bigger woman's ferocious grasp. 'You're doing well,' she tried to reassure the mother-to-be.

'Try not to push,' Jack told Mary. 'I'm going to give you a drug that will hopefully delay delivery at least until we get you to hospital. I'll top it up every thirty minutes.'

Ruby retrieved a vial from the pack and handed it to Jack.

Mary gasped, 'Are you taking me to Nelson Hospital?'

'Sorry, it's Wellington for you,' Ruby told her.

'But my GP's in Nelson. My family are there. My friends.'

Ruby helped her sit up and swing her legs over the side of the bed. 'I'm sure you'll be transferred to Nelson later on, but first we need to get you to proper care and Wellington is closer.' The difference in distance wasn't too much but Ruby hoped to calm Mary because there was no choice in their destination. 'You do want what's best for those little ones, don't you?'

'Of course. I just never thought I'd be going anywhere else.' Her eyes widened. 'How will Colin get there? Is there room in the helicopter for him?'

'Unfortunately not,' Ruby replied. 'We need the space in case you start to deliver.'

Mary stood up awkwardly, her thighs pressed together, as though afraid her babies might drop out. 'But I need Colin with me.'

'I'll leave in the boat the moment you're airborne, love,' Colin tried to reassure her.

'What happens if the babies decide to come while we're flying?' Mary asked.

Ruby had never seen such a white face.

Jack's brow puckered, his eyes narrowed. The look he got while trying to think of how to word something so as not to upset anyone. It was such a familiar expression that Ruby's heart tipped sideways. The last time she'd seen that look had been when he'd told her, 'Goodbye, hope it all works out for you.'

'I've delivered a few babies in my time. We'll manage, okay? Try to relax.' He smiled that smile that usually won over even the most stubborn people. 'You're thinking what would I know about what you're going through? Right?'

Outside Ruby clambered onto the back of the truck, leaving Jack to squeeze in beside his patient. 'You okay back there?' he asked. 'I can swap places.'

'You're needed inside. I'll be fine. It's only a short ride.' Ruby sat down on a very wet pile of sacks just as Colin lurched the vehicle forward. She grabbed for a rail and held on. Cold moisture seeped into her jumpsuit, making her shiver. *Great. Now I'll look like I've wet myself.*

On board the helicopter they quickly made Mary comfortable. Then, as Chris and Slats began the start-up procedure, Ruby called Wellington Hospital A and E on the radio and filed Mary's details so the appropriate staff and equipment would be waiting for them when they touched down.

The next thirty-five minutes took for ever as they banged into a strong headwind. Every time Mary groaned, Ruby held her breath. A mid-air birth would not be fun for any of them. Slowly the drug took effect and the contractions abated. But for how long?

She took another BP reading and showed it to Jack. 'No change.'

He nodded. 'You're doing fine, Mary.' Sitting back on his haunches he mused, 'Twins, eh? Double trouble. Or double fun. I reckon it would be great to have two babies at once.'

Ruby gaped at him. 'You'd like twins?' When had he

decided he'd like babies at all? They had never discussed having children. Her heart sank. What had they learned about each other? Absolutely nothing, it seemed.

'If I was having children, yes, I reckon I would. They'd always have a mate, someone who understood them, someone to look out for them all the time.'

'Like you and Steve?'

'Something like that but more.' A far-away look washed through his eyes, lightening their slate-grey colour. Had Jack missed out on friends while he was growing up? Had his life been dedicated to making sure his father and brother were happy? So that they didn't leave him?

She couldn't ask him. He'd turn away from her, his eyes would snap with disapproval. So Ruby nudged him. 'And what about the extra work? All those nappies, all the extra bottles of milk, the crying late at night when one wakes the other?'

'I'd be there, doing my share.' He turned that dreamy gaze on her. 'Don't you ever think about having a family of your own, Red?'

Stunned, Ruby could only swallow and shake her head. He'd said babies and Red in the same sentence. Did that mean anything? Or nothing? She sank back on her seat and reached for the safety harness. No, she was getting way ahead of the ball. 'Can't say I have.' She had enough on her plate with the house and Zane.

Sure she did. Her eyes scoped Jack. An unbidden thought unfolded, expanded, took hold. Kids. Her very own children. With Jack. Wow. This was something she'd never considered, didn't know what to do with.

Because it was never, ever, going to happen. Children, with or without Jack. How did a woman who'd given her mother such a hard time bring up her own children?

A few hours ago she'd ordered cookery books that she

didn't know how to use. How could she raise kids? For starters, they'd need feeding. How old did they have to be before they ate pizza?

No, no, no. Maybe she needed to go back to the SPCA and get Zane a playmate. Two dogs should keep her few free hours full, and at least she could buy them ready-made dog food.

Just over a week later, Julie placed a courier package on the tearoom table in front of Ruby after they'd handed over to the next shift. 'This arrived for you today. You and your books. You're going to have to build a library in your house.'

Ruby smiled happily. All taken care of. Three shelves in one of her new kitchen cupboards would be allocated to recipe books. She lifted the parcel, felt the weight of the books. Solid hard-cover ones. 'The bathroom's next. I'm not living through another winter without fixing that up. I get into a piping-hot shower at five in the morning, then snap-freeze the moment I step back out.' She shivered ex-aggeratedly. 'How did people survive eighty years ago?'

'They were hardy.' Jack tugged open the fridge and handed around beers, putting one back when Ruby shook her head. He sat on the opposite side of the room and looked around at all his colleagues, except Ruby. 'What's everyone got planned for their days off?'

'I'm going to sit in my new kitchen and gloat.' Ruby tipped her chair onto its back legs. He mightn't be looking at her but she could still answer. 'If it's finished.'

'How many days has that taken?' Jack asked.

'Three.' Every night she'd gone home and stood in the middle of her changing kitchen space and absorbed the clean blue and white lines of her new cabinets. And last night she'd rubbed her hands over the sensuously smooth, black granite benchtops.

'We should have a kitchen-warming party,' Chris supplied.

'What? And have you lot tramping around on my beautifully varnished floor?'

'Are you actually going to use this kitchen?' Jack asked. 'As in turn the stove on, cook meals?'

Just you wait and see, she gloated to herself. Which reminded her. What was the time? Oops, time to go. She leapt up. 'Must fly. Things to do, places to be.'

'You're not coming to the pub for a meal?' Jack looked around the room. 'Isn't that what we're all doing?'

'Rain-check.' Ruby nipped over to her locker and tugged out her bag as everyone else confirmed they were on for the pub. 'See you all next week. Enjoy the days off.'

Out in the car park she swung up into her truck. She had to go to the supermarket, walk Zane and change out of her uniform, all in less than an hour.

Jack's face appeared at her side window and she lowered it reluctantly. Any delay would have a serious impact on her plans. 'Yes?'

'What's the hurry?'

She wanted to keep the cookery lessons secret until she'd mastered a few simple techniques. 'I'm running late. I'll get growled at if I don't get a wriggle along.'

'Oh, sorry, didn't mean to keep you.' Jack stepped back, looking as though she'd slapped him.

'You're not.' Ruby smiled, trying to erase that frown between his eyebrows. Putting the gearshift into drive, she added, 'Have a good two days off. See you later.'

Her wheels spun on the wet tarmac as she sped away. She winced, screwing up her face. Now Jack would really think her date was extra-hot. She glanced at him in the rear-view mirror. Oh, hell. He stood staring after her, an angry figure in the partially dark car park, her courier package in his hand. The books she'd forgotten in her rush to get away.

CHAPTER SEVEN

THE following morning, package in hand, Jack wandered through Ruby's front yard towards the back of the house, wondering why he was bothering. It was obvious from last night that Ruby had a life that had no place in it for him. Had she been on a hot date? He fervently hoped not.

But he'd seen that glint of excited anticipation in Ruby's eyes yesterday when Julie had handed over the parcel and knew she'd want it. Yeah, right. Any excuse to see her. Whether he'd be welcome was a very different story.

But today he felt oddly ready to take some chances. Nothing he could explain, but it was almost as though he had unfinished business with Ruby. When she'd headed to the States he'd believed their break-up was final with no chance of a reunion later on. Any time someone had left him it had been final. Like the day his sister had died. That had been a cold day in hell even for a seven-year-old. A cold day followed by a cold week and an even chillier year. He'd missed Beth so much. Her cheeky grin, the way she'd hung around her brothers all the time.

Then there'd been his mum. Distraught beyond belief with the loss of Beth, she'd gradually fallen apart right before his eyes. The laughter and fun that had been her trademark had never returned. Then there'd been the day he'd woken to silence. Trotting through the house, he'd found every room empty. Mum had gone. Out in the garden his father sat hunched over, a forlorn figure with nothing left inside him to console his frightened son.

Some time in the following days and weeks Jack had learned to make himself indispensable to his father and to Steve. No one else would ever leave him behind again.

Until Ruby.

Her departure had been agony. Even as an adult he'd struggled to deal with it. Oh, he'd told himself he understood, but beneath his bravado he'd hurt badly. No matter how he'd cushioned the truth, Ruby had left him. And he hadn't put up a fight, any more than he had for Beth or his mum.

But now Ruby was back. Not for him. But she was here. And it was wonderful to see her. A living, vibrant Ruby. A calmer, happier Ruby. But his fledgling hopes of maybe spending time with her dived to his toes. She had history. History she was working hard to fix. But he'd seen the doubt float through her eyes when she'd hit problems with the kitchen. If Ruby didn't believe in herself, didn't trust that she'd make it, how was he supposed to?

Voices penetrated his dismal thoughts. Children? Surely not. Jack rounded the corner and Zane tore at him, barking crazily. Jack took the impact in his legs and leaned down to scratch behind the dog's ears. 'Hey, boy, slow down.'

'Who are you?' a young voice demanded.

Jack lifted his head and found himself staring directly into the quizzical faces of three boys. They stood shoulder to shoulder, assessing him. Were these guys the hot date? He chuckled. His shoulders lifted and he studied the trio. Did they think they were guarding Ruby? They all had blond, curly hair and the same piercing blue eyes, as well as similar miniature tough-man stances. 'I'm Jack. Who are you?'

'Are you Ruby's friend?' the tallest asked.

'Yes. We work together.' Jack straightened up.

'Are you a pilot?' the same boy asked, a flicker of excitement in his direct gaze.

How easy it would be to win this lot over. Jack shook his head. 'Sorry, I'm only a doctor.'

'Ruby's a sort of doctor,' he was told.

Another brother said, 'No, she's not. She's a para-thingy.'

'Paramedic,' Jack supplied. 'How old are you boys?'

'Seven.'

'Six.'

'Five.'

'What are your names?' They were kind of cute.

'Toby.'

'Thomas.'

'Tory.'

'Nice to meet you all. Where's Ruby?'

Toby stepped forward. Or was it Thomas? 'She's inside, making us hot chocolate.'

Jack hoped these kids had cast-iron stomachs. 'Sounds yummy.'

'Ruby makes the best chocolate drink. She puts marshmallows in it so they melt and go gooey.'

So the boys had survived previous drinks here. 'Think she'll have enough for me too?'

'Hey, Jack,' Ruby called out the kitchen window. 'You run out of things to do at your place?'

Nope. The lawn needed mowing. The recycling stuff required taking to the tip. The path could do with a sweep. And the basement would look better with a new coat of paint. 'Yeah, something like that.'

'He wants a hot chocolate,' one of the boys yelled, so loud Jack's ears reverberated.

'Lucky I've made a pot full, then. You'd all better come in. Take your gumboots off on the porch, boys. I don't want mud tramped inside my kitchen.'

'Ruby's fussy about the floor at the moment,' one boy told Jack with a serious face.

'You say the same things that Mum tells us,' Thomas grumbled at Ruby.

'Then I must be right.' Ruby grinned before shutting the window.

'You forgot your parcel in your hurry to get away last night.' Jack placed it on the table, trying not to stare at Ruby. Dressed in butt-hugging jeans and a green merino jersey that matched her eyes she appeared not much older than her young charges. The apprehension he'd felt since the day he'd learned he'd be working with Ruby unravelled a little.

'Thanks.' A faint pink hue coloured her cheeks.

As she took the package he quickly shoved his hands in his jacket pockets. No accidental touching today. 'Where do your little friends come from?'

'Over the road. I offered to have them while their parents go out for lunch and some couple time, which is pretty hard to get with these three little men.'

'That's a nice thing you're doing.'

Ruby handed him a mug of steaming chocolate with the anticipated marshmallows bobbing on top. 'It's not exactly taxing. The boys spend most of the time playing with Zane, which gives him extra exercise and wears him out for me.'

'It hasn't taken you long to establish yourself in the neighbourhood.' Envy stabbed him. He hadn't got to know any of his neighbours. Like him, they were all too busy building careers, and barely took the time to wave at each other when they put the trash cans out on Monday mornings.

'Knowing my neighbours is essential if I don't want to live in isolation. I want to be able to knock on the boys' door and invite them and their parents over for a barbecue in summer, or take Mrs Crocombe some new spuds for her dinner.'

'You've never had that, have you?' Jack recalled how Ruby used to watch families at the beach with such a hunger in her eyes he had always been surprised it hadn't devoured her. Even with his screwed-up family he'd felt he belonged in his community. Despite keeping aloof, he'd known deep down there were people who'd have helped him if he'd ever been desperate enough to ask.

Ruby handed drinks and a soft smile to each of the lads. 'I have now.'

One of the boys flicked a marshmallow into his mouth and grinned. 'Yummy, yummy, I've got mallow in my tummy.'

'Can we take Zane to the beach later?' Toby asked.

'Have you got warm jackets?' Ruby asked. At three solemn nods she said, 'Okay, sounds like a plan to me. Jack, want to join us?' Her breathing stopped as she waited for his reply.

'Count me in. We used to enjoy walking along the beach.' Holding hands, laughing.

'You always said you'd get a dog one day.'

'You beat me to it.' His gaze followed Ruby as she turned back to the bench, suddenly intent on wiping up some spilled water. Did work colleagues usually go to the beach with someone else's kids? Not exactly keeping his distance from Ruby. Another thought blinded him. When they'd first met and got together, had Ruby felt the sense of helplessness he did now? Had she fought getting involved?

Had she even thought about how she'd eventually leave him? How well had they known themselves back then, let alone each other? He didn't know himself now. Six months ago, if someone had said he'd quit A and E, he'd have sent them for a brain scan.

Excited chatter filled the air. Jack tried to focus on the boys. They talked a foreign language, kid stuff, arguing and giggling as they slurped up liquid chocolate.

What he couldn't get his head around was how effortlessly Ruby handled them. They did everything she asked in preparation for leaving, finishing their drinks and putting the mugs in the sink without a single protest, gathering their jackets and getting into the back seat of the twin-cab truck.

Jack closed the back door of the truck and got in beside Ruby. The boys obviously adored her. Why wouldn't they? She was adorable. And funny, playful. What's more, she seemed to know exactly what they liked doing. If he had to pick a mother for his children, he'd choose Ruby.

Jack swore. Hard. Silently. His hand reached for the doorhandle. Going to leap out of the vehicle? He might land on his head and knock some sense into it. Something needed to. Was he crazy? Where did these weird ideas come from?

'Everyone belted up?' Impervious to his silent rant, Ruby glanced over at the boys and didn't engage the truck in gear until they'd all said yes, including him.

He watched as she carefully negotiated the busy Saturday-morning traffic, and said lamely, 'You love driving this truck, don't you?'

Tossing him a grin, she said, 'People actually take notice of me in this, especially as I'm darned fine at reversing. Men stand around watching, thinking I'm going to make a total clot of myself. I so love getting it right first go. Their jaws drop and they turn away in such a hurry they trip over themselves.'

Jack tried to laugh, but it stuck in his throat around the lump that had sprung up when it had struck him he wanted kids with this woman. 'You've never been invisible.'

Her eyes widened along with her grin. 'Thanks. I think.' She negotiated a speed bump in the road, glanced in the rear-view mirror. 'I don't like Zane being on the deck but he loves it.'

'He doesn't attempt to jump off?'

'He's chained up, but if I have to stop in a hurry he'll slam into the cab.' She slowed for a corner, turned onto Oriental Parade and parked by the beach. 'Here we go, guys. Everyone out. Watch for cars.'

'Bossy britches.' Jack slid out and opened the back door for the lads, who tumbled out in a flurry of arms and legs, shouting about who would take Zane's lead first.

Chuckling, Ruby took the lead herself. 'Last one on the beach is a smelly egg.'

Jack loped along behind everyone, making sure he was the egg and not little Tory, who had the shortest legs and was struggling to keep up with his brothers.

Sticks were thrown for Zane and naturally the boys tended to toss theirs towards the sea. Zane repaid them by shaking salt water over everyone. Finally Jack took the boys in hand. 'Let's skim stones over the water.'

'Yes, please,' three voices yelled.

'I'll take Zane to the end and back. Wear off some of his energy.' Ruby jogged away down the beach, leaving her charges in his hands.

He glanced after her in amazement. Ruby and exercise had never gone together before. She'd believed people only ran if they were being chased by something terrifying. So those firm muscles he'd felt the other day when he'd held her in his arms weren't just from swinging a hammer. No wonder she looked so delectable in her jumpsuit.

Jack spun away, heaved the stone in his hand across the wavelets as hard and far as he could. It slammed through the crest of the first wave and sank.

Thomas jumped up and down with glee. 'You got it wrong, you got it wrong.'

I sure did, buddy. I should've stayed at home and cut the lawns. Then I wouldn't have this melting sensation in my gut. Or feel powerless. I wouldn't be wondering how soon I can kiss Ruby again. Ruby, you're making my heart pound, making my knees knock, all over again. Tell me why I'm going away in October. Will you cry as I go through to the departure lounge, as I cried for you?

Jack looked as though he was thoroughly enjoying himself as he told the kids a joke about a hairy monster. Ruby shifted on the park bench, trying to get comfortable. It was spooky how right this felt. The kids and the dog and Jack. Cosy and warm. Like a family. She spluttered into her soda can. A repeat image of her and Jack and their babies slammed into her mind, brighter than before.

'Back off,' she growled under her breath. This was totally crazy. Jack needed a woman who could make him open up and share his feelings, something he'd never done with her. He needed a partner who'd be there all the time for him. Her fingers curled tight around the can. Her heart thumped a little harder. She'd had her chance, and she'd blown it. Jack didn't need her in his life. Whatever he chose to do in the future.

'What are you going to do after your stint at Scott Base?' she asked abruptly.

'I'm not sure yet. I've applied for a few jobs overseas.'

He scrunched up a burger bag and tossed it at the rubbish bin. 'Nothing's really grabbed me yet, though.'

The soda can pinged as Ruby's fingers pressed a dent into it. How was it that when she finally stopped running and wanted to stay put, Jack had come up with this idea of going off to see the world? 'You never wanted to travel before.'

'Excuse me?' Jack's eyebrows shot upwards.

And when he continued to stare at her like she'd grown another head, she explained, 'I can't remember you ever mentioning going overseas. You always said you had too many commitments here for that. Your dad, Steve. Your career.'

'I did, didn't I?' The eyebrows slowly returned to normal. 'I can gain a lot of experience working in other countries.' He gathered up the boys' discarded wrappers and bags, stood up and tossed them into the bin.

So that was that. She could stop mooning about families and accept Jack had a very different agenda these days.

'Let's go.' Jack nodded at the boys and picked up Zane's lead.

'Sure,' she muttered as she followed them back to the truck. She hated it that he wouldn't talk to her about his plans, even as a friend. Wanting to know more about his life since she'd gone away, Ruby asked as she drove down the road, 'How's your dad? Still working for the immigration department?'

Jack settled himself into the corner, turning to face her. 'You'll never believe it but Dad's moved to Auckland.'

'Really?' Mr Forbes leaving Jack and Steve? Leaving the people who supported him? Wow.

'He met a lady when she came down here to work in the department and…' Jack snapped his fingers '…just like that he was head over heels in love. I wouldn't have believed it if I hadn't witnessed it. After twenty-three years on his own my father lost his heart.'

'Do you like this lady?' Mr Forbes had replaced one support system for another and in doing so had let Jack down.

'Absolutely. She's wonderful to Dad. The only snag was that he had to move to Auckland as she has commitments up there, but that didn't faze him at all.'

'You must miss him heaps.'

'I do but I can't begrudge him his happiness. You should see them together, like a couple of lovestruck teens.'

Ruby thought of the sombre man she'd known. 'I'm pleased for him. He deserved a break. So with your dad gone and Steve only here occasionally, you're free to do what you want now.'

No wonder Jack appeared restless. All the people he'd put first in his life had slipped off the radar. And he didn't know what to do with himself. A focused man when it came to his family and career who had no idea how to live his own life—for himself. Did he even know what he wanted?

'I always knew what I wanted.'

Reading her mind?

He continued, 'To be the best at emergency medicine I could be. I've achieved that. Taking this temporary position might be a sideways step, but it's still emergency medicine.'

'You are happy, right?' She flicked a sideways glance at him and saw him blink.

'Why wouldn't I be?' He pushed against his seat.

'Something I'm sensing. Could be because I'm still getting used to the idea of you going away.'

'You're saying that what I set in motion as a teenager about to start med school has to remain my plan for ever?'

'Me? Hardly. Being the biggest changer of plans I've ever met, that would be hypocritical.' She sighed.

'You've certainly done a total rollover of your life. From upping sticks on a regular basis you now say you're putting down roots, never to disappear over the horizon again.'

Back to her and his disbelief that she might have changed. At least he had talked a little about his dad, a first in their relationship. 'Like I said, circumstances have altered. I should've listened to Mum.' A cold lump clunked in her stomach.

'It's probably natural that you never accepted her version of someone so important to you.'

'I was wrong.' The lump grew, rolled around her belly. 'This is where I was the closest to being content. Mum's buried here. I go talk to her every week. It would take something cataclysmic to move me out of Wellington now.' Mentally she crossed her fingers, afraid she'd tempted fate.

Jack's eyes bored into her as she turned into her street. What was his problem? She'd told him too much, but at least it was the truth. 'Ruby…' his voice caressed her '…I know how badly you wanted your father to be a part of your life.'

She stared at the road, blinking away the sudden mist in her eyes. That gentle understanding undid the lock on her determination to keep the sorry story to herself. 'It was worse than that.' Slowly a piece of her unravelled and she told him what she'd never told another soul. 'I did have a fairy-tale picture of my father. But it was a cover-up. Ever since I can remember I blamed myself for him leaving. I thought he hated me. I believed Mum's inability to make a home for us in one place was because she was heartbroken and looking for him.'

'He left before you were born. How could he hate you?'

Her mouth was bitter. 'He'd been calling on Mum whenever he came through Christchurch, until Mum got pregnant. She never saw him again once she told him. She went on the road, moving from town to town every couple of years. Once I was old enough to learn the facts, I blamed myself. Unfortunately those facts were totally skewed and fed to me by my grandfather, whom I adored.'

'He shouldn't have done that. You'd have been too vulnerable.'

'Granddad was bitter. His precious daughter heartbroken. He reacted as many loving fathers would.' But not hers. *He'd* never acknowledged her, not even when she'd tracked him down. Oh, no, he'd been terrified her appearance would wreck the comfortable life he'd built for himself using his trusting father-in-law's daughter and wealth. 'The Greaser deserves every last drop of Granddad's bitterness. And more.'

Jack's hand touched her leg, his fingers spread across her thigh in a gentle touch that warmed her and threatened to turn the mist to a flood of tears. 'You know something? You've come through this and you're different. Calmer, more sorted, if you know what I mean.' His hand remained on her leg. 'You've still got attitude, though.' And he muttered, 'Thank goodness.'

Did he like the new her? They used to get on so well, maybe he preferred the uptight, unhappy Ruby. Not likely. 'I feel as though a whole world of trouble has gone. My life's looking up and, yes, I'm content.'

Especially since Jack was in the truck with her, his warm hand so right as it touched her. Sharing the day with him had brought the sun out in her heart, despite getting carried away in the confession department. 'Thanks for spending the day with us,' she said, then added, 'You surprised me when you agreed to come.'

'Surprised myself.' Jack slowly removed his hand. 'It's been fun.'

In the back of the truck the boys were playing paper and scissors amid loud shrieks. Ruby grinned at them through the rear-view mirror. 'These guys are so cool, I love them.'

Jack glanced over his seat. 'You're right, they are. Bet they must be a handful for their parents at times. None of my friends have kids of an age that I can play with yet. They've all got babies, those that have got family.'

That reminded her. 'I wonder how Mary's twins are doing. They must've grown a teeny bit by now.'

'Shall we call into the hospital later? Do you ever do that with any of the patients you bring in?'

Ruby parked outside her gate, hauled on the handbrake, unclipped her belt. 'Sometimes. It depends on the situation, whether they were conscious and talking while I was with them. But I'd like to see those girls.' She laughed. 'Colin Archer won't know what's hit him when they all go home. In the space of a year he's gone from a lone man living on his island to having three females around the place.'

'Bet he has those girls delivering lambs before they're even talking.' Jack swung out of the truck and let the boys out before getting Zane down. Like he'd been doing this all his life.

Ruby watched him, her heart squeezing for the sad and troubled boy he must've been, the unsettled man he'd become. He'd had to watch out for Steve a lot while trying to make their father give them some space to grow up in. Apparently old man Forbes had lived in fear of losing his sons after his wife had gone away. According to Steve, he'd clung to the boys to the point he'd almost strangled them.

And now Jack's dad and Steve didn't need Jack like they used to. No wonder he was lost. Would he find whatever it was he wanted at the rescue base? Or at Scott Base? In another country?

Darn, she'd finally realised what she wanted more than anything. Not the job, the house or even, at a pinch, Zane, bless him. She wanted Jack, every little piece of him. And he was planning to disappear on her.

Ruby gazed in awe around the heaving pub Jack had brought her to on Courtney Place. 'We used to stop in here on the way home from work. It's gone all upmarket and fancy.'

'The same doctors still frequent it but they earn more so I guess the proprietor saw an opportunity and grabbed it.' Jack leaned back in his seat and twirled his icy bottle of beer between his hands. Those days they'd thought they'd be together for ever. Correction. He'd thought that. Ruby had always intended on moving on.

Ruby slouched down in her chair and an eloquent shiver rolled through her upper body. 'You wouldn't think it was snowing up in the hills after how sunny it was earlier at the beach. Weather forecasts are less reliable than having your tarot cards read.'

Jack spluttered. 'You get your cards read?'

'The only time I did I was told I had a great future ahead of me as a truck driver.' She rested her chin on one finger. 'Or was it *with* a truck driver? I probably should've asked for my money back.'

'I reckon.' Jack chuckled and relaxed further. He liked it when Ruby was being funny. 'Though you do call your vehicle a truck so maybe there's something in it.'

'Maybe.' She grinned.

Jack looked around the room, trying to ignore Ruby's delectable mouth and the warm feelings it engendered deep inside him. 'That open fire makes it nice and cosy in here.'

Ruby's bottle banged loudly on the tabletop. She straightened up, her cheeks colouring fast.

Instantly Jack knew what she was remembering. Nice and cosy. Something to do with a sheepskin rug, a bottle of wine that she'd swapped for a lager, and nakedness. Heat blasted through him. Why did everything they talked about bring back its own special memory? Those seven months had been the best of his life. He must've been mad not to have gone with her to the States, even if he'd believed qualifying was the most important thing in his life. Hell, why hadn't he asked her to wait a few more months?

Because he'd been afraid she'd say no. Afraid to lay his heart on the line. Even more afraid than he'd been of being left alone. And because of his reticence she had gone, taking his heart with her.

It wasn't too late to rectify everything. He could stay here, not go off into the wild blue yonder. Except it wouldn't work. Getting involved with Ruby again meant living on a knife edge, always wondering if she'd still be lying beside him when he woke up in the morning, never knowing what might trigger her next disappearing act.

No, he couldn't do that. Not if he wanted to stay sane and remotely happy.

Huh, did he really think he could be at all happy without her? Well, he'd find the answer to that soon enough. October was rapidly approaching and he'd be gone.

CHAPTER EIGHT

'JULIE, you're late. I hope you've got a good reason.' Jack raised his voice so he would be heard out on the tarmac where his office lady stood chatting to Ruby.

He saw Ruby give Julie a sympathetic look, heard her ask, 'What's up with him? You leave him too many letters to sign last night?'

As Jack's temper increased, Julie glanced nervously at him. 'Guess I'd better find out.'

'Isn't being late to work a good enough reason to call you out?' Jack growled at Julie as she approached.

Ruby followed, the packs slung over her shoulders. Her step was as jaunty as ever. Did nothing upset her these days?

'I'll be with you shortly.' He scowled at Ruby, before turning to Julie and dropping the level of his roar a decibel. Not enough if the way Julie flinched was anything to go by. 'Where have you been? I'd hoped to see the mail before I get called out.'

Julie stared up into his face, two red spots staining her cheeks, and said breathlessly, 'I don't officially start until nine. Most days I'm early because I drop the kids off at school and come straight on here. Today I had other things to do first.'

Jack started, gulped down his shock. 'I see.' Why hadn't

he known that? He was such an idiot. All because he'd had a sleepless night trying to decide what to do when he returned from Scott Base. The idea of heading down south without definite plans for afterwards had begun eating at him, creating an urgency within him that he didn't know how to fix. The idea of wandering aimlessly to somewhere else was panicking him.

Julie rocked back on her heels. 'There isn't any mail today.' And she walked into her office.

Jack knew he was being watched and spun around to encounter Ruby's hot, angry gaze.

'What was that all about?' she demanded.

'I got something wrong, that's all.' *None of your business, Red. Ruby. Damn it. Ruby.*

'Then you'd better apologise to Julie.' Ruby turned into the storeroom, dropping the bags onto the floor.

'Don't be so heavy-handed with those,' Jack bawled after her. 'Broken vials cost money to replace.'

Ruby slapped her hands on her hips, her chin tilted at a dangerous angle. 'You fall out of bed this morning? Or burn the toast, over-fry the eggs?'

All of the above. Because of his foul mood. He jammed rigid fingers through his hair. 'Damn it.' His long strides ate up the distance to his office. The door slammed, satisfyingly rattling the walls.

He stabbed the 'on' button of his laptop and paced back and forth across the tiny room until the desktop icons appeared. He'd be decisive. All this uncertainty was tearing him apart. Once he had a plan in place for the next twelve months he'd be able to cope with Ruby, would manage to keep her from getting under his skin and making him wish he could stay here with her.

He quickly found the folder labelled 'The Future' containing three job applications. Click, send. Click, send.

Click, send. All three were on their way, whizzing through cyberspace. Surely he'd get something from one of them. Then he'd know what the hell he was doing.

Ruby waved up at Jack as he peered down from the helicopter. His foul mood was still bubbling between them, but right now he should get over it. They were on a job. 'Take the hook away,' she snapped into her mouthpiece before starting across the slippery boulders. She was heading to the man huddled against the rocks, sheltering from the spume coming off the sea. Another man lay sprawled beside him. The shattered hull of their boat rested upside down five metres away. Ruby shuddered. These men were incredibly lucky to be alive. According to the report that had come through to the helicopter, the driver of the boat had cut too close to the shoreline and crashed into submerged rocks.

A dented scallop dreg lay on a tangle of ropes. Ruby didn't know the exact quota for private fishermen but she'd bet there were hundreds more scallops strewn over the scene than these two were entitled to. Picking her way carefully, the pack heavy on her back, she called out, 'Hi, guys. I'm Ruby, a paramedic.'

'About time you showed up. Where the hell you been? Stop at the pub on the way, did ya?' Judging by the slurred words, he was the one who'd been drinking.

Ruby studied him carefully. Drinking and boating made a dangerous combination. Probably the reason for this predicament. But it wasn't her place to criticise. She was making a judgement call that could be very wrong. 'We came the moment we got the call. I guess it seemed like a lifetime, waiting for us to turn up.'

'You can cut the nice-girl stuff and get on with helping

me. I reckon I've broken me arm.' His left arm was tucked against his chest.

Ruby walked past the belligerent man and approached his mate lying face up on the rocks. 'I'll be with you in a minute, sir. Your friend looks like he's unconscious.' Or deceased. Blood had pooled beside the man's head but no wound was obvious from this angle.

'I could've told you that. Doesn't take a rocket scientist to know he's out for the count. Why are you looking at him? He can't feel anything. My arm's hurting like hell.'

Ruby knelt beside the apparently unconscious man and searched for any signs of life, eventually finding a very weak carotid pulse. Speaking into her mouthpiece, Ruby told Jack, 'Need the stretcher, one collar and the back-board.'

'On the way.' Still terse.

'Hey, girlie, you listening to me at all?' The man loomed above her, reeking of fish and booze.

A flicker of concern washed over Ruby. Where was Jack? This man's menacing attitude made her uncomfortable. Plastering on the sweetest smile she could raise, she told him, 'I'll be with you shortly, sir. Can you tell me your names?'

'What's names matter? You should be fixing me up.' The slurring seemed worse.

'Do you remember how long ago you crashed?' For all she knew, this guy might've been knocked out too.

'I don't know. Hours ago.'

'Has your friend been unconscious all that time?'

'I guess. I dragged him away from the boat in case it went up in flames. The fuel went everywhere.' He tried to step closer, staggered and sank down on his rump. His injured arm banged onto his knees, and his roar of pain made Ruby cringe. His cussing was long and loud, turn-ing the air blue.

'Sir, are you a diabetic?' she asked. He appeared to be about fifty and had a very rotund figure, a prime candi-date for the disease. She needed to check his blood-sugar level. A raised result could explain his slurred speech. But there was no denying the strong smell of alcohol.

'No, I'm not. What's that got to do with me arm?' He managed to get back on his feet, swaying in all directions, his good arm raised at her.

Ruby held her breath, and kept her mouth shut. Saying anything at all would only crank his anger levels higher. Heck, she was surrounded by angry men. Finally, when this particular one didn't move towards her, she spoke quietly into her mouthpiece. 'What's keeping you, Jack? I've got a problem here. Alcohol involved. But not sure if he's had too much or if he has an insulin crisis.'

'Onto it.' Jack's voice, laced with fury, came through her earpiece. Like she needed his attitude right now. She had another patient desperately requiring attention. But as Ruby started towards the unconscious man a heavy hand grabbed her shoulder, flipped her round. Pain stabbed her bad knee as it twisted, and she couldn't hold in a groan.

'Leave him,' her tormenter snarled, his face only inches from hers. 'Deal with me first.'

Spittle covered his chin, big bloodshot eyes filled Ruby's vision, and the stench of sour alcohol made her nauseous as her stomach clenched in fright. For all his bulk he'd moved fast, surprising her from behind. What was this guy about? He wouldn't, couldn't, hurt her. Not when she was there to help. She opened her mouth to talk him down, but no words came out.

A fist came into sight to her left. She ducked. The man

swayed on his feet, missed connecting with her, and she hurriedly stumbled backwards.

Jack could barely control his fury as he charged reck-lessly across the slippery rocks. If that idiot touched Ruby again there'd be no accounting for what he might do. When the maniac had grabbed Red, fear had gripped him, stopped his breathing. Stopped his heart. All the anger he'd been directing at himself for his appalling behaviour back at base was now focused on this man. What chance did tiny Ruby have if that guy took another swing at her and connected? She might act tough but she was minus-cule against her assailant. Jack skidded, righted himself, charged ahead. He could see Ruby straightening up, shock turning to rage in her expressive face. *Don't, Red. Don't antagonise him. Play it safe. Go for quiet, calm. If any-one's going to knock his block off, I will.*

How could anyone in their right mind think of hurting Ruby? She was trying to help, for pity's sake. Jack stopped a metre from the man, sucked a breath, then another, and said, 'Hey, there, how are you doing, mate?'

The guy whipped around, stumbled and sat down hard again. The language that followed was colourful.

Jack reached out, touched Ruby's arm. 'You okay?'

Her eyes were large in her very pale face and she swal-lowed hard, but all she said was, 'What took you so long?' Then she headed to the other patient.

He stared after her, a grin beginning deep inside him, some of his fury abating. *You're one tough woman, Ruby Smith.* Then his grin stopped. She was limping again.

Dropping to his haunches in front of the problem pa-tient, Jack bit down on a few sharp words and said, 'Got yourself into a bit of a pickle here, I see. I'm Jack, by the way. A doctor.'

That really focused the guy. 'So why'd you send the

girlie down first, then, eh? I need a real doctor, not one of those poncy medics who think they know everything. She hasn't even looked at my arm, reckons me mate should be looked at first.' He started pushing up on his feet.

Jack shook his head at the guy's total lack of concern for his friend. 'Can you remain sitting, sir, while I take a wee drop of blood from your thumb?'

'What for? What kind of doctor are you? It's me arm you should be worried about, not me blood.'

'I want to check your sugar levels,' Jack reassured him. 'You're a bit wobbly on your feet.' Thank goodness or Ruby might now be lying stretched out on the rocks. He snapped open the glucometer case. *Calm down, Jacko. There's nothing to be gained by giving this idiot what for.* Except he'd feel a heap better. With a wry smile Jack quickly pricked the guy's thumb and placed a drop of blood on the tab for the meter to read.

Ruby grimaced. The rocks dug into her knees as she examined the unconscious man, taking his BP, pulse rate. A massive haematoma had formed above his left eye, but no other injuries were evident on the top side of his head. A pool of blood had congealed around the man's shoulder. Feeling through a slash in his heavy oilskin jacket her gloved fingers encountered soft, torn tissue. Further examination revealed many cuts, some bone deep, on the man's torso, arms, legs. There'd be internal crush injuries for sure. She slit the trousers and winced. A line of bruises ran directly below both knees. Was this where the boat had hit?

Ruby's nerve endings flared in sympathy. When his pal had dragged him out from under the boat, he'd caused further abrasions. If this man hadn't been unconscious before that move, he'd surely have passed out from pain then. She reached for her pack and the IV kit.

Jack crouched down beside her, his shoulder gently nudging hers in support. 'What have you found so far?'

Ruby quickly ran through her observations as she inserted the cannula and ran a line in. 'According to our friend over there, the boat landed on him. Any spinal injuries might've been made worse when he was dragged clear.' She explained about the leaking fuel.

'Since he's already been moved, let's get the collar on and stretcher him ASAP. We'll give him fluids once we're on board. The sooner we get him to hospital the better.'

Working together, the patient was soon ready to be winched aboard. Ruby glanced at their now subdued second patient. 'You hit him over the head with a rock?'

Jack grunted. 'Painkiller.'

'His blood sugar?'

'Slightly high, not the cause of his speech impediment.' Jack dragged out the last word.

'Why do some boaties drink when they're out here? Haven't they got any brains in their skulls?' Ruby checked her patient's harness again before nodding at the other man. 'Think he'll go easy in the winch bucket?'

'Only one way to find out.' Jack crossed to check on the man. 'How're you doing, mate?'

'Get me off this place, will you?' The man glanced around at the carnage. 'That boat was me pride and joy. More fun than the wife.' His gaze reached the scallops and his head jerked around. 'Reckon you got room in that helicopter to take me shellfish? I'll give you some.' A harsh, smoky laugh followed. 'Them fisheries officers won't be looking for me at the airport.'

'Come on, let's get you and your pal on board.' Jack ignored the man's protests and rising temper over not being able to take his catch with him.

Ruby muttered under her breath as she prepared to be

winched up first, 'Maybe the wife would like us to leave him out here.'

'Ruby Smith, you wicked girl.' Jack smiled at her briefly.

'Just telling it as I see it.' But she turned her head away, smiling. She could do wicked if that was what turned Jack on. High heels, black fishnet stockings, one of those figure-hugging body suits all in lace.

Jack muttered, 'Let the guys know what's going on. Slats can help you if our pal gets stroppy.'

The depth of concern for her in Jack's eyes brought tears welling up. Just a short while ago he'd been angry with her. She was so mixed up that she didn't even answer.

They didn't make it back to base. Another call came through minutes after offloading the boaties. Jack read the screen in the cockpit. '"Hiker in the Tararua Ranges, male, thirty-four years old, suspected broken pelvis from falling down a ravine yesterday. Stat three."'

'He's probably hypothermic. It rained during the night.' Ruby spoke through the headphones. 'What was the low last night, Chris?'

'Four degrees in the city, but probably closer to zero in the ranges, with sleet higher up. Better hope our man had a survival blanket with him.'

'Surely if they're smart enough to carry an emergency locator beacon they'll have a blanket.' Jack peered through the window at the desolate hills coming into view below. 'A night out in the ranges in the middle of winter is not my idea of fun. They probably take that tasteless, dried food with them as well.'

'The food would be right up Ruby's alley.' Chris studied the transponder, ignoring the spluttering going on in their headsets from Ruby.

'Getting a signal yet?' Jack asked. Standing behind the pilots, he studied all the dials in front of him. Some he knew from flying the Tomahawk, most didn't make any sense at all. He did recognise the transponder but didn't know how it worked.

'Yep.' Chris pointed. 'That needle directs me to the spot, and hopefully we'll find a clear patch in the bush with our patient in the middle. If not the patient then his companion should be there, ready to lead you to the guy.'

Jack told him, 'According to the search and rescue boffins, there were three hikers altogether. When our man fell the other two shifted him to a flat area above the river. One person stayed and put their tent up over him, while the other hiked out to get help.'

'Why are we only now going out on retrieval if that's the case? We could've got to him before nightfall. The weather wasn't an issue yesterday.'

Jack understood Chris's frustration. 'The woman walking out for help got lost, then darkness fell and she had to wait for daybreak to find her way back to the track.'

'Trouble comes in threes.' Chris grimaced. 'Here's the next problem.'

'What's wrong?' Ruby's voice zapped Jack's brain.

For a brief moment he'd forgotten she was there. How had that happened? These past weeks had been all about Ruby. Working with Ruby. Walking the dog, attacking her kitchen floor, sharing a beer at the pub with the team— and Ruby. He hadn't had any respite when he'd gone to bed either. She followed him there—unfortunately only in his head—and when he finally did manage to drop off to sleep she crawled into his dreams.

Chris was talking. 'The wind has returned. By the way those beech trees are lying over, the gusts are very strong.

I don't like your chances of being winched down at the moment, Ruby.'

If there was any danger involved then Ruby wasn't going down. No argument. Jack twisted around to face her. 'I'll go.'

Her chin shoved forward. 'Jack, it's my day for going down first.'

'I'm pulling rank.' And losing respect. 'Please, Red.'

Those green orbs glittered. 'Don't even go there,' she ground out through clenched teeth. 'I know what to do.'

Chris's calm voice interrupted. 'No one's going unless I think it safe enough. I'm not having anyone hanging on the end of the line when one of those gusts hits. We'll wait a bit and see what the wind does. If we're lucky it'll be a brief squall.'

Jack's heart plummeted. He couldn't imagine flying away, leaving behind an injured person. 'Do your best to get me down.'

'Pardon?' Ruby retorted.

'Us down.' Anything to placate her.

Chris told them, 'If we get a window of opportunity I want you prepared and ready to go. No mucking about. Load and go. If the tent's not packed and ready, leave it. If you get down and the wind returns, I'll have to leave you with the patient.'

Chris's professional attitude settled Jack. He'd been wrong to try and replace Ruby. It was her drop and he shouldn't be bringing in personal concerns while on a job. But he'd worry fit to burst the whole time she was on that wire. And still believe he should've gone.

Jack pushed through to the back. 'Get hooked, Red.' *And stop glaring at me. I know I called you Red but right now I'm more concerned about your health and safety than what the pilots might think of what I call you.* 'If you need me down there, call up.'

She knows that, you idiot. She's been doing this stuff for a lot longer than you have. But not with him there to worry about her. Which she'd absolutely hate. And charged emotions were unsafe in this environment.

Ruby stood up and quietly got ready, but after she'd clicked the hook in place she reached out and touched his shoulder.

Why? Thanking him for giving in? For caring? For *showing* he cared? Jack dredged up a smile. 'Look out for yourself, okay?' He knew full well she'd ignore him but he'd had to say it. Hadn't been able to stop himself.

'It's looking good.' Chris's voice sounded in his ear. 'I'm going round. Get ready.'

They pulled the door open and waited. Jack's heart thudded dully. His finger traced a line over her hand, felt her shiver. 'Go well, ruby red girl.'

Chris again. 'Okay, Ruby, I'm over the spot. The moment you're unhooked I'll back off until Jack's got the stretcher ready. Good luck.'

And Ruby was over the edge and dropping as rapidly as the winch allowed. A short gust of wind rattled things inside the 'copter and Jack watched, his heart thudding in his ears, as Ruby spun out of control on the end of the wire. Her slight body offered no resistance to the wind. Jack's teeth bit painfully into his bottom lip as she swung close to the top of a huge beech tree. His imagination drew a horrific picture of Red splattered against those thick branches.

The helicopter lifted quickly, taking Ruby out of harm's way. Then as suddenly as the wind came up it dropped and Chris was edging Ruby down to the ground.

Seconds later she was on her feet and unhitching the

wire. 'Pull it up, Jack.' Her urgency came through the headset loud and clear. He responded instantly.

Ten minutes later he was bringing the laden stretcher inside and lowering the hook again to retrieve Ruby and the other person on the ground.

'Phew. Well done, everyone,' Slats said as the 'copter rolled sideways and turned for home. 'That was a very fast turnaround.'

Jack focused on the patient and his broken pelvis, trying hard to quell the shaky feeling in his hands, the gnawing sensation in his gut. When that gust had caught Ruby he'd been utterly helpless to do anything for her. He, who always put himself out there for those he loved—cared deeply about—hadn't been able to do any more than watch. He'd been desperate to swap places with her. And now that she'd returned to the helicopter, safe and unscathed, he wanted to hold her tight and never let her go.

Like that was ever going to happen.

Ruby stretched her legs out straight, trying not to wince. That landing back on the Tararuas had been a little too hard, jarring her teeth and jolting her wonky knee. Coming on top of the twist it had received back at the boat-crash scene, her knee might take a bit of rest and relaxation to settle down this time. She seemed to have been giving it a few too many knocks lately.

Please don't let it be the start of the problems the doctor in San Francisco had warned her about. Arthritis would naturally set in as she got older but, hey, that was light years away. The doctor, a serious man who believed she should leave dangerous ambulance work to the men, had told her in no uncertain terms that too many bumps and she'd find herself in need of a knee replacement.

'Problem?' Jack asked. 'That's the second time you've rubbed your knee.'

'Chris didn't give me a lot of time to unhook myself.'

Her headphone crackled as Chris growled light-heartedly, 'Yeah, right, blame me, why don't you?'

'I've noticed you limping a few times. How did you damage it?' Jack wasn't easily deflected.

She sighed. 'Not through working on the helicopters, that's the truth.' The last thing she needed was Jack going all protective on her. Like he'd already done twice today. The first time with that drunk idiot had made her feel all soft and gooey inside, and had stopped her from doing something to the idiot she'd regret for the rest of her life.

But Jack had gone too far when he'd said he'd swap places with her on the winch up in the hills. He'd over-stepped the boundaries. Boss or not. She was as capable as anyone on the base of doing the job under difficult circum-stances. If Chris had said it was a no-go then she'd have accepted his advice. But to be told she couldn't do a drop because Jack was worried about her? That was wrong. It would show her up as a second-rate team member.

Silence descended between them, the whine of the rotors suddenly loud. Finally Jack tapped her knee. 'You going to tell me?'

Maybe if he heard the story he'd understand how capable of looking after herself she was. 'Some screwball on a drug high attacked me and my crew partner late one night in San Francisco when we were called to pick up a cardiac arrest at a house. He freaked us out by knocking on the windows while we were trying to resus our patient. When we carried the stretcher outside he held a knife to my partner's throat, demanding drugs.'

'Blimey, Red. What did you do?'

'I kind of kicked him to make him drop the weapon.'

'You kind of kicked him?' Jack's eyes were popping, his mouth twitching. 'Where it hurt the most?'

'Definitely.' She grinned. 'He wasn't happy and when he'd got his breath back he chased me out onto the road where I tripped, trying to dodge around a moving car. I went down hard, and had to have surgery, which put me on light duties for two months.'

'He didn't attack you again?'

'The car I was avoiding hit him.' The whole thing still gave her nightmares at times. 'By the time the drugs cleared out of his system he was in jail with a broken ankle.' She shuddered. 'It was all a bit freaky.'

'You ever go out on night calls again over there?'

'Not until I'd done a judo course.' Not easy with a dodgy knee but definitely good for the confidence levels when approaching drunks on the street late at night. But today when that boatie had swung at her, her training had seemed to evaporate and all she'd done had been to duck his arm.

Jack chuckled. 'That I'd pay to see. Tiny Ruby hoisting some big, uncooperative male over her shoulder. Remind me never to upset you again.' Then his smile faded. 'You restrained yourself today.'

Tiny Ruby? She conceded she only came up to Jack's chest. Had always tucked under his arm with room to spare. Glancing up, she found his gaze lingering on her and muttered distractedly, 'No, I blew it. Didn't react as I should've. I could do with some practice.'

'Want a partner? I've done a little tai kwon do.'

Ruby's pulse picked up speed. She and Jack on a mat, practising moves and throws? Up close and personal? Twisting their legs around each other. Pulling his body over her shoulder. Being pulled over his, their jackets sliding past each other. Her tongue began doing laps of her mouth.

The radio interrupted. 'Another call,' Jack muttered.

Ruby sighed with relief at her lucky escape from having to answer his invitation. 'No rest for the wicked.' Why was wicked coming to mind so much today?

CHAPTER NINE

AT HOME Jack tossed his keys on the dining table and picked up the pile of mail Johnny must've collected. Idly flicking through the envelopes, he headed for a cold beer.

'Rates, car registration, Visa card bill.' He tossed those aside. Everyone wanted his money.

Pulling open the fridge, he snatched up a beer and butted the door closed with his hip. The last envelope in his hand was white with the Antarctica Project logo emblazoned across the bottom corner. Jack stared at it. He'd been waiting weeks for this, wondering if the boffins running the summer programme were ever going to make up their minds about staffing and finalise his contract.

Hooking out a stool with his foot, Jack sank down at the breakfast bar, turning the envelope over and over. And over. He twisted the top off his bottle and drained half the contents.

'Dr Jack Forbes,' he read. So here it was. The result of two interviews for the most amazing job on the planet. Summer down near the South Pole.

Open the damned thing. Sign the contract. And move forward. Jack dropped the envelope onto the counter. Looked around the ultra-modern kitchen and felt nothing. No pride in ownership. No sense of home. Merely a place to put his head down at night after a hard day at work. Nothing like Ruby's villa, full of character, filled with Ruby, her scent, her laughter, her presence. Yes, she had made a home for herself.

Tugging his wallet from his pocket, he found the photo he'd carried for three years. Long sherry-coloured hair flowed over Ruby's shoulders where his arm rested. Her sensual mouth had split into a wide grin and for once those beautiful eyes held no tension. He visualised the short black dress she'd worn that night, how it had fitted like a second skin—and teased him all evening. His gaze slid sideways and he studied himself. Happy, in love and totally out of his depth with the woman in his arms. No change, then.

He slapped the photo down. None of this had anything to do with the letter in front of him. Draining the bottle, he reached into the fridge for another. And slit the envelope open, shook the letter out. Picking it up, he stared at the folded pages.

'Hey, buddy.' Johnny strolled into the kitchen, tugged open the fridge for a beer. 'How was your day?'

Jack set the letter aside. 'Busy, and dangerous.'

'See you got a letter about that summer job. What did they say?' Johnny plonked his butt on a stool at the other end of the bar.

'I was just getting to it.' Jack finally unfolded the letter. Read it with a sinking heart. 'Damn.'

'Aw, man, you didn't get the job? I thought it was already decided.'

'This is the contract.' Jack skimmed over the details. 'I leave from Christchurch on October twenty-first.'

'That's fantastic. You must be stoked. Let's go to the pub and celebrate.'

'No, think I'll stay in. Got a few things to do.' Like what? His friend studied him over the top of his bottle. 'Aren't you meant to be jumping with excitement? You wanted this big time.'

'I still do.' *I think.*

'It's Ruby, isn't it? She's got to you again.'

After taking a swig, Jack banged his bottle down. 'Not at all. She has nothing to do with this. Nothing, do you hear? I do want to go to Scott Base. This is a once-in-a-lifetime opportunity. It'll be awesome down there.'

'The man protests too much,' Johnny said around the mouth of his bottle.

The problem was it was impossible to fool a close friend. 'Some pea-brain threatened her today. He was drunk and belligerent. Then…' Jack sucked air into his lungs. 'Then she had a hairy ride down to a patient in the middle of the bush.'

'And you not signing this contract…' Johnny stabbed the letter '…will help her how?'

Jack shivered. 'That's just it. It won't.' Ruby didn't need him there to hold her hand, protect her back, keep her safe. She managed perfectly well without him.

But could he manage without her in his life now? He'd begun looking forward to her ribbing him every day. She was there full of unwanted advice whenever they had a bad day on the job. His days off were spent doing fun things with her.

'Twelve weeks. Not a lot of time to be away.' Johnny's reasonable tone broke into Jack's rising panic. 'You'll be back before you know it and probably wishing you could stay down there for longer.'

'You're right.' Twelve weeks without Ruby in them. What had happened here? He'd been hoping for this job for so long and should be crazy with excitement.

'So that's a yes, then? You'll go?'

'I guess.' The break from Ruby might be for the best.

He was becoming too fond of her again, spent too much time thinking about her. She was settled in that house of hers, with her crazy mutt and the kids over the road. Ruby didn't need him as he needed her.

There was the scary thing—admitting he needed her. But what to do about it? He and Ruby had fitted together well three years ago. Now that fit seemed to be growing more cohesive, more right. *Ruby's essential to you, Jacko. Yeah.* He shoved a hand through his hair. That was the problem. Ruby was his rock. Always had been, always would be.

So option one—he'd go away, put the distance between them. A shiver rocked him. He'd sent other applications that morning for jobs he could get seriously interested in. He might be about to embark on years of living away. Reaching for a pen, he quickly scrawled his signature across the contract and shoved it into the prepaid envelope. Sealed it.

Jack spun off his stool, snatched up his keys. 'Your offer of a trip to the pub still on, Johnny?'

'The twins were so cute. Even with all those tubes and things.' Ruby hugged herself as Jack parked his car outside her house on their next day off. The tiny girls looked utterly defenceless in their incubators, while Mary and Colin had been exhausted. 'Ruby and Jackie. How cute is that? No one's ever named their child after me before.'

'Not sure how I feel about Jackie.' Jack grinned.

'The girls will be all right, won't they? I'm sure they're a bit bigger than last time we visited.'

'Early days yet, Ruby. Their lungs need to develop. Thirty-one weeks is very prem. You know that.'

'Yes, but—'

'It's a waiting game. They'll be monitored continuously.'

Jack switched off the engine and turned to face her. The preoccupied look hovering in his eyes for days now was still there. 'We did a good job, rescuing them. Now it's up to the twins to fight for themselves.'

'I know.' Something like pain snagged Ruby. She'd hate it if something ever happened to her babies. She wanted babies now? When had that happened? *Get out of Jack's car and go and see Zane. He's your baby.* 'Want a coffee?'

Darn it. So much for keeping her mouth shut around Jack. Spending most of her days off with him was only frustrating her. She longed to hug him, kiss him, make love with him. She wanted to speed up the getting-to-know-him process. She'd got it bad.

Her gate was off its latch. A prickle of apprehension slid down her spine. 'Zane? Here, boy.'

She rounded the corner and stopped. Seated in a row on her back porch were Toby, Thomas and Tory. Their small faces were red and puffy, and tears had made tracks down their cheeks. In unison they looked up at her, then dropped their heads again. Sniff, sniff.

'What's up, guys?'

The boys shuffled closer together, almost sitting on top of each other.

Jack laid a hand on her shoulder, moved closer to her. 'Any guesses?'

Ruby looked around the yard. 'Zane?' No answering woof. No beloved dog bounding across the wet lawn to put his muddy paws on her shoulders. No ball pressed into her hand. Her heart started banging crazily, painfully, against her ribs. 'Where's Zane, boys?'

'We're really sorry, Ruby.' Toby.

'We meant to shut the gate.' Thomas.

'It's our fault.' Tory.

Ruby stared at the boys, her breath stuck in her lungs. 'Is Zane hurt?' Please say no. Please.

Three little heads nodded. Three noses sniffed. 'Dad's taken him to the vet,' Thomas whispered.

The vet? Fear clutched Ruby. Zane couldn't be injured. Could he? What had happened? Oh, no. Was he alive? Pain sliced through her as she struggled to remain calm. Zane had to be all right. He had to be.

Jack's arm slid around her waist, held her upright. 'Easy. We'll find out everything.'

'Mum said we had to wait here for you,' Thomas continued. 'Are you going to be angry with us?'

Leaning into Jack, Ruby tried to quell the panic tearing up her throat. *Be strong, be tough.* Glancing down at the boys again, she saw their fear, their guilt; and her heart went out to them. Whatever had happened, they were only little boys.

She dropped to her knees and spread her arms out to encircle them. Her hug was fierce, filled with fear for her pet and her need to let these kids know she still cared about them too. 'It's okay, boys. I'm sure you didn't mean anything bad to happen to Zane.' Leaning back so she could see their faces, she asked, 'Did you?'

Three heads swung left, then right, and back. 'No.'

'I knew you wouldn't. You all love Zane like I do.' Ruby forced patience into her voice while inside she was screaming out, *What happened?* 'Did you leave the gate open?'

'We didn't mean to.'

'Did Zane run out on the road?' she asked.

Three nods. 'A car came and ran over him.'

Her blood chilled. Ran over him? A sob broke from her throat. He might be big but he wouldn't withstand that. Her poor baby. At least the boys' father had taken him to the vet already. Another group hug and she stood up. 'You'd better go home and get warm, boys.'

Jack immediately put his arm around her again. 'Do you know which vet to go to?'

'I'll ask the boys' mother but I'm guessing the one at the bottom of the hill. That's where I take Zane for his vaccinations.'

With Jack holding her hand, they escorted the boys home and learned from a very embarrassed mother that Ruby had surmised correctly. Then Jack put Ruby back in his car and drove her to the veterinary clinic.

'Zane's being operated on,' Rod, the boys' father, told them when they arrived. 'His front left leg's broken and needs pinning.'

Ruby's mouth dried. When she tried to speak nothing came out. Her body began trembling. Tears welled up, dripped down her face.

Jack wrapped her in a hug, and asked over her head, 'Are there any other injuries?'

'I don't know,' Rod answered quietly. 'The vet took X-rays but he hasn't told me any more.'

A flicker of hope wove through the chill cramping Ruby. She squeezed her eyes shut and sent Zane a message. *Please be all right, my baby. Hang in there, for me, for you, Zany.*

'How were the boys?' Rod asked.

Jack answered, 'They've gone home. They did really well fronting up to Ruby.'

'Hopefully they'll have learnt something from this.' Rod ran a hand through his hair. 'I guess we're in for lots more trouble before they reach adulthood.'

Ruby managed a weak smile. 'Would you have them any other way?'

'Today? Most definitely.'

They all sat down in a corner and waited for an interminable amount of time. Ruby was frozen with terror. When at last a door behind Reception opened and a man swathed in blue theatre scrubs emerged, she was afraid to look at him in case she saw bad news in his eyes.

The vet crossed over to her. 'Ruby, Zane's going to be fine. There's some bruising around his ribs and his broken leg. He'll have a limp to go with that blind eye but otherwise he's one very lucky dog.'

'Really? You're telling me the truth? There's nothing you're missing out?'

Jack interrupted with a crooked smile, 'Ruby and Zane, matching limps. I like it.'

Ruby batted him with the back of her hand. 'Thanks, pal.'

The vet smiled tiredly. 'Come through and see Zane for yourself while I explain what I've done. He's still out for the count but I understand you want to touch him and feel his chest rising and falling before you fully believe me.'

Ruby hesitated, turned to Rod. 'The boys will be relieved.'

'I'll go and tell them the good news.' Rod grimaced. 'And, Ruby? I'm sorry they went to see Zane while you were out.'

'Don't be. Boys and dogs. You can't stop them. I've always encouraged them to play with Zane.' Ruby took Jack's hand and tugged him into the operating room with her, still needing his support. So much for being strong and tough. The moment Jack was around she leaned on him. Everyone relied on Jack. Maybe they shouldn't. But he had never complained. If he had, would he be so restless now?

* * *

'Why are you so jittery?' Jack asked Ruby when they arrived back at her house. Her hands moved constantly on her thighs, her head turned left and right as she peered through the stormy night. She couldn't still be worried about Zane. She'd seen him, stroked his head until he'd have had a headache if he'd been awake, and knew his injuries weren't life-threatening.

Ruby shoved the door wide, hesitated. 'Do you want a beer?' There was a catch in her voice. 'Or a coffee? I can heat up something to eat.'

Realisation crashed through his brain. Ruby didn't want to be on her own. Because she was upset about Zane? Or didn't she like being in the house alone at night? Could be why she'd got a dog in the first place. 'A warm drink would go down a treat. I'm freezing.'

As Jack locked the car he thought back to when they'd lived together. No memories came to him of Ruby not wanting to be home alone. But then they'd shared the flat with others to save money so the chances were she'd never been by herself.

Inside she headed for her kitchen and plugged in the kettle. 'Can you light the fire for me? This house is colder than a freezer.'

'I'm onto it.' It was almost warmer outside in the icy wind.

When she passed him a mug of steaming coffee her hand shook. Jack's heart oozed love for her. He patted the couch beside him. 'Zane's going to be fine. It won't be long before he's dropping that raggedy old tennis ball at your feet and demanding you toss it for him.'

'I know, but seeing him like that was horrible.' She plonked down heavily beside him, putting his coffee in jeopardy. 'My lively, never-sit-still boy knocked out and looking dead.' Big fat tears oozed out from the corners of her eyes, trailed down her pale cheeks and dripped off her chin.

Jack put his mug on the floor and wrapped an arm around her slight shoulders, gently tugged her closer. 'Zane is not going to die. The vet was adamant about that.'

'Knowing that and reliving the fear I felt when I first saw him are two different things. I'd be devastated if—' She trembled like a sparrow balancing in the wind.

'I know, Ruby, I know. You've really taken to this fella. He's your baby, isn't he?'

Against his chest her head nodded. 'I love him. He's so generous with his affection and all he wants in return is love, food and warmth.' She sagged a little closer. 'It feels like I'm being tested all the time. First the kitchen plans went awry, now Zane's been hurt. What's next?'

'Ever considered those are normal, everyday things that happen to people?'

'You think so?'

'I do.' He watched her sipping her coffee, her hands shaking.

Her gaze roamed the room, pausing at a photo of her mother, moving on to the water stain darkening the wallpaper above the door, to the worn patch in the carpet at the doorway where people had trodden for tens of years. 'There's so much to do,' she whispered. 'But I really want to achieve it all, put my mark on this place.'

The grief, the uncertainty, the angst seemed to slip out of her and she relaxed back against the couch. Not against him now. This was a Ruby he didn't know. Strong. Tough. For the first time since he'd met her years ago he believed she was happy within her space, comfortable in her own skin. That she liked the life she'd carved out for herself. Surprise rolled through him. Ruby had made it all happen despite the mixed-up, tormented girl she'd once been.

Pride for her overlaid his surprise. Maybe this time she really wouldn't tear away somewhere else the moment life turned difficult.

Ruby said, 'I love this house. It's mine, and it has history for me. I don't know if I could leave, even if I wanted to. Which I don't.'

You left me, even when you apparently didn't want to.

'It wasn't easy, was it?' She turned deep green eyes onto him.

Had he spoken aloud? Or were his feelings so strong she'd read them in his face, felt them in the air? He'd left her too, remember? 'No.'

'Breaking up like we did, agreeing we each had very different paths to follow, it still hurt.' Her eyes darkened further. 'Sometimes, when it got really awful with my father, I wondered if I'd done the right thing.'

And? Don't leave him hanging. Tell him it had all been a big mistake. But then where would they go from here? Did he want to start again with her? Yes, if he could only take the risk. No, he was too restless to settle down now. Talk about ironic. 'We did what seemed right for both of us at the time. And we're different for it now.'

'You think?'

'I know. Look at Zane's accident. You were fantastic with the three Ts today.' The boys had been expecting a blasting from her. *He'd* been expecting her to react wildly. Instead she'd been so understanding and caring it had lanced his heart as she'd hauled the boys in for the hug they'd desperately needed. She'd make a brilliant mother one day. And that was something he shouldn't be thinking about. Kids? And Ruby? With Ruby? His heart crashed into his ribs. He was falling in love with her all over again. He wanted to be with Ruby for ever. Only this time he'd want the whole deal. House and kids. Dog and truck. With Ruby at his side.

He stood and crossed to sit on a chair. He had to maintain some semblance of control.

'The three Ts? Is that what you call the boys?' Ruby's green orbs sparkled and her beautiful, full lips twitched with suppressed laughter, totally unaware of what was going on in his mind. 'The three Ts. I like it.'

She'd ignored his compliment about how she'd handled the boys. The Ruby of old wouldn't have. She'd have taken it and analysed it until it no longer meant anything. She'd been so unable to believe a good thing about herself back then.

Now she scrambled to her feet. 'I'll put a casserole in the oven to heat. I'm starving.'

'When aren't you? That's something that hasn't changed about you. Where do you put all the food you manage to swallow?' He could do everyday conversation. Just.

'One day, when I'm fifty, I'll balloon into something the size of a house and you'll be able to say you told me so.' She spun out of the room, leaving him staring after her.

As if he would be around in twenty-four years' time to know what had happened to her. That thought saddened him. Now that he'd found Ruby again, he didn't want to lose touch. He cared what happened to her. Which reminded him…

Following her into the bright, shiny new kitchen, he leaned against the cupboards and asked, 'Are you okay, being here at night without Zane?'

The spoon she was stirring the casserole with clattered against the dish. 'Why wouldn't I be?'

'Because if you aren't, I can sleep on the couch.'

'You're a bit long for that old lumpy thing.'

'There's the spare bedroom, though it's probably cold enough to freeze my lungs. Steve and Johnny won't miss me. They're going to a party tonight.' One he should be attending too. The guys would give him grief tomorrow when he explained he'd been with Ruby.

Ruby was stirring the life out of their dinner. 'If you don't want to go home, that's fine by me.'

'Where are the sheets? I'll go make up the bed now, and leave the door open so some warm air has a chance to make its way down the hall and inside the room.'

'Linen cupboard's next to the spare room.' Ruby put down the spoon and lifted the dish into the oven. Her shoulders relaxed and she began humming.

Jack grinned. She'd never admit she was glad to have someone in the house with her overnight. Where had this fear of the night come from? It didn't matter. He'd see she was okay. He should've told her he'd be better placed to protect her if he slept in her bedroom.

His grin slipped. As if he'd be sleeping then. Face it, he wasn't going to get much sleep just being in the same house as her. He shouldn't have offered to stay. Toughen up. One night. He'd manage.

Hell, what if Zane didn't come home tomorrow?

CHAPTER TEN

RUBY sat upright. A loud crack had snatched her out of the cosy dreamlike state she'd succumbed to. What was that noise? Wind rattled her windows, rain pelted the glass. Everywhere was black. No hall light. The green numbers of her bedside clock were gone. Blood pounded in her ears. What had happened? Had someone deliberately turned off her power?

Crack.

She jerked around, stared through the pitch dark at where the window should be. Someone was out there. Why wasn't Zane barking? Duh. Zane was at the vet clinic. So where was Jack? He was supposed to be looking out for her. 'Jack?'

'I'm here, Ruby. You okay?'

Crack.

'No, I'm not. There're no lights anywhere. And what's…?' she hiccuped. How embarrassing. 'What's that loud creaking sound?' Yikes, now her voice sounded like a screeching soprano's.

Her bed rocked. 'Can't see a thing,' Jack growled in the dark.

If she hadn't been in such a panic his sexy voice would've had her scrambling to haul him under the sheets with her. Great cure for panic. She moved and reached out in the dark for him. The bed moved sideways, tipping her backwards. 'What are you doing?'

'Trying to reach you.'

'I'm on the bed.'

'Yes, Ruby, I got that.' A warm hand touched her leg. 'If this isn't you then I'm in big trouble.'

He sounded too darned chirpy. She was freaking out. 'You're okay, it's me.' And think what she liked, his hand on her knee felt right. The thumping in her ears slowed, quietened. Replaced by a steady crashing in her chest.

'Have you got a torch handy? The power must have gone out. All the streetlights are out too.' His hand made it up to her arm.

Jack's practicality steadied her, even her fickle heart. 'In the top drawer of my bedside cabinet.' She rummaged around in the dark, finally finding the torch. 'Note to self, leave torch on top of cabinet in future.' Jack's welcome face sprang out of the dark as she flicked the beam on. 'Hi.'

'Hi, yourself. Let's go and get that fire roaring. That'll give us light and warmth. We could drag your mattress into the lounge, put it in front of the fire and be really snug.'

Gulp. Snug with Jack. Sounded too good to be true.

Creeeeak. Crack. Crash.

The house jolted, rocked. The sound of breaking glass could be heard over the other noises.

Ruby jumped. 'What was that?'

Jack reached for her hand and stood up. 'Let's find out. Could be the wind's coming from a different direction than usual and causing trees to scrape against the house.'

'That wouldn't make the house shake, though. It wasn't an earthquake, was it?'

'Definitely not.'

She waved the torch around, feeling better as familiar things sprang into sight. She tightened her grip on Jack's hand. His warmth helped enormously to banish the chill inside her; his strength gave her strength.

'Oh.' Ruby stared at the devastation before her when they stepped out onto the porch. The huge walnut tree lay twisted and broken, filling her yard with its massive branches. Her torch highlighted the wooden fence now broken where a large branch had crashed on it. 'My beautiful walnut tree.' The torn trunk loomed eerily out of the dark. 'I loved that tree. Granddad hung a swing off it for me when I was little.' Sadness twisted through her gut.

'Your grandfather lived here?' Jack gaped at her.

She nodded slowly, before directing the torch at her laundry room. 'There's the explanation for the breaking glass.' A branch had pushed through the window. 'Lucky Zane isn't in there tonight.' A gust of wind slammed into her, forcing her back a step. She tugged her top tighter around her neck. The air was arctic.

Jack ordered, 'Direct the torch onto the fence. I want to see if the tree has hit Mrs Crocombe's place.'

'She's gone to stay with a friend for the weekend.' Thank goodness, or else she'd have been terrified when the tree came down.

'Looks all right from here,' Jack said. 'Let's get that fire cranked up. There's nothing you can do outside until the morning.' Jack's voice was so reasonable it angered her.

'Sure.' She slammed the door shut behind them.

'What's up?'

'Do you really have to ask?' Ruby leaned back against the door. What was he blind? 'How do I clear away all that huge tree? My vegetable garden is under those branches, all my plants no doubt squashed out of recognition. Did I mention my laundry now has a gaping hole where the window used to be? More work, more money.' Tears pricked the backs of her eyelids. Her hands balled into fists. 'It's never-ending. It's like something out there wants me gone.'

Jack's arm draped across her shoulders. 'Come on, you'll get through this. You're strong. If you want something badly enough, I know you'll make it happen.' He led her into the kitchen. 'Have you got another torch? I've changed my mind. I will go outside and check on the house.'

Dragging her shivering body away from his warmth, Ruby tugged a drawer open and withdrew a box of candles. 'I'll light some of these so you can take the torch.' He thought she was strong. If only he knew how much she depended on having him nearby to boost her confidence.

When Jack headed outside she couldn't hold in her despair any longer. Her fists banged the bench time and again. Her frustration erupted. 'Why pick on me?' Thump, thump. 'What have I done to deserve this? I want to establish my home, not have to fight for every step of the way.' Her hands ached with the pounding they were getting on the granite bench.

'Hey, take it easy.' Jack stepped up beside her. 'What's this all about?'

'I was looking forward to collecting walnuts for years to come.' Even hanging a swing for those kids she'd started thinking she might have one day.

'I'll buy you a new one. Not quite the same, I know, but it will be with you for years, while that old one was going to have to come down some time soon.'

'It'll be ages before I get the yard cleared enough to plant another tree.' Or made her vegetable patch workable again. But she mustn't give up on her dream. *Be tough, be strong.* She'd taken two hits today. Tomorrow was another day. Hopefully a darned sight better one.

Jack started towards the lounge. 'Let's make the place

a bit warmer. And you can tell me how you came to be living in the house your grandfather used to own.'

She trailed after him, slightly ashamed of her outburst. 'When it came on the market, the lawyer looking after Mum's estate emailed me in the States and I had to have it. I'd have paid twice the price if necessary.'

'Back up. Did your grandfather live here when you were in Wellington with me?'

'No, he died when I was ten. Mum occasionally brought me to visit when I was little but they didn't get on very well because of how Mum was always on the move. Granddad said it wasn't the right way to bring me up and they had a big fight about that.' Ruby automatically flicked on the light switch as she moved into the lounge. 'Duh, stupid,' she muttered.

'You? Or your mum?'

Her mind was whirling. 'You know something? I always figured I moved a lot because I needed to find my father, but did I learn the habit from Mum?'

'I suppose if you've never stopped in one place for long you wouldn't know what it's like. And yet you're managing it now.' Jack moved the couch back to make room for her double-sized mattress.

Shock jolted Ruby. 'You're starting to believe me?'

'I got it loud and clear when you mentioned the swing your grandfather made for you in that tree.' His smile was endearingly crooked. 'I finally understand how much this place means to you.' Jack wrapped her in his arms. 'You're here to stay.'

'For ever.' If only that included being in Jack's arms for ever. But despite getting to know each other again he obviously didn't feel she could provide what he needed. Slowly stretching up on her toes, Ruby placed a soft kiss on his cheek, restraining from giving him the full-blown lips-to-lips kiss she ached for. She whispered, 'For ever.' She'd wait for him anyway. She had no choice.

Sliding down his body, she stepped away from those strong, supportive arms, and went in search of blankets and pillows.

Jack awkwardly manoeuvred the mattress and dropped it in front of the fire, sending a gush of flame-laden air up the chimney. 'That's heavy.'

Ruby rolled herself into one of the blankets before nodding to the other. 'Here, tuck that around you to keep the draughts out.' She'd keep temptation at bay with her arms pinned in the cocoon.

Jack smiled as he did as he was told. 'Sure you'll be warm enough? I mean, you had about fifty blankets on your bed, now you've got one.'

'But it's wrapped around me more than once. I probably look like an Egyptian mummy.' Lying down on the side closest to the fire, she cracked a grin. 'Besides, I've got the best place. Those flames will keep me cosy.' There was that word again. Cosy. Like snug, it made her want to curl up against Jack and slide her arms around his warm, muscular body, bury her face against his chest and pretend this was how they always spent their evenings.

Rolling onto her back, she stared at Jack, suddenly remembering other nights lying in front of a fire together. Nights of passion. Nights when she'd believed she had it all, hadn't understood how easy it would be to lose everything, everyone, she cared about. The flickering flames cast shadows over the firm planes of Jack's face. Tugging an arm free, she ran her palm over his cheek, his chin, felt the light rasp of the beginning of whiskers.

Jack turned his head slightly so his lips were on her palm. He kissed her hand. He stroked her hot skin with his tongue. A tremor rippled down her arm. Followed by another. And another.

He laid his hand over hers. Desire rolled through her as she swam in the long-forgotten sensations swamping her. His eyes closed as he sank down closer to her, still stroking the palm of her hand. Such a small action, such a huge response. Ruby arched her back, squeezed her leg muscles tight as the sweet, hot desire continued rolling through her, building, building, building.

And then Jack was lying beside her, so close it was as though he was a part of her. Somehow he unwound her blanket and their bodies meshed, legs tangled, chest pressed to breasts, hips to hips, arms holding each other closer and closer. Warmth became heat. So hot they were about to combust.

Light flooded the dark.

Ruby jerked, pulled back, blinking. 'I left that switch on.' She checked out the room. It looked normal, while she felt totally abnormal. Out of sorts. About to make love with Jack. Had the light saved them from making a mistake? Jack looked startled, then relieved. Acute disappointment flared in her tummy. So he wasn't really ready to get too close to her, and certainly not for the lovemaking that went with the kind of deep, meaningful relationship she wanted.

His beautiful eyes locked with hers, the glazed look slowly disappearing. He had wanted her. She'd felt it in his hands caressing her, his lips devouring hers, the sharpening of his muscles under her touch.

Ruby put space between them as she studied him. She wasn't about to throw herself at him, had to protect her pride. His mouth was swollen from their kisses. To have been tasting Jack after all this time had been wonderful. And was never going to happen again if the look now filtering into his eyes was anything to go by.

'Ruby?' Her name croaked off his tongue.

Funny that it hurt now he'd got used to calling her by her proper name. Every time he'd used Red it had given her hope, despite her ranting at him to use Ruby in front of others. A tiny piece of her believed that as long as he used the old affectionate name they'd had a chance of returning to their previous loving relationship. Now she understood there was no going back, only forward. What she needed to know was if Jack would ever come with her on that journey, but tonight wasn't the night to be asking.

Pulling further away, she got up and put another piece of wood on the fire. The raging heat of passion of moments ago had gone. If the power hadn't come on for a few more minutes they'd have been down and naked, and then there'd have been no stopping her. Sadness and a sense of loss gripped her. She didn't know if she was coming or going with Jack. 'I think we should go to sleep now.'

'You're right.' His words snapped through the air.

Behind her he tucked himself up and settled on the far side of the mattress, not touching her at all.

The fire crackled and hissed as it devoured pine cuttings. Ruby watched the red-and-yellow flames dancing before her. So pretty, so dangerous. Was everything in life like that? Good and bad in every situation? As with Jack, being with him was wonderful, but every minute in his company put a strain on her heart, on her determination to leave him free to pursue his dreams. The dreams that would soon take him away from her.

'You've all got visitors.' Julie met Crew One as they disembarked after carrying an MVA victim to hospital the following week.

'We have? Who?' Jack asked as he handed down the pack to Ruby.

'It's a surprise, okay?' Julie looked smug.

Perplexed, Jack followed Julie inside. As station manager he'd have thought he'd be told prior to any one coming on base. 'Any ideas?' he asked Ruby.

She shrugged. 'Could be anybody.'

Stepping into the tearoom, Jack stopped at the sight of Lily Byrne and her parents sitting at the table, looking happy and, more importantly, healthy. At least Lily did. Her mother still wore a cast on her leg. 'This is a nice surprise.'

'We made you a cake,' Lily told him shyly.

Jack's heart lurched at the sight of the little girl. She was so cute with her shaven head now covered with a light growth of blonde hair. He hunkered down to her level. 'I love cake. How's your head?'

Lily smiled at him. 'It hurts sometimes and I cry but Daddy says it will stop soon.'

'I am very glad.' Jack straightened up and shook hands with Lily's parents. He didn't ask the questions raging around his head about the child's outcome. It wasn't his place. She looked fine, though he knew how deceptive that could be. Behind him he could feel Ruby pushing past. She immediately knelt down with Lily, chattering to her about the ballerinas printed on her pink dress.

Mrs Byrne spoke up, her eyes bright and glittery. 'Lily's going to be absolutely fine. The doctors don't expect any long-term effects from her injuries.'

Relief poured through Jack. A happy outcome. Yes. This was why he did his job, for the good days. 'That's fantastic. And your leg?'

'Netball is off the programme for the rest of the season.' Lily's mother smiled softly. 'But that's so unimportant compared to getting Lily back to normal. I'd have broken both legs, if I'd had to, to save her.'

'Which is why we're here.' Mr Byrne placed a hand on his wife's shoulder. 'We wanted to thank you all for picking up Lily that day. Without the helicopter she'd have been a lot longer without the right treatment and the outcome might've been very different.'

Jack dipped his head at their pilot. 'Chris and Slats are the men you've got to thank for that.'

Chris shook hands with both parents. 'It's a team effort. I've got the easy job. Jack and Ruby here do the real work.'

'The doctors told us that you'd all helped to save Lily's life. When she had those fits she could've choked if you hadn't been there.'

Jack felt their anguish, as he had the day they'd lifted Lily off the road. He'd known it deep down as they'd flown to hospital, helping Lily fight for her life. He'd dreaded the outcome going the other way and these parents suffering as his had when Beth had died. He said gruffly, 'I'm thrilled we were in time.'

Ruby shook hands with the parents too, then grinned. 'Who's for coffee? That cake is begging to be eaten. Lily, what flavour is it?'

'Chocolate.' The little girl peered over the table. 'Do I have to have coffee too?'

Ruby clapped her hands. 'I'll find you some juice. And thank you for making my favourite cake. I love chocolate.'

'Me too.' The girl followed Ruby to the cupboard for a glass and then to the fridge for the juice. She stood by Ruby as she put the kettle on and spooned coffee granules into mugs. She got the milk out when Ruby asked her.

Jack waved everyone to a seat. Inside he felt warm, happy, as he watched Ruby with her little shadow. Ruby looked happy. She really had found her place in life and didn't need to go out in search of anything any more. His heart flipped. He thought of the job applications he'd started hearing back about. Emergency Specialist positions in Australia, England and on the African continent. Every week he added more advertisements to his file, and every week he deleted the expired ones. Apart from that day when he'd sent off three applications, he'd done nothing about seriously getting work for next year once he'd finished in the Antarctic. Something held him back from putting words down, prevented him posting his CV away. Something or someone?

Ruby?

When the family finally left, and with no callout to take his mind off whatever was bothering him, Jack headed for his office to tackle the stack of mail Julie had left on his desk.

And to check his inbox for any new job ads.

'Okay, so who's going to the ball?' Jack tossed the invitations on the staffroom table a short time later.

'What ball?' Ruby reached for the pamphlet that lay under the invitations.

Chris stretched his legs under the table and leaned back in his chair. 'It's organised by our charity trust to raise money for the Rescue Helicopter base. We're all expected to go.'

'All of us? Think I'll be washing my hair that night.' Ruby grinned. 'Can you imagine me all togged up in heels and a dress? Dancing?'

Jack nodded at her. 'Yes, I can. Remember that dinner-dance night we went to for the Wellington Hospital doctors? Correct me if I'm wrong, but you wore a dress that night.'

Heat spread across Ruby's cheeks. She'd worn a very short black dress with a low-cut neckline that had left little to the imagination. Her sherry-coloured hair had swirled around her, touching her waist, sliding across Jack's hands. He'd been stunned when he'd first set eyes on her that night. He hadn't recovered all evening, desperate to get away and take her to bed. 'That was back when I was young and fearless.' Or stupid. If she had to wear a dress this time, it would be something more subdued.

'You can't wear your overalls and boots.' Chris laughed.

'And you are going. With me. I'll make sure you don't renege.' Jack sauntered out to his office.

Ruby stared after him. 'What happened to asking nicely?'

Jack looked back over his shoulder. 'You'd have said no.'

'Of course I would've.' She couldn't go to the ball. Her? With Jack? They weren't dating. No, just lying together in front of the fire and getting as frustrated as it was possible to get.

Chris began texting on his phone. 'I'm letting Sandra know about it. When is the ball?'

'Three weeks' time. It's short notice but I think they've been selling tickets for a while now,' Jack called out.

'Typical. We're the last to find out anything and we're expected to turn up.' Ruby rinsed her cup. A bubble of excitement moved through her. A real ball. Dancing with Jack. Maybe she could find an exciting dress. It didn't have to be as provocative as that other one. She'd buy gorgeous shoes, new make-up and get her hair done. She shook her head. The hair thing might have to take a miss. Not enough to do anything glamorous with. Just because she usually wore jeans or jumpsuits it didn't mean she didn't love dressing up. She turned to Chris. 'What will Sandra think about this?'

'She'll love it. We had a great time last year, and everyone danced themselves to exhaustion. Seriously, Ruby, you'll enjoy it.' Then Chris's face fell. 'Whoops, better check the roster first. Just our luck we're on that night.'

They weren't. And later, when Jack told them he'd arranged for a crew from Nelson to come over and cover so that no one missed out, Ruby's excitement began to grow. This could be fun. She texted Sandra. 'Want 2 go dress shopping?'

Sandra replied instantly. 'Sat am. Pick u up 9.'

That night Ruby studied her meagre wardrobe. Forget ball dress, she really didn't have that many clothes full stop. When had she last bought something new? Some time in San Francisco. And because she hadn't been dating anyone there, her clothes had tended to be practical, not designed for fun.

She'd definitely splash out. Shoes were a priority. Her work boots, runners and sneakers didn't cut it for a ball. Roll on Saturday. There'd be some more serious damage done to her bank account. After the vet bills, paying for the laundry window to be reglazed and replacing some of the planks in the fence, her account looked a little sick. Thankfully Chris and the guys had all pitched in with chainsaws to cut up the fallen tree, while she and Sandra stacked the wood behind the house to dry for next winter's fires. But she might have to put that new lounge suite on hold for a while.

She shrugged. She couldn't wear a lounge suite. Couldn't wow Jack with one of those. And wow Jack she would.

'There's ice in that rain,' Ruby muttered, zipping her jacket collar as high as her throat allowed. 'Half an hour to go until I'm out of here. A hot roast at the pub for dinner tonight, I reckon.'

Chris growled, 'Now you've jinxed it for sure. No calls for three hours and I'll bet you that dinner we'll get one in the next few minutes.'

Someone's pager sounded loud and shrill. 'Darn,' Chris muttered. 'Didn't even get time to shake on the bet.'

Ruby and the men scrambled to their feet. Jack read his pager. 'Fisherman on a trawler twenty kilometres off the coast. Injured in the chest by a flying winch.'

Chris touched the computer screen, brought up the met forecast for the area they were about to head for. 'Marginal. There's every possibility that once I put you on board I'll have to leave you there until there's a break in the weather. It's the wind that's the problem.'

Jack rolled his eyes. 'Wonderful. But at least we'll be able to make the seaman comfortable. Hope the guy hasn't broken his ribs and punctured a lung.'

Ruby swallowed. 'Do they have roast meals on the trawler?' Not that she'd be eating one. She headed for her locker and retrieved a small bottle of seasickness tablets just in case she did end up staying on board.

'Got a spare one of those?' Jack asked from behind her.

She spun around. 'You get seasick too? You never mentioned that when we went out to the ferry on your first day.'

'I didn't get a chance. We were up and away so fast I had to hope we'd be as quick on board the ship.' He took the bottle of tablets she held out to him. 'Like you, I get motion sickness only at sea.'

'Let's hope this is a fast turnaround, then. Wouldn't look good for both of us to be puking over the side when we've got a patient to deal with.' She shoved the bottle at the back of her locker.

'You dropped something.' Jack bent down and stilled. 'You've still got this photo. That was taken at the doctors' dinner-dance.'

Ruby's cheeks warmed. She snatched the photo from his fingers. 'It's my favourite.'

Straightening, Jack pulled his wallet from his back pocket and flipped it open. 'Snap.'

Stunned, she stared at him. 'You kept a photo of us? Together.'

He shrugged. 'You kept a photo of us. Together.'

Her throat ached when she swallowed. Wow. What did this mean? Tucking her copy in her locker, she slammed the door and locked it. Peering up at Jack through her eyelashes, she found him watching her with the same question in his eyes.

He smiled. 'Wow.'

Chris yelled, 'You two coming?'

The flight was bumpy. Every time Ruby glanced at Jack he was staring at her. Because of those photos? That dinner-dance? She thought about the upcoming ball and her dress. Excitement sizzled through her veins. She'd completely got over not wanting to go, could barely wait for the night to arrive. What would Jack say when he saw her all dressed up? Would his eyes go all glittery and bright shiny grey? Would he hold her close, really, really close? Bring it on. She was going to make a statement.

Chris's voice interrupted her glee. 'Here we go. The wind's quieter out here so let's make this a quick and safe turnaround.'

Ruby peered over the edge as Jack was lowered to the heaving deck below. Three crew members stood ready to help him the moment his feet touched down. Then Ruby joined Jack and they were led below decks to the sickbay, moving awkwardly along the narrow corridors of the rolling ship.

It was ten o'clock before Slats put the 'copter down on the tarmac back at base. 'Home, sweet home,' he drawled.

'So much for my roast.' Ruby shoved the door open and reached for a pack. 'Not that my stomach is too keen on that idea any more.'

'You still feel nauseous?' Jack placed the second bag beside hers.

'Settling down. But that was the worst I've ever felt. I'm glad we didn't have to stay on board overnight.' She dropped to the ground. Pain jagged her knee, and she gasped.

'Ruby? You okay?' Jack landed beside her.

'Sure.' Her teeth bit hard into her bottom lip as she waited for the pain to pass. Why hadn't she used the step? She'd already tweaked the knee landing on the trawler's deck. And it had been so good over the weeks since picking up that hiker.

'Let me take that bag.' Jack slung both packs over his shoulder and took her elbow.

She pulled away. 'I'm fine. I don't need mollycoddling.' But the pain wasn't diminishing as quickly as usual, and she hobbled cautiously towards the hangar.

'Don't be stubborn, Ruby. No one's going to think less of you because you've got a damaged knee.' Jack took her elbow again.

No one but me. 'My knee's fine.'

'You seen your doctor about it lately?'

'I get regular check-ups.' The last one had been when she'd first arrived back in Wellington, more than four months ago now. She couldn't take time off every time it hurt. She'd never be at work.

'When's the next one?'

Resisting the urge to spin around in front of him and

poke a finger in his chest, Ruby snarled, 'Drop it, Jack. I know what I'm doing.'

I'm protecting my job, the job I love more than any other I've had. The job that's a part of the new life I'm putting together. I can't risk losing it, not when the house keeps tossing up unpleasant and costly surprises, not when Zane is hurt. What if I did get grounded? What would I do then? I'm not leaving Wellington, that's for sure.

Really? asked a voice in her head. A voice she recognised as the one that had so often sent her packing and moving on.

'Really,' she snapped, clenching her jaw. 'Really.'

CHAPTER ELEVEN

JACK strolled into the conference hall, which had been decked out in red for the ball. Red, the colour of their helicopters. Red, the colour of Ruby's hair. Red, the girl who'd got to him again, knocked down his defences when he wasn't looking. He scanned the crowded tables, searching out his colleagues.

Looking for Red.

She'd managed to wriggle out of coming with him. Something to do with being late finishing at the hair salon. How long did it take to fix stunted hair? Ruby and Sandra had got ready together, at Chris's place. Ruby doing girl things with Sandra was nice. She'd not had a lot of that in the past.

Jack scanned the room for brilliant red hair. Surely that traffic-light colour had to stand out even in this crowd?

He found Chris first. He was standing at a table with a beer in his hand and talking to Slats, who looked distinctly uncomfortable. Jack started heading towards the pilots, constantly looking for Red.

Pow. A punch to the ribs. He jerked to a stop. And stared. What the hell had happened? Ruby stood on Chris's other side. Ruby in a black dress. *The* black dress. The one that she'd worn to the doctors' dinner-dance. The one that had taken his breath away back then. No air was draw-

ing into his lungs now either. His feet were stuck to the
floor as he stared at the beautiful apparition before him.
The dress appeared to be painted on that splendid body.
Just like last time. Except tonight she wore a wide red belt
cinched at her narrow waist.

Ruby in a dress. His gaze trailed downwards and a surge
of laughter rolled through him. Ruby's shoes were an exact
match for her belt, with heels about a metre high. How did
she balance up there? Could she breathe the rarefied air?
As for dancing on those things—impossible.

'Hey, Jack.' Ruby waved to him.

'Great to see ya, ruby-red girl,' he whispered, and began
pressing forward again, his eyes glued to her. How had he,
even for a fraction of a second, believed he'd got over Red?

Not only did he want to haul her into his arms and rav-
age her right here, right now, but he wanted to be around
so he could hold her through all the ups and downs. He
craved her body, her laughter and teasing, her loyalty, everything about her. He wanted to share his life with her.

Hell, a simple black dress had slammed him between
the eyes, woken him up to what had been right before him
all along. He smiled at her, his heart stuttering with love.

She blew him a kiss and gave a big, knowing wink.

Jack elbowed people out of his way and reached Ruby.
Startled, he gaped at her. How had he missed that? 'Your
hair.' That glittering red had vanished. It was coloured as
close to her natural sherry gold shades as possible. His
heart pumped hard. His mouth dried. The little minx. Red
was setting her sights on him. He lifted his hands in sur-
render. He was all hers.

'Hey, Jack, isn't this awesome?' Ruby stood before him,
grinning, her face a lot closer to his than usual thanks to
those shoes. There was a cheeky twinkle in her eyes, a
knowing, cheeky twinkle.

'Your hair. It looks fantastic.' Even cut so short, the colour brought back undimmed memories of running his hands through the silky layers. He groaned. This was going to be one heck of a night. Just keeping his hands to himself would be next to impossible. So why try?

'Let's dance.' He scooped her into his arms and glided across the floor. 'I hope you remember how much we danced last time you wore that dress.' Looking down, he saw her eyes widen, and heat flush up her neck endearingly. He ran a finger down her cheek. 'Because tonight we ain't going to stop, lady.'

And who knew where that would lead? At the dance three years ago they'd finished the night making love. Tonight? Who knew? But he had a damned good idea.

Ruby flopped down onto a chair, a brimming plate of food in front of her. But it was the cold drink she went for first. 'That's divine. It's so hot in here.'

Jack grinned back at her. 'Can't keep up?'

If she hadn't noticed the thin veneer of sweat on his brow she'd have thought Jack had been training for weeks. 'I can match you every dance step of the way.' Glug, glug. The cool water was heavenly in her throat. If only she could ignore the throbbing in her knee.

'That's good. There's plenty more where those last moves came from.' Jack sat down beside her, his suit jacket draped over the back of his chair.

'I'm up for anything once I've eaten this delicious-looking food.' She had to replenish her energy levels somehow. And give her leg a break.

Jack leaned close and whispered, 'Anything?'

'Anything on the dance floor.'

'Retracting your statement?' He winked.

'Just clarifying it.'

Sandra sat down on Ruby's other side, dabbing her eyes. 'I haven't had a night like this in ages.'

Ruby laughed, glad of the break from Jack's all-seeing eyes and double-edged banter, which she was rapidly losing control over. If she'd ever had any control.

Sandra leaned closer. 'Your Jack's a smooth mover.'

Her Jack? Since when had the base staff decided that? 'He seems to know what he's doing.'

Pine scent wafted past her nose. 'You bet I do,' the man himself whispered beside her ear.

Gulp. This really had to stop. Right here. Right now. But hadn't she set out to wow him? Didn't she want him in her bed tonight? Of course she did. So stop being coy. Pushing aside her barely touched plate, she grabbed for Jack's hand. 'Let's dance.'

'Red, I'm starving.' He blinked at her.

'So am I.' But not for hot ham and Parmesan-coated chicken. She backed onto the dance floor, drawing Jack with her. Her hands met behind his neck, her tummy pressed into him and her feet began moving in time with the music, quiet dinner music that most people were ignoring while they ate the meal. Jack's warm, hard body was all she needed right now. Jack was all she wanted to devour. He was the main course and the dessert.

His hands settled on her waist, drew her even closer to him. 'Ahh, Red. Some things just don't change, do they?' His lips kissed her forehead.

'But they do get better,' she whispered back, wondering how she would last the next few hours here without dragging Jack outside and into the back seat of his car. Talk about acting like a teenager. But that was how he made her feel, all hot anticipation and excitement. Her body tingled as his lips trailed kisses down her cheek.

The music stopped. Ruby tripped over her own shoes

when Jack stopped too. His arms steadied her. 'Easy. How do you manage to stay on those stilts?'

'Stilts?' She leaned back in his arms and glared up into his laughing eyes. 'That's so not sexy.'

'Exactly. I'm trying to defuse the situation so we can get through the remainder of the evening.' He leaned closer. 'But they are the sexiest shoes I've ever seen.'

Her mouth dried. She managed to stutter, 'Th-that's better.' For a moment there she'd thought she'd been losing her touch when it came to teasing Jack.

'Ruby, come on, we've got to join the others for the speeches. It won't look good if the base manager is missing.'

'I hate it when you get all practical and proper.' But she took his hand and walked back to their table, struggling not to limp and wondering how late they had to stay. They didn't see the ball out.

They couldn't take the strain of dancing together so close they were as one, without wanting to get even closer. Jack drove fast, straight to Ruby's house. It was nearer than his. If he didn't get there in a very short minute he'd implode with needing her. Dancing with her had wound him tighter than a coiled spring. Hours of holding her body against his had raised his desire to impossible levels. Absorbing her scent had nearly tipped him over the edge—very publicly.

He braked sharply at Ruby's gate. Waving the automatic-locking device at his car, he raced up her path with her hand wrapped in his. If the car hadn't locked, too bad.

Ruby had her front door open faster than a burglar. They tore down the hall to her bedroom, not stopping for kisses on the way. They were way past needing to hold each other, or to kiss and take their time allowing the passion to build.

The passion was there, barely in control, sizzling along his veins. Jack tossed his jacket, tugged his shirt out, up and off. Caught Ruby to him as she reached the bed and felt behind for her zipper. 'Let me,' he murmured against her neck.

She swivelled around under his hands. 'Hurry.' And she shimmied out of her dress, her butt touching, teasing him.

Jack pulled her back against his chest; his hands found and kneaded her breasts. She arched them into him while her backside touched his manhood, pushed closer. Teasing, taunting, making him ache for her. Her hot hand slid between them, found him, rubbed him.

He wanted her, wanted to be inside her. Now. His hand slid downwards, caressing that silky skin from breast to navel, over her belly to the mound above her core, under her panties and into the warm, wet centre of the woman he loved. 'Ahh, Ruby,' he whispered against her neck, tasting her, spreading kisses over her hot skin.

Under his hand she moved, rocked onto her toes, rolled forward, back, forward, back. Between their bodies she continued to rub him. Jack gritted his teeth, attempting to hold back the desire roaring through him and threatening to spill out into her hand.

He'd waited a long time for this. He'd wanted Red from the instant he'd set eyes on her again a few months ago. A few more minutes were nothing. He couldn't fall off the edge without taking Ruby with him. They were finally together again. They would finish this night wound around each other, their bodies blended into one.

Bracing himself, pulling her hand away, he concentrated on Ruby and only Ruby. Her moans of pleasure curled around him, and he turned her so he could taste her sweet mouth. 'I've missed you so much,' he groaned against her lips.

She kissed him back as though this was for the first

time, for the millionth time. Fiercely, greedily. Tenderly, sweetly. All rolled into one life-changing kiss. Her breasts pressed against his chest, her hands clasped behind his neck, she tugged him backwards.

Jack backed her onto the bed and dropped down beside her, covered her body with his and slowly slid inside. Slowly slid home. Home where he belonged, had belonged all along.

Ruby put the phone down, marvelling that Jack hadn't been woken when Chris rang. Unless he was lying in bed, waiting for her to return for some more serious lovemaking. A warm glow settled over her. Last night it had been as though they'd never been apart, like they loved each other as much as ever. More than ever. Hands on hips, she stretched, arching her back, easing all her sweetly aching muscles.

She hopped over to the sideboard, saving her bad knee, and tugged open the drawer containing an assortment of bills, letters and brochures. She scrabbled through them until she found what Chris had asked for and tossed it over to the table, then turned to the fridge. If Jack wanted her back in bed he'd just have to wait while she cooked up a storm of bacon, eggs and hash browns. He'd always had a big appetite after the night before.

While the bacon sizzled gently she found a tray big enough to carry their breakfasts back to bed. A bubble of happiness grew inside her, pressing on her lungs, squashing her tummy, widening her smile. Her feet tap-danced a circle, her hands punched the air. Yee-ha.

Crack, two eggs in the pan. Suddenly Ruby's smile slipped. What if Jack wanted nothing other than the bed stuff? What if he didn't come home after his southern sojourn? Take it one day, one hour at a time. Jack was asleep in her bed after a hot night making love. She'd make the most of the moment and worry about the rest later.

Waiting for the eggs to cook, she eased her bad leg out straight. Sucked air through her teeth as her knee protested. All that dancing had turned it into a hot, throbbing glob in the middle of her leg. Shards of pain stabbed outward, up and down, slicing at her calf muscle, at her thigh. 'My own fault for doing the whoopee dance.'

Reaching up to a high shelf above the microwave, her fingers closed around a small bottle. Two painkillers would lighten the pain for a while. At least until Jack had left. The last thing she needed was for him to start nagging her about seeing a doctor. She already knew what her specialist would say, and she wasn't ready. A knee transplant would mean time off work, would probably mean the end of her career on the helicopters.

As she swallowed the tablets the injustice of everything began roiling in her stomach. Did reality mean she had to give up the job she loved? Was any job worth wrecking her body for? Her happiness slowly deflated.

She plonked down on a chair at the table and dropped her head in her hands. 'I'm not going there yet. I can't. Not after all the effort I've put in so I can have the right house, the perfect job. I'll have to take more care, not get so carried away. There's too much at stake.' Her happiness and heart.

'Trying too hard to convince yourself to stay, Ruby?'

Her head jerked up. Her eyes clashed with Jack's glinting ones as he leaned against the doorframe. 'I don't need convincing to stay in Wellington.'

'Sounds to me much like last time. Just as things are going very well you want to take a hike.' His face tightened, his lips pressed together. 'Just when I'd begun believing in you.'

'I'm still here, aren't I?' Slam bang went her heart against her ribs.

'For how long, Ruby? A week? A day? An hour?' His face was white. 'Save us a load of bother and go pack your bag.'

'You're quick to judge. Doesn't the night we've just shared mean anything to you? Or was I a way of easing your frustration?' She had thrown herself at him, but she'd believed they were on the same page.

His eyes narrowed as his gaze slid over her. 'How do you explain that little conversation I overheard you having with yourself? If that wasn't about leaving then I'm damned if I know what it was.'

Ruby slapped her hand on the tabletop, and let her temper get the better of her. 'My knee is giving me grief big time. The time is rapidly approaching when I have to have replacement surgery. And I'm not ready. I'll never be ready. I don't want to give up my work. I don't want to give up any of the things I'm trying to achieve here.'

His gaze dropped to under the table but he didn't say anything.

Goaded by his silence, she cried out at him, 'You don't want to understand. You don't care. You enjoyed last night, all of it, and don't even begin to deny that.' She stabbed the air between them. 'But already, almost before you've woken up, all you want to do is protect yourself from me. Fine, get out of here. I'll change crews for the rest of your time on the base. I don't need you in my life, Jack Forbes.'

He flinched, straightened and began to turn away. Stopped, turned back, his eyes widening as he stared at the table. Two long strides and he stood beside her, his hand snatching up the brochure she'd got out minutes ago. He flicked through it, his cheeks blanching.

Ruby stuttered, 'I—I can explain.'

'I bet you can. But I don't want your lies.' He slapped the brochure down. 'Why is it so hard for you to come out and say it? When were you going to tell me you're planning to move to Australia?' His finger stabbed the advertisement for staff at the flying doctors' base circled with blue ink. 'Is everything still about you? Your job. Your house. It used to be your father.'

'You're wrong.' She wasn't going to beg him to hear her out.

'How does it make you feel when you let people go from your life?' He played dirty.

'I came back because of you, Jack.' The instant disbelief in his eyes stabbed her through the heart. 'I do love my house and I'm proud of what I'm achieving with it but it's only a house. Same goes for my job. I'd leave it all for you.'

His eyes rolled towards the ceiling. 'And Zane? You going to dump him too?'

'He goes with me. Where are we going?' Her heart had stopped. He really didn't want to be a part of her life. His harsh goading hurt.

'You're going to Queensland. I'm going south.'

That was low. Anger stirred again, kick-started her heart. 'I don't owe you an explanation. You wanted honesty. How about trust? If you can't give me that then we have nothing.'

'Too right.' And he was gone, the back door slamming behind him.

Ruby folded her arms on the table and sank her head onto them. And gave in to the tears she'd never thought she'd have to cry over Jack again. The only man she'd loved. The man she still loved, stronger than ever. There'd be no more chances. She'd used up her last one.

* * *

Ruby crawled into her bed, concentrating on the throbbing in her knee in a vain attempt to ignore the agony in her heart. Stretching her legs out carefully, she rolled into the space where Jack had slept the last hour of last night. Pulling the covers up tight around her neck, she curled onto her side, tucking the pillow he'd used against her tender breasts. Her whole body ached from their lovemaking. It should've been a delicious sensation but now it felt bitter-sweet.

Inhaling his scent, she gave in to another wave of tears. One night with Jack and she'd been in heaven. He'd made love with a skill that had taken her breath away. Often. Very often. He'd given so freely, as if it was the only way he knew to share himself.

A doggy nose pressed against her back. Slowly she rolled over and came nose to nose with Zane. 'Hey, my boy. I still have you. It's back to you and me again.' If it had ever really been any different.

Zane plopped his head on the side of the bed and gazed at her adoringly. His head felt silky under her shaking hand. His eyes were full of love and trust. So much trust, so easily won with affection and food and warm shelter.

'Why can't he be like you?' *Hey, wake up, Ruby, smell the air. Your dream of getting back together is over before it even left the ground. Jack's heading out of town, without you. He won't be looking back.*

Exactly as she'd done. Except she had looked back. Often. And finally she'd returned.

Sitting upright, she yanked at the covers as they threatened to slip off her. Red haze filled her head, coloured her sight.

Jack had no right to do this to her. He couldn't treat her so badly and expect to get away with it. No way. Who did he think he was to make love to her all night and then walk out on her? Not when he knew first hand how that felt.

She wasn't going to give up without a fight after all. If she won him back, anything she did now would be worth it. Urgency gripped her. She had to find him, make him talk to her, listen to her. They belonged together.

Tearing down the hall, she veered into the bathroom where she turned the shower on to heat up while she cleaned her teeth. She'd take an hour to prepare herself and to calm down or she might do more damage to their strained relationship when she saw him. Because they did have a relationship, one with good history. Jack was perfect for her. She was right for him. Hadn't he told her how she'd saved him that night years ago?

'I'll use my mallet on his head to make him see sense if I have to.'

She ducked into the shower box. 'Ahhhhhhhh!' She leapt straight back out. Grabbed a towel to wrap around her. Her teeth chattered, and goose-bumps covered her skin. The water was freezing.

Turning the shower off, she tried the hot water in the basin. Cold. Out in the kitchen the same result and the old hot-water cylinder was definitely on. The fuse hadn't popped on the meter board. The lights came on when she flicked switches so there was still power.

'Another disaster, but this one I'm going to suck up. I can deal with it. Easily.' She gave herself a quick, cold sluice before pulling on a thick jersey and tight-fitting jeans. She shoved her feet into thick woollen socks and tied on her boots. Then she rang the plumber.

'I've got a bit of a problem.' By the time she hung up her head was hurting. Hot-water cylinders didn't come cheap. Of course they wouldn't. That would've been working in her favour and so far today showed no signs of being at all friendly. *Be tough, be strong.*

She debated for two seconds about walking around to Jack's house. 'Sorry, Zane, you'll have to wait for your walk. I'm taking the truck.' The truck would be quicker. And it gave a boost to her confidence to be seen behind the steering-wheel, made her feel a few sizes taller. And she was going to need all the confidence and good luck and patience she could muster when she came face to face with Jack. She had to get this right or she'd spend the rest of her life debating with herself how she could've done it differently to keep Jack.

She'd have charged inside without knocking if his front door hadn't been locked. Instead she leaned on the bell until she heard the door being unlocked.

'Jack, what do you think you're...?' She spluttered to a stop, staring at the man standing in front of her, his eyes chilly, his face blank. 'Steve.'

'Ruby.' Jack's brother made no move to let her enter.

'I didn't know you were home.'

'Why would you?'

Jack might have mentioned it last night when they were still getting on. She shrugged away her disappointment. Same old Jack, not talking about anything going on in his life. 'Can I come in? I need to see Jack.'

'He's not here. He won't be back until late tomorrow night.' Was that a flicker of sympathy in his face? Not likely. Steve had never been her friend.

'Are you sure he's not here?' Steve would be loving her desperation. He'd done his best to come between her and Jack three years ago and he'd never hidden his delight when he'd learned she was leaving.

'Jack left half an hour ago for Auckland.' Steve held the door wide. 'Want a coffee? I've just made a pot.'

Her eyes popped. What? Steve inviting her in? To prove Jack really wasn't here? Or to be friendly? Either way, she wasn't staying. 'No, thanks. I just needed to see Jack, explain something to him, but it'll have to wait until work on Tuesday.'

She turned for the stairs and her truck. How would she get through the weekend? Go to Auckland? Definitely not.

'Ruby,' Steve called. 'Wait.'

'What ever for?' That red haze was returning. These brothers stuck together no matter what, never giving an outsider a chance.

'Give Jack a break. Hear him out when he gets back home. Please.' Steve was pleading with her?

'Hear him out? Getting him to talk in the first place would be a start.'

'He gave you a chance three years ago, Ruby. He worked hard at seeing things your way, broke his heart over you because he knew it was right to let you go. Please.'

'Please' twice in one conversation, in one lifetime. Her mouth dropped, the haze retreated. Steve wanted her to give Jack a chance? Steve was helping her with Jack? What was this about? 'About that coffee?'

She followed Steve through to the kitchen and perched on a barstool, watching him fill a plunger with grinds and boiling water. 'How long are you back for?'

'A week. My next leave happens when Jack's gone to Scott Base so I figured I'd come home now.'

'I'm still struggling to believe he's going there. It's so not Jack.' She got off the stool, wandered across to the bay window and gazed out at the harbour way below.

'Who knows? It could be the best thing for him. Dad and I kept him tied here, looking out for us, for too long. It's time for him to sort out what he wants to do for himself.' Steve lifted his head, his eyes connecting with hers.

'I'll rephrase that. Jack needs to admit to what he already knows he wants and go after it.'

'And what would that be?' Obviously not her.

'You'll have to ask him.' Steve pushed a full mug in her direction.

When she sipped the hot liquid her eyebrows rose. 'You want to teach Jack how to make coffee this good before you go away again?'

'That sounds like you intend coming around here some more.' Steve leaned his elbows on the bar.

'That's up to your brother.' If he opened up to her after she explained about the brochure. After she told him how much she loved him.

'You two need your heads knocked together. Hard.' Steve's mug banged on the bench. 'Whatever happened to sitting down and talking things out like normal adults?'

Ruby squirmed on her stool. Steve wasn't just mad at her, he included his brother in the equation. 'You want me to sort things out with Jack? Once and for all?'

He rolled his eyes heavenward. 'At last, the woman gets it.'

CHAPTER TWELVE

'ARE you stopping over in Auckland tonight, Dr Forbes?' The flight attendant hovered over Jack, her breasts pushed almost into his face.

'Yes, I am.'

'Alone?'

'No.' *Now leave me alone. Go pick on some other bloke.*

Jack watched her slink down the aisle, relieved she'd got the message, guilty for being so abrupt. But he wasn't in the mood for idle chit-chat. He was angry. At Red? Who else? He swallowed the hot lump in his throat, slumped further down in his seat. No, not at Red, at himself.

He was an idiot. Too busy protecting his heart to think about the hurt he'd inflict by walking out on her. After snarling cutting criticism that had sliced into her. Oh, yeah, he'd seen the instant the pain had struck.

But what else could he do? Admit how much he needed her? How her strength was his pillar? That would terrify her. A sure way to get her packing up again.

Be honest, Jacko. Red isn't leaving. You're the one running away and it feels bad. Feels totally, totally wrong. How had Ruby done it so often?

Different scenario, Jacko. She was searching for her father, not running away.

He tried stretching his legs in the cramped space under

the seat in front of him. Gave up. Airplanes weren't designed for anyone taller than—than Ruby. Leaning his head back, he closed his eyes and immediately saw Red. She was dancing by, laughing, teasing, waving at him in that black dress. He blinked. Red didn't disappear. Now her face had crumpled with sadness, but that chin was still jutting out in defiance. Gutsy. Strong. Lovable.

She'd said she'd go anywhere with him, give up her job and house for him. And he'd stomped on her words. Did she give second chances? He'd have to dig deep, open himself up to her in a way he'd never done in his life. It'd be excruciating. It would be worth it if she listened.

'Ladies and gentlemen, shortly we'll be landing in Auckland.'

Jack popped his eyes open. Auckland. Dad. Family.

What about Wellington? Ruby. Family. And a house, a wacky dog and maybe a job in February.

At the airline counter Jack was gutted when told he'd have to wait till the next day to return to Wellington. 'Are you saying all the flights are full?'

The assistant shook her head in disbelief. 'You've just landed and you have to ask why there are no flights?' He must have looked stunned because she added, 'They're about to close the airport. Wellington shut half an hour ago. Didn't you find your flight very bumpy?'

He'd had more important things on his mind.

By Monday afternoon Ruby was so tense she thought she'd go crazy if she didn't see Jack soon. But despite the zillion texts she'd sent, he hadn't answered.

She spun the truck's steering-wheel and parked outside her gate. Letting her head drop back against the seat, she grimaced. At least she'd sorted some things out in town, had begun the processes for major changes. Changes she'd never thought she'd make and now that she'd instigated them she felt surprisingly light-hearted about them.

Her cellphone chattered. Grabbing it, she read the name flashing back at her. Not Jack. Tossing the phone into her bag, she picked up her grocery bags and eased down to the road carefully, favouring her knee.

Zane barked as she pushed open the gate and rubbed his ears. 'Hey, boy. Did you miss me?'

Thump. Thump. Thump.

'What's that?' Straightening up, Ruby followed the heavy sounds to the corner of her house where she stopped abruptly. Leaned against the wall for support. And ogled the view.

Jack, shirt off, swung an axe at the stump of her old walnut tree. Swing, slam. Swing, slam. My, oh, my. The man had some muscles. They rippled down his back. They flexed in his arms. They held his stomach taut. Her mouth dried, her tongue did circuits. He'd felt good, strong and hard, during their lovemaking on Saturday night, but now? Now she had to restrain herself from rushing over and running her hands all over that sweat-coated body.

Flip-flop went her heart, like a tadpole out of water. Heck, she could go on watching him for ever, drinking in the sight.

Zane had other ideas. He picked up his ball and trotted over to Jack, nudged his thigh. Jack slammed the axe into a root and turned to pat Zane. That was when he saw her. His gaze clashed with hers. His face filled with uncertainty. 'Red, I hope it's okay to start on removing this stump.'

She blindly placed her bags on the porch and advanced slowly towards Jack. Her heart started an erratic beat. 'It has to come out some time and I can't get a bulldozer out here to haul it from the ground.'

'That's what I thought.' His eyes still held hers.

'You have nothing better to do with your afternoon?'

He swallowed. Nodded. 'Yeah, I did. But you weren't here.'

'You knew I wouldn't have gone far, right?'

'Zane told me.' He looked away, looked back. 'Yeah, I knew. I don't know what that brochure was about but I already figured you wouldn't lie to me. You never have. I got it horribly wrong so I figured I'd got other things wrong too.'

'To clear up one thing, the brochure belongs to Chris. He's got a surprise trip organised for Sandra. He couldn't leave them in his locker at work because she's in and out of it as often as her own.'

Jack crossed the lawn to stand in front of her. 'I'm not very good at talking about me.'

His blunt statement took her breath away. 'It's okay.'

'No, it's not. I hated it when you left to go to the States. I wanted to ask you to stay a few more months so we could go together. But that would've meant telling you how afraid of being left behind I was and why. I couldn't do that. To tell you that everyone left me at some time in my life would've made me look like a loser, like the kind of man no one wanted around for ever.'

'Jack, no. Don't ever think that. People don't leave you. They go out into the world on their own journeys, strong from your love and knowing you'll always be there for them.' Ruby reached for his hands, held them tightly. 'They're not running away from you. They haven't stopped loving you. I never stopped loving you. Not for one second.'

'So why didn't you come look me up when you got back?'

She grinned, a slightly strained grin but one nevertheless. 'The blonde sticking plaster.'

'What?' He stared at her as though she'd grown a third eye.

Ruby quickly explained, and Jack relaxed, pulled her close and wrapped his arms around her. 'You're my only love, ruby-red girl. Always have been.' They stood in the spring sun, holding each other until Zane nudged them.

Ruby wiped her eyes. Somehow they'd become damp. 'You weren't the only one at fault. I should've talked to you before I went away. I wanted to wait for you but didn't think you'd agree to go with me.'

'I think now that I would've.' Jack kissed the tip of her nose.

'At the time I was so antsy. And the Greaser was my battle. I don't think I wanted to share him.' She kissed Jack's mouth. There'd been a lot of things she hadn't shared. From now on she'd tell Jack everything. So, 'I've been to see the base doctor today. My knee has been getting worse. A few bad landings, a lot of dancing. I've made a decision.' She sucked air, again surprised that this didn't hurt much. 'I'm quitting the helicopters and going to work on the ambulances. There's a job coming up in the city next month.'

His face registered surprise. 'I knew you were having trouble but I thought you'd keep on jumping out of helicopters for a long time to come.'

She shook her head. 'I want to dance with you again. Often. I want to be able to run on the beach with my kids. Knee replacements are all very well but let's not go there any sooner than necessary.'

His mouth covered hers. A deep, lingering kiss, only to be interrupted by Zane again. Jack laughed and took Ruby's hand, turning her round. 'Look, there in the corner by your vegetable patch.'

'A new walnut tree. Awesome.' Ruby stared at the tree, a giggle rolling up her throat, breaking free. 'With two toy plastic swings hanging on the branch.' She swivelled around to Jack. 'A pink one and a blue one. Jack, what are you planning?'

He counted on his fingers. 'Making you my wife. Having a baby with my wife. Having another baby with my wife. Starting back in A and E in February after I've been on my honeymoon with my wife.' His smile was so male, so self-satisfied. 'I'm still going south so I thought…' he glanced at her '…hoped we could get married as soon as I get back.'

Ruby threw herself into his arms and started a thorough kissing campaign.

Zane finally gave up trying to get their attention and went to study the contents of Ruby's grocery bags. When the humans finally came up for air the dog had devoured the steak Ruby had planned on having for dinner.

Ruby laughed out loud. 'Naughty boy.' She patted his head. 'Now I'll have to cook something else. You like lasagne, Jack?'

'Why don't I take you out somewhere? We can leave the heat-and-eat stuff for another less important day.' He wisely stepped back, out of arm's range.

Ruby wagged her finger at him as she approached. 'I'll tell you this for nothing, Mr Smarty Pants. I've been taking cooking lessons and I can rustle up a fine meal any time I like now.' She sprang at Jack, catching him as he tried to dodge sideways.

They went down in a heap on the lawn. As Jack wound his arms around Red again he grinned. 'Now I know this day is a total dream. I'm going to wake up and find two-minute noodles on the table and you standing over me with a whip until I eat them.'

'Do I get to wear black stockings and a lacy body suit?' Ruby covered his oath with her mouth and kissed him senseless.

* * * * *

THE DOCTOR, HIS DAUGHTER AND ME

BY
LEONIE KNIGHT

MILLS &
BOON

*Many thanks to Heather and Ian, retired dairy farmers
and a wonderfully generous couple, who helped me
with the details of life on a farm. Also for Shellee and Margaret.
You are truly inspirational.*

First published in Great Britain 2012
by Mills & Boon, an imprint of Harlequin (UK) Limited.
Harlequin (UK) Limited, Eton House, 18-24 Paradise Road,
Richmond, Surrey TW9 1SR

© Leonie Knight 2012

ISBN: 978 0 263 89788 3

Harlequin (UK) policy is to use papers that are natural, renewable
and recyclable products and made from wood grown in sustainable
forests. The logging and manufacturing process conform to the
legal environmental regulations of the country of origin.

Printed and bound in Spain
by Blackprint CPI, Barcelona

'Is there room in your life for anyone else to love you?'

Ryan knew he was moving too fast but he had to know. If she said no without hesitation then he might as well give up. Tara could be stubborn, and if she made up her mind about something it was extremely difficult to change it.

But she hadn't answered.

Her cheeks were pink and she was looking at a point somewhere on the opposite wall. He moved a little closer to her and grasped her hand.

She refocused and mesmerised him with her deep grey-blue eyes. Was it desire he saw in their depths?

'You mean you?' she finally said.

'Yes.'

Tara leaned across, rested her head on Ryan's shoulder and sighed.

'Oh, Ryan. Why did you have to come back? I had my future mapped out. I thought I was as happy as I could be. And I honestly can't think of love. Not now. It's too hard.'

Ryan gently stroked her silky hair and resisted the temptation to put words into her mouth. *She* had to say it.

He waited…

Dear Reader

I was born and bred in the city, but have spent nearly two decades living and working in the country. During that time I've come to know many true heroes and heroines who have done the best they can to make a go of it on the land. In this story I have tried to impart a sense of the struggle many country people have to deal with as a backdrop to the romance between Ryan, a city orthopaedic surgeon, and Tara, a country GP.

Their journey takes them from a life-changing event in the past, and having to deal with the fall-out of that event, finally to a future full of love, hope and impossible dreams come true.

I hope you enjoy this story.

Leonie K

PS I love to hear from my readers and you can contact me via my website: www.leonieknight.com

PROLOGUE

Dr Tara Dennison closed her eyes, took several deep breaths and tried to relax as the physio's thumbs dug deep into both sides of her neck. She was close to tears but it had nothing to do with the massage. She'd decided she couldn't put it off any longer. She would tell Ryan tonight. And then they would both be free…free of the guilt, anguish and pain that held them together in a fragile relationship that had mercilessly sapped the strength from both of them over the past three months.

'Ouch,' she said as the pressure on her spine amplified and teetered on the edge of pain.

'You're tenser today than you usually are. Is there anything wrong? Soreness anywhere?'

Tara opened her eyes. She definitely wasn't about to reveal that *everything* was wrong. That she loved her husband so much there was no way she could deny him the future he deserved—the loving *perfect* wife, sexual fulfilment, the children he'd always wanted…

'No, I'm fine. I think I may have overdone it in the gym yesterday. Perhaps we could call it quits now?'

'Good idea. I'll catch up with you in the pool tomorrow afternoon.'

'Yes, the pool…'

But before she had time to finish her sentence the physio

had left, and a few minutes later she heard familiar footsteps heading towards her room. Her heart did a somersault and landed squarely in the pit of her stomach.

Now.

She'd made up her mind. She would definitely tell him *now*.

Ryan felt good. The time was right. He clutched an enormous bouquet of delicately scented yellow roses in one hand and the list he'd laboured over for the past week in the other. With the information he had, and Tara's all-time favourite flowers, how could she possibly refuse?

But when he reached her room, drew back the curtain and saw the expression on her face, he began to have doubts.

'Hi, beautiful.' He placed the flowers on the bedside table, leaned forward and kissed his wife on the mouth, holding the simple but intimate connection for as long as he could. Her mouth was immobile, her lips cool, and when he finally drew away her sombre expression flattened his mood like a burst balloon.

'What's the matter?'

She was looking at the roses as if he'd given her a bunch of stinging nettles.

'I have something I want to tell you.'

'That's great.' His gentle smile did nothing to thaw the icy expression on Tara's face. 'I have something to tell you too.'

Some of his previous joy at finally tying up all the loose ends of his plan that would give them the chance of a rosy future returned. His love for Tara had never waned. They had survived a horrific accident and were both miraculously alive; he'd been there every step of the way through the lengthy and arduous rehabilitation programme; he'd supported her through bouts of debilitating depression and he'd found a way for them to live out the happily-ever-after of their dreams. If she'd just let him explain…

'I'll go first.' The list he had made seemed redundant now, but he knew once she'd realised they weren't stuck in an inescapable rut…

'No, Ryan. Let me.'

Her eyes, which were usually wide open windows to her feelings, were shuttered.

'Okay,' he said slowly as he reached for her hand, but she snatched it away.

'I want a divorce.'

Ryan shook his head in disbelief. Just when there was a possibility they could get their lives back on track? Had he heard wrong?

'No!' The word came out more forcefully than he'd planned. 'Sorry,' he added, and this time Tara let him hold her hand. She was shaking.

'Why?'

She took a deep breath and looked him straight in the eye.

'Because I'm disabled, Ryan. I'm a different person to the perfect woman you married. I think and feel differently and I could never be a mother to your children—'

'But…' He squeezed Tara's hand tight. 'But none of that matters…if we love each other.'

Tara looked away and shifted restlessly in her hospital bed.

'Tara? Love…it's what has sustained us through the bad times as well as the good.'

Tara's gaze swung back to Ryan. She sighed.

'That's the problem, Ryan. I don't love you any more. And I can't live in a loveless marriage.' She cleared her throat. 'I want a divorce and I'm not going to change my mind.'

CHAPTER ONE

Eight years later.

RYAN DENNISON wasn't trying to avoid the inevitable confrontation, just delaying it. He circled the car park looking for an inconspicuous space from where he'd still have full view of the entrance to the clinic.

How long had it been since he'd seen Tara? He did a quick mental calculation. It was nearly eight years. Back then, he'd told her he was prepared to be there for her all the way, no matter the sacrifices. He'd had a workable plan for their future. But she'd insisted she wanted a divorce. He thought he'd found a way to overcome all their problems but he'd had no answer to her simple statement: *I don't love you any more.* And she'd been right; they couldn't stay together in a marriage without mutual love.

After several weeks of agonising self-doubt, guilt and pleading with Tara, she'd held her ground and become more distant as time went on. He knew her grief had been as gut-wrenching as his, but she hadn't seemed to understand the anguish he'd suffered at being pushed away, at having to endure years of remorse.

Yes, he'd agreed to end their marriage, but his heart still bore the scars of being rejected by the woman he'd loved with his whole being. His attempts to contact her by e-mails and phone calls in the first few years had been ignored, as if she'd been frightened of having any communication with him. His phone calls to her home phone had always been coldly blocked by her parents, who'd told him their daughter didn't want to talk to him, and she must have recognised his mobile number as his texts and calls went unanswered. In the end he'd stopped trying.

No one was to blame.

Well, that was what he'd kept telling himself—until the words almost lost their meaning.

But Tara's parents didn't believe it and he suspected Tara nursed doubts as well.

He parked the car and then glanced at his watch—four twenty-five. He'd done his homework. She finished at four-thirty but he'd come prepared for a wait. She would be busy, popular and almost certainly run overtime. Scanning the cars in the disabled section, he came to the conclusion hers would be the people-mover—the only vehicle big enough to take an electric wheelchair and be fitted with the gadgetry for a paraplegic driver.

Paraplegic… Oh, God, if only things had been different. Despite his outward calm he still had nightmares, replaying the horrors of that terrible evening. In the past week he'd woken nearly every night in a lather of torment, grief and with a vivid image of twisted metal. It was a painful reminder of how he was feeling about seeing his ex-wife again.

He took a sip of bottled water to cool the burning dryness in his throat.

He couldn't change the past. Now he was going to be working in the same building with her he hoped she'd at least talk to him. But unless she'd had a turnaround in her personality she'd be stubborn and cling fiercely to her independence. The fact she'd finished her training and found a

job was testament to her determination. She didn't need—
or want—him any more. She'd made that clear when they
parted.

The guilt stabbed painfully again.

He closed his eyes for a moment and when he opened
them he saw her, just as beautiful as she'd been the
day he'd met her. The years had been kind to her. Her
strawberry-blonde hair, streaked with gold, was cut shorter,
so it fell in tapered wisps to her shoulders. He could see her
arms were muscular and her shoulders a little broader than
he remembered, but it didn't detract from her femininity.
Grimacing with concentration, she skilfully manoeuvred
to the driver's side of the vehicle, opened the door and positioned the wheelchair so she could haul herself into the
driver's seat. Then she smiled and said something to the
young woman accompanying her, who opened the rear
door and put the chair on a hoist which lifted it into the
luggage space. The woman waved as she returned to the
building and Tara reversed and drove slowly away.

What now?

He'd seen her. That had been pleasure, not pain. But he
still had to speak to her. Tell her he was soon starting sessional work in the specialist rooms attached to her practice. What a strange turn of fate that the position of visiting
orthopaedic surgeon had come up in Keysdale, of all
places. As the most junior partner in his practice, without
any country attachments, he'd been offered the job and
been expected to take it. Initially he'd had doubts, as it
would mean bringing up traumas of the past he'd thought
he'd laid to rest, but after thinking long and hard he'd realised it might be a way of achieving closure to confirm
Tara had no feelings for him.

And now he was back, and he didn't want to present her
with any nasty surprises like approaching her in the car

park. It would have to be at her home—her parents' home. He cringed at the thought of a reunion with the two people he'd believed had liked him and approved of his marriage to their only daughter. But after the accident they'd not bothered to hide their abhorrence of him. *They'd* blamed him and then callously ignored him. Or at least her father had.

If there was any other way…

He decided to have a coffee in one of the cafés in the main street, go through in his mind what he would say, and then drive the ten kilometres out of town to the Fielding farm. He couldn't put it off any longer.

'Is Dad still working?' Tara asked as her mother helped her into her wheelchair.

'Yep, but he should be here any minute. He's been fixing fences down near the creek and said he'd finish the job after milking.' Jane Fielding closed the back of the car and followed her daughter towards the homestead.

'How was your day, love?' her mother asked, as she did every afternoon when Tara came home from work. Tara loved her mother dearly, but sometimes felt smothered by her protectiveness and yearned for a home of her own.

But Tara was realistic; leaving the family home wasn't practical. She'd need a purpose-built unit and help from an able-bodied person for things that most people took for granted—like transferring to her chair, shopping in a supermarket, hanging out washing or gaining access to immediate help in an emergency. Of course there were ways around these difficulties, but even the most basic tasks took longer when you were confined to a wheelchair. She'd have to rethink her schedule to incorporate cooking, housework, washing and ironing—all the things her mother did without complaint. Her life wasn't perfect, but it was a better option than moving out on her own. She was used to the routine. And her parents had made sacrifices, including nearly losing the farm, to cater for her needs and extra expenses in the early years. She would probably never be able to repay them.

'Oh, you know—the same as usual; nothing out of the ordinary.' She parked next to the kitchen bench where her mother began preparing a late afternoon tea.

A moment later she heard the sound of her father's boots being flung into the corner of the veranda near the back door.

'I'm home,' he shouted unnecessarily. You'd have to be deaf as a farm gate not to notice his comings and goings. Her mother always said it was a *man thing*—slamming doors, throwing things like a ball to a hoop and stomping around like an army major.

'We're in the kitchen. Tara's just come home and I'm making tea.'

'Rightio.'

Tara laughed. The word was so old-fashioned but suited her father perfectly.

Jane put fresh-brewed tea and a plate of orange cake on the bench as Graham Fielding entered the room.

'Have you washed your hands?' Tara's mother was quick to ask—as she always did when Graham came in from working on the farm.

'Yes, I've washed my hands,' he said as he held them up for inspection, before kissing Tara on her forehead. 'How's my best girl?'

Tara frowned. She hated the way her father often treated her as if she was still his little girl.

'Fine, Dad.' She reached for her cup of tea as her mother passed the cake. 'How did you go with the fences?'

'All done, but I won't move the cows until after milking tomorrow morning.'

'Want a hand?'

Though she was quite able to handle a quad bike to get around the farm, and knew the routine of milking back to front, she guessed her father would say no. As he always did. She was sure she could manage most of the work from her wheelchair with a simple modification to raise her height. She'd developed strength in her arms and shoulders to rival any man's.

But her father had refused to let her near the dairy after the accident. He didn't seem to understand that her help would give him more time for the heavier work that neither Tara nor her mother could manage. For him, there was a non-negotiable line between men's and women's work that she'd almost given up trying to cross. His one concession was letting her mother help out now they could no longer afford to hire a dairyman.

'No, love. It won't take long, and you deserve your free time on the weekends.'

He had good intentions but was seriously lacking in subtlety. Another one of those *man things*, as her mother would say. He had no idea, though. She hardly needed to keep a social diary. Her life had settled into a comfortable equilibrium of work, home and the occasional outing to the shops or the pool at the physio's in Bayfield, fifty kilometres away. And at the end of her working days she hardly had any energy left to party.

Their conversation was interrupted by a car pulling up at the front of the house.

'Are you expecting visitors?' Graham glanced at his wife.

'Might be Audrey. She said she'd come round some time

this week to return those preserving jars. But she usually drives around the back.'

A car door slammed and a few moments later there was a crisp knock on the front door. 'I'll go and see who it is,' she added.

Graham stood up, an imposing thick-set man of six foot three. 'No, I'll go. You get another cup of tea poured.'

Tara heard her father talking, but not what he was saying. She could tell he was angry by the sharp rise and fall of his voice. The visitor was male, that was all she could tell, and clearly unwelcome.

'Doesn't sound like Audrey,' her mother said with eyebrows raised.

They stilled at the sound of the front door slamming and her father clomping, barefoot, down the passage.

'Who's that?' Jane asked. She'd already poured a cup of tea for the visitor and looked disappointed.

'You don't want to know.' He scowled and shifted his gaze to Tara. 'It's Ryan.'

It took Tara a few moments to process the information.

'Ryan?' The word escaped as a husky whisper and didn't require an answer. She'd tried to put her feelings for her ex-husband on hold since their dramatic parting, but rarely a day went by without her thinking of him, dreaming of what life *could* have been if she'd not rejected him so coldly. She'd made the right decision, though. She'd heard Ryan had married again and started a family. She was happy for him.

But she'd never stopped loving him.

So she'd have to make sure she remained cool and detached and not let her true feelings show.

But why was he here? And why now? She felt her heart

pumping as a film of sweat broke out on her forehead. She felt winded.

After all these years!

She took a deep breath and attempted a steady voice. Both her parents were looking at her, waiting for her re-action. She tried to restore her usual calm.

'Ryan Dennison?'

The angry fire in her father's eyes answered her question.

'He's waiting outside, insisting he talks to you, says he won't go until he's seen you.' He paused as if gauging her reaction. 'I'll send him away—even if it means running him off the property with the shotgun—'

'No, Dad, I'll see him.' Though the last person she wanted to see was her ex, she knew her father wasn't jok-ing about the gun. 'I'll go outside. There's no need for him to come in.'

He seemed to accept her suggestion as a sign of her dis-approval of her ex-husband and conceded.

'All right, but you be careful.'

Tara wasn't sure what her father meant.

At the time of their separation her thoughts had been clouded by the devastation of losing so much—the use of her legs, her career, the baby they'd so desperately wanted to make their family complete.

Ryan had had his whole life to live. She hadn't wanted to take that away from him. He'd just started his specialist training in orthopaedics—his dream career. If he'd become her full-time carer, as he'd said he would, the future they'd planned before the accident would have been shattered. She'd felt she had little choice, especially in the early days when the pain had been so acute, and in retrospect she'd probably been depressed, not capable of making rational decisions. Back then there'd been no way she could have deprived Ryan of his dreams of a career, a happy marriage to a healthy wife and the children he had wanted so much.

The best thing had been to divorce. It had been easier that way. She hadn't wanted to find out if Ryan was capable of coping with living with a woman who was disabled. He'd always described her as *perfect in every way.*

But she wasn't *perfect* any more, not since the crash, and her scars were more than just physical. Yes, the sadness and pain, both physical and emotional, had lessened as the years passed, but memories still lingered of the man she'd loved with every part of her heart and soul.

Why was he here? The thought tumbled into her mind again.

She felt light-headed as she opened the door and the familiar clawing of panic descended like thick smog. Her heart began to pound and she gagged on the taste of bile at the back of her throat. A shard of irrepressible fear mixed with long-suppressed hurt stabbed at her heart and threatened to take control of her mind.

She stopped in the doorway and began taking slow, deep breaths.

'What's the matter, Tara? Are you all right? You look pale.'

For a long moment she'd been so preoccupied with losing control in front of Ryan she'd forgotten where she was. By now it was too late. A man she hardly recognised crouched in front of her. This was a successful man in his mid-thirties, with thick brown hair clipped short, clean-shaven and dressed in a conservative charcoal-grey suit, white shirt and silver tie. He looked nothing like the relaxed young man she remembered.

She was beginning to feel normal again, but couldn't bring herself to smile. Her emotions were too raw. She felt the slowing of her heartbeat and the fuzziness clearing from her head.

He still had the same deep blue eyes, though, and right now they were full of concern.

'I'm fine,' Tara replied. She hated the fact she'd let down her guard and revealed how vulnerable she could be before they'd even said hello. 'I just get a bit light-headed sometimes. It never lasts for more than a few minutes.' The tension in Ryan's face relaxed. 'Dad said you wanted to talk to me.'

Ryan stood up with an expression that was almost but not quite a smile.

Damn his charisma and amazing good looks. She was determined not to expose her emotions, though. He mustn't know she still had feelings for him, but already she knew the spark was still there.

At least he wasn't focused on her humiliating physical response to him. But that was the thing with panic attacks. She'd thought she had them beat but they could be triggered by the most unexpected and sometimes insignificant things.

'There's something I thought you needed to know.'

Her confidence was coming back.

'I'd better sit down.' Tara had become used to making jokes about her condition, to break the ice for people who weren't comfortable with her disability, but this time it didn't work. The frown on Ryan's face was set in stone.

'*You'd* better sit down, then.' She pointed towards an old swing seat suspended from the rafters. She now felt calm and in charge of the emotions which had threatened to be her undoing a few moments ago.

'Do you need any help?'

'No.'

She set the chair in motion and forced him to move out

of the way. Finally he sat down on the swing opposite her chair.

'So, what is it you want to talk to me about that's so important you were prepared to brave Dad and his threat to run you off the property?'

Ryan smiled.

But it didn't last long.

'He said that?'

'Mmm, he did.' She paused a moment, wondering how much of the past she could raise without ramping up the tension that already buzzed in the air between them. On reflection, she realised she had nothing to lose. It wasn't as if she was trying to impress Ryan, and he was well aware of her parents' dislike for him.

Ryan gazed into her eyes and she jolted at the unexpected connection. The feeling was from the past—something that had been exclusive to them alone—an understanding that she and Ryan had used to consider a sign of their closeness.

But it served no purpose now. She wasn't going to reveal how she really felt.

He finally spoke.

'I'm going to be working down here. I start in two weeks in the new specialist rooms attached to your clinic.'

He stared, as if trying to gauge her reaction. And she produced the goods in the form of a violent blush. Her heart began to race again, but she was determined to keep her cool despite the overwhelming shock of his revelation.

'I thought it was better for you to know in advance, rather than just bumping into me at work one day.'

She swallowed and concentrated on the calm evenness of her breathing.

'You could've easily phoned.' She wondered at his motives. She'd not heard from this man for nearly six years—

since he'd finally got the message she didn't want to be reminded of the past by his e-mails and calls. All she knew of him was through the medical grapevine—he was a successful orthopaedic surgeon, three years after they broken up he had remarried, and the last she'd heard he was overseas.

'I wanted to see you…'

Tara found that hard to believe.

'Why?' That gnawing pain in her heart that visited her every day was demanding an answer. Anger surfaced unexpectedly. 'Were you frightened of what you might see?'

Ryan looked genuinely hurt—a totally unanticipated reaction. She hadn't meant to be cruel, but her emotions were ruling what came out of her mouth.

'Sorry,' she muttered.

'No… You're absolutely right. I should have phoned. I didn't realise seeing you without warning would upset you.' His pupils dilated, which made their rim of blue the colour of bright sky reflected in black ice. 'I'm the one who should be apologising.'

She still wasn't quite sure why he'd gone to the trouble of driving all the way to Keysdale and then out to the farm. It wasn't the sort of visit a person would plan on the offchance. She suddenly felt resentful that he'd upset the ordered balance of her life.

He looked down at his hands clasped in his lap and said quietly, 'How are your parents?'

It was a question she wasn't expecting. She thought a moment before replying.

'You're not part of our lives any more. I'd describe Mum's attitude to you as ambivalent, and Dad…well… you saw what he was like when he answered the door. But I don't think they actually hate you… It's what happened—the accident—they both still blame you for that.'

Ryan reached for Tara's hand but she snatched it away. Seeing him was traumatic enough. She didn't want any physical contact because…because she wasn't sure how she'd react. The old desire she thought she'd buried long ago was still there. It frightened her.

'And you?'

Tara closed her eyes and took a deep breath. She was hurting. Why was Ryan trawling through what had happened so long ago? No one was to blame for the accident. He was a good driver and had done what most people would have—tried to avoid their collision with a kangaroo. With devastating consequences. Her situation was a cross she had *chosen* to bear without him, and up until ten minutes ago she'd been managing perfectly okay.

She opened her eyes but didn't look at Ryan.

'You know I've never held you responsible.' She sighed. 'It happened, it was regrettable, but I'm over it and I think you should be too.'

Ryan brushed a piece of fluff from his sleeve.

'Of course you're right,' he said. 'But it isn't enough to stop me feeling it was my fault. Can you understand how difficult it is for me to see you like…?' The words seemed to stick in his throat and he swallowed.

Tara looked into the distance, trying to take on board what Ryan was saying. He was hurting too.

Neither of them could ever forget the crash and its aftermath, and sometimes Tara thought Ryan had been more damaged than she. His dreams had been blown apart—his career, the life they'd planned together, the children they'd so desperately wanted. They'd talked about her completing her GP training part-time. She'd been off the pill for a couple of months and the heartbreaking irony was that her period had been a week overdue. She'd planned on doing a home pregnancy test the following week, but the day after the accident she'd bled...and bled...and bled...

Another tragic loss.

It had been as if her lifeblood had drained from her, but she'd always put on a brave face.

Of course they both knew she was still physically capable of conceiving and bearing children. She'd assumed she was no longer sexually attractive to him, though, and even if she did have a child she would need help to look after it. With the long hours Ryan worked she would be effectively a single parent. Combined with her disability, the whole scenario was unworkable.

To her alarm, she was close to tears. She needed to change the direction of the conversation.

'So you'll be doing sessional work, I guess?'

He also seemed grateful for the change of subject.

'I'll be operating on Thursdays and consulting Fridays, with the option to do an extra theatre session on alternative Saturday mornings. I'll stay overnight.'

'Where are you planning to stay?' she asked, purely out of curiosity.

'I thought one of the motels. But if you can suggest anything better?'

She thought for a moment.

'The Riverside is the best of the three motels in town. It's off the highway and not far from the clinic.' That was all the advice she was prepared to give.

'Right. I'm staying over tonight, so I can check out the consulting rooms and meet with the manager to go through all the paperwork tomorrow morning. I can book in to the motel you suggested. I plan to head back about lunchtime.'

To his wife.

Tara wondered what she would think of her husband

working away. But she certainly wasn't going to delve into his personal life.

'Can I pick you up and take you out to lunch before I leave?'

No way! What on earth was he thinking?

Tara tried not to let her disbelief show on her face and mustered a smile.

'No, thanks, I'm busy all day tomorrow,' she lied. 'And I'm sure you'll be keen to get home to your wife and family.'

'Pardon?'

Hadn't he heard her or didn't he understand?

'You'll surely want to get home,' she repeated.

'To my wife and kids?'

Tara nodded.

'That's what I thought you said.' His brow crinkled in a frown. 'Of course—I shouldn't have assumed you'd know.'

'Know what?'

'Shannay and I divorced over a year ago and she has custody of our daughter.'

He was waiting for a reaction but what did he expect? Should she express regret at the breakdown of his second marriage? This was too much for her to deal with. She'd had the idea, set in her mind, that Ryan would find the perfect woman, that he would have the perfect family. But divorce! It had never been in the equation.

'Sorry,' she finally said. 'I heard you'd married again, but—'

'To separate was the best option for both of us. We weren't compatible and it wasn't working out,' he muttered.

He stood to leave. He was obviously uncomfortable talking about it.

'I'll get going, then,' he added.

'Yes. I work Tuesday, Wednesday and Friday. so I'll

probably bump into you when you start your Friday sessions.'

Before she had a chance to recoil he leaned down and placed a brief kiss on her cheek, and his questioning eyes lingered on hers for a moment before he strode down the steps and headed for his car.

He'd certainly changed, but in a lot of ways was still the same Ryan Dennison she'd fallen in love with. That was all in the past, though, dead and buried.

But he was single.

Of course that didn't alter anything, did it?

Seeing Tara again was like a rebirth.

Ryan had to deal with all the raw emotion, the painful memories, the turmoil of indecision he'd held inside for so long. To overcome the reality of the wretched, haunting past that intruded into his dreams, that followed him during every waking hour of every day, was a challenge he wasn't sure he was ready for.

Did he blame himself?

How could he not?

He'd had control, he'd been at the wheel and his reflex reaction had resulted in the horrendous collision that had left Tara without the use of her legs.

The moment he'd realised Tara's future had been snatched away from her he'd desperately wanted to turn back the clock. If he'd seen the kangaroo twenty seconds earlier, if he'd reacted faster, if the massive tree had been a few metres further along the road, if they'd left the party ten minutes earlier, if he hadn't insisted they stop to buy a bottle of wine on the way home, if he could change places with her, if... There were so many ifs he thought he'd dealt with, but deep down he still nursed a guilt that was so sharp, it cut directly into his heart.

Visiting Tara had made him wish he'd tried harder to convince her she'd been more important to him than a career or money or a tribe of kids. He'd felt sure they could pick up the pieces, but had been rejected when Tara had told him her love had dried up. He'd been devastated, but in the end had genuinely believed he'd done what was best for them, what Tara wanted. She'd not wanted to even give him a chance to provide the love and caring he'd thought only he could give. Tara had been determined and immovable in her resolve that getting a divorce was the only way she could put the past behind her.

And, in a way, she'd been right.

She now had a fulfilled life with a satisfying job and she was more beautiful than ever. It wouldn't surprise him if she had dozens of admirers and could have the pick of the bunch. In fact Ryan was surprised she hadn't remarried.

But that was her business.

He had no right to interfere with what she'd worked so hard to achieve.

It wouldn't be easy, but he'd just have to ignore the churning deep in his belly and the ache in his heart and get on with his own life. Thinking that there was even the remotest chance they could get back together was an aberration. Tara's attitude to him had verified that.

Ryan slowed down as he reached the outskirts of the town. He suddenly felt exhausted. It had been a long day and he'd had an early start, which made the prospect of a hot cup of coffee and a soft bed very attractive.

The Riverside Motel, Tara had said.

He travelled slowly through Keysdale's sleepy town centre until he saw a sign pointing east towards the river. After about half a kilometre the motel came into view, and he shifted his focus from ruminations about Tara to the practicalities of organising his accommodation for the night.

Two rows of tidy units nestled on the banks of the Keysdale River. Most had views of the lush green paddocks beyond and it was quiet, away from traffic noise and had an air of relaxed tranquillity about it.

He pulled up in front of the office, got out of his black sports car and stretched. He'd done too much driving that afternoon, and his right hip ached from the bursitis he got when he sat for too long. A bell above the office door tinkled as he opened it but there was no one inside. He gazed around, noting the tourist brochures advertising the history museum, a dairy called The Milk Factory, white-water rafting and half a dozen local restaurants.

He took a double-take and grabbed a leaflet, but before he had a chance to look at it more closely a plump, middle-aged woman emerged from a back room.

She smiled and greeted him.

'Hello, sir. Do you want a room?'

'Yes, just for tonight.' He explained his requirements for regular accommodation and they came to an arrangement.

'Here's your key. Your room's nice and quiet with a wonderful view.' She paused to take a breath. 'Dinner is served from six-thirty to eight-thirty and there's a menu in your room for breakfast orders.'

'Thank you.'

The woman glanced at the leaflet he was still clutching in his hand.

'Well worth a visit if you've time.'

'Maybe next time,' he said as he turned to leave.

'Enjoy your stay, Mr Dennison.'

'I'm sure I will,' he said cheerily, trying to convince

himself, but he knew he'd spend most of his spare time soul-searching.

Before he climbed into his car he had a closer look at the brochure.

THE MILK FACTORY.
EXPERIENCE A WORKING DAIRY FARM FIRST
HAND
Ten kilometres south of Keysdale, on Hill Park Road.

He scrutinised the photo then unfolded the leaflet.

Open for tours. Devonshire teas.
10 a.m. to 5 p.m. weekends and public holidays
Dairy tours including real-life milking 3 p.m.
Proprietors: Graham and Jane Fielding

He hadn't even noticed.

There would have been signs. How could he have missed them? He must have been so focused on seeing Tara he'd been oblivious to anything else.

But it made him think.

Were the Fieldings struggling to make ends meet?

Did Tara *have to* go out to work?

Did the accident have anything to do with their situation?

He felt discomfort in the pit of his stomach.

So much had changed in the years since he'd lost contact with Tara and her family. His ex-wife certainly had.

He drove to his unit, grabbed his briefcase and overnight bag and let himself in. He rummaged in a tiny cupboard above the sink, found a sachet of instant coffee and filled the kettle. When the brew was made, he opened the sliding door which led to the veranda. The setting sun cast long shadows across the river and a cow's gentle mooing echoed in the quiet. He seemed to have the place to himself.

With time to think.

About Tara.

It was impossible to erase her, and all the reasons he'd fallen in love with her more than a decade ago, from his mind.

She was even more beautiful than he remembered, and her fighting spirit had not been dulled by circumstance or time.

It suddenly occurred to him that he'd found out what he needed to know—he still loved her.

But he didn't have the faintest idea what to do about it.

After Ryan left, Tara needed some alone time to gather her thoughts, so she stayed on the veranda and watched a golden sun sink slowly towards the horizon.

Why?

Why now?

She'd mourned her decision to send Ryan away every day. The flame of her love for him still burned brightly, and seeing him again… It was like a dam bursting—as if time had stood still for those eight years and suddenly she was looking into the eyes of the man who, for her, would always be her soul mate.

How should she react?

He was divorced, but there was no way they could start again. She had a satisfying life she'd worked hard to achieve and Ryan had his life in the city. It shouldn't be difficult to act cool and detached and very professional. After all she would rarely see him.

Yes…cool, detached and professional. She could do that.

Couldn't she?

CHAPTER TWO

'THE new orthopaedic surgeon starts today,' said Kaylee, the young receptionist, as she operated the pneumatic lift that moved Tara's wheelchair from her vehicle and placed it on the ground. Tara preferred to use her electric chair at work, as it provided greater manoeuvrability, but getting it on and off her vehicle was one of the few things she couldn't manage herself and had reluctantly learned to live with.

'I know.' Tara had been counting the days and psyching herself up for her first meeting with Ryan in the workplace. None of the staff were aware of her history with him. Of course some of the close-knit community knew she'd been married, but Ryan was a city man, born and bred. He'd hated the idea of any kind of fuss and had always been a reluctant participant in their rare visits to the farm. And, the way she was feeling right now, it was a good thing. She didn't want the burden of gossip to stress her any more than she was already. She certainly wasn't prepared for a public airing of her past, which she'd spent the best part of the last eight years trying to forget.

Not yet. Not today.

She'd also had time to think about his visit to the farm two weeks ago and had pondered on his motives. In fact she'd questioned long and hard about why he would choose a job in Keysdale when not only did he hate rural life but he probably had the pick of any position he wanted?

The questions burned and she needed some answers… from Ryan.

Her thoughts were interrupted by the young receptionist.

'And Jenny said he's gorgeous.'

Kaylee positioned the wheelchair next to the driver's seat and stood back as Tara used the strength in her arms to shift into it. The girl seemed oblivious to the flush of embarrassment that warmed Tara's cheeks and prattled on.

'Jen met him when he came down a couple of weekends ago. She said he's really nice, as well as good-looking.'

'What about the paediatrician? Isn't she starting today as well?'

Tara was desperate to change the subject. She didn't need to know that her ex-husband had already charmed at least one of the female staff, and probably the whole Saturday morning team.

'Yeah, this afternoon. Val's putting on a special lunch to welcome them both, and she's asked their receptionist not to overbook on the first day so they'll have time to meet us all.'

'Oh.'

Tara had prepared herself for the possibility that she'd bump into Ryan at some stage during the day. The brand-new specialist offices, although housed in an extension to the GP clinic building, were separate and self-contained. They had their own reception area, procedure room and consulting suites, but the lunch room was shared. She'd planned to eat a sandwich in her room and catch up with her paperwork, but that wasn't an option now. She'd be expected to make an appearance, at least.

Kaylee walked beside her as she steered through the

self-opening doors and made her way to the busy waiting area, past Reception then to the doctors' rooms beyond.

'See you later,' the teenager said as their paths diverged.

Tara nodded and forced a smile, eager to reach the privacy of her consulting room so she could take a minute or two to compose herself. She'd never had a panic attack at work and she wasn't about to change that today.

Ryan scanned the room full of chattering staff but couldn't see Tara. He lingered a moment in the doorway, taking in the table laden with a bounty of home-cooked food, but was soon approached by the principal doctor at Keysdale Medical Clinic, Rob Whelan. The man greeted Ryan with a welcoming grin.

'I'll introduce you to the mob, and then you can eat...' his grin broadened '...and mingle.'

Rob reeled off a long list of names Ryan would never remember to associate with the endless stream of nodding, smiling faces. Then, his gaze automatically following his colleague's, he turned, and it was as if the waters parted. People moved out of the way as Tara wheeled herself into the room with a barely suppressed scowl on her face and rosy colour in her cheeks.

'And last but not least...' Rob said, resting his hand lightly on Tara's shoulder. 'Dr Tara Fielding.' He glanced at Ryan. 'This is Ryan Dennison, our new visiting orthopaedic surgeon.'

Thank God Tara had reverted to her maiden name, averting a possible problem he hadn't thought of until now.

At that moment Rob's attention was taken by the timely arrival of Karin Hooper, the new paediatrician. Rob began the introduction ritual all over again, and Ryan was grateful the spotlight had moved away from him and Tara, who was still right next to him, waiting for her turn in the short

queue for the food. She reluctantly shook his offered hand
as he leaned over to talk to her.

'I'm glad to finally meet you, Dr Fielding. I've heard so
much about you.' It was an attempt at humour to lighten
Tara's mood but he wasn't sure if it had worked.

She answered him with a cool smile as she released his
hand from a momentary grip of steel.

'Ouch,' he couldn't help exclaiming.

'Sorry.' She was grinning now but still looked tense…
guarded. 'Sometimes I forget my own strength.' She picked
up two plates and handed one to Ryan, who promptly discarded the fleeting thought of offering to serve her food.
He had much to learn.

'How has your day been so far? Not too snowed under
with Keysdale's unique brand of orthopaedic problems?'
It was inconsequential small talk.

He laughed politely. 'You mean crush fractures from
being stepped on by livestock and strain injuries from
overdosing on fencing?'

'You've got the idea.'

While he was talking Ryan watched in wonder as Tara
effortlessly multi-tasked, deftly moving her chair into im-
possibly small spaces while at the same time loading her
plate with enough to feed a professional athlete.

She paused a moment and looked at his empty plate.

'Aren't you hungry?' she asked.

'Oh…er…yes.' He stuttered his reply, not prepared to
admit he'd been too busy watching her. After shoulder-
ing his way through the tightly packed occupants of the
small lunch room, he began to select food from the abundance before him. By the time he'd filled his plate Tara
had moved to the other side of the room and was deep in
conversation with a woman he remembered, from her name
tag, was a physiotherapist.

Balancing his plate in one hand, he headed in Tara's direction but was stopped midway by a tap on his shoulder. He turned.

'Sorry to desert you,' Rob Whelan said amiably. 'I wanted to have a word with you about the possibility of you doing some extra consulting—maybe on the Saturday mornings you're not operating?'

If Ryan's appointment book was anything to go by, the services of an orthopaedic surgeon in the town were desperately needed, but he was over-committed as it was.

'I'm sorry, I'm on call at St Joseph's one weekend in four, and…' He hesitated, deciding whether Rob, a relative stranger, needed to know about the custody arrangements he had for access to his daughter. As it was, he only saw her one weekend a month, and that time was precious.

If things had been different… He sighed.

'And?' Rob raised his eyebrows, as if he sensed Ryan's discomfort but his curiosity overrode tact. Maybe it was the country way—that everyone had a God-given right to know everyone else's business. But it wasn't Ryan's way.

'I have regular family commitments on most of my free weekends.' His use of the word *free* was somewhat tongue-in-cheek, but the vague comment was all he was prepared to give at the moment. 'And I think you'll find things will settle down in a month or two, once I work through the backlog of referrals and start seeing follow-ups.'

Rob rubbed his chin and pressed his mouth into a thin line.

'I thought as much.' The older doctor's grin reappeared. 'But, you know, if your situation changes the offer stands.'

'I'll bear that in mind.'

At that moment Ryan noticed Tara heading off, and he wanted to talk to her. He felt oddly jilted. But he didn't have any claim on what she did.

'If you'll excuse me, I just want to…' His voice trailed off as one of the other GPs in the practice cornered Rob Whelan and let Ryan off the hook. Ryan dumped his barely touched food onto the table to follow Tara, but she'd vanished in the space of a few seconds. He went in pursuit and found her room off the corridor leading to Reception.

He knocked quietly but there was no response.

Maybe she hadn't gone back to her room.

He knocked again, a little louder.

'Tara?' He opened the door but her spacious office was empty. He glanced around and noted the modifications that had been made because of Tara's disability. Shelves and cupboards were no higher than shoulder-height. There were two patients' chairs but a notable absence of a seat for the doctor. The examination couch was also low, and the pedal that raised or lowered the bed had been modified to accommodate hand controls similar to those used for hospital beds. In fact just about everything in the room was reachable from a wheelchair.

He heard movement from behind a door on the far side of the room, and then the sound of a toilet flushing and water running. The door opened, apparently remote-controlled, and Tara wheeled herself into the room, concentrating on the small joystick that controlled the direction of her chair. She obviously hadn't seen him as he stood quietly by the door.

He cleared his throat and the muscles of Tara's shoulders visibly jerked. She scowled as blood rose to her neck and coloured her face.

'What the—?'

'Sorry, I knocked. Twice.' He cleared his throat again.

'Well, did you want to see me for something?' Tara said after they'd eyeballed each other for what felt like an age but was probably less than twenty seconds.

'I…'

What was supposed to be a relaxed greeting and a little ice-breaking chat on his first day working in the Keysdale clinic wasn't working out the way he'd planned.

'I just wanted to touch base…er…in a professional capacity, of course.' He smiled uneasily. It sounded ridiculous now. 'But you disappeared before I had time to say much more than hello just now.'

Tara tilted her head slightly and the steely look in her eyes blocked any access to what she was thinking. Then the expression on her face softened, as if she'd had a change of mind. It was too much to expect she'd had a change of heart.

'You took me by surprise,' she said bluntly. 'I have a fairly rigid routine at work. It means I can use my time here the most efficiently.' She hesitated.

'Oh, I'm sorry. I didn't mean to—'

'You weren't to know. After all, a good many years have passed since we last saw each other and a lot has happened since then. We've both been living our own lives and I'm not the same person I was back then.'

She was unable to hide her quick downward glance. He didn't blame her for being bitter. Thoughts that had been tumbling through his mind over the last two weeks returned.

If he could change places with her, he would—a hundred times over; if he could turn back the clock; if only things had been different.

He felt totally helpless.

'Yes.' It wasn't often Ryan was lost for words. He was now.

Tara fiddled with some papers on her desk, arranging them in a neat pile. Then she repositioned herself in her chair.

'Well, while you are here, have you a minute to discuss a patient?'

'Yes, of course.'

The atmosphere had definitely lightened. The tension of discussing the past evaporated like summer rain falling on hot asphalt.

'Her name's Pippa Morgan and I've asked her to make an appointment to see you but it could be a couple of weeks down the track. I've been told how busy you are, and that you're booked up for the next month.'

'Tell me about her.'

Tara swung around to face him.

'She's nineteen. Juvenile rheumatoid arthritis was diagnosed when she was six years old. She's been managed by a rheumatologist from the early stages.' Tara paused to take a breath. 'Of course I've only known her as a teenager, and she's been under the care of Liam Taylor for the past two years. She's had just about every treatment in the book to control her pain and inflammation—non-steroidal anti-inflammatories, Prednisone, Methotrexate, a trial of a DMARD as well as joint injections.'

Ryan had treated many patients with the inflamed and sometimes deformed joints of the chronic rheumatic condition rheumatoid arthritis, but rarely saw children or young adults with the disease. Treatment by surgery was usually kept in reserve for when all else failed. And the bulk of his experience had been with the middle-aged and elderly.

'Liam's one of the best adult rheumatologists around.'

'It was he who suggested she may need a hip replacement in the next year or two.'

'And you want my opinion?'

'That's right.'

Their conversation was interrupted by Ryan's mobile phone. He answered the call from his receptionist.

'Sorry, there's an emergency. A child with what sounds like displaced fractures of tib and fib.' He looked at his watch and noted his busy afternoon consulting was due to start as well. 'I'm going to have to go.'

'Of course.'

'We'll talk about Pippa later.' He paused in the doorway on his way out. 'I'll ring you.'

As Ryan strode down the corridor he tried to file thoughts of Tara Fielding deep in the back of his mind so he could focus totally on his work.

'I'm taking two patient files with me tonight. Also, would you mind checking if we have a referral letter for a nineteen-year-old named Pippa Morgan—and have you typed out the theatre list for tomorrow?' Ryan glanced at the wall clock behind his receptionist, eager to leave. He'd had an early start and a long day.

Liz extracted a file from the cabinet and leafed through a dozen sheets of paper before she found the letter Ryan had asked for.

'Here it is. I'd have remembered if I'd scanned it into the computer records because I'd have made a file for her.' She stood up. 'I'll just do you a photocopy.'

The efficient middle-aged woman smiled. She was a Keysdale local, and today was the first time he'd met her, but she'd certainly proved her worth. She seemed to have the ability to think and act one step ahead of him.

'So you don't trust me to return it?'

'I'm sure you have the best of intentions but I know how busy doctors are.'

'And it might get overlooked?' He returned her smile.

'Something like that.' She handed him the copy of the letter as well as the theatre list, and jotted down the names of the patient files he'd laid on the counter. 'And there's one more thing.'

'What's that?'

'I won't be a moment,' she said as she turned and headed for the back room, returning with a loaded plastic carry-bag. 'You won't need to think about what to eat this evening. There was so much food left over from the welcome party, and the girls didn't want to waste it. Someone noticed you rushed off without touching your lunch so they thought you were a worthy recipient.'

Ryan took a quick peek in the bag and noted there was enough food to last for the next week.

'Thanks, that's a really kind thought, but I can't possibly eat all of this.'

'It'll only get thrown away, so you might as well take it.' He took the bag.

'Okay, thanks, Liz. I'll see you next week, then.'

When he arrived in the car park he offloaded the food and his gear in the back seat, climbed in and turned the key in the ignition. But instead of firing on the first turn the engine groaned and his state-of-the-art luxury car gave up.

'Damn, this is the last thing I need,' he muttered. He tried again with the same result, wondering if his usually reliable car had been interfered with. 'The last thing I need...' he muttered again, trying one more time to fire up the engine.

He phoned his roadside call-out service and was given the number of a local auto repair shop. When the mechanic arrived the news was not good.

During Tara's busy afternoon every patient seemed to take longer than their allotted time, and at the end of her list she was running nearly an hour late. It was well past five o'clock. If she was running too late her parents worried. She understood why. The accident had fuelled what had become their almost obsessive concern about the safety of their only child, their precious, perfect, beautiful daughter—but it didn't make her life any easier. No matter how many times she'd tried to persuade them she was capable of looking after herself they still waited up for her when she had the occasional date or night out with her friends. And she had to tell them where she was going, especially if she was driving on her own.

Right now she had to live with it. Tara owed her parents big-time and she didn't want to cause them any more stress than they already had.

She packed her things in readiness to leave and headed to Reception. When she was barely out of her room Ryan burst through the outside door as if he was being pursued by a pack of rabid dogs. He'd certainly found a novel way of attracting attention.

'Is there a taxi service in this town?' he said in a voice laced with frustration and impatience.

Tara wheeled slowly closer, but Ryan hadn't noticed her and went on without waiting for a reply.

'My car won't start. There's something wrong with the ignition system and it needs to be towed to the local garage to be repaired—'

'I've got some jump leads in my car if that's any help,' Jenny offered.

Ryan sighed. 'I wish… Apparently the computer and security system is so complicated you need an auto electrician to reset and reconnect it, even if it's simply a flat battery. Which won't happen until tomorrow.'

Some of the edginess had gone from Ryan's voice and he looked worn out. He'd obviously had a busy day and it appeared it wasn't going to get any better.

Tara was at the counter now.

'I'm just leaving and can drop you off. Taxis here are notoriously unreliable unless you make an advance booking. Where are you staying?'

Ryan looked stunned, as if Tara was the last person he'd expected to see, let alone offer a simple solution to his predicament.

'Ahh…'

Three sets of eyes were fixed on him, waiting for a reply, and Tara began to wonder if her offer was a mistake.

'You could help me with my chair.' Tara was the one to break the uncomfortable silence.

'I'm at the Riverside. I could probably walk, but I have a lot of gear to transport.' He hesitated. 'And it would just be for tonight. A hire car is being delivered to the motel in a couple of hours.' His expression softened. 'Thanks, Dr Fielding.'

When they reached her car Tara couldn't help noticing Ryan's gaze drift to her legs and then to the hand controls of the car. Suddenly she felt she had something to prove to Ryan—that she could manage perfectly without him. She didn't want pity, or sympathy, or even admiration. She just wanted her ex-husband to accept her for who she was.

'What do I need to do to get your chair into the car?' he said, after he'd moved a couple of plastic crates, his medical case and two supermarket carry-bags from the boot of his now useless car to the back seat of her vehicle.

Good. The practicality of the transfer from chair to car was the perfect diversion from thoughts of Ryan encroaching on her personal space. She wheeled close to the driver's door, opened it and lifted herself into the seat.

'When you open the back you'll see the platform. The

controls are hooked onto the driver side just below the window.'

Ryan was already at the rear of the vehicle. He opened the door.

'Is this it?' He waved the handpiece.

'Yes. All you have to do now is press the down arrow button and the platform is programmed to slide out and down to the ground. Simply strap the chair in and press the up button.

'Ah, yes, I can see it.'

A few seconds later he was at her side. 'Is there anything else I can do?'

'Thanks, but I can manage now.'

Tara felt her jaw tighten, and her words did little to disguise her feelings, which were churning around like a newspaper caught in a whirlwind. She'd had no idea being in close proximity to Ryan—alone—would have such an unsettling effect on her. She'd programmed herself to keep him at a distance and now he was sitting a handspan away from her.

At that moment she wondered if she'd made a mistake. She wished she could drive straight home.

But she couldn't.

Though Ryan was grateful for Tara's offer to help him out, he got the impression she wished she was anywhere but sitting next to him in her car.

What could he do to help her relax? After all it wasn't his fault his car had broken down and she'd offered him the lift. She might be taking him back to his motel, but it wasn't as if he then expected her to sleep with him…

Where had that come from?

The thought did hold some attraction, though. He glanced in her direction and dismissed the idea from his mind. The scowl on Tara's face suggested she'd more likely suffer being thrown into a pit of deadly snakes than have the slightest physical contact with him.

But why?

He'd been pleasant and polite without being over-friendly. He'd made no demands on her, and he hoped he'd dealt with his ex-wife in a non-confrontational way.

But she'd changed. The openness they'd always shared in their relationship had been replaced by a cautious hesitancy; the love of life she'd had in bucketloads seemed to have dried up; taking risks and trying new things had been supplanted by the rigid routine enforced by her disability. And she certainly wasn't to blame. No one was to blame. Ryan repeated the words that had become a mantra in the months following the accident.

No one was to blame.

Did Tara believe that?

He truly wanted to find out and, if the barriers were still up, shielding the intimacy they'd had in the past, then maybe he should just try for friendship. Now he had seen her again he knew he at least needed to talk to her. And perhaps he had the ideal opportunity tonight. After all, the worst that could happen was that she'd simply refuse, and he could live with that.

They were pulling into the driveway of the motel so he didn't have much time.

'I really appreciate you helping me out, Tara. Can I repay you for the lift?'

'Pardon?' She glanced briefly in his direction before bringing the car to a halt in front of the office.

'I want to repay you.'

'What do you mean?' Her stare was ice-cool.

'Liz gave me some leftovers from lunch and I have way

too much to eat myself. Would you like to share them with me?'

The stare turned into a frown and then she looked straight ahead, moving the gearstick from 'Park' to 'Reverse'.

'Which unit is yours?'

Any kind of thaw seemed a long way away, and Ryan accepted the fact he'd just been handed a refusal. Nothing lost, nothing gained.

But then her expression changed. Still cool but the ice was melting.

'Okay. I have that patient I mentioned earlier I wanted to discuss with you. Would you mind—?'

'Of course not.' Ryan had the feeling he had nudged a little closer to first base.

And what could be more innocent than two colleagues discussing a patient over a bite to eat? Tara shouldn't feel threatened by that. Ryan's face broke into a smile as he realised what he'd thought was going to be a gloomy end to his long day had the potential to shine.

CHAPTER THREE

PART of the reason for Tara's decision to share a meal with Ryan was because over the last two weeks, since he'd catapulted back into her life, she'd been thinking about him constantly. She also had some questions she needed answering, and it wasn't the sort of discussion that could take place in the lunch room at the clinic.

Her all-consuming concern was…why?

Why was he back when she'd worked so hard to make her life as good as it could be without him?

Why had he accepted a job in Keysdale when he could choose any job he wanted?

Why had he married, fathered a child and then divorced a few short years later?

And the last question she could only answer herself—why did she care so much when she'd thought she was well and truly over him?

She tried to rationalise by telling herself it was perfectly reasonable that she held a gnawing suspicion about his motives. But were those emotions that were surfacing from another time in her life an indication she still had feelings for her ex-husband?

It scared her.

She was also annoyed that her balanced, well-ordered world was beginning to tilt on its axis a little. Her life was complicated enough as it was and she didn't need any more problems.

To clear the air she definitely needed to at least talk to Ryan, so she could clarify her own feelings. All she knew now was that the man sitting next to her with a genuine smile on his face, had forced her to revisit a time when she'd been married to the only man she'd truly loved. While he'd been married to a stranger, settled more than two hundred kilometres away and living the life she'd always hoped he'd have, she'd overcome the pain and uncertainty of wondering if he sincerely believed, as he'd told her a hundred times after the accident, *she* was more important than anything else in his life.

Ryan cleared his throat as he opened the car door and she wondered if he'd been watching her.

'I'll get your chair and then I'll unload all my stuff.'

'Thanks,' she said quietly, forcing a smile.

Ryan was a quick learner. In just a few minutes he had the chair where she could easily transfer into it and was rummaging in the back of the car, unpacking his bags and boxes.

'Would you mind carrying the food?'

'Fine.' He definitely did learn fast, and was doing his best not to make a big thing of what Tara *couldn't do* and focusing on what she *could*.

After locking the vehicle, Tara propelled herself to the small entry of Ryan's unit and waited while he unlocked the door, went inside and turned on the lights. She cast a quick glance around the compact living-dining area and noted that her host was obviously not expecting guests. The small desk in one corner was littered with papers and a large overnight bag decorated the single settee. She could see jeans and a couple of tee shirts strewn on the bed, with a cup and a juice box sitting on the bedside table. At least the bathroom door was closed. She didn't want to conjure up any thoughts of Ryan that tipped outside the boundaries she'd decided to impose for any contact outside work.

'Sorry about the mess.'

Ryan's clichéd reply brought a small smile to Tara's face. He'd always been messy.

Ryan put the food in the kitchen, stowed the rest of his gear in the bedroom and closed the door. He was staring at her intently.

'What's so amusing?'

Damn. She'd let her guard down. She restored what she hoped was a neutral expression. The last thing she wanted to do was to tell Ryan her thoughts.

'Nothing at all. However, I should ring my parents and let them know I'll be home late.

'Yes, of course you must. I'll go and get changed while you do and then we'll eat.'

Tara watched him disappear into the bedroom and sighed, hoping she'd have the courage to start to put her life back on course. She rang her parents' number.

As Ryan pulled on a pair of jeans and a crumpled polo shirt a jumble of thoughts he'd previously managed to suppress scuttled through his mind.

Thoughts of the past.

He now realised that his years with Tara had been the best of his life, but she'd changed; her body had changed. Ryan knew it shouldn't make any difference but it did. Although *his* feelings for *her* were strong, Tara was guarded and cautious around him. He didn't seem to be able to get it right—the balance between friendly helpfulness and the undeniable protectiveness he felt for her. She seemed to want to be treated only as a colleague, but he couldn't ignore their past.

He was responsible for the way things were now. The thought kept flashing in his mind like a neon sign that wouldn't go away.

It added to his remorse.

In the end, he decided to let the evening chart its own course and he'd suffer any consequences. After all, it was unlikely they'd have the opportunity to spend much time together at work. Already he had a good idea he'd have little spare time to socialise during the couple of days he spent each week at Keysdale. In fact he'd been prepared for a knock-back when he'd asked Tara to share a meal with him.

Tara… She was rapidly turning into an enigma. He remembered how self-contained she'd been when he'd watched her get in her car and drive away without any idea he was in the car park on that Friday afternoon a couple of weeks ago. But he'd also seen traces of anxiety mixed with vulnerability during the brief contacts he'd had with her since. His natural instinct was to offer to help, but her independence stood firm as a barrier to his good intentions. He took a deep breath and opened the bedroom door. Tara had moved his bag and settled herself in one corner of the settee.

She glanced at him, blushed and then focused on the bags on the kitchen bench. She was more ill at ease than he was.

'The food smells delicious.'

Small talk was definitely a good idea.

'They seem like pretty high-quality leftovers. I hope you don't mind?' Ryan stood awkwardly, not sure what to do next. He began unpacking the food.

'Of course not.' She scrutinised every dish.

'Are you happy to eat now?'

'I don't mind. Whatever you want to do.'

Tension buzzed in the air. It was almost as if they were on a first date.

'I somehow managed to miss out on lunch and I'm starving.' He cleared his throat. 'My brain functions better on a full stomach.'

He began to lay out two place settings on the tiny kitchen gate-leg table, but then realised there would be more room on the coffee table.

'I'll spread the food out here. There's much more space and we can serve ourselves.'

'Yes, that's a sensible idea. I'm hungry.' She paused a moment, then smiled. 'I hope you don't mind women with hearty appetites.'

Ryan couldn't help doing a quick appraisal and it reinforced his first impressions. He was pleased with what he saw. Tara wore trousers and a tailored shirt with the top two buttons open, revealing a hint of cleavage which he hadn't noticed earlier in the day. Her upper body was lean and well toned. He imagined she exercised regularly to keep in shape.

She was an attractive woman...and very sexy.

His heart thudded uncomfortably at the realisation. Sex had been an important and joyous part of their relationship. Making love with Tara had always been a deeply sensual experience—he smiled—laced with a unique sense of fun that he'd never experienced with his second wife, Shannay. With the benefit of hindsight and the lingering pain of a second divorce, he realised his feelings for his second wife had been based on a blinding infatuation, probably arising from a need to escape his grief.

There was no hint Tara had any similar feeling towards him, though. She was looking at him impatiently, waiting for his reply.

'No, definitely not,' he said at last.

Once the food was set out they both loaded their plates and ate their fill.

When Tara put her empty plate on the table, Ryan cleared the dishes and left them on the sink to deal with later.

He sat down next to Tara.

'So tell me about your patient.' It was neutral territory and unlikely to open any old wounds.

'Yes, of course.'

Focusing on something other than Ryan was exactly what Tara needed.

Reaching over to her wheelchair, where she'd left her bag, she extracted Pippa Morgan's file. She opened volume two to the section containing test results, investigation reports and specialist letters.

'Do you want a recap on her history?'

Ryan nodded. 'Good idea,' he said.

Tara repeated what she'd told Ryan earlier—that the teenager had suffered from the painful and debilitating condition of juvenile rheumatoid arthritis since early childhood, and that her joints had degenerated to the point where her specialist was considering the possibility of surgery to relieve the increasingly severe pain in her right hip.

'The rheumatologist has exhausted all the possibilities in his repertoire?'

'Yes, Pippa's had just about all medical treatments available. Even a course of injections of an experimental antimetabolite. They worked for a while, but her liver started showing signs of stress.' Tara extracted a radiology report from the file. 'This is her latest X-ray report.' She paused as Ryan took the two sheets she handed him, containing a long and detailed assessment. 'The patient has the original films, but I've asked Pippa to bring her most recent X-rays when she comes to see you.'

Ryan was silent and his face immobile as he read the report. It was impossible to tell what he was thinking. Finally he looked up, his expression bleak.

'She's only nineteen. Poor kid,' he said softly as his brow furrowed into a frown.

'They're awful, aren't they? Her left hip is nearly as bad.'

Ryan nodded. 'About as bad as I've seen in someone so young.' He hesitated, closing his eyes and rubbing his forehead as if attempting to erase what he'd seen in the X-ray report. He took a deep breath as he opened his eyes. 'You know I mainly see adults?'

'Pippa is an adult. And a beautiful young person who has had to grow up fast,' Tara couldn't help adding. Against all that she'd been told in her training, Tara had developed a bond with Pippa that went beyond the usual relationship between doctor and patient. Their connection was all about shared disabilities which had robbed them of many things healthy, able-bodied people took for granted. Tara understood exactly what her young patient was going through. No matter how much they strived to live a normal life they would always be considered different, and often a burden to those who cared for them. And Pippa was a teenager, with all the baggage associated with her stage in life—the transition from childhood to adulthood; the need to be accepted by peers; rebellion against parental control; preoccupation with appearances and the related issues involving self-esteem, making choices about her future. The list was endless.

'You know what I mean,' Ryan answered.

'Sorry, of course I do. Anyone under fifty is young when it comes to considering a hip prosthesis.'

'Just based on the report, she must have a high level of pain and loss of joint function. And I agree the left hip doesn't look too great either.'

'The pain is the deciding factor for her. Some days it's an ordeal to get up in the morning, and her slow, stiff movements are more to do with the fact her joints are hurting so much than limitation due to the disease.'

'Quality of life?' Ryan asked with a sigh.

'She finished Year Twelve last year—amazing to be only a year behind her peers when she's had so much time off. She gained the marks to get into uni and has enrolled in a teaching degree at Bayfield.'

Ryan leaned back in his chair and studied the report again.

'Remarkable. She must have good family support. Even travelling for a couple of hours a day must be difficult.'

'Her father's principal of the local high school and her mother's a pre-primary teacher.' Tara smiled at the recollection of Pippa's stubbornness in her insistence she embark on a career in teaching. Tara suspected teaching was in her blood, and she had encouraged the young woman to pursue her dream by example. Nothing was impossible if you wanted it enough. 'Her father has organised for a lot of her coursework to be done online, so she only has to travel one or two days a week. The last six months, when the rheumatoid has been really active, she's resorted to using a wheelchair a few times.'

'A wheelchair?' Ryan's eyebrows elevated.

Tara nodded. 'Only as a last resort. She's really tried hard to overcome her condition, and considering her age—'

'She has her whole life ahead of her.'

'Exactly.' Tara fiddled with the hem of her blouse for a moment, suddenly overcome with emotion at the thought of what Pippa had gone through and the future that lay ahead. 'Do you think a hip replacement is an option?'

'Without seeing her, my thoughts are that surgical treatment would be effective in getting rid of her pain, and would probably restore mobility to the joint...'

'But?'

Tara could tell he had doubts.

'But she's so young. Even with the latest prosthesis, and the possibility of replacing the joint without cement, she'd be lucky to get twenty years out of a new joint. The best scenario would be that she'd be in her forties and need surgery again.'

Tara hesitated before voicing her own thoughts.

'Twenty years without pain is better than twenty years of agony. That's my personal opinion.'

Tara's simple statement cut to Ryan's core, and the few moments' silence seemed to stretch way too long. Her face was serious and Ryan tried to read her thoughts.

Was she talking, just a little, about herself?

Eventually he spoke.

'She's a little like you, isn't she?'

Tara fidgeted, and then looked up straight into his eyes with poignant honesty. She cleared her throat.

'Maybe a bit.'

'Was I part of your pain?'

Ryan could see the pulse in her neck and it was accelerating.

'I don't understand what you mean?'

He decided to be brutally direct. There were still things about the accident and the aftermath he didn't understand.

'Removing me from your life lessened your pain, helped you cope?'

'In a way,' Tara said in barely more than a whisper. 'I'd

lost so much… Having to deal with your distress and un-certainty as well as my own was just as bad as the somatic pain of my injuries. Can you understand that?'

Ryan nodded, swallowing the lump that had lodged in his throat.

She continued. 'I'm sorry if I hurt you, but it was for a reason. In some ways the divorce was a relief. The last thing I wanted was for you to stay with me out of guilt or duty.' She looked away. 'And I believed you'd stopped lov-ing me, despite your insistence that you'd do anything for me. I was scared witless of messing up *both* our lives.'

Her eyes were moist but Ryan needed to know.

'Do you still think that? That I stopped loving you?'

Tara took a deep breath and continued to fix her gaze on the window.

'I…I don't know. It's been eight years. Some of my memories are blurred. We're both different people with completely different lives compared with back then. It was a shock to see you again. You remarried. You have a child. And I'm coping in the best way I can—better than that, I am succeeding. If we'd stayed together there was no way of predicting if we'd be happy over the long term. I felt the odds were stacked against us.' She paused. 'I'm happy with my life now.'

'Are you?'

'Of course I am.'

'How did you feel about me marrying again?' He hesi-tated. 'I couldn't commit to a new relationship for a long time. It was over three years after we split before I met Shannay.' The question was blunt but Tara didn't have to answer if it was too painful.

She swung her gaze back to him and said with purpose, 'I was pleased. It's what I wanted—for you to find some-one else who could provide the happiness that I couldn't.

Someone who could give you the children you always wanted—'

'The children *we* always wanted.'

She looked away.

'That I could no longer provide.'

Ryan knew that wasn't strictly true, but he wasn't about to start an argument.

'I never loved Shannay.'

'Why did you marry her, then?'

'I thought I loved her. She was beautiful and charismatic and young. Too young, really. I was still grieving over the accident and losing you. I know that now. Shannay and I weren't compatible. She got bored with me and she was the one who wanted us to separate.'

'But what about your daughter? Shannay must love her.'

'Of course she does. But I sometimes think Shannay's too…er…flighty to be a good mother.'

Tara looked truly devastated, and Ryan realised he'd said the wrong thing. He remembered how passionate Tara had been about having children. She'd sworn she'd not make the same mistakes as her parents. And he'd believed it could have worked. It wouldn't have been easy, but if the passion had been there they could have at least tried. He now had a greater understanding of Tara's reasons for wanting him out of her life at such a momentously traumatic time. It made him want to be there for her now.

And he'd *never* fallen out of love with her.

Tara rubbed her hands nervously across her thighs.

'There's something I need to know, Ryan.'

He remained silent while Tara appeared to be summoning up the courage to go on. She had the hint of tears in her eyes, but bravely fought them back. She swallowed.

'Why are you here, Ryan? I don't understand. Why have you chosen to work in Keysdale when you hate the country

and with your qualifications and experience could have
just about any job for which you applied? To me, opening
old wounds serves no purpose, and if you simply wanted
to reassure yourself that *my* life wasn't in tatters, and you
had absolutely no cause to be guilty, a visit or two would
have sufficed.' She sucked in a breath and clenched her
hands together in her lap. 'Why, Ryan? Why have you done
this to me?'

Tara's poignant and emotive outburst had a similar effect to being hit in the guts with a sledgehammer. She
thought he had a hidden agenda—which was the last thing
he would have dumped on her. He needed to salvage his
credibility.

'I… I…' But he battled to find the right words. Tara's
tearful gaze didn't help. 'I couldn't really refuse—'

'I don't believe that for a minute.' Tara's distress had
morphed into a look of steely determination. The only answer she would accept would be the truth.

'Just listen for a minute.'

'Go on.' Tara nodded.

'I've only worked for Southern Orthopaedics for just
over a year. Before that I was in New Zealand for six
months in a specialised lower limb unit. I'm literally the
new kid on the block, and I have what the senior partners
consider minimal family commitments. It's almost a rite
of passage for a junior consultant to spend time overseas
and be seconded to a rural practice. If you refuse you tend
to stagnate and you are not considered for the more…er…
esteemed—'

'You mean promotions.' Tara interrupted. She had been
listening intently and seemed to believe him. 'And the position in Keysdale just happened to come up?'

'The past…our history…it was purely coincidence…'
With a decent lashing of fate.

Tara's hands relaxed and she rubbed one forearm with her other hand.

'You've never been good at lying, Ryan, so I doubt you'd have made it up.' She gathered together Pippa Morgan's notes. 'I believe you.'

She began to lift herself on to her wheelchair.

'It's time for me to go home.'

She looked tired and stifled a yawn.

'Can we at least be friends?' Ryan said with apprehension. He had no idea whether he had gained any ground with Tara.

She looked at him with a penetrating gaze but said nothing.

'Right, then. I'll help you put the chair into the car.'

Tara positioned herself comfortably in the driver's seat and as soon as Ryan had loaded the chair reversed and set off down the road at a speed just short of burning rubber. On the way she glimpsed the local mechanic's van and the old wreck the garage staff used for pick-ups and deliveries heading for the Riverside. Ryan's hire car, no doubt. She chuckled. But it wasn't her problem.

The return of her ex-husband into her life was, though. No matter how hard she tried she couldn't clear him from her thoughts.

Removing the man she'd once loved from her life had been a major contribution to deadening the emotional pain resulting from the loss of many of the things that had been important to her—her physical strength and agility, her independence, *her attractiveness*. The biggest blow, though, had been to her self-esteem.

Now Ryan was back he'd rekindled some of those feelings that belonged in the past. Feelings that went deeper than a platonic friendship, than simple physical attraction.

She felt the same intimate connection they'd shared before the accident—the ability to know what the other was thinking, the desire to comfort when the other was hurting, the yearning for mutual happiness and the sharing of goals in a future that stretched *until death us do part*.

Was that love?

It wasn't worth even trying to answer the question. Even if it was, loving Ryan again would almost certainly mean more pain. There were too many reasons why the relationship wouldn't...*couldn't* work. Geography, lifestyle and a small child who had probably had more disruption in her life than most adults.

She wished she could believe the old saying that *love conquers all*, but she had a feeling a future with Ryan now would be more likely to fail than eight years ago. Both she and Ryan had new and different lives, and it was dangerous to even think about taking risks.

She'd just have to work harder at making sure her heart was impenetrable.

There was no point in falling for this intelligent, charming, sensitive man all over again even though she could feel it happening. An attraction based on the past could only lead to disaster. She had to nip her feelings in the bud before they began to blossom.

Tara was surprised her mother and father didn't come out to meet her, so she honked her horn twice—the signal she used to alert them she was home. A few minutes later Jane appeared in the doorway, a worried expression on her face, and Tara prepared herself for the inevitable grilling.

'Thank God you're home,' Jane said as she opened the car door. It certainly wasn't the greeting Tara was expecting. Had something happened? Some bad news?

'What's the matter, Mum?'

'It's your father. He's had an accident and he's refusing to go to the hospital.'

Tara's heart began to thud irregularly, and she felt the blood drain from her face, but the light-headedness only lasted a few seconds. It was at times like this she missed being able to leap out of the car and run inside. The wait for her mother to get her chair so she could go in and see for herself what had happened was an agony of uncertainty.

'What happened?' She couldn't help the impatient note in her voice.

'Darby was in one of his bad moods,' Tara's mother said breathlessly as she wheeled the chair from the back, not bothering to close the door. 'And today your father wasn't quick enough to get out of the way. He's got a chunk out of his leg, and I think he's either badly sprained or broken his wrist.'

Tara processed the information as she lifted herself out of the car.

Darby, a now aging pony, had been a gift for Tara's eighth birthday and she had loved him to bits—still did. He'd probably been a substitute for the siblings she'd never had, and she'd treasured the solitary rides they'd shared when she'd chatter away to him and reveal her deepest secrets.

He'd been literally put out to pasture since Tara had stopped riding him, and was usually placid. Over the last six months or so he'd been prone to stubbornness and the occasional temper tantrum where he'd kick and try to buck. Tara had laughingly said he had equine Alzheimer's. She doubted he'd be capable of causing any major damage, though.

Her mother, casting worried looks in Tara's direction, led the way into the house and Tara followed her to the kitchen.

It took Tara only a few seconds to take in the blood-soaked towel on her father's shin and the roughly applied elastic bandage on his left wrist. Graham's expression was a mix of frustration, pain and anger.

'It's not as bad as it looks,' he said in an unusually quiet voice, doing his best to hide a grimace. 'Blasted horse,' he added, as if apportioning blame made it easier for him to cope.

'Let me have a look.' Tara wheeled over to where her father sat in a spindle-backed chair next to the kitchen table. 'Are you in a lot of pain?'

Tara could tell he was, but he was unlikely to admit it. It was one of those crazy man things, to deny pain.

'Just a bit. Mainly in my leg,' he said through clenched teeth.

Tara carefully removed the towel from her father's leg and it took a great deal of effort to suppress her gasp.

A chunk of flesh the size of the palm of her hand had been torn away from his shin just below the knee, exposing bone and muscle. There was no deformity, so she hoped the bones were intact. Her mother had obviously cleaned the edges of the wound as best she could, but there were flecks of dirt and possibly manure embedded in the exposed area and a steady ooze of blood from one side of the wound. For his leg alone he needed X-rays, cleaning and debridement of the wound, a tetanus booster and antibiotics. There was a real possibility he would need a skin graft.

Tara took the clean towel her mother offered and covered the wound, instructing her to apply pressure while Tara began to unwind the bandage. To her relief, the skin of Graham's hand wasn't broken, and again there was no obvious deformity, but there was some swelling of his wrist.

'How did you do this?' she asked calmly.

Her father seemed to have succumbed to his fate and replied meekly, with what she thought was a hint of a smile on his face, 'I tried to give Darby the same as he gave me.'

Tara thought for a second.

'You mean you tried to kick an elderly pony that was having a temper tantrum?'

Her father nodded. Why didn't that surprise her?

'And I slipped,' he added.

'And landed on your outstretched hand?'

'Yeah, that's right.'

He winced as she prodded the dip in the back of his hand near the base of his thumb—over his scaphoid bone.

'That hurts?'

He nodded again.

'Anywhere else?'

He shrugged

She manipulated his wrist and asked him to flex and extend his fingers but couldn't find evidence of any other injuries.

'Dad, you're not going to like what I'm about to say, but Mum's right—you need to go to hospital, and you might even need surgery. That wound on your leg is deep, and you've almost certainly done some damage to at least one of the small bones in your hand.'

Her father scowled but seemed accepting.

'Tonight?' he grumbled.

'The sooner the better.'

Tara's father, not surprisingly, refused her suggestion they call an ambulance. By the time she'd phoned the hospital, organised Rob Whelan—the on-call doctor covering emergencies—to meet them in the small ED of the local community hospital and supervised her father's transfer from house to car, it was nearly ten o'clock. Graham tried to manage the short walk to Tara's car unassisted, and even using Jane on one side and a broom on the other as a crutch she could tell he was in a great deal of pain. He'd definitely need a wheelchair when they arrived at Keysdale.

With her father in the back seat, her mother driving and Tara settled in the passenger side they set off.

Tara glanced behind her and noticed her father had his eyes closed but was still grimacing. He'd refused to take anything for the pain, which was just as well as it was likely he'd need surgery—if only to clean and debride his wound. If that was the case he'd need a drip, and analgesia could be given through the vein. Fortunately Rob could do a simple debridement, but if Graham needed more complicated surgery he'd have to be transferred to the regional hospital in Bayfield. She wasn't looking forward to his reaction, even if his injuries turned out to be minor.

'Nearly there,' her mother said, attempting cheerfulness. They turned off Hill Park Road onto the highway heading towards the town.

Her father groaned as they jolted over a pothole.

'Sorry,' Jane said. 'I didn't see it.'

Graham's silence was an ominous sign that indicated he either didn't have the energy or was too focused on his injuries to complain.

They pulled up to the front of the hospital and parked in the area designated for ambulances. Laurie, the night orderly, and Kath, one of the ED nurses, stood waiting with both a gurney and a wheelchair. Graham had obviously noticed.

'I don't need those things. I'm quite capable of getting inside under my own steam.'

'Like you were at home?' Jane was quick to reply, the strain showing in her voice and on her face.

Graham attempted to move his leg and this time the movement was accompanied by a string of expletives.

Laurie brought the chair next to the car and then glanced at Tara. 'Is this okay to transport your father, Dr Fielding?'

At that moment Rob Whelan arrived, leaped out of his car and strode towards them. To Tara's relief, after acknowledging her and her mother's presence, he took over with an assertiveness that defied protest.

While Graham was carefully moved to the wheelchair without the clamour of expected complaints, Jane brought Tara's chair from the back of the car and stood by while she transferred. Once Tara was in her chair she noticed her mother had begun to tremble. Reaching out, she gave her hand a squeeze.

'He'll be all right, Mum. You know he's in good hands.'

Jane took a deep breath and her hands steadied.

'I know that, love.'

'Why don't you go inside and I'll lock up the car?'

'But—'

'Just go and be with Dad. He needs you.'

In the five minutes or so it took Tara to make her way inside to the Emergency Room, Graham had been undressed, his grubby clothes replaced by a hospital gown, and Kath was opening a dressing pack. The blood-soaked towel had been replaced by a large sterile pad of gauze, and Rob Whelan was busy inserting an IV. He glanced at Tara.

'I've done a lightning examination, but he needs analgesia and the quickest way is into the vein.' Then he smiled. 'But of course I don't have to tell you that.'

'No, but I'm sure Mum and Dad would appreciate you explaining things in layman's terms.' Tara resisted the temptation to quiz her colleague about the seriousness of her father's injuries as he'd probably barely had time to take a history and would no doubt do a more thorough examination once the pain had eased.

Jane stood silently on the other side of the couch, looking pale and tired. She'd most likely put up with at least an hour of Graham's undiluted anger while they waited for Tara to arrive home.

'Of course.' But Rob's conversation was still directed to Tara. 'I've asked Meg to phone the radiographer.' He lowered his voice. 'I suspect he's cracked his tibia and almost certainly has a fractured scaphoid.' He cleared his throat. 'And Meg's also going to see if she can contact Ryan Dennison. He has a short list tomorrow, so I assume he's still in town.'

'No! I don't want that man touching me!' Graham said in a loud, angry voice.

Four pairs of eyes fixed on him, but Tara's were the only ones wide with horror at the realisation of how deep her father's dislike of Ryan was, even after all these years. Rob looked stunned. He had no idea. He'd taken the helm of the practice nearly five years ago, when old Doc Harris retired. Rob was a relative newcomer and had no knowledge of her history with Ryan.

'Why? You know Dr Dennison?' Rob said.

Graham scowled.

'I thought I did.'

Tara felt the heat of her father's stare as his gaze shifted to her and fixed on her legs.

'Before he crippled my daughter.'

CHAPTER FOUR

THE main reason Ryan couldn't sleep was because it was so quiet. His city residence, a second-floor apartment in South Perth, was on a busy street, and he hadn't realised background noise was his default setting. In his restless state of insomnia, his thoughts were only of Tara.

What a determined, courageous woman she was. Despite the limitations imposed by her paraplegia, she'd not let it hold her back and had embraced life with an enthusiasm he admired. But he doubted she had much in the way of positive feelings for him. When he'd asked her if she still believed he'd stopped loving her, she'd been vague and skirted around the issue. Their love had been shattered to pieces in a few seconds in which his reflex response had been the wrong one…and he could never put it right.

But he did still love her.

He flung the quilt off the bed and pulled the sheet up to his waist in an effort to get comfortable enough to entice sleep. It made little difference. In the deathly silence of the outskirts of a country town at eleven on a Friday night he was yearning for at least a little traffic noise.

So it was almost a relief when his mobile phone rang.

'Ryan Dennison,' he said, not recognising the number of the caller.

'Hello, Dr Dennison. It's Meg Davies, a casualty sister at the hospital. I'm sorry to disturb you so late.'

'The hospital? I'm sorry, which hospital?'

'Keysdale.'

'Oh. What can I do for you?'

It hadn't been written into his job description that he covered orthopaedic emergencies after hours, but Rob Whelan had negotiated an agreement that he would attend emergency patients during the two or three days a week he visited the town.

'You'd be lucky to be called out at night more than once a month, and major trauma cases go directly to Bayfield,' Rob had said jovially while he was filling out the paperwork granting him admitting rights to Keysdale hospital.

Tonight was only his second day working in the town. His so-called operating session the previous day had been an orientation day, where he'd met some of the hospital staff and been shown the facilities; he had no post-operative inpatients. The call was most likely an emergency.

He heard the nurse clear her throat and what sounded like raised voices in the background.

'We have a patient here Dr Whelan was hoping you could come in and see.'

'Okay, can you fill me in with a brief summary?'

There were more noises in the background, muffled as if the nurse had covered the handpiece of the phone.

'Dr Fielding wants to talk to you. She'll be able to explain better than I.'

Tara?

What on earth was she doing at the hospital at this hour of night? He had a fleeting thought that she was the patient, that she'd been injured. He was usually calm in times of crisis but he felt the effects of adrenaline surging through his circulation.

'Hello, Ryan, it's Tara.'

Ryan exhaled a breath that had somehow caught in his throat.

'What's happened? Why are you at the hospital?'

She hesitated a moment before replying, as if she needed time to formulate what she was about to say. Almost as if she was going to impart bad news.

'It's Dad. He had an altercation with Darby, my old pony. Rob's just got the X-rays back and he has an undisplaced open crack fracture to his right tibia. He also has a scaphoid fracture, and the radiographer says there's at least two millimetres displacement.'

She sounded understandably anxious, her voice high and staccato.

'I'll come straight over. I should be able to get there in about ten minutes.'

'No, Ryan. There's a problem. If you could just give some advice over the phone…'

'A problem? What problem?'

'Er…Dad's creating a bit of a fuss. He refuses point-blank to see you.'

Ryan took a moment to take in what Tara had just told him. It made sense. Not only did Graham dislike him, he obviously nursed a deep mistrust of his one-time son-in-law. It was unfortunate that lack of trust extended to include Ryan's professional skills. But he wasn't about to let a strong-willed, one-eyed farmer put him off.

'Like I said, I'll be there in ten minutes and we can sort Graham's issues when I get there.'

After he ended the call, without giving Tara time to reply, he felt a little guilty. But he needed to see the X-rays to know if Graham required surgery. If that was the case, the ideal situation would be to put him on the end of his operation list the following day. At worst it would simply mean referral to a surgeon in the nearest regional centre.

He pulled on the jeans and tee shirt he'd been wearing earlier, travelled the two strides to the bathroom and splashed cold water on his face. Finger-combing the spikes from his tousled hair, he grabbed his medical bag, slipped into his shoes and headed out to… He suddenly remembered that his mode of transport, delivered not long after Tara had left, was a battered, noisy work ute lent to him by the mechanic because neither of the two Keysdale vehicle rentals was available until the following day—by which time he'd been assured his own car would be back on the road.

After a clunky gear-change he rumbled off, and ten minutes later was pressing the after-hours buzzer at the entrance to the ED of the hospital.

'You stay with Dad,' Tara said with a weary sigh.

Ryan was busy writing up Graham's notes and reorganising his theatre list. He'd been a prince of patience and reason, the way he'd calmly explained the different options available to the stubborn farmer. The threat of sending Tara's father to Bayfield and the possibility of having long-term problems with his hand and wrist if the scaphoid fracture wasn't fixed promptly had won out. Fortunately Jane's attitude to Ryan was less hostile, but the seeds of blame and guilt were still embedded in her heart, and Tara knew the relationship her parents had with her ex-husband would never be the same.

'But—' Jane croaked in a voice laced with tiredness.

'No buts, Mum. I'm quite capable of getting into Ryan's car. He can leave my chair in the car and I'll use the manual one when we get home. I've got a spare key so Ryan can move it away from the ambulance entry.'

Tara's gaze shifted from Jane to her father, who was snoring softly, no doubt due to the effects of the morphine that was coursing through his veins. If he'd been aware of the arrangements she was making for Ryan to drive her home he'd have blown his stack, but thankfully he was peacefully sleeping.

Her mother looked too tired to protest, but it had been her choice to stay with her husband at least until he was settled in the ward.

'Oh, all right.' She suppressed a yawn. But then she was suddenly wide awake, with a panicked look on her face.

'What, Mum? What's the matter?'

'Milking…the herd…I'll have to come home. The cows aren't going to wait.'

She began gathering her things.

It took seconds for Tara to realise that the problems the Fielding family were about to face didn't only involve Graham. And it took her less than a minute to formulate a plan—a plan she would have considered totally out of the question if she hadn't spent the evening with Ryan. She had a gut feeling he would help without her having to ask him. After all she'd used to know him with an intimacy that was only present in a committed couple who were deeply in love.

She placed her hand on her mother's trembling arm and felt the tension in Jane's muscles, strung taut like new fencing wire.

'Mum.' Tara's voice was steady, with a tone she hoped conveyed control. Her mother relaxed only a fraction, and the look of dread in her eyes conveyed more than mere words. 'Forget about the farm. What do you really want to do?'

Her mother opened her mouth to speak but the words seemed to stick in her throat.

'I can't forget about the farm,' she finally said, withdrawing her arm from Tara's hold and gathering up her handbag. She fumbled with the zip, and when she finally opened the bag she couldn't find what she was looking for. It was the last straw. She began sobbing.

Tara leaned across and drew her mother close at the same time as Ryan quietly slipped into the cubicle. He didn't speak, but his presence was oddly reassuring.

'*I* can manage,' Tara said softly, with a conviction that defied argument.

She paused, waiting for her mother's response. But Jane said nothing, as if making decisions was too much for her after such a long and stressful day.

Tara glanced briefly at Ryan. 'And Ryan can help me with the few things I can't do on my own. It will only be for the morning milking. Tomorrow I'll be able to organise some local help.'

She heard Ryan catch his breath but he gave nothing away. He didn't show any signs of surprise, or confusion, or incredulity—the emotions he was probably experiencing as a result of her sudden, unexpected request. It was as if she'd simply asked him to make her a cup of tea. He nodded his agreement.

'So, what do you *really* want to do, Mum?' Tara repeated.

Jane pulled away and took a deep, sighing breath.

'I want to be with your father.'

'Right, that's settled, then. I'll see you tomorrow—and *don't worry about the milking.*'

Tara kissed her mother on the cheek before she reversed out of the cubicle, raising her hand in a wave. Meg was at her desk but she stood when she saw Tara and Ryan.

'We're ready to take your father to the ward.' A look

of concern crossed her face. 'Are you going to be able to manage on your own?'

She wasn't on her own, though. For better or worse, she'd roped Ryan into the latest Fielding family drama and it was too late to bail out. She needed him. The thought was scary, and strangely exciting at the same time.

'Yes, I'll be fine. Dr Dennison is going to help out.'

There was no mistaking the meaning behind Meg's quizzical look and the momentary upward twitch of her eyebrows. Tara suspected several versions of the news of the favour Dr Ryan Dennison was granting her in the small hours of Saturday morning would be all over town by the end of the weekend.

But there was nothing she could do to stop it.

Ryan wasn't sure what he'd let himself in for when he'd agreed to Tara's request to take her back to the farm and help with the milking. If she'd asked him to speak at a conference, or organise a meeting with the local politician, or even charm his way into a late booking at his favourite waterside restaurant in the city, he'd be in his element. He'd been raised in the Big Smoke and knew the drill.

He didn't actually hate the country…or farming…or getting dirt and sweat on his freshly laundered clothes. He thought of his attitude as being more like a fear of the unknown. In fact he could use exactly the same phrase to describe his feelings towards Tara at the moment.

Fear?

He couldn't get rid of the anxiety niggling at the edge of his usual calm demeanour—and, yes, he was a little frightened of being alone for the rest of the night with Tara. It was all to do with the fact he'd used to know this woman intimately. And earlier tonight she'd been frank with him to the point where she had come close to opening her heart.

He needed time to think through his next move with her. She wasn't a stranger, but he had to get to know this new Tara Fielding all over again. He had the feeling it would take more than charm for Tara to allow him into her present-day world. And he wanted to do it when *she* was ready.

They made their way to the ute.

'Sorry about the transport. It was all Keysdale had to offer at short notice.' Ryan doubted she'd complain. She'd been raised on a working farm after all.

'No problem.' She stopped on the passenger side, waiting for him to open the door.

'Once I'm in, you'll remember how to strap my chair onto the hoist and park it in my car, won't you?'

'Yes, I'm pretty sure I can manage.'

She held out a bunch of keys, singling out the car key. 'And if you wouldn't mind shifting the car into the car park. The hand controls don't interfere with using the floor pedals. You just drive it like a normal car.'

'Oh, okay.'

He seemed to be learning new things about Tara and her lifestyle at a rate of knots that he was battling to keep up with. He wondered how she had learned to cope all those years ago, when she'd been so resistant to his many offers of help. Back then he'd not had the strength to stand firm. He'd been a prisoner in his own guilt-ridden anguish and had succumbed to Tara's wishes without more than a token protest. Now he wished he'd been more persistent. Trying to contact her without being confrontational by phone and e-mail in the first couple of years after the divorce hadn't been enough. He should have put aside his fear of having to deal with Graham's and Jane's anger as well as another rejection from Tara and forced her to talk to him. Doubts surfaced. He wondered if it was too late to start all over again? But his circumstances were different—he had a child to cope with now.

He opened the borrowed vehicle and went to reach across his companion to open the door, but she beat him to it. In what he guessed were less than a couple of minutes she'd shifted from her chair to the dusty, work-battered seat and was in the process of buckling her seat-belt. He paused to admire her and she looked up with a nervous smile.

'What's up? Is everything okay?'

'Yes, fine.' He certainly wasn't about to tell her that everything was far from being okay. That his mind was becoming increasingly scrambled with feelings he didn't understand. And it had nothing to do with the tiredness that hung heavy like early-morning mist. He fumbled to release the brake on her chair and finally managed to move it to Tara's vehicle.

'You remember the way home, don't you?' Tara asked as he positioned himself behind the wheel.

Home? Of course *her* home was the farm, and had been since her discharge from the rehabilitation hospital. That had been several months after their divorce and was a part of her life he knew nothing about.

He remembered when *home* had been a shabby two-bedroom flat near the university that he and Tara had shared with another couple who were also struggling students. He recalled the excitement when they'd moved into a smart townhouse by the river after they were married, and the joy they'd shared in choosing furniture, in packing the small courtyard garden haphazardly with dozens of plants, and filling their lives with dreams and plans for a future—a future that had been cruelly stolen from them.

'You *do* remember the way to the farm?' she repeated.

Ryan had been so swept up in his own thoughts he'd not answered.

'Yes, of course,' he said, a little more brusquely than he'd planned, and his terse response put an end to their conversation until he turned onto the gravel road leading to the homestead. 'I made my own way here a few weeks ago, didn't I?'

He pulled up as close as he could to the ramp without getting in Tara's way, and was grateful someone had had the forethought to leave an outside light on. There were also several rooms bathed in a welcoming golden glow.

Tara was again handing him her keys. This time she'd separated a brass door key from the rest.

'My other wheelchair is in my bedroom. Do you remember where that is?'

Of course he did. How could he forget those stolen moments of tantalising intimacy on the few occasions they'd visited the farm when they'd been students, uninhibited with their affections and so much in love.

'Vaguely.'

He had a sudden idea, and the words were out of his mouth before he had time to think of the implications.

'Look, why don't I just carry you inside? If you need the chair I can find it when you're settled.' He paused, waiting for her reply, but it didn't happen. Her face was in shadow, so he couldn't see her expression. He figured he had nothing to lose. She hadn't agreed, but she also hadn't refused. 'And I don't mind putting you to bed. It's been a long day and I'm feeling dead on my feet.'

Dead on my feet...

How insensitive was that?

Tara turned towards him and he could now see the icy

look on her face, the steely defiance in her eyes. He'd hit a raw nerve and he braced himself for the consequences.

'I'm not a child, Ryan,' she said quietly. 'I don't want to be carried, let alone put to bed like a helpless baby. I'm quite capable of putting myself to bed, on my own, just like I've been doing for the past eight years.'

Despite the gloom Ryan could see her red cheeks and the veins standing out on her temples. He suspected her rosy complexion was more to do with anger than embarrassment.

His heart filled with regret. He certainly hadn't planned to hurt her.

'I'm sorry, Tara. I didn't think...' he said meekly. He took the offered key and climbed out of his car. 'I won't be long,' he added as he strode towards the house, wondering how he could have got it so wrong.

Tara had become used to her predictable life with its strictly regimented routine. That wasn't to say she was completely happy with it, but at least she knew there would be few surprises.

The first shock had been Ryan appearing on her doorstep and telling her he was about to edge his way back into a part of her life she'd thought she had control of. Then, even scarier, had come the revelation he was divorced with a child, and that information was all tangled up with the realisation she still found her ex-husband attractive. Up until now she hadn't believed that to be a problem, because all she had to do was have as little contact with him as possible.

But now!

She'd shared a meal with him at his motel, he was the treating specialist for her stubborn and hostile father, and he was about to spend what was left of the night with her.

Oh, God.

Her privacy, her independence, her fragile self-confidence was crumbling around her.

She was grateful Ryan had gone inside to get her wheelchair as it gave her a few moments to rein back her emotions and think about how she was going to handle the next five or six hours. Had she been too harsh with him when he'd offered to carry her inside?

Carry her!

She wasn't ready for that kind of close physical contact and didn't trust how her body would respond to being cradled in his arms. Better she just keep her distance—both physical and emotional. Ryan would be heading back to the city after his operating session and then they'd be in a better position to know how long her father would be out of action. The crisis at the farm would be over, or at least reduced to a manageable drama by the end of the weekend. She looked forward to some semblance of normality being restored.

Her thoughts were interrupted by a knock on the window. Ryan stood sheepishly behind her chair. She opened the car door. 'I'm sorry—'

'There's no need to apologise.' He had a tentative smile on his face, as if waiting for permission to go on. 'You're tired and have had an incredibly stressful night. I understand.'

Tara's first reaction was to recoil from words that could be interpreted as condescending. But he was right. Stressed and tired was exactly how she felt. Add a handful of guilt at not being home for her parents when her father had been injured, and it wasn't surprising her judgement was skewed.

'That still doesn't excuse my...er...grouchiness.'

His smile morphed into a grin.

'You always had a quick temper.' He paused and rubbed his forehead. 'But it never lasted for long. And I like a woman with spirit.'

'Enough,' she said quietly, feeling the edginess coming back. Ryan seemed to understand, and busied himself with positioning the chair as close to the car as he could.

She pulled herself into her chair and headed towards the open front door of the house, leaving Ryan to lock up the ute and follow her. The first thing she did when she got inside was to check there was fresh linen in the guest room. She also glanced in the bathroom and noted there were towels, fresh soap and a new toothbrush. She gave a silent cheer for her mother's efficiency, and as she turned to come out of the room nearly bumped into Ryan.

'Whoops,' he said as he moved aside. 'I just seem to keep getting in your way.'

She ignored his comment and stifled a yawn. 'We should try to get a few hours' sleep. I'll set my alarm for five, because we need to be in the milking shed by six at the latest. What time does your theatre session start?'

'Half past eight.'

The yawn she'd tried to suppress a minute ago returned but she ignored it.

'Good. If you're a fast learner...' which she doubted— he'd always shied away from any manual work involving more energy than moving the occasional plant pot '...you might have time to grab a bite to eat before you go back to the hospital.'

She thought of apologising for volunteering him for pre-dawn hard labour, but she was too tired and would think about an appropriate way to thank him in the morning. He obviously hadn't missed her yawn, and she harboured the thought that she didn't look her best after a long hard

day, let alone one which had turned into an even longer
and demanding night.

'To bed, then.' A cheeky smile appeared on his face and
he added, 'You must be exhausted.'

'I think you're familiar with the guest room,' Tara muttered. and waved her arm in the direction of the room
they'd just left. 'You should have everything you need—
feel free to raid the kitchen if you're hungry.'

'Thanks.' They both hesitated, Ryan appearing as uncomfortable as Tara felt. 'I'll see you in the morning.'

He started off towards his room, but then stopped and
turned. Two strides and he was back at Tara's side, and before she had time to stop him he'd leaned over and planted
a warm, firm kiss on her lips.

Ryan had kissed her!

It was brief enough to be simply a goodnight kiss between friends but long enough to hold the promise of
more… If she wanted it.

Did she? But Ryan didn't give her the opportunity to
decide.

'Sweet dreams,' he said as he closed his door.

When Tara finally fell into a restless sleep she dreamed
of Ryan's arms around her, his mouth on hers, his lips caressing. It was the sweetest dream—until he began to undress her and saw her injured legs. Then the sweetness
evaporated and all she was left with was the same empty
loneliness she'd endured for the last eight years.

CHAPTER FIVE

WHEN the loud buzz of Tara's alarm jolted her into consciousness the following morning it felt as if she'd only just gone to sleep. She stretched, rubbed her eyes and looked at the clock on her bedside table. Yes, it *was* just after five a.m. Time to get up. Her mother's words echoed in her mind—*the cows aren't going to wait.*

By the time she'd hauled herself out of bed, washed and attended to her usual morning ablutions, it was close to half past and she hoped Ryan wasn't still a heavy sleeper. When she knocked on his door he opened it with a wide-awake, cheerful smile. He'd obviously showered as he was towelling his still-damp hair and droplets of water trickled down his chest.

His bare, lean, muscular chest.

The noise that involuntarily emitted from Tara's suddenly tight throat was a cross between a moan and a gasp. All he wore was a pair of navy boxer shorts and a mischievous grin.

'It's not as if you haven't seen it all before.' He discarded the towel and pulled on jeans and a shirt.

By this time Tara's cheeks were burning, but she couldn't bring herself to look away. Memories flooded back. Bittersweet memories of carefree times when she'd felt no embarrassment over nakedness—hers or Ryan's.

Back then she'd been comfortable with her body. She'd revelled in the sensuousness of just looking at Ryan naked; in the warm pleasure of unexpected arousal and lovemaking—in the shower, on the floor, leaned up against the front door, breathless and impatient, or lazily in bed on Sunday mornings.

But now? The thought of revealing her damaged body to Ryan—or any man—made her stomach turn.

Another blow to her fragile self esteem.

And why should Ryan be any different? A feral thought entered her mind associated with a vivid image of a very young, very energetic, nubile and sexy Shannay. The other ex-wife, who seemed much more real now she had a name. How could she compete with that?

'I wasn't expecting you to be awake.' She managed to salvage a morsel of control.

'You said we had an appointment at six with a herd of impatient cows. I don't want to keep the ladies waiting.'

He then had the audacity to wink. He was flirting with her. *And she liked it.*

She glanced at his bare feet in an effort to take her mind off the rest of his body.

'There'll be a pair of spare wellies in the dairy and I'll lend you some thick socks,' she said. His designer running shoes would be ruined within five minutes in the milking shed.

'Thanks.' He slipped on his shoes without bothering with socks. 'Anything else we need to do before we go?'

'I'll need a couple of cushions—'

'So you can relax and watch me do all the work?' He laughed and, surprisingly, seemed to be enjoying the novelty of helping out.

She didn't want to burst the bubble and tell him he was in for at least an hour of unremitting hard toil. Tara ig-

nored his remark as she reversed out of the doorway, Ryan
not far behind. She did a quick detour to get the socks and
cushions, which she piled on her lap.

'I'll take the quad bike. It's parked in the tractor shed.
Then if you could put my chair in the truck…' She grabbed
a set of keys from a hook near the back door and threw
them at Ryan, who caught them clumsily. 'Then follow me
to the dairy.'

There was something exhilarating about driving an old,
beat-up farm truck along a potholed dirt track in the milky
pre-dawn light. Ryan could make out the silhouettes of
scattered trees on the blurry horizon, and he inhaled the
heady smell of livestock and wet grass while he battled
to keep up with the jolting tail-lights glowing just ahead.

He followed Tara around a broad bend, and in the sweep
of his headlights witnessed an amazing sight.

The rising sun back-lit the dairy shed and bathed it in a
golden glow. Behind the shed the ground in the paddock
sloped up to a backdrop of gently rolling hills. In the distance he could see an army of cattle making their way towards them, a small brown dog running from one side of
the herd to the other.

He parked the truck next to Tara, and as the cows moved
closer he was embraced by the noise of them clomping
and mooing in the otherwise quiet dawn. He glanced at
his watch. Five forty-five. They'd arrived in good time.

Tara looked impatient to get started, so he lifted her
chair out of the tray of the truck, unfolded it, positioned
what seemed like a mountain of cushions on the seat and
wheeled it over to the quad bike.

'If you could just help me onto the cushions?' she said.
Once she was on her chair, the cushions added an extra

twenty centimetres to her height and when she turned the lights on in the dairy he understood why.

All the equipment, as well as the cattle stalls, was raised nearly a metre above ground level—he presumed so that the farmer and his helpers didn't have to constantly bend. Unfortunately the design didn't take into account the height disadvantage of a paraplegic worker. Hence the cushions.

'Why did you bring the bike?' Surely Tara could have just as easily travelled with him.

'Sometimes Jacko sleeps late—'

'Jacko?' he said. Who the hell was Jacko? Was Tara expecting hired help to arrive at any minute? A jolt of something very like jealousy surprised him.

Tara chuckled. 'The dog. Didn't you see him in the paddock when you pulled in?'

'Oh, yes, of course.' It made sense now. Farmers used motorbikes to round up stock. Tara used the quad bike if and when the energetic little Kelpie overslept—which he doubted happened very often.

After he was kitted out in wellies, rubber gloves, a plastic apron and disposable cap, Ryan followed Tara into the shed. It was like entering a different world, full of stainless steel surfaces, machinery for milking, pipes seeming to go in all directions and a huge tank at the end of the run.

Tara seemed to know what she was doing, though.

'What can I do to help?' he said as she spun wheels, checked dials and wheeled up the work area that ran between the stalls where the cows would be milked.

'I've just done a flush of the system to clean it, and the cows will start coming through soon. Then it'll be non-stop.'

'Until we finish?'

'That's right. When one hundred and twenty-three cows are milked and back in the paddock.'

'You count them?'

'Every day. But it's done electronically nowadays. It's a way of keeping track of them. If they're not all accounted for it can mean trouble.'

She sighed, but Ryan could tell she was experiencing a buzz from being up to her ears in hard physical work. Somehow he couldn't imagine Graham Fielding letting Tara have free rein in the dairy, even if she'd been able-bodied. Her father had been protective of her all the years he and Tara had been together. It had been easy for her to move away to go to university, but the wheel had turned full circle.

He could only envisage what it must be like for her now, and had a new respect for how she was coping.

He felt her tugging at his sleeve and turned to see what she wanted. The cows were patiently waiting outside the shed so he assumed the milking was about to start.

'We'll take a side each. Your inexperience should balance with my being in the chair, so hopefully we'll synchronise.' She pointed to a gate on his side. 'Time to open up. I'll show you what to do with the first cow and then you're on your own.' She smiled. 'Watch closely, learn and then do it yourself, as my grandpa used to say.'

The next hour flew by in a blur of teats, milking cups, feed bins, cow excrement and noise. There wasn't time to talk even if Ryan had wanted to. Tara had been right—they got into a rhythm of sorts that they both could manage.

When the last half-dozen cows were released he felt as if he'd worked a twelve-hour shift moving rocks up a mountain. He'd discovered muscles he never knew he had and hoped he'd not have to use again any time soon. He stretched, wiped hot sweat from his throbbing forehead and groaned. Tara manoeuvred to face him.

'You did really well. I'm impressed. Especially since you always seemed to be glued to the city with orthopaedic cement.'

'Don't sound so surprised.' He detected a touch of sarcasm in her comments but chose to ignore it. All she did was shrug and reach her hand to massage a very attractively muscled shoulder. He wondered what it would be like to have her strong fingers kneading his own tender muscles. 'And I assumed this was a one-off. An emergency. I couldn't exactly refuse.'

The smile on her face disappeared, and Ryan wasn't sure if it was because he'd said the wrong thing, or because she was disappointed he wasn't planning on making a habit of early-morning milking.

'What now?'

'I'll clean and disinfect the tubing, if you could hose out the stalls.' She looked at her watch. 'And we might even have time for a quick breakfast.'

Tara decided to leave the bike at the dairy, saying she would get the dairyman to bring it back in the afternoon.

'The dairyman?' Ryan was curious. He'd assumed the Fielding family ran the farm single-handed. He squinted at the low morning sun, concentrating on negotiating potholes that seemed to have multiplied since he'd made the trip in the dark.

'We open the farm on the weekend to tourists, or to groups of schoolkids by appointment on weekdays, so that they can see how a working dairy farm runs. One of the neighbour's boys comes over to help.'

Of course. Ryan remembered the leaflets he'd noticed at the motel. He stole a glance at his companion. She was coiling a tendril of hair between her restless fingers.

'Haven't your parents got enough to do—?'

'They have,' she interrupted tersely. 'It's to do with money—you know, making ends meet.'

So his suspicions were confirmed—they had been struggling. It made Graham's injuries all the more serious…and distressing. If he was out of action and they had to employ someone else it would make their situation even worse.

'I'm sorry. I didn't realise,' he finally said.

They travelled the rest of the short journey back to the farmhouse in silence. When they rounded the bend on the approach to the homestead they saw Tara's car parked out at the front.

'Mum's back,' Tara said, her brow furrowing in a frown. 'I only hope Dad's—'

But her words were interrupted by the sight of a tired but smiling Jane emerging from the front door. She waved and started down the steps as Ryan pulled up next to the car.

Tara opened the door and hugged her mother with a down-to-earth affection he'd never known from his own parents.

'How's Dad?' Tara asked as she sat back and sighed.

'As well as we can expect. At least he's accepted the wisdom of having surgery. The driving force is his getting back to work as soon as he can. He seemed to forget about the milking, though, thank goodness. I think his brain was a bit numbed by the morphine.' She paused and held her daughter at arm's length. 'So how did the milking go?' Then she glanced at Ryan and smiled, but without any sign of the affection she'd shown towards her daughter. 'Thank you so much for helping out.'

He returned her smile. 'My pleasure.' To his surprise

he realised the words had a ring of truth. He had actually enjoyed the hour of gruelling hard labour with Tara.

'So how did it go?' Tara's mother repeated, her eyes still fixed on Ryan, almost challenging.

'You'd better ask your daughter.'

Tara was positioning herself, ready to climb out onto her chair.

'A bit slow, but we managed.'

It was hardly a compliment, but the circumstances had been difficult.

'Good. Have you two got time for some breakfast? I've got scrambled eggs ready to cook. It'll only take five minutes.'

Country hospitality obviously outweighed her reticence to accept Ryan and all the baggage he still carried involving the Fielding family. The thought of fresh-cooked eggs had Ryan's mouth watering, but he looked across at Tara to see if she approved.

'Have you got time?' she asked.

'I'll make time,' he said graciously as he climbed out of the truck and hoisted the wheelchair from the back.

'Good.' Jane turned to go back into the house and Ryan found himself alone with Tara again. He wheeled the chair to where she waited, but stopped a few feet away.

'What's the matter?' she said.

It was a simple question, but it was enough to unleash an unexpected flow of raw emotion in Ryan; as if a dam had burst. She looked so beautiful—a smudge of dirt smeared on her neck, her hair enchantingly dishevelled, clothes damp with sweat. She smelled of fresh milk, hay and wholesomeness.

But now was not the time to tell her *everything* was the matter. He wanted to hold her in his arms, kiss her senseless and love her...make love with her. But he knew his thoughts were pure fantasy. He'd had his chance and would have to work hard for a second one.

He hesitated.

'Nothing,' he replied.

And all he could do was look away into the distance. What hope did he have of making up for the traumas of the past?

Very little.

Freshly showered and with a full stomach, Ryan drove back towards Keysdale. He would be late starting his operating session but it couldn't be helped, and stressing about it wouldn't change things. None of the three cases were emergencies, and half an hour either way wouldn't make any difference.

Huh?

Stressing about it wouldn't change things?

Normally stress was his driving force, but his stress meter had been reset and he felt unusually calm. Pretty damned tired as well, but calm and alert and surprisingly content with the world. The physiological reason was probably to do with the release of endorphins, the body's happy hormones, after a morning that could be compared to a full-on, two-hour gym workout, or running the City to Surf, or... No, he wouldn't go there. There was no point in going back to that long-ago place and time when a night of lovemaking with Tara would leave them both breathless and exhausted but somehow renewed.

He eased his foot onto the brake, slowing down as he approached the intersection of Hill Park Road and the highway. A long-haul, fully loaded prime mover sped by in a cloud of gravel dust as its inside wheels skimmed the road shoulder. It wavered for a moment before finding the blacktop and its stability again.

In an odd way that was exactly how Ryan felt—wavering close to something precariously dangerous, with an outcome that could go either way. He could play it safe, drive slowly, not take any risks and maintain a professional but friendly distance from Tara. Or he could put his foot down on the accelerator, follow his heart and steamroll into something he had no control over that could easily end in disaster.

The second option was definitely risky, the first not worth considering. He would just have to look for a middle road. Yes, that was what he would do. Try and get to know Tara again and to understand her life, with its challenges and successes. But it would be up to her. She was the only one who could decide whether to let him into her life again.

And if she said no?

Well, he'd deal with that when it happened.

The effect of the happy hormones was beginning to wear off.

When Ryan arrived at the hospital he quickly changed into crisp green scrubs and emerged from the change rooms to see his first patient being wheeled through into the operating theatre. Dylan Payne was a young mine worker and football player who needed a shoulder reconstruction. Ryan enjoyed surgery and hummed softly as he began the ritual of scrubbing up. A few minutes later, frothy yellow antiseptic running down his forearms, he reversed into the efficient bustle of people preparing for the operation.

He looked around at the team: the anaesthetist—Jim Fletcher, one of the GPs he'd met briefly the previous day; an anaesthetic technician who doubled as a general helper; a scrub nurse who introduced herself as Kelley; and a junior nurse named Janine. They all greeted him civilly and he suddenly felt bad about not being punctual.

'Sorry I'm late,' he said. But he wasn't about to explain that his lateness was due to lingering too long over a huge plate of perfectly scrambled eggs with all the trimmings while in the dizzying company of Tara Fielding.

He could tell they were curious, though, and hoped it was to do with how he performed in the operating theatre—not where he'd spent the night and the early hours of the morning.

But he was wrong.

He should have known news spread like wildfire in a town like Keysdale, where the community thrived on knowing everybody else's business.

Once Dylan was asleep and Ryan had started prepping the young man's skin Kelley began the inquisition. At least that was what it felt like.

'The last patient is Dr Fielding's father?'

It was a rhetorical question but was a way of letting him know the news was out.

'That's right,' he said as brightly as he could. 'I'll be internally fixing his scaphoid as well as cleaning up his leg wound and applying a cast with a window over the wound.'

'Mmm…we heard it wasn't the only emergency you were called out to last night.' The middle-aged nurse's eyebrows elevated and her eyes twinkled.

Ryan was less than impressed by the familiarity the woman assumed. He had no doubt she was referring to his overnight stay with Tara and his subsequent involvement in the milking, but he wasn't the sort of person to discuss his personal life with a complete stranger.

'Scalpel,' he said sharply, and was promptly handed the

instrument he'd requested as well as sponge-holding forceps loaded with gauze.

'How did Tara and her mother cope?'

'Pardon?'

Was she talking in generalities or specifics? He decided to answer as vaguely as he could and suddenly yearned for the session to be over.

'As well as can be expected. I gather the loss of a skilled pair of hands on a family-run farm like the Fielding's can be pretty tough.' He looked across at the nurse and smiled, hoping she registered his expression despite his mask, then continued concentrating on exposing the damaged ligaments and tendons in his young patient's shoulder. 'But I imagine in such a close knit community as Keysdale you'll pull together and help.

Ryan didn't wait for Kelley's reaction. He glanced at the anaesthetist.

'Everything going okay your end?'

'Perfect. Stable obs. What you'd expect with a healthy twenty-year-old.'

'Good.'

Kelley left Ryan alone after that, and despite her inquisitiveness turned out to be a very capable assistant.

Though the morning seemed unusually long, the first two cases on Ryan's theatre list went predictably well. After Dylan an elderly lady was scheduled, with severe deformity and increasing pain from bunions. Ryan removed a piece of bone from her right foot and fixed the straightened bones with a K wire. The relatively simple procedure would make life easier for eighty-seven-year-old Elsie Tanner, who had worked hard in her family's market garden for most of her life.

His third and final patient for the morning was, of course, Graham Fielding.

Ryan had called in to see him briefly before beginning his list and his attitude, though still complaining, was significantly subdued compared to the previous night.

'I only agreed to this because of Tara,' he'd said gruffly without a scrap of gratitude. 'And because I haven't got time to mess around with referrals to the city.' He'd then lowered his voice and conceded, 'And Tara said you were a dab hand with the knife.'

Ryan had laughed inwardly. He appreciated Tara's confidence in his ability, despite the fact she'd never seen him operate as a fully qualified orthopaedic surgeon.

Pity.

As a student she'd always been interested in the procedural side of medicine. It was one of the reasons she'd chosen the rural stream of general practice training—so she would have the skills to do an emergency anaesthetic or remove an inflamed appendix. They'd talked about her assisting him with surgery. But their plans had been quashed. The accident had changed everything.

But…

Ryan had the seed of an idea.

Why couldn't Tara assist in the OR now?

Operating often involved standing in one place for the duration of the surgery.

Surely a chair or stool could be modified for a surgical assistant who didn't have the use of her legs? After all, she had full use of her hands, and her wheelchair gave her a degree of mobility that amazed him. It could be a way to show her he still cared about her and admired and valued her skills as a doctor. There was also the element of surprise. It was unlikely she'd even think of the possibility of having a useful role in the operating theatre.

But enough of daydreaming. He had work to do

and would have to file away his germ of an idea until another time.

Graham's surgery went as well as could be expected. The fracture in his scaphoid—a small bone in the hand notorious for causing long-term problems if a fracture was missed or not treated appropriately—was fixed with a small screw. After his leg wound was thoroughly cleaned, it was dressed, then a plaster cast was applied from his foot to mid-thigh with a window over the wound to allow inspection and dressing. He'd need a more permanent fibreglass walking cast once the swelling settled. Treatment of Graham's bones had been relatively simple, but the size of the defect in the skin on his shin would almost certainly need a skin graft. That would mean referral to see a plastic surgeon in Bayfield or the city, and Ryan wasn't looking forward to breaking the news to Tara's father.

The operating session finally finished at half past one, and he was due to call in to the garage and collect his car any time after midday. Despite the inconvenience, the competence and efficiency of the mechanic had impressed him. After stripping off his gloves and gown he headed towards the change rooms.

He yawned, suddenly overcome with the kind of satisfying tiredness that came after a job well done. As he changed into civvies his mobile phone rang, and he sighed as he recognised the number.

'Hello, Shannay. What's up?'

Whenever his ex-wife rang him while he was working he had a sense of doom. She was usually embroiled in some self-centred mini-crisis that involved off-loading their daughter at short notice. Of course he didn't mind. He loved Bethany and treasured any extra time he had with her. But sometimes it just wasn't convenient—like now. He reminded himself he shouldn't jump to conclusions.

'Nothing serious,' she said breathlessly, as if she was in a hurry. 'I just need to talk. Is it convenient?'

'I guess so.' He began walking down the corridor towards the hospital exit.

'Right. Well, I have some really good news.' She paused, as if waiting for a response, but Ryan waited for her to continue. 'Some fabulous news.'

He reached the vehicle and opened the door, settling into the driver's seat to hear Shannay's *fabulous news.*

'Yes?' he finally said, in an endeavour to hurry her up. His stomach gave an impatient growl.

'I went for an interview last month and didn't think I had a chance but they contacted me this morning. I rang you twice but the dragon who had your mobile said you were operating and you could only be disturbed if it was a life-or-death emergency.' She giggled and Ryan realised Shannay was still just as immature as when they'd divorced. 'I thought of making something up.'

'Who? Who contacted you?'

She'd successfully aroused his curiosity, but he wondered why it was so important to inform him.

'The airline. Trans Jet. I'm sure I told you. I really want to become a flight attendant, you know, before I get too old.

That was news to him. His heart dropped but he had to ask.

'What about Bethany?'

'Well, that's the thing. I have to move to Sydney for training. My hours are going to be all over the place and I start next weekend. Ah…you'll have to take her. That's why I wanted to let you know as soon as I found out—so you'd have time to make arrangements.'

'A week!' He couldn't keep the frustration from his voice.

'The training's only for three months. A trial period. And if everything goes okay I might get to be posted back here.'

'Look, I'll be back tonight and I'll come round to see you tomorrow.'

The anger welled in his gut but he didn't want to get into an argument. With Shannay it always ended in tears, and there was never any satisfactory resolution. He needed time to think.

He needed time to work out what was best for Bethany.

CHAPTER SIX

RYAN wasn't sure whether to grin or snarl. He'd been to see Shannay and was bitterly disappointed he'd been denied the pleasure of seeing his daughter. Beth was away on a play date with one of her young friends.

But the visit had definitely been worthwhile. Despite what he could only construe as a misguided attempt by Shannay to seduce him, he'd gleaned the information he needed.

Yes, Shannay was packing her bags and moving to Sydney in a week's time.

No, there was definitely no alternative to Ryan taking over his daughter's care.

Yes, of course Shannay would miss the lively four-year-old, but it was *a once in a lifetime opportunity.*

And, yes, Ryan would find some way of caring for his daughter, even if it meant taking time off work.

The icing on the cake was that he'd negotiated to apply for full custody of Beth, and to his surprise Shannay had offered little resistance. She was focused on the present and her own needs, and was as self-interested as when they'd divorced. Their ten-year age difference seemed more pronounced than it had ever been.

Ryan put on a soothing classical CD and made himself a strong cup of coffee.

He closed his eyes. He'd do it, but he wasn't exactly sure how.

'Can I have a quiet word with you, Tara?' Rob Whelan said in his usual calm but assertive voice.

Tara wasn't the least surprised when her employer requested he talk to her privately. It was Sunday afternoon and she was visiting her father, who was as grumpy as ever after receiving the news that heavy farm work was out of the question for the best part of the next two months. Despite Tara's protests he had apparently told Rob all about her marriage to Ryan and the circumstances surrounding their divorce as an explanation for his dislike for the man who had so skilfully treated his broken bones. Rob had taken on the role of moderator.

'Dr Dennison wanted to see you personally, but he was called away to a family emergency. He asked me to give his apologies and tell you everything went very well, but he wants you to see a plastic surgeon.'

Rob had patiently explained the reasons to her father, and handed him a referral letter for a Perth specialist who consulted at Bayfield once a fortnight. Fortunately Graham had a deep respect for the experienced GP. Although Tara's father obviously hadn't liked what he was hearing, he'd managed to control his temper and agreed to travel to Bayfield as soon as an appointment could be made.

As Rob left the small private room Tara glanced at her mother, who sat holding Graham's hand. She then shifted her attention to her father.

'Dr Whelan wants to talk to me. I'll be back as soon as I can. Okay, Dad?'

Graham nodded and Tara felt his gaze burning into her

back as she left the room. She knew her father would never change, but she also knew that if you tried hard enough to penetrate his crusty shell you might find he actually had a heart—a big heart—that was capable of breaking. She didn't want that to happen again, but she had the feeling if the Fielding family's dirty washing was aired publicly it would result in considerable pain—and not only for her father.

Rob waited outside the door and directed Tara to the small meeting room at the end of the ward. She wheeled her way along the corridor and into the room. Her companion followed, closed the door and sat down opposite her. He took a deep, sighing breath.

'I suppose you have an idea of what I want to talk about?'

'Ryan Dennison…and me…'

'That's right.' Rob Whelan paused and rubbed his forehead, but the creases of his frown remained. 'You might think it's none of my business—your personal life before I met you, before I employed you—but I feel if we discuss it now things are less likely to get out of hand.'

'Things? What things?' Tara was aware of an increase in her heart-rate and the overpowering need for fresh air. She began to perspire, and could feel the anxiety building inside like a balloon about to burst at any moment.

Rob picked up on her distress.

'Are you all right, Tara?' He laid his hand on her forearm but it gave little reassurance, and the more she tried to control her panic, the more out of control she felt.

'Er… It just feels stuffy in here. I feel hot. Maybe I've had too many coffees. And I haven't had much sleep in the last couple of days.' She managed a shaky smile. Her history of panic attacks was something else her boss didn't know about, and she didn't want him to find out now.

Rob left his seat and opened the window. It took a couple of minutes because the catch was jammed. Tara used the precious time to take some slow, deep, relaxing breaths and focus her attention away from her symptoms. Without any conscious effort she began to think of Ryan, and Rob's words rattled through her mind.

How had he explained Ryan's rapid departure after his Saturday morning operating session?

A family emergency?

She'd been preoccupied with her father and his negative attitude to everything and anything but she felt sure that was what Rob had said. Her heart missed a beat as she speculated what it could be. Had something happened to his parents; his ex-wife; his younger sister…or his daughter?

A light breeze brushed her cheeks and the coolness was like an injection of the calm she desperately needed. Suddenly she wanted to know.

Rob came back and sat down, a look of concern on his face.

'Feel better?'

Tara nodded. 'You said Ryan left yesterday because of some emergency? I know I'm probably out of line asking, but—'

'It's okay. Dr Dennison told me he had to go back at short notice to look after his daughter. He didn't give me the impression it was a secret, so I'm sure he wouldn't mind me telling you.'

'His daughter?'

'Yes. You knew he had a child from his second marriage, didn't you?'

Tara cleared her throat.

'Of course. So it wasn't really an emergency?'

He grinned. 'I was the one who called it a family emergency. And what I've told you is all I know. Sorry. But we're getting off track. I wanted to talk to you about how you feel about Dr Dennison working in Keysdale. I gather it's not general knowledge in the town that you were husband and wife and…well…with your father's attitude, I need to make sure what happened in the past isn't going to affect your work in any way.'

'Oh.' She understood where her boss was coming from but wasn't sure how to answer. The presence of Ryan in her life after an absence of almost eight years had certainly scrambled her emotions, but she hoped she'd be able to make sense of what was happening and that it wouldn't interfere with her work. Of course it all depended on how quickly the gossip spread through the close-knit town once the connection was made between Ryan and her accident. She was prepared to brace herself for the worst. She still hadn't answered Rob's question.

'I can't think of any reason it should.' A little white lie wouldn't do any harm, she thought as she bravely continued, 'I no longer have strong feelings, either negative or positive, towards Ryan Dennison, so my work wouldn't be affected. After all, we'll probably rarely see each other. I assure you, you have no reason to be concerned.'

'And if history turns into gossip?'

'I think we should deal with that if it happens,' Tara replied, more confidently than she felt.

Rob Whelan smiled and briefly laid his hand on hers.

'Good, that's settled, then. I'll let you go back to see your father.'

Although fitting the early-morning milking into her already full routine was a challenge for Tara, it at least stopped her from thinking about Ryan. In fact she had little time to think about anything other than work on the farm, her time at the clinic and her efforts to placate her father's frustration at being so helpless.

It was a week to the day since Graham's accident and he'd been discharged from hospital the previous morning—on the condition he limited his activities to simply walking with crutches and carrying out the twice daily exercises the physio had recommended. He'd also been provided with a list of things he *wasn't* allowed to do, and Jane had been given the unenviable job of supervising him.

As if she didn't have enough to do.

Of course he grumbled about everything, despite the fact his co-operation would expedite his recovery. Fortunately one bright light shone out of the gloom. The plastic surgeon was happy with the wound on Graham's leg and pronounced that a skin graft wasn't necessary. If kept meticulously clean and free of infection the wound should heal naturally, he'd said.

Tara shifted her thoughts to the working day ahead as her mother followed her out to her car. She'd negotiated with Rob Whelan to start her clinic sessions an hour later and finish later, but even with the extra hour, and the help of the dairyman on the days she worked, she still battled to get ready for work on time.

'Have you got a busy day today?' Tara's mother asked wearily as she moved the wheelchair ready to put in the back of the car.

'Close to fully booked when I last checked before I left on Wednesday.'

Tara sighed.

She loved her work, but the strain of extra duties on the farm, her father's grumpiness, her mother's self-sacrificial patience and the messy business of her past relationship with Ryan Dennison threatening to come out in the open for public dissection added another dimension to her ever-present weariness.

'So you'll probably be home late?'

'I'm sorry, Mum. If there was any way I could take time off, I would. But with Lindley on maternity leave and the new registrar not starting until next month I feel I'd let the team down.'

'I know. I'm not complaining. Dr Whelan and Ryan have shown endless patience with your dad, so I have nothing but praise for them. And I know how important your work is for you.'

Yes, it was. Her mother was right. Not only was her job satisfying but it got her out of the house, away from the farm; it gave her a sense of self-worth in an environment in which she at least had some degree of control.

Tara smiled and nodded agreement.

'I'll see you this evening.' She paused a moment. 'And don't let Dad get you down.'

Her mother frowned. 'He's getting under my feet already and it's only his second day home. But we'll survive. We've coped with a lot worse than this.'

Tara reached out through the window, grasped her mother's hand and gave it a quick squeeze before she drove slowly off, Jane's words echoing in her mind.

We've coped with a lot worse than this.

Did she mean the dreadful experience of Tara's birth, when Jane had nearly lost her precious daughter? Tara's mother had only told the story once—probably because it was so painful for her to remember that with the complicated delivery of her first baby she'd sacrificed the chance to have any more children. Or was she referring to the anguish, pain and grief her parents had endured after her accident? Did she mean the loss of a future, loss of the rose-coloured dream she'd had for her only child? Jane had had more than her fair share of suffering and disappointment.

But there was no point in dwelling on a past she couldn't change. All Tara could do was play the cards she had left in the best possible way.

Tara slid a pop-rock CD from the early noughties into the player and turned the volume up loud, but the music didn't have the effect she wanted. Rather than filling her mind with pleasant thoughts of vicarious love, hope and fantasy, it just brought back memories. Ryan had given the disc to her. She'd lost count of the times she and Ryan had slow-danced to the caressing monotone throb of the female lead singer's voice. The number of times that seductive, rhythmic intimacy had led to…

She jabbed the off button with her index finger and accelerated down the narrow country road in silence. When she arrived at Keysdale Medical Clinic she had her emotions back in order. Grabbing her mobile phone from her pocket she dialled the familiar number.

'Hi, it's Tara,' she said brightly. 'Can you come out and help me with my chair?'

Pippa Morgan.

The teenager's name had been added to the end of Tara's morning consulting list in the space which was reserved for 'book on the day' patients: those who were not seriously ill but who had problems that needed dealing with urgently. Tara wondered if Ryan would be prepared to offer advice if the girl's problem was related to her arthritis. She decided she'd give him a quick call before his morning got too hectic.

She dialled the number of the specialist clinic and waited for several rings before the message on his answer-machine kicked in. Tara recognised the voice of

Liz the receptionist stating that the rooms were unattended until one p.m. and to leave a message or ring the hospital number if it was an emergency.

Strange.

The previous week Ryan had started at eight-thirty. But there was most likely a simple explanation. Maybe he'd been called to an emergency; perhaps he'd reorganised his operating times; or he could be sick. There'd been a particularly virulent flu going around Keysdale the past few weeks, and doctors, especially out-of-towners, weren't immune to illness. She glanced at her watch and noticed it was after ten. She was already running late and decided she didn't have time to dwell on why Ryan had taken the morning off. In fact it was none of her business. If it turned out she needed his advice, she'd ring later.

Her morning consulting went smoothly, and she was only running half an hour late when she called her last patient in at one o'clock.

'Pippa, come in.' Tara smiled at the young woman and beckoned her to proceed down the corridor. Although she was walking unaided, Pippa's body tensed every time she put weight on her right leg and her limp was more pronounced than Tara remembered from when she'd seen her patient about a month ago.

When they reached the consulting room Pippa went in and sat down slowly. It looked as if every movement aggravated her pain, but Tara vowed to remain cheerful and positive. There was always a bright side, no matter how bad things seemed to be, she reminded herself. Tara had been in the same place Pippa was in now, and had survived without someone who knew what it was like to show the way.

'Good to see you on your feet.' Tara offered an encouraging smile. 'But it looks like you're struggling. What can I do to help?'

'I've run out of my painkillers. Sorry to bother you with something like this, but I was booked to see the new specialist today and I thought he might prescribe something different.'

'You had an appointment to see Dr Dennison?' Tara's curiosity was aroused.

'That's right. But Liz rang yesterday and said Dr Dennison wasn't coming in this week at all. The earliest she could make another appointment was three weeks away. I couldn't wait until then.'

'No, of course not. I wouldn't expect you to wait a couple of days, let alone weeks. You did the right thing.'

Pippa grimaced as she repositioned herself on the chair.

'Is the pain still mainly in your hips?'

'Yes, though I'm still getting stiffness in my hands. Probably something to do with the cold mornings we've had lately.'

Tara thought of how chilly it had been in the milking shed the last few mornings and gave an involuntary shiver.

'I mentioned last time about warm water, didn't I?'

Pippa laughed. 'Mum won't let me forget it. She reckons you're a genius. Sometimes I wish I hadn't *shared* with her.'

'You mean you have no excuse for not washing the dishes in the morning now?'

'You guessed it.' She paused, and then continued with a serious face. 'Having my hands in warm water for ten minutes or so in the morning really helps.' The smile returned. 'But Mum says the downside is that she's had to postpone getting the dishwasher Dad promised a few months ago.'

Tara admired the teenager's positive attitude and never-ending courage. It was one thing to cope with limited mobility, but to be in near constant pain… Well, Pippa deserved all the help she could get.

'What time of day is the worst for you?'

'Probably the evenings—especially on the days I travel to uni.'

Tara made a minor change to Pippa's prescription for analgesia and printed it out.

'I've increased the quantity you get each month, so you can take an extra one or two tablets of the short-acting painkiller if you need it.'

'Thanks.' Pippa took the prescription, folded it and put it in the pocket of her jeans.

'Is there anything else you need?'

'No, and I really appreciate you seeing me at short notice. Thanks again.' She made a move to get out of her chair and struggled to stand, but once she was on her feet her movement was freer. She walked slowly to the doorway and when she reached the door paused and turned.

'Is Dr Dennison a good surgeon?' she said with a slight smile.

'Excellent. One of the best. If you need an operation you'd be in safe hands.'

'Good.' Pippa's smile turned into a grin. 'I've heard he's drop-dead gorgeous, and single as well.'

Tara smiled. 'Just what the doctor ordered,' she said quietly as Pippa set off slowly down the corridor.

CHAPTER SEVEN

THE previous week had turned out to be a disaster for Ryan. Organising childcare at short notice had not been as easy as he'd hoped. And Shannay was no help at all. Once she'd made the decision to hand over responsibility for Bethany to him, her sole focus of attention had seemed to be on Sydney and her exciting future as a flight attendant. Ryan couldn't help wondering how long her enthusiasm would last—especially when she discovered that, as well as the veneer of glamour and limitless free travel, there was actual work involved. At least their daughter wouldn't be subjected to yet another series of disruptions, though.

Would she?

Not if he could possibly help it.

But as the week drew to a close the odds seemed to be stacked steeply against him.

All he needed was a nanny who was prepared to do the odd hours he was requesting, including around-the-clock care while he was away. He also wanted someone who would be available at short notice when he was summoned to the hospital on the nights and weekends he was on call. The ideal situation would be a live-in nanny who had no weekend or evening commitments and a non-existent social life on the weekends.

But such a person didn't seem to exist.

Was he asking the impossible?

Then a totally unexpected notion popped into his over-stressed mind. He tried to dismiss it, but it kept bouncing back.

What he needed was...*a wife*!

A totally preposterous idea. Where on earth had the thought come from?

He'd tried marriage—twice—and had proved he was no good at it. He'd been rejected by his first wife because she couldn't even envisage continuing to live with him after what he'd done. And Shannay... He'd been blinded by her charisma and infatuation and not realised they'd been too different to sustain any kind of long-term relationship.

No, he definitely *didn't* need a wife. He was going to do the best he could and give everything he had to make sure Bethany had stability in her life as well as an abundance of love.

He could do that.

As a *single* dad.

But, despite all the rational reasons he shouldn't, he still burned a candle for Tara, and wondered if she'd been telling the entire truth when she'd revealed she was pleased he had remarried and had a child. She would make a wonderful mother, and it was a tragedy she seemed to be denying herself the experience because of her physical problems. He felt sure there'd be a way to overcome them. He held the old-fashioned belief that loving parents in a stable home was the most important thing in bringing up children.

Would Bethany be a complication in their tentative new friendship? Did he have the courage to ask her how Tara really felt? Was she envious of him?

Maybe he'd never know.

But he wished he had someone to talk to now—to give him advice; to tell him he was doing the right thing; to

reassure him there was no need to panic. And he wished
that person was Tara. She would know what to do.

He'd reluctantly cancelled his sessions at Keysdale for
the week and had spent the morning interviewing the last
of the candidates the nanny agency had sent. He'd not
been comfortable with any of the five women he'd seen
and he was starting to feel desperate. He was picking up
Bethany that afternoon and had planned to be back at work
on Monday, in fact he had a full theatre list which would
be difficult to cancel. Liz had competently taken care of
his Keysdale days.

'Don't you worry about a thing at this end,' she'd said
with a confidence he'd already come to trust. 'Just do what
you have to do.' She'd hesitated. 'And if you need any more
time off—'

He'd assured her a week was enough, but now he wasn't
so sure.

He was due to pick up Bethany in less than an hour.
Fortunately it was his usual access weekend, so he wasn't
on call and was looking forward to spending quality time
with her. But he still hadn't managed to find someone suit-
able to pick Bethany up from day care or stay over when
he was on call, let alone look after her on the days he went
to Keysdale.

A cloud of gloom descended. Perhaps he'd made the
wrong decision. Maybe he should have insisted Shannay
give him more time. Maybe the prospect of finally acquir-
ing custody of Bethany had clouded his judgement.

He wondered if it was too late to change his mind.

He went to the kitchen to make a cup of coffee. He
needed a boost before he made the short journey to collect his daughter. As he was about to sit down to drink the
hot black brew his mobile phone rang.

'Hello—Ryan Dennison,' he said wearily, not recognising the caller's number.

'Dr Dennison.'

He identified the voice immediately and wondered what Liz could want at four o'clock on Friday afternoon. He assumed she was calling from her own personal phone.

'Liz, what can I do for you?'

'It's more what I can do for you.' She chuckled and he let her go on. She'd already aroused his curiosity. 'Do you still need someone to look after your daughter while you're working?'

Something snapped inside and he felt like pouring his heart out to the middle-aged woman he'd met barely a week ago. But he didn't want to burden her with his troubles, so pulled himself together and said calmly, 'I am. Why do you ask?'

'Well, when you told me last week what you were looking for—the unusual hours, being available at short notice—I suspected it was going to be no easy task to find someone.'

'And? Go on.' Ryan found himself steadying his suddenly erratic breathing and praying for an unlikely miracle.

'I put some feelers out and thought of my cousin, Christine.'

'Your cousin?'

'She's about my age, widowed, has one grown-up son away at college and lives locally. In fact she's living with us at the moment, because she's just finished a job as a governess on a cattle station in the Pilbara.'

Liz paused for breath but Ryan wasn't about to interrupt. So far the woman sounded perfect. He was waiting for the catch.

'The family's youngest child left for boarding school

at the beginning of term, so Christine found herself out of a job and without a home. She has excellent references and loves kids. She would have had a tribe herself if her husband hadn't been killed in a farm accident.'

'She never remarried?'

'No. She says she's set in her ways now, and as long as she has a job involving children... But it's probably best you ask her yourself. That's if you're interested?'

'Oh, yes, I'm definitely interested.' Ryan tried, unsuccessfully, to quell the overwhelming relief in his voice. 'When can I see her? I could drive down to Keysdale tomorrow, or Sunday. Of course I'd have Bethany with me, but that shouldn't be a problem, should it?'

'Hang on—slow down. There's one thing I said I'd mention before you get too excited,'

Ryan's heart dropped. There was always a 'but' and he was about to find out what it was. He suspected the picture Liz had painted of her cousin was too good to believe.

'And what's that?'

'She would prefer a live-in job. Otherwise she'd have to find a place to rent in the city. She basically said she couldn't afford it.'

Ryan's crinkled brow relaxed and he broke into a grin. She sounded better than perfect.

'So when can I meet her?' he repeated. The future had suddenly taken on a rosy glow, and if Liz had been standing in front of him he would have enfolded her in the warmest hug laced with gratitude and hope. It now seemed at least possible to give Bethany the kind of consistent and loving environment she deserved.

'She's already booked on the morning train to Perth. She has some business in the city to attend to and we thought maybe you could see her then. You said you wanted to go back to work next week—'

'Would she be able to pack a bag?'

'But—'

'I trust you, Liz. If you recommend your cousin, I'm sure it will work out.' He rubbed his forehead with his thumb and index finger, not wanting to think of any other possibility. 'And if for some reason it doesn't happen I'll cross that bridge when I come to it. Thank you.'

'My pleasure.'

Ryan could almost feel Liz's warm smile bouncing along the airwaves.

The gates of Shannay's townhouse were closed but the front door was open. Ryan spotted Bethany sitting on the step as he cruised past, looking for a space to park. His daughter was perched on top of a pile of boxes and bags which he assumed contained the material detritus of four years living with Shannay.

He felt an unsettling mixture of excitement and nerves as he parked and climbed out of his car. A whole new episode in his life was about to begin, and he hoped he'd be able to live up to the challenge and deliver the goods he'd promised.

By the time he reached his ex-wife's home Bethany was standing at the gate, presumably having recognised his car.

'Daddy! Daddy!'

His baby's voice was remarkably loud, considering her diminutive stature. The noise was certainly effective in bringing Shannay to the door.

Ryan opened the latch and scooped Bethany up into his arms. She plonked a wet kiss on his cheek and then positioned herself on his hip as he made his way towards the front door and Shannay.

'Mummy said I was going to live with you.'

Ryan's gaze locked for a moment with Shannay's before he looked down at the eager face of his daughter.

'For ever!' Bethany added loudly and triumphantly.

Ryan felt an instant of sadness at the fact his daughter seemed to have no regrets at dismissing the time she'd spent with her mother so casually. *For ever*, she'd declared. He wondered if the reality of leaving her home of over four years would kick in when she realised she wasn't coming back on Sunday afternoon. And Ryan was struck by the realisation that *his* life would never be quite the same.

'Are you okay?' he said to his ex-wife. She was unusually quiet.

She shrugged. 'I'm fine. I just want to get it over with.'

And that was it. He finally had custody of his daughter and it was the beginning of a new stage in his life.

The news had filtered through to Tara that Ryan's absence from Keysdale was tied up with problems he had with his daughter. Apparently the child's mother had handed her back to Ryan and he'd been doing his best to arrange care for her while he worked.

Ryan's child…

Tara imagined a pint-sized version of Ryan, with soft brown curls, sparkling blue eyes and a personality that would melt hearts.

Ryan's child…

If things had been different *she* could have been the mother of Ryan's children.

She wiped away a tear and silently reprimanded herself. She'd decided long ago she wouldn't burden Ryan—or any man, for that matter—with a child she was incapable of looking after, no matter how much she yearned to have a baby of her own. How could she cope with the full-time demands of a baby, the exuberance of a toddler, the respon-

sibility of a child? You needed to be able to run to a child
in danger, to rescue a toddler from the top of a slide, to
act quickly with speed and agility. Which she didn't have
and never would. Children were unpredictable, and the
fabric of Tara's life was woven with routine and knowing
exactly what was going to happen next. She wasn't one to
take risks, not now.

She turned off her computer screen and began to pack
her things away. She'd somehow managed to get through
another busy week of extra work on the farm and her father's continuous grumbling. A small step forward was
Graham's reluctant agreement to help with the farm accounts. It had amazed both Jane and her that once he'd got
the hang of the computer he seemed to enjoy it. At least it
gave them a break from his grumpiness.

Tara sighed as she dumped her bag on her lap and
headed for the door…just as the phone started to ring.

'Damn,' she muttered. She should have left half an hour
ago, but had decided to stay and clear the pile of paperwork she'd been ignoring all week. The thought crossed
her mind to let it ring, but she knew she'd feel guilty and
worry that she'd missed something important.

Rather than do a U-turn, she reversed back to her desk
and picked up the handpiece.

'Hello?'

'Hi, Tara.'

She instantly recognised the voice and her heart-rate
involuntarily jumped.

'It's Ryan.'

She cleared her throat. 'Yes, I know.'

'I thought I might have missed you.' He paused only
long enough to take a breath. 'My last patient for the day
is your friend Pippa Morgan and I wondered if you wanted
to sit in on the consultation.'

'I...er...'

'Of course I understand if you haven't got time. I can ring you. And you'll receive a detailed letter.'

He was providing her with an out, as if he'd sensed her unwillingness. He wasn't to know that the reason for her reluctance was not because she'd had a long day and wanted to get home, nor that she had another commitment. It was because she could already feel her legs metaphorically turning to jelly at the thought of seeing him. In fact she'd managed to evade him the previous Friday and thought she'd succeeded in avoiding him again.

And her reluctance for face-to-face contact was all to do with failed marriages, lost opportunities and children.

'I was about to leave, so your timing is perfect. I'll be over in five minutes. And thank you. Pippa is a very special patient of mine.' She somehow managed to keep her voice calm, telling herself that sharing the care of a patient was a normal part of the association between a specialist and the referring GP. And that was how she planned to keep their relationship.

Strictly professional.

Now that their past was common knowledge and she had nothing to hide there was no reason why that should change.

'See you in five,' Ryan said just before he hung up.

Tara propelled her chair along the corridor connecting the GP clinic to the specialist rooms. The doors slid open as she approached and she stopped, mesmerised. She shook her head to make sure she wasn't imagining what she heard. But it was definitely real. Liz's unmistakably mature voice was attempting to harmonise with the remarkably tuneful singing coming from the mouth of a young child. She paused a moment longer to listen to the simple words of an ancient nursery rhyme about stars and diamonds, night skies and the curiosity of children. The scene touched a raw spot in her heart.

The song ceased abruptly as she began to move again. The child must have heard the almost silent whirr of her chair's motor.

'What's that?' the little girl asked loudly as Tara approached cautiously.

Unpredictable small children and electric wheelchairs weren't an ideal combination, but she needn't have worried. A delightfully pretty little girl with straight black hair, cupid lips and huge brown eyes peered around the side of the reception desk. Was it Ryan's child? She looked nothing like him. Maybe she was one of Liz's grandchildren.

Tara smiled. How could she not when the girl beamed, her animated face crinkling in what could only be described as mischievous curiosity.

'Hello, and what's your name?' Tara's tentative enquiry brought the child out from behind the desk, but just enough for her to get a better view of the strange lady in a motorised chair.

'Um…Beffny…and I'm…' she took another curious step forward '…and I'm waiting for my daddy to finish work. Um…he's a very important doctor, who fixes up bones and stuff like that. When they're broken.'

Tara glanced at Liz, who hadn't said a word during the mostly one-sided conversation.

'Ryan's daughter?'

Liz grinned like a proud grandma. The diminutive four-year-old, although she looked nothing like her father, had obviously inherited his charm.

'Yes. Her name's Bethany. Isn't she an angel?'

'Definitely cute, but—'

Tara was about to say they'd only just met and she would reserve judgement until she got to know the girl better.

A barrier had gone up because she didn't want to get too charmed by Ryan's little girl. Not yet. It was just as well she was interrupted as the words on the tip of her tongue suddenly seemed pompous and totally inappropriate.

'Can I have a ride on your chair thingy?'

'Maybe later, darling.' The timely rescue by Liz certainly didn't come too soon. 'This lady is a doctor too, and she has *very important work* to do with your daddy.'

The child seemed to accept the explanation and turned to face Liz, whom she'd obviously had no trouble bonding with. Tara felt an unexpected jolt of jealousy.

Jealousy? Why on earth should she be envious of the freely given affection dealt out to the middle-aged receptionist by a child she'd only just met?

She promptly rejected the notion that because Bethany was her ex-husband's child she represented the children Tara could never have. She wasn't the kind of person who would bear a grudge. Not after all the years of trying to cast from her mind any thoughts of the future with Ryan that was lost for ever.

'You can go straight in, Tara. Dr Dennison is expecting you,' Liz said after a brief phone conversation with her boss.

Tara knocked softly, then opened the door as Ryan spun around in his chair.

'Thank you for coming.' He indicated the space between Pippa and her mother with a casual sweep of his hand. 'I've just been talking to Pippa and Mrs Morgan about Pippa's arthritis and there are a couple of questions I'd like to ask you. I understand you've been Pippa's GP for a number of years now?'

'Yes, of course.' Tara looked across at her patient and gave her what she hoped was an encouraging smile. 'Pippa transferred from Dr Fletcher the year I started with the practice.' She stopped to think a moment. 'Nearly five years ago. Pippa was in Year Eight.'

Over the next forty minutes Ryan proceeded to take a detailed history, performed a thorough and complete examination, paying particular attention to the teenager's hips, and embarked on a sensitive discussion of her treatment options including surgery.

'I'd like to order an MRI of both hips, as well as blood tests, before we make any definite decisions.'

Pippa grimaced but remained silent while her mother spoke.

'I've heard about MRIs, Doctor, but could you explain what an MRI is?'

'MRI stands for magnetic resonance imaging, and it uses magnets—not X-rays—that produce magnetic fields that bounce off the body and are turned into very accurate images by a computer. I want a detailed picture of Pippa's tendons, ligaments and the membrane lining her hip joints, as well as the bones.'

'Are there any side effects?'

'No—apart from some people getting a rare reaction to the dye that is sometimes injected.'

Ryan rummaged in one of his desk drawers and produced a leaflet.

'This should explain what you have to do to prepare and what to expect when you have the actual test. I've referred you to Bayfield and I understand it can take a few weeks to get an appointment. Which is not as long as if I'd referred you to one of the city hospitals. Any questions?'

Both Pippa and her mother looked satisfied with the explanation.

'And I stay on the same medications?'

Ryan looked across at Tara and smiled. 'Yes, Dr Fielding is doing an excellent job of managing your tablets, so if there are any problems before your next appointment I'd recommend you see Tara.' He directed his gaze back at the patient. 'And I'll see you again in a month.'

Mrs Morgan stood and helped her daughter out of the chair.

'Thank you, Dr Dennison. At last I feel as if we're moving forward,' she said, with gratitude shining in her eyes.

Ryan certainly had a great bedside manner, Tara thought as she watched him escorting the two women out of the consulting room. By the expression on their faces he'd acquired two adoring fans for no other reason than simply being the Ryan Dennison he'd always been. Her mind began to wander as memories of Ryan bounced in and out of her head—as an impetuous and charismatic uni student, as an attentive and exciting lover, as a loyal husband and now as a competent and caring doctor...*and a devoted father*.

'Penny for them?'

Ryan's words broke into her thoughts and startled her. 'I...er...I—'

Fortunately a small dynamo launched into the room like a pyrotechnic rocket. Ryan's attention was diverted to his daughter, who climbed onto his knee and began relating, in considerable detail, the story of her day.

'Hey, young lady, haven't you forgotten your manners?'

Ryan swivelled the child around so she was facing Tara. Bethany, suddenly lost for words, buried her head in his chest, but the little girl's erratic behaviour didn't seem to worry her father.

'Dr Fielding, I'd like to introduce you to my daughter, Bethany,' he said loudly, with a mischievous grin on his face. It did the job of rekindling his daughter's apparent wish to be the centre of attention.

'Hello.'

Tara chuckled.

'We met earlier, and I must say Bethany has a lovely singing voice. I particularly enjoyed her special rendition of "Twinkle, Twinkle Little Star".' She paused. 'Will Bethany be coming with you to Keysdale from now on?' Tara was curious as to his childcare arrangements.

Bethany grinned with pleasure at what she obviously perceived as a compliment about her singing. She climbed off her father's knee and sidled over to Tara, grasping her hand in what could only be interpreted as a childish way of demonstrating her acceptance of Tara.

'No, this weekend is the exception,' Ryan said with eyes slightly narrowed, as if he was defending his actions. 'Bethany usually stays in Perth when I come to Keysdale. Christine—you probably know her; she's Liz's cousin and now Bethany's nanny—has come down this weekend and is staying with Liz. Christine needed to collect some more of her things she wants to take back and at the moment is attending an appointment in town. I didn't see any problem with Bethany staying here for an hour or so. Liz was quite happy to supervise.'

'So I noticed.' She glanced at the child in an effort to include her in the conversation. 'And you were being very good for Liz and your daddy when I came.'

In the next minute or two Bethany managed to climb onto Tara's knees, and she was suffused with a warm glow of pleasure at the child accepting her so readily.

Too readily?

'Can I have a ride now?' Bethany's eyes beseeched in a way that was impossible to refuse, but Tara glanced at Ryan before she replied. He nodded.

'Okay, but you've got to hold on tight.'

Tara executed a perfect three-point turn at the same moment Liz appeared at the doorway. The older woman's eyes widened as she took in the scene. A very cosy scene...

'I was just—'

'You don't need to explain. I can see you've made a new friend and I don't want to interrupt.' Her attention turned to Ryan. 'I've finished for the day and wondered if you could lock up and set the alarm? You're welcome over any time after six.' She smiled, tousled Bethany's hair and then added, looking at Tara, 'Would you like to join us for dinner?'

'No, I'd better get home. I'm running late already and Mum and Dad worry.' The response was automatic.

'It's nothing fancy. Just a casual barbecue out by the pool.' Liz wasn't about to accept her refusal easily. 'We'd love you to come.'

'Yes, love you to come.' Bethany echoed Liz's words, and that beseeching, impossible-to-refuse expression returned to her face. 'Ple-e-e-e-ase,' she added.

Tara laughed. 'Well, I guess if you put it like that... how can I refuse?' She leaned down and gave Bethany a hug and it felt good. In fact Tara hadn't felt so content in a long time. It felt like... She shuddered in disbelief.

It felt like coming home.

CHAPTER EIGHT

'Do you know where Liz lives?' Ryan said tentatively. Liz had already left and Bethany was fidgeting at the door, impatient to get moving.

'Yes. She's been a good friend of Mum's for as long as I can remember. I used to play with her kids. I haven't been there for a while. In fact the pool's a new addition,' she added as she headed for the exit. 'If you're ready to go I could do with a hand with the chair.'

He nodded. 'Of course.' His tone was polite. He didn't want to put her off. It was a breakthrough that she'd accepted Liz's invitation without a protest.

'And I'll need to ring Mum,' she muttered as she cruised through the door.

But then she stopped, reversed and said something to Bethany he didn't hear. A moment later his daughter was comfortably seated on Tara's lap.

'I promised Bethany a ride. Is that okay?'

'Sure, go for it.'

His daughter started giggling as they sped towards the exit.

His heart skipped a beat.

They looked so relaxed together—his daughter and the woman he had never fallen out of love with.

He gathered his bag to follow them, dismissing any

thoughts of reconciliation from his mind. Tara had already made it quite clear how she felt about him, but that didn't stop the fantasies slipping into his mind when he least expected them.

Which included thoughts about a future…that included Tara.

He locked the doors of the specialist rooms and set the alarm before hurrying down the corridor. The scene that greeted him when he stepped outside amazed him, to say the least. Tara and Bethany were doing the two-wheeled equivalent of wheelies around the near-empty car park and his gut reaction was to stop them. It was dangerous. Wasn't it?

But Tara's face was lit up with the child-like joy of fun times from the past and Bethany screamed with laughter as they did a one-eighty-degree turn. Tara appeared to know what she was doing and he didn't want to break the moment. It didn't last long, though. Tara noticed him staring and she slowed down, making her way sedately back to the vehicles. She was breathless when she pulled up beside him, and Bethany began to grumble a protest.

'Sorry,' Tara said. All the excitement that had lit her face a few moments ago disappeared. 'I promised Bethany a ride and I just got a bit carried away.'

'Yes, well…' He looked at the recalcitrant pair sternly. 'Don't let it happen again.'

Ryan's mouth twitched with a hint of a smile as Bethany's expression mirrored almost exactly the mix of the contrition and defiance on Tara's face.

'Apology accepted.' He turned towards his car and clicked the remote. 'Let's get you strapped in, Beth.'

The next five minutes were taken up with sorting out Tara's move into her car and loading the chair in the back. He let her drive off first, and as he reversed out of his space his daughter piped up cheerfully from the back, 'What's the matter with that nice lady's—?'

'Her name's Tara, sweetheart,' Ryan said, hoping for an extra moment to compose his answer, cursing himself for not realising how naturally curious and uninhibited small children can be.

'Okay,' she said slowly. Ryan could almost hear the cogs turning in her head. 'What's the matter with Tara's legs? Why can't she walk? Why does she have to ride in that chair all the time?'

He had no idea what was the appropriate thing to say. He'd just have to wing it.

'She had an accident, Beth, and hurt her back and her legs so bad they don't work properly any more.'

'Oh.'

Ryan tried desperately to think of something to change the subject but he was too late.

'You'll be able to fix them, then, 'cause that's what you do.'

Ryan was lost for words.

If only he could.

Seeing Ryan with Bethany, having the young girl offering the kind of simple, unconditional friendship only a small child could give, and the prospect of spending the evening with father and child had Tara's heart fluttering with a combination of anticipation, nerves and a dash of hope thrown in for good measure. The fact that since Ryan had been back she'd realised she still loved him with the same joyful passion she'd had before the accident had been a revelation for her. She was confused. With her heart, she wanted Ryan in every sense of the word. She'd even dreamed of making love with him and it was magic.

But…

Would Ryan ever want *her*?

Aside from all the rational, sane reasons why another relationship with him would be doomed before it started, she was getting signals that her ex-husband wanted at least to be friends and that he wasn't put off by her disabilities. Might he even regard her as attractive? It was a question she hadn't even considered asking herself until now.

Was meeting Bethany what had changed things for her? Seeing Ryan fall so naturally into the role of father had been a revelation for her. His love for his daughter seemed so natural. Fatherhood only served to make him more attractive to her.

She pulled into the driveway leading up to Liz's house, parked the car and suddenly remembered she hadn't rung her parents.

Enough dreaming about things that were about as likely to happen as the sun rising in the west. She removed her phone from her pocket and dialled her parents' number. Her mother answered.

'I won't be home for dinner, Mum. Sorry about the short notice.'

'Oh, that's a pity. I've made the baked chicken breasts you like.'

Tara refused to feel guilty. She was a grown woman and entitled to have a life of her own. Why hadn't she realised before? Why had she led such a cloistered life? Was it to please her parents? Or to protect herself from more hurt? Or maybe the life she now led had simply become a comfortable habit?

But habits could be broken. Old relationships could be given new life—to her surprise her mind was still full of Ryan.

She took a deep breath and suddenly felt a new freedom—a lightening of her heavy heart, a sense of breaking free. And it all had to do with the man who was about to accompany her on the first night out she'd had for months.

She focussed back on the conversation with her mother.

'That's a shame.' Tara hesitated. 'I'm always up for leftovers. You know my appetite. I'll have what's left for lunch.'

The light-hearted approach didn't seem to be working.

'Where are you going?'

'To Liz Tate's place. She and Steve are having a family barbecue and asked me if I would like to come over. It was a spur-of-the-moment invite and I thought it would be nice. I haven't seen their revamped entertaining area…'

How many other thirty-five-year-olds had to account for every move they made to their parents? She suddenly felt claustrophobic and rebellious.

'I might be home late, but I'll be up early enough to help in the dairy.' She knew both her parents wouldn't settle until she was home, tucked up in her own bed. 'Bye, Mum. See you later.' She hung up before her mother could start grilling her. That could wait until the morning.

A few seconds later Ryan pulled up and parked beside her. She opened her door and began to move towards the edge of her seat in preparation for the transfer. Ryan released Bethany from her booster seat and the child stood quietly watching as her father lowered the chair and wheeled it to the driver's side.

Tara managed the transfer easily, and his daughter seemed fascinated by the whole procedure.

'Daddy said your legs don't work because they were hurt. But he can fix them 'cause he's a bone doctor and that's what he does.'

Tara glanced at Ryan. Why on earth would he tell Bethany that? He shrugged and shook his head.

'That's her take on what I said—which wasn't anything about fixing them.' He looked bewildered and embarrassed, but didn't have time to dwell on what Bethany had said and the implications.

The child, now much bolder than earlier, walked over and gently touched her legs.

'Can you swim?'

'Yes, I can swim.' Tara laughed at Bethany's audacity. 'In fact I'm a very good swimmer.'

'Good, because Daddy said I could go for a swim in the pool, but I want you to swim with me.'

What had father and daughter been plotting on the short journey to Liz's? There was no way she was going swimming, and Ryan should have realised that and not got Bethany's hopes up.

'Sorry, darling, but maybe another time. For a start I haven't got my bathers with me—'

'Oh…'

The child looked disappointed, but Tara wasn't going to change her mind. It was easy to distract her, though.

'Let's go inside. It's getting chilly out here.' Ryan came to the rescue.

When they reached the front door and rang the bell Liz appeared and greeted the threesome warmly. They made their way to the back patio where she introduced Ryan to her husband, Steve, her son, Gus, and Gus's wife, Rachel.

'The splash maniacs in the pool are our two kids, Bonnie and Daisy,' Gus informed them, after shaking hands vigorously with Ryan and kissing Tara lightly on the cheek.

'And you're expecting your third?' Tara glanced at Rachel's noticeable bump, which she estimated to be five to six months along. 'I don't think I've seen you since you fell pregnant.'

'No, I see Dr Fletcher, and he does his antenatal clinic

on Mondays. What with two kids, the farm and a *demanding* husband...' she looked over at her husband and winked '...I never seem to have enough time in the day.' She squeezed Tara's hand and added, 'We must get together for a cuppa some time, or maybe a girls' day out at Bayfield.'

'Yes, we must.' But Tara suspected it wouldn't happen any time soon. Rachel led a busy life. Maybe after the baby was born. 'Do you know the sex?' Tara asked. Most couples were more than happy to find out the gender of their unborn baby fairly early in the pregnancy, and by the gleam in Gus's eyes...

'It's a boy,' Gus said.

A cloud of envy hung low over Tara as she observed the happy family. But it didn't last for long. Bethany suddenly overcame her shyness when Christine emerged from the house.

'I want to go swimming.'

Christine smiled and bent down to pick Bethany up.

'You said you'd bring my bathers.'

The child wriggled to get down and stripped off her soft grey and white striped hoodie, fumbled with the fastenings of her lolly-pink denim overalls. Practical but cute—and very *girly*, Tara thought. How wonderful it would be to go shopping with a little girl like Bethany.

'Hang on a minute—you can change in my room,' Christine said.

At that moment Steve appeared with an ice-filled coolbox of drinks and a large tray of meat balanced on his other hand.

'If you don't mind serving yourself with drinks, I'm about to start cooking.'

Liz added, 'It'll probably be at least half an hour until the food's up. Why don't you two go for a swim? The pool's solar-heated. Steve can lend you some board shorts, Ryan, and I have a one-piece suit that would fit you, Tara.'

'No.'

The single word was out of Tara's mouth before she had time to stop it, and six curious eyes were directed her way, waiting for an explanation. She couldn't tell them her gut response to Liz's innocent offer was all to do with Ryan, though. That she'd been imagining what it would be like to renew an intimacy, with all its associated fervour of needs and desires. But she knew lovemaking would never be the same and she wasn't ready to strip off. There was no way she could expose her body and her vulnerabilities to him. *She definitely wasn't ready.* Not yet.

'Um, sorry. I'd much rather be a spectator tonight.'

Liz threw her an understanding glance, but Tara couldn't bring herself to make eye contact with Ryan.

'No problem,' Liz said quietly. She pointed to the other side of the pool, where her daughter-in-law sat, keeping an eagle eye on Daisy and Bonnie. 'I'm sure Rachel could do with some company.'

As Tara made her way around the pool she saw him on the edge of her peripheral vision, and when she turned to look at him Ryan's eyes locked with hers and she knew exactly what he was thinking. It was like the old days.

He wanted her.

She could see the desire fizzing in his eyes and rippling in the muscles of his slick, bare chest.

He wanted her?

If she was right, what the hell was she going to do about it?

When Ryan summoned up the courage to make an appearance in oversized Hawaiian-print board shorts held up by a tenuous waist cord, with a lime-green bathtowel slung over his shoulders, Bethany was waiting at the side of the pool. He took a moment to search for Tara and noticed her heading for Liz's daughter-in-law. God, she was beautiful. He imagined her in a sexy, skimpy swimsuit moulded seductively to her curves.

At that moment she glanced at him and they connected... She blushed, quickly wheeled herself towards her friend and became engrossed in serious conversation.

What was that all about?

There was definitely a spark. Something new. Something that gave Ryan a morsel of hope he'd not had till now.

But he didn't have time to ruminate.

'Daddy. What's the matter? I want to swim.' Bethany's demand was non-negotiable. 'The water's warm, Daddy. And Christine says I can borrow some of Daisy's floaty things 'cos she can swim already and doesn't need them any more.'

Bethany had obviously had no trouble making friends with the junior members of the Tate family. In fact one of them was doing a fast dog paddle towards them. She climbed onto the step.

'Is that your dad?' The girl wasn't one to mince words.

'Yes,' Bethany said proudly, to Ryan's amusement.

'And is that your mum?'

Ryan's head spun around to look in the same direction as Daisy, but Bethany still had her attention firmly fixed on her new friend.

'My mummy's gone away for a long time to...um... where has she gone, Daddy?'

'To Sydney, darling.' He managed to drag his gaze back to his daughter, but wasn't totally successful in erasing from his mind his imagined vision of Tara's super-fit body in a swimsuit.

'Who's that, then?' Daisy pointed at Tara.

Bethany turned to see the focus of Daisy's attention and her face broke into a broad grin. 'That's daddy's new friend. She's a doctor too.'

'Is she your daddy's girlfriend?'

Ryan was only half listening to the girls' conversation. He felt a tugging on his shorts and looked down at his daughter. She was frowning.

'What, Beth?'

'Is Tara your girlfriend?'

It took him a moment to take in what she'd said.

'No, she's not,' he said, but right at that moment he wished she was.

Daisy climbed out of the pool and came back a few moments later with a pair of blow-up floaties that she plonked in the shallow water next to him, and then swam away to where her young sister had discovered how to blow bubbles under water.

Ryan positioned the inflated devices on Bethany's upper arms.

'You should ask her to be.'

Fortunately he wasn't required to reply as Bethany's attention reverted to the pool.

'Who's coming swimming?' he said with a grin.

Bethany needed no further invitation as she slung her arms around Ryan's neck and they moved smoothly into the water, where they splashed and spluttered and scooted back and forth across the pleasantly warm water.

As Ryan floated in the soothing water he saw Christine slip into the pool and paddle towards him. When she was a couple of metres away she stopped to tread water and nodded towards his wriggling cargo.

'If you want to have a few minutes to swim on your own, I can look after Beth.'

His daughter made the decision for him as she reached her arms out to her nanny and boldly plunged into the water.

'Thanks,' Ryan said, and his gratitude was rewarded with a wink.

'It's not always easy to relax when you have a four-year-old in tow.'

Christine didn't wait for his reply and headed towards the shallow end, where the other girls were playing, leaving Ryan to do laps. And to think…

He glanced in Tara's direction, but she was still engrossed in conversation with Rachel.

The shimmering reflection of the patio lights in the pool danced across her lightly tanned skin and reminded him of an ethereal fairyland. In some ways she had more going for her than many able-bodied women.

Tara was truly beautiful and alarmingly attractive.

She was strong and courageous.

She was intelligent and caring, and often selfless when it came to dealing with those she perceived as being in trouble.

And she would be a wonderful parent, if her dealings with Bethany were anything to go by.

His heart did a clumsy somersault as a startling realisation struck like a king wave in an otherwise calm and predictable sea. He felt totally winded.

Not only did he love her with every fibre of his being but he wanted to spend the rest of his life with her.

He wanted to care for her, to protect her, to be there for her if she needed a shoulder to cry on or to share the beauty of a spring sunrise, the taste of a fresh-picked peach, the gently caressing waves of a balmy ocean on a hot, mid-summer afternoon.

He wanted to be an enduring part of her life again.

But he doubted it could ever happen because Tara had made it clear she didn't want *him* in *her* life in any meaningful or long-lasting way. For her, pragmatism appeared more important than love.

Ryan dived to the bottom of the pool and stroked along underwater until he saw three sets of small chubby feet dangling at the side of the pool.

'Daddy, come on—let's play bucking horses.' Ryan's thoughts were interrupted by the impatient demands of his daughter. He grinned and then rolled onto his stomach, letting Bethany tumble into the water, scooping her up again before her face went under. She gasped, and then squealed with laughter as he lifted her so she straddled his shoulders. He began lurching from side to side.

'More, Daddy, more!' she shrieked as he bobbed her in and out of the pool, splashing great gouts of water in all directions.

The game continued for a few minutes more before they were interrupted by the deep, cheerful voice of Steve.

'Food's up in five minutes, everybody!' he yelled.

Ryan looked around for Tara but she was nowhere to be seen. She must have left the pool area when he'd been engrossed in his watery game with Bethany. He recognised the stab of emotion he felt as disappointment, but knowing what it was didn't make it any easier to bear.

'I'm hungry, and Mr Steve says dinner's ready,' his daughter announced, promptly putting an end to Ryan's introspection. He swam to the steps, deposited Bethany on the top one and lurched out of the pool.

Watching Ryan and his daughter frolicking in Liz and Steve's pool had evoked a mixture of joy and envy in Tara. She felt a little on edge, but also revived. Life was definitely worth living when you could spend a pleasant couple of hours in the company of friends who expected nothing more of you than that you have a good time.

Of course she had no idea what Ryan's expectations were. It was probably big-headed of her to think he had any expectations at all. He was friendly enough, but his focus—and rightly so—had been on his daughter, who was an absolute delight. Maybe she'd imagined the sensual connection she'd felt buzz between them earlier.

She suddenly felt the chill of a clear, moonlit night and realised the front of her shirt was soaking, and she had a substantial damp patch on her trousers from bouncing a small but very wet child on her knees a few minutes ago. Rachel had excused herself so she could help her daughters into dry clothes and Tara realised she should change herself.

She wheeled herself into her hostess's kitchen, where Liz and Christine were tossing salads and adding garnish at the last minute.

Liz looked up when she heard the door slide open. She smiled.

'Enjoying yourself?'

'Definitely.' Tara paused, reluctant to interrupt the food preparation, but she was feeling colder and battled to keep her teeth from chattering. 'I wondered if I could borrow a towel—maybe a pullover? I seemed to have got a bit wet.'

Liz left what she was doing and came close enough to do a full inspection. At that moment Tara could no longer stop the shivering.

'Oh, you poor love. You need a dry change of clothes. Come with me.'

'But—' Liz read her mind and glanced at the food.

'That can wait for a few minutes. Your wellbeing is more important.'

Tara followed her down a passageway and was led into

the master bedroom. Liz spread an array of clothes across the bed, fetched a fluffy towel and said she would leave Tara to get changed. Liz closed the door, but Tara felt more comfortable sliding the lock on the knob to ensure her privacy.

In the *en-suite* bathroom she peeled off her wet clothes and dried herself as best she could, leaving her still slightly damp trousers on. She glanced in the three-quarter-length mirror and quickly looked away. She usually avoided appraising herself naked. In fact she kept away from mirrors that displayed more than her head and shoulders because she was scared of being reminded of what she had lost. Her pale, thin legs were a symbol of the things she couldn't do any more.

Then she looked back and studied the image she saw— broad, lightly tanned shoulders, well-muscled arms, firm rounded breasts and an acceptably flat stomach. She touched her right breast, tentatively at first, and then with a cautious boldness she hadn't experienced since before the accident. She explored the soft milky skin, the crinkled dark area around the nipple, and then the nipple itself, which was suddenly hard and exquisitely sensitive.

A vivid image of Ryan touching, stroking, exploring and pleasuring her flashed into her mind. Like old times.

There was a soft knock on the door and Tara snatched her hand away, grabbing the towel to cover her nudity. She knew she was fantasising, and logic told her that her dream could never turn into reality.

Ryan had his own life to live.

'Are you okay? Do you need any help?' Liz's quiet voice was reassuring.

'No…' Tara cleared the husky embarrassment from a throat that didn't seem to want to work properly. 'I'll be fine. I'm just getting dressed and I'll be out in five or ten minutes.'

'Great. No need to hurry. Steve's estimate was a tad ambitious when he said five minutes. It'll take at least another ten minutes until we're ready to eat.'

'Thanks, Liz.' Tara's voice was back to normal but her emotions certainly weren't. Her thoughts drifted back to her reflection in the mirror, to the body she'd denied had any worth for so long. To the ugly but also to the beautiful. She wasn't usually a negative person, but since the accident she'd been blinded to the fact she had to accept what she was, the good and the bad, before she could move on. It was as if a part of her that had been locked away for more than eight years had been released.

She was capable of feeling attractive.

She had sexual urges.

She had feelings for her ex-husband.

But could they ever be reciprocated?

What was happening to her? Whatever it was, she knew she had to nip it in the bud before she added another complication to her life—which was overloaded with them already. Her moment of self-discovery was overshadowed by confusion as she slowly and methodically dressed. She combed her hair and then ruffled it into some kind of order with her fingers, rubbed her cheeks to restore some colour to her pallid face and then, taking a deep, calming breath, she wheeled herself through the door and back out to the... unknown.

CHAPTER NINE

RYAN suspected it was more than chance that he and Tara ended up sitting next to each other at dinner. Although he didn't have much time to have any kind of personal interaction with her, he was acutely aware of her presence, her closeness, the hint of chlorine mixed with the fresh smell of a light lavender cologne that drifted into his airspace, the aura of sensuality she didn't even know she had.

'Bethany's a real darling,' Liz said as she passed the potato salad down the table.

It was the kind of statement that didn't need a reply and jolted Ryan back to the reality of the here and now.

'I'd second that,' Tara said with a little shyness in her voice, but Ryan had no time to dwell on her comment.

'She's been no trouble at all,' Christine chimed in. 'Considering what she's...'

It was obvious what the woman was about to say, and Ryan felt embarrassed for her as her cheeks turned a rosy pink. 'She's been used to going to day care and having a nanny, so she takes to new people—especially ones she likes,' he added with a smile, 'really easily.'

He glanced over at the small table where the three little girls were quite happily sitting, eating their way through a plate of chipolata sausages, chunks of marinated chicken and several mini-bowls of salad. Bethany whispered something and the two other girls giggled before the threesome resumed their intimate chat. They were getting on like a rabble of Labradors at their first puppy obedience class—exuberant, curious and totally uninhibited.

'She's made new friends in Bonnie and Daisy too,' Liz said thoughtfully. 'In fact I just had an idea.' She glanced across at Gus and Rachel, who were absorbed in their own conversation. 'Bonnie and Daisy are staying tonight. How about Bethany sleeping over too?'

The offer was unexpected, and something Ryan hadn't even contemplated. When he'd taken on his daughter's full-time care he'd decided to spend every spare minute he could with her. But his daughter had certainly been used to staying at her grandparents' before they'd moved interstate. Beth seemed to be more interested in the company of Bonnie and Daisy at the moment than she was in his. And if there were any problems he was only a phone call and at the most ten minutes away.

'I'm not sure.'

Liz sent him a look of understanding. 'Maybe we could ask her? You've got an early start tomorrow, and your list probably won't finish until mid-afternoon, so she'll be here for most of the day anyway.'

'All right. I'll ask her after dinner.' It was a shame to interrupt the girls when they seemed to be huddled in a *tête-a-tête* of whispered secrets and shared laughter.

Liz smiled knowingly as the conversation drifted on to the current state of the economy and how it affected the region's primary producers and the very ordinary performance of the local football team the previous weekend. Before long Liz began collecting dishes. Rachel yawned and Steve unsuccessfully tried to refill Tara's glass. Bethany definitely looked droopy, and Ryan suspected her supreme effort to stay awake more than an hour after her usual bedtime was to do with wanting to keep up with her young friends.

'I'd better see what Bethany wants to do before she falls asleep.' Ryan kind of liked the idea of not having to wake a sleepy child and pack her off to Christine before Beth had even had her breakfast.

Bethany must have heard her name, because she stood up, stretched, and then toddled over on slightly wobbly legs to where Ryan sat. He hoisted her onto his knee.

'Have you had a good time tonight?' Ryan knew the answer.

To the adults' amusement she punched the air with a small fist and said sleepily, 'The best.' She yawned. 'Can I come here tomorrow while you're at work?'

Ryan stroked her hair and then kissed her forehead. 'Would you like to stay here tonight and I'll pick you up tomorrow afternoon after I finish work?'

For a moment Bethany's eyes opened wide and she beamed. 'That would be…' Her eyes crinkled in thought. 'That would be awesome, Daddy.'

Christine had obviously tuned in to their conversation and was already bundling the two other girls together, ready to settle them in for the night.

'Let's get you girls off to bed, then.'

Bethany followed Christine without question, and when the woman returned about five minutes later she was smiling.

'Would you believe they were all too tired for a bedtime story? They're sound asleep.'

'Who's for coffee and cake?' Liz asked enthusiastically.

Tara was the first to refuse.

'I really should be going, Liz. I usually don't stay out this late and I've got an early start tomorrow too.'

Ryan checked his watch. Even though it was only just

after nine o'clock, he wasn't surprised at Tara's comment. He imagined Graham kept fairly close tabs on his daughter's whereabouts.

'Oh, what a shame.' Liz smiled. 'I'll pack you some to take home.'

'I'll be heading off too,' Ryan said, with the idea of helping Tara. He stretched out his hand to Steve and then gave Liz a brief hug. 'Thanks so much for the meal and the company—and for having Bethany stay the night.'

'Make the most of it while you can.' Ryan thought he saw the hint of a wink before Liz added, 'There's nothing like an uninterrupted night's sleep when you're a parent of a pre-schooler as lively as Bethany.' She paused and then put her arm around Tara. 'And don't leave it so long between visits, young lady.'

Ryan barely heard what she said next as she leaned close to Tara, but the gist of it was something to do with having a social life and cutting the umbilical cord. If he'd heard right he couldn't agree more.

And perhaps he could have a hand in broadening Tara's social horizons.

Maybe he could start tonight.

The realisation suddenly struck Ryan that if he embarked on a physical relationship with Tara it would mean a commitment much more binding than his token attempts in the couple of brief relationships he'd had since his second divorce.

Could he handle that?

It would mean significant changes to his already topsy-turvy world.

It would also mean offering Tara a future she could cope with, both physically and emotionally, and their plans would have to be made together.

How would he handle rejection?

In the best way he could. There were no valid alternatives.

He had to be patient, which was the last thing he felt like being at the moment.

Tonight…?

He'd ask her in for coffee, prepare himself for a knock-back, and if she accepted? Well, he'd just let the evening happen.

At that moment Christine appeared with two plastic dishes containing what looked like huge slabs of chocolate cake with a big dollop of cream on the side.

Ryan suddenly began to doubt whether he had the courage to ask Tara back to his place.

He rubbed the back of his neck, took a deep breath and reminded himself he had nothing to lose.

Tara was acutely aware of Liz and Steve standing on their front veranda as Ryan lifted her chair into the car. She turned the key in the ignition with a sense of disappointment. It was a little like the old days when she'd been a teenager and single. Before she'd met Ryan. An outing with friends would sometimes end with the feeling that the night wasn't finished. That there was a party somewhere they could go to, or a nightclub that stayed open until the small hours, crammed full of music and dancing and possibilities.

She felt wound up and ready to party. After all it was Friday night and just after nine o'clock—about the time cities woke up. But country towns like Keysdale closed up for the night.

She sighed. She wasn't looking forward to the prospect of recounting every detail of her night out to her parents, but there was absolutely no alternative.

Glancing in her side mirror in preparation for reversing, she saw Ryan heading towards her.

'Don't forget your afters,' he said with a grin, thrusting
a container in her part-open window.

She wound down the glass.

'Thanks.'

She expected Ryan to head straight for his car but he
lingered, swaying slightly from one foot to the other, as
if he had something to say but hadn't decided whether he
would or not.

'Is there something else?'

'Ah…yes there is.' He cleared his throat.

Tara's curiosity was definitely aroused.

'It's still early and I wondered if you might like to come
back to my place…er…to the motel, for a coffee?'

Tara was totally taken aback by Ryan's bumbling invitation. He was usually so confident and together. She was
the one who was prone to bouts of nerves. In fact her heart
had begun to thud at the knowledge that Ryan could no
longer be *just a colleague*. Whether he knew or not, the
fantasies Tara had had at Liz's, the possibility Ryan could
become her *lover*, had put their relationship on a different
level.

She ached for his strong arms to enfold her in a tender
embrace.

She yearned to feel the passion of his searching lips on
hers.

She wanted him in her bed, exploring the new and re-
discovering what they'd cherished in the past. Ryan was
the only person she wanted to travel the path of her re-
awakening, and there was an opportunity for their journey
together to begin tonight.

'Yes, I'd like that,' Tara finally said.

She let out the sighing breath that had been struggling

for release. Ryan glanced back at the house and she followed his gaze to the veranda, where she was just in time to see the front door close.

'I'll meet you at the Riverside, then.'

'Yep, I'll follow you there.'

When they arrived back at the motel, apart from scattered lights and the monotonous drone of television, the place was quiet. Ryan had followed Tara's slow drive to the motel and she'd pulled up next to his unit. Once Tara was settled in her wheelchair he marched ahead to turn the lights on and crank up the heating as there was a definite chill in the air.

'Welcome to the Dennison mansion,' he said with a grin as she wheeled past him into his unit.

She laughed, but Ryan could tell she was on edge. 'It hasn't changed since last time.' Her voice was a little unsteady, and she had a flush of colour in her cheeks despite the coolness of the night 'Except it's a bit messier. Which makes me think this is a spur-of-the-moment invitation,' she added.

'Right. I haven't had time to organise the soft music, candlelight, chilled wine.' It was his attempt to open the door to the possibility of a romantic evening together. He flicked the switch of the main light but left the softer kitchen light and a small table lamp on.

'That's better.' Tara parked next to the sofa. 'Is it okay if I move to the settee?'

'Yes, of course. Do you need any help?'

She visibly relaxed and smiled with a gentle understanding. Ryan felt content that Tara's hackles appeared to be down. She seemed comfortable in his presence, which was a total turnaround since the last time they'd been alone together.

'Do you mind if I watch how you do it?'

She glanced at him enquiringly. He'd expected at best a reluctant acceptance but she seemed to have acknowledged his ignorance of the practicalities of her disability and was now willing to let him into her world—a world he'd been locked out of for the last eight years. He hoped that at last they were surfing the same wave, aiming for the same place on the shore.

'Why should I mind?'

Tara removed one of the arms of her wheelchair and lifted herself onto the seat with a quiet strength and grace that tripped a switch in Ryan's heart. As she settled—arranging her legs, positioning a cushion at her lower back and moving from side to side until she found the place that was most comfortable—Ryan went over to the small kitchen.

'Coffee and cake?'

'I'd prefer a cup of tea, but a definite yes to Liz's cake.'

'Coming right up.'

Ryan was aware of Tara's gaze following his every move as he boiled the kettle and made the drinks, retrieved milk from the small fridge, rummaged in several cupboards looking for a tray, and finally brought the drinks and set them on the coffee table. He then sliced the rich chocolate cake and served it on two plates with the generous dollop of cream that his kind, multi-talented receptionist had provided.

'Looks delicious—although Liz might well be killing us with kindness. All that sugar and cholesterol… I'll have to work out for twice as long tomorrow.'

'You work out?'

'Every day, if I can.'

Tara forked a piece of cake into her mouth and then licked a trace of cream from her upper lip. Ryan could barely suppress a groan of pleasure, but he managed to keep a straight face as she continued with her explanation.

'I have a small gym of sorts in a room off my bedroom. It used to be a walk-in wardrobe. I do weights. I have a rowing machine, and another piece of motorised equipment a bit like a bike, which helps maintain flexibility and mobility in my legs.'

Wow. No wonder Tara was in such good shape. She'd always been slim, but now she was much fitter. She leaned over to reach for her cup. Ryan's gaze flicked to the smooth, inviting expanse of Tara's neck and the seductive fullness of her perfect breasts.

'You're a very beautiful woman, Tara, and I don't just mean on the outside,' he said quietly, and then paused, gathering his thoughts. There was something he needed to know but he didn't want to upset Tara by asking insensitively. He decided to go ahead anyway. 'I don't understand why you've not married again or at least had a boyfriend? Because you were so adamant you didn't want me after the accident I hoped you'd find someone else.'

She looked at him for a moment, before focusing on the wall opposite.

'I… Because…there was never anyone…er…' Tara cleared her throat, her eyes damp with threatening tears. 'I didn't fall in love again.'

Ryan swallowed some cake that threatened to stick in his throat and then followed it with a mouthful of tea. Tara had not had any serious relationships since they'd parted because *she hadn't fallen in love again*? He felt guilty, and partly responsible for what must have been eight years of loneliness. No wonder her attitude to him when he first arrived had been distant.

But *he* had been Tara's first and only love and she his. He'd already told her he'd never loved Shannay.

'You know that I never stopped loving you and that I still do.' It had to be said—he wanted to make it clear—before friendship turned into something more. He moved a little closer to her and grasped her hand. She mesmerised him with her deep grey-blue eyes. Was it desire he saw in their depths?

Tara leaned across, rested her head on Ryan's shoulder and sighed.

'Oh, Ryan. Why did you have to come back? I had my future mapped out. I thought I was as happy as I could be. And I honestly can't think of love. Not now. It's too hard.'

Ryan gently stroked her silky hair and resisted the temptation to put words into her mouth. *She* had to say it.

He waited.

'There are so many reasons not to even begin a relationship with you. You live and work in the city, you have a daughter. My life…' she paused and a single tear trickled down her cheek '…and my family, my roots, are here.' She moved away so she was staring directly at him. 'There's too much at stake. I'm in a wheelchair, Ryan. I have different needs in a relationship to a normal woman.' A second tear followed the track of the first and she wiped away the moisture with the back of her hand. 'But—'

'Can we try?'

She shivered and then closed her eyes.

'Yes,' she answered in a husky whisper.

Ryan lowered his head and planted the gentlest of kisses on her cheek, feeling close to tears himself. This was one remarkably brave woman, and she deserved so much more from life than being tied to her parents and the family farm.

'Do you really want to?'

The question was loaded with deep respect and a profound love Ryan had never experienced before—not even with Tara. In a way it was a positive that what might be a new beginning, depending on Tara's answer, would be the gateway to a whole new life; a challenging one, certainly, but one that had the potential to have more fulfilling highs to balance the inevitable lows. He had no idea whether it could work, but the only way to find out was to try.

'I think I do.'

Ryan's heart burned in his chest and a warm glow spread to every tingling part of his body. He'd had no idea he would feel so elated, so blown away with euphoria at the sound of those four simple whispered words. He hugged her close.

'Here? Tonight? Can we start to learn to love each other all over again?'

Tara's reply was husky, but her answer sent his heart racing with anticipation and joy.

'We can only try.'

Tara knew the emotional stakes were high and she was taking a huge risk, but for once she was making an important decision for herself, and she was determined to follow her heart regardless of the consequences.

'Do you want to finish your dessert? I can make a fresh cup of tea.'

Tara was grateful for Ryan's sensitivity and amazed she felt so comfortable with him, considering they were about to embark on something that could be the basis of a whole new life for Tara.

But definitely first things first.

He was looking at her with tenderness and an empathy she'd never seen from him before. In some ways it was just like old times, but in other ways they had so much to learn about each other. He had the insight to let her call the shots—at least initially. The problem was she didn't know what the shots were. All she knew was that she nursed a white-hot desire, originating somewhere deep in her chest, filling her with a need she'd only dreamed of experiencing over the past eight long years of celibacy. And she'd given herself permission to act on that need.

Oh, how she wanted him.

He ran his fingers softly down her cheek.

'Your skin is so smooth and kissable.'

Before she had a chance to respond Ryan sighed, and kissed the track he'd made with his fingers. His touch was a magical mix of gentleness and wonder. It sent shivers down Tara's spine so acute she felt a trembling in her unfeeling toes.

She opened her mouth as his lips explored, and his tongue probed and searched until he found a spot so arousing she stiffened and a guttural moan escaped from her throat.

'Shall we go to the bedroom?' he said, kissing her again. 'Remember I'm still on L plates.' He sent her a giftwrapped, cheeky smile and raised his eyebrows.

She laughed. The thought of two worldly wise adults in their mid-thirties who had been married before—to each other—starting over like a pair of star-crossed virginal lovers had a levelling but also a very titillating effect. She had no expectations because she didn't have any idea what to expect. All she knew was, whatever happened, she wanted it to happen with Ryan.

'Yes, and it's okay to carry me.'

He simply nodded, before scooping her up in his arms and then tenderly laying her on the bed. He was primed for her already, but he gave no hint of impatience.

Tara lay on her back and reached out to Ryan. 'Come here. I want to undress you,' she said, with a shyness that dissipated as soon as her lover moved close.

Ryan lay on the bed beside her and she rolled onto her side as her deft fingers worked their rekindled magic on the buttons of his shirt. She ran her palms down the bare skin of his chest, savouring the warmth of his body and the wiry texture of his chest hair. He grasped her upper arms in a token gesture to stop her before she unzipped his fly and peeled off first his trousers and then his straining briefs.

He helped her complete the task and smiled cheekily as he said, 'My turn now.'

She rolled onto her back and he began to undo buttons and zips and hooks until he'd exposed her nakedness—and, remarkably, she didn't feel embarrassed at all.

Being with Tara—being *in bed* with Tara—brought Ryan back to a time when making love with her had been the affirmation of a love so strong, so exquisitely all-encompassing, it had never failed to take his breath away. Was tonight going to prove that Tara had the same depth of feeling for him as he had for her? Was it going to mark the beginning of a new commitment to each other?

Perhaps he was expecting too much.

He ran his index finger gently down the sensuous curve of her neck and took a sharp intake of air.

'My God, you are so beautiful, Tara.'

She looked at him and smiled with a warm flush of what he hoped was desire that seemed to wash over her whole body.

'And so sexy—'

She put her finger up to his lips to silence him and then moved her hands slowly, seductively down his chest to his groin, in a way that made him feel he was about to explode with the passion he'd bottled up over all the years of being apart.

He moaned.

'Stop. I want this to last,' he whispered, before nibbling her earlobe. 'I want to savour every moment.' *And to rediscover the glorious past but also to find out how she had changed.*

Ryan explored nearly every inch of Tara's body, and they discovered that in the parts where sensation was unaffected by paralysis her response was heightened. Ryan straddled her hips and blew gently on one of her nipples. It was enough to have her gasping for more.

'Don't stop,' she demanded as her grip tightened on his backside.

So he sucked and nibbled until she cried out in an uninhibited agony of pleasure, and then he continued his journey all the way down to her toes. Although she couldn't feel his caresses she watched, initially with a look of trepidation on her face and then with apparent delight.

Ryan remembered how she'd loved him massaging her calves, finding the pressure points on the soles of her feet and sucking her toes. Although it was different now, those same caresses sent a bolt of need through his whole body and he wanted…he wanted tonight to last for ever.

'Can I roll you over?'

She nodded and grinned. 'It's wonderful, Ryan, beyond my dreams.' She sighed. 'I never thought—'

'I did,' he said softly as he gently helped her move.

When she was lying on her stomach they found pleasure points behind her ears, on the tips of her shoulders, down the length of her spine and, surprisingly, just above the small of her back at approximately the level of her injury.

They made amazing love, with Ryan watching every moment of her pleasure—and the experience was beyond his dreams. At that moment he knew he would move heaven and earth to win her back.

Tara was incredulous. Although she didn't climax she felt a deep warmth inside when Ryan orgasmed. The most amazing thing, though, was that her disabilities didn't seem to matter any more. She was a desirable and sexy woman. And the person who had brought about the transformation was Ryan…her ex-husband…the man she'd tried so hard to erase from her memory and her heart.

'Shall we finish the cake?' Ryan said dozily as he nuzzled into the crook of her neck. 'I'm hungry.' He chuckled as she raised her eyebrows. 'For food.'

'Okay,' Tara said, and a few moments later they sat propped up in the small double bed, sipping tea and spooning cake into each other's mouths. 'And thanks for tonight.'

'The pleasure was all mine.' Ryan leaned over and licked the crumbs that had settled between Tara's breasts. 'We'll definitely have to make a habit of this.' He grinned. 'Coming back to my place for coffee and cake.'

'I wish it was that easy.' Some of the pleasure and the sense of freedom at being with Ryan evaporated. If she continued to see Ryan her parents were going to be her biggest obstacle. How would she tell them? What would she tell them? She certainly wasn't about to reveal she'd slept with him. But she wanted so much to continue their relationship—at least for the time being.

'What are you thinking?' Ryan said softly.

'I'm wondering what the future holds for us. Revisiting the physical part of our relationship means a great deal to me. Since the accident I've never felt attractive in that way.' She took a deep breath. 'But to be perfectly honest I want more from a relationship than sex, no matter how good it is.'

She blushed. It had obviously taken a good deal of courage to lay her thoughts on the table.

'I want more too, and I'm sure if we both want something enough we can make it work—no matter how many obstacles are thrown at us along the way. Maybe we should just take it slowly until we get our heads around what's happened tonight?' He reached down and found her hand, intertwining his fingers in hers, but their conversation was interrupted by the sound of his phone ringing. A worried expression appeared on his face.

'Hello? Ryan Dennison.'

Tara could only hear it was a woman's voice, and that Ryan was punctuating an animated monologue with single-word replies. Just before he ended the call he said, 'Thanks for telling me, Liz. I appreciate it.'

'What did Liz want?'

'She rang to let us know that your parents rang her, worried about you and the fact they couldn't raise you on your mobile.'

'Oh, I think the battery's flat.' Tara sighed, her heart suddenly sinking to her boots. She turned on the bedside light and looked at her watch. 'Oh no—it's nearly midnight and I bet they've stayed up for me. I'll have to ring them.'

'What will you tell them?' Ryan said, reaching for her hand.

'I have absolutely no idea, but I don't think they're ready for the truth.'

CHAPTER TEN

TARA couldn't handle trying to explain her way out of spending the evening and half the night with Ryan, so when the phone rang five minutes later he answered it.

'She's just left,' he fibbed, with a calm confidence that Tara could never have managed. She could hear the edginess in Jane's voice, though she could only make out a few of her words.

'I'm sorry I kept her out so late. I understand how worried you must be. But we just got talking and time ran away from us. It's entirely my fault, Mrs Fielding.'

He winked as Tara balanced on the side of the bed to put her shoes on. With Ryan's help Tara had managed to get dressed in double-quick time, and as soon as the phone call ended she'd be in her chair, out the door and on her way.

'*I'm* not sorry.' She mouthed the words and Ryan smiled as, still naked, with his phone pressed to his ear, he walked through to the living room, brought in her wheelchair and positioned it where she could easily slide in to it. He was a fast learner.

A few moments later he finished the call.

'Was Mum okay?' Tara was feeling guilty about giving Ryan the task of bending the truth.

'Anxious, but otherwise quite reasonable. I could hear

Graham in the background and I think your mum knew he'd blow his stack if he got near the phone.'

'Thanks.'

She reached out and stroked her fingertips over the smooth curve of Ryan's buttocks and nuzzled a kiss into the wiry fuzz of his pubis. She inhaled the intoxicating scent of soap and their recent lovemaking. As he began to stir he pulled away.

'Hey,' he said softly. 'Don't get me going again or your parents will be organising a search party. We'll have the local police knocking on the door.'

He pulled on his briefs and slipped sandals onto his feet.

'They'd do that, you know. It's not as outrageous as you think.'

'Which is why we should be getting you on the road.'

Tara wheeled towards the door and let Ryan open it for her. It didn't take long to load the chair, settle in the car and dissolve into Ryan's brief but deeply evocative kiss.

'Now who's delaying my departure?' she said with a wink.

Ryan moved away from the car and sighed.

'Go,' he said. 'Or I won't be accountable for my actions.'

She laughed, wound up her window and reluctantly pulled away, thinking how wonderful it would be to spend the night with Ryan, wake up to the comfort of his warm body pressed against hers, to be his lover. To be his wife?

As she turned into Hill Park Road she wondered if there was any point in dreaming. She was battling to make sense of what tomorrow would bring, let alone speculating about the rest of her life. Her lovemaking with Ryan had been a life-changing event for her. Did Ryan mean it when he said he wanted more from a relationship than simply sex? What she really wanted was the full romantic, happily-ever-after fantasy of marriage to Ryan. She wondered if the reason she'd never contemplated it with anyone else was because she had the same feelings for her ex-husband as before the accident. Had she nursed that frustration for all these years without realising?

And there were so many things standing in the way. It would mean a huge change for both of them, mainly because of her situation, and Tara was fearful of any significant alteration to her structured, rigid lifestyle.

But Ryan had said, 'If we both want something enough we can make it work.'

It made sense and it could happen if… Maybe…?

A dozen questions tumbled through her mind as she turned into the road to the farm.

She needed a clear head to think about the options, and right now she had her parents to deal with.

Both Jane and Graham were waiting on the veranda when Tara pulled up in front of the homestead. Lights blazed from just about every room in the house, and the yard spotlight illuminated the driveway and its surrounds for about a hundred metres.

She knew the atmosphere at the Fielding farm would be tense and she wasn't looking forward to the inevitable confrontation. At any other time the lights would be welcoming, but under the present circumstances Tara had a sudden understanding of the blinding numbness kangaroos felt when they froze in headlight beams.

A moment after she stopped the vehicle Jane was at the window, with Graham hobbling not far behind. Her mother opened the door and leaned close, whispering so that her husband wouldn't be able to hear.

'I wasn't worried, love—well, only a little—but your father started getting a bee in his bonnet about ten-thirty.

I told him you'd ring if there was any problem, but when we couldn't get through on your mobile—'

'You imagined the worst. I'm sorry, Mum. I didn't realise the batteries in my phone were flat. I should have let you know what I was doing.'

The choice was between an apology and an argument, and Tara didn't have the energy to protest. Saying sorry to Jane was unlikely to placate her father, though. He was leaning on his crutches just behind Jane, the deep furrows in his brow and the tight line of his mouth reflecting his mood. He was not a happy man.

'Where the hell have you been...?' He paused to squint at his watch. 'Until half past midnight?'

'Shush, Graham. Let's get inside out of the cold. I'll make us all a cup of hot chocolate.' Jane hesitated. 'Or maybe it would be better to wait until the morning to... er...talk.'

Tara had a sinking feeling in the pit of her stomach. She wasn't quite drowning but it was no easy task to come up for air.

'Mum, Dad.' Tara's gaze shifted to her father. 'I appreciate you staying up for me. If there was any way I could get into the house without your help... Um...I'm tired and we all have to be up before dawn so I'd really like to go straight to bed.'

'Yes, love. That would be best. I'll get your chair.'

Graham remained silent, but it wasn't difficult to guess how discontented he was. He turned and headed towards the house, and as he reached the steps of the veranda she heard him mutter, 'I'm not going to let Ryan Dennison take her away from us again.'

Ryan had a full operating list on Saturday, and with the addition of two emergencies and a ward round of his pa-

tients in the hospital he probably wouldn't finish his working day until well into the afternoon. With his late night in
the company of Tara—gorgeous, seductive, wonderfully
sexy Tara—and his full-on day he felt exhausted. The
prospect of the long drive back to the city with his lively
young daughter minus her nanny had become less attractive as the day wore on.

During a short mid-afternoon break he made a decision. First he rang the motel to check his room was available that night, which it was, then he rang Liz Tate's place.
He spoke to Christine and apologised for being late. Ryan
had agreed he would take over the care of Bethany when
he finished work on Saturday.

'I plan on staying over and driving back tomorrow. Does
that suit you?' he asked Christine.

'Thanks, but I think I'll stick with the arrangement of
going back on the first train Monday morning.'

'Good, that suits me. You'll be back in time to pick Beth
up from day care?'

'Of course,' she assured him, and he wondered what he
would do without her.

The practicalities sorted, his mind began working overtime. He desperately wanted to see Tara before he left, and
toyed with the idea of asking her to go on a picnic with him
and his daughter. Tara and Bethany had seemed to get on
well the previous evening, and Beth would act as a buffer
between them. Not that *he* needed one, but he thought it
might be reassuring for Tara's parents that they wouldn't
be on their own.

At that moment the scout nurse appeared in the doorway of the surgery staffroom.

'Your next patient's ready to go, Dr Dennison.'

Right—two more patients, a quick ward round and he'd
be finished for the day.

'I'm on my way.'

He'd ring Tara before he picked up Bethany. That would hopefully give them time to talk without the distraction of his garrulous daughter.

Ryan crossed his fingers as he strode back to the operating room. He desperately wanted Tara to agree to his plan.

When he'd finished his hospital duties and dialled Tara's mobile phone number he felt fluttering in his stomach and had to concentrate on stilling the tremor threatening his hands.

Tara's phone rang a dozen times and then went to voice-mail.

'Damn,' he muttered, ending the call without leaving a message. He needed a moment to compose one, which was more difficult than he thought.

Last night was wonderful and I'm suffering every moment I can't be with you.

The truth—but way too corny. He knew Tara's mind and it would put her off for sure.

Ring me. I need to talk to you.

Too abrupt. After she got over being annoyed she would most likely worry.

I'm staying over tonight and wondered if you could join Bethany and me for a picnic brunch. Ring me when you can.

That was more like it. Letting her know his plans without being too wordy. She'd have time to think about whether she wanted to accept his invitation before she answered. And if she didn't phone that afternoon? He'd be devastated.

He was about to press redial when the phone began ringing. It was Tara's number. He knew it even without the prompt from the small screen. He cleared his throat.

'Hello…Tara.'

'I'm returning your call. Sorry I couldn't answer. I was just winding up the dairy tour. We've had a busload of Japanese tourists. With Dad out of action, Mum and Pete—from the neighbouring farm—have been doing the milking and I'm the tour guide. I think you know what I mean when I say Dad's not great with his people skills.'

She paused, but began again before he could get a word in. Was she nervous?

'What did you want? I can't speak for long. I have to go back to the homestead and help Mum with the Devonshire teas.'

'Oh.' He'd finished his work for the day but she was obviously still going full-pelt through hers, and he suspected she'd probably started before dawn. With her late night she must be totally exhausted, he thought. 'I can ring back later.'

'No, back at the house Dad seems to be watching my every move. Best if we talk now. At least I've got a bit of privacy.'

Ryan heard the rumble of a vehicle and the gentle lowing of contented cows.

'How will you get back?'

He could *feel* Tara's all-knowing smile and imagined what she was thinking—that he didn't have a clue—well, maybe not much more than a smidgeon of a clue—about the practicalities of her life.

'I'm on the quad bike. Mum helped me and is on her way back to the house. It was weird, though. The visitors seemed to be more interested in me and my disabilities than the milking. I could tell they wanted to take photos but were too polite to ask. So when I gave them permission they went wild with their cameras. I felt a bit like I was on a celebrity photoshoot.'

Ryan was smiling now. Her enthusiasm for the farm and letting others share it was palpable.

'Sorry, what did you want? I'm talking too much.'

Which didn't worry Ryan. He could listen to her all day.

'I'm staying over in Keysdale. I didn't fancy the long drive this afternoon and I wondered if you would like to come with me and Bethany on an early picnic tomorrow? I thought about ten, and I'd have you home before the afternoon milking.'

There were only a couple of moments of silence before she replied, but it seemed like an age to Ryan.

'Um…'

'I understand if you have to check with your parents.' Silence again. 'And that it's short notice, but—'

'Yes, I'll come.' There was a note of defiance in her voice. 'I'd love to. Will you come and pick me up or would you like me to come to the motel?'

Ryan had been expecting her to *um* and *ah* and was surprised by the confidence of her reply. It was as if he'd handed her a pair of scissors to finally sever the apron strings. Even if she hadn't completed the cut yet, she was at least on the way.

'Whichever you'd prefer.'

'Maybe I'll go to your place. I doubt Dad would give you much of a welcome, and it would be easier for me if we took my car. Would that be okay? I'm pretty sure we haven't any tourist bookings tomorrow. I can bring scones. What time did you say?'

It was like conversing with a tornado. He had to catch his breath, and he wasn't the one talking at a hundred miles an hour.

'About ten?'

'Fine. I have to go now. Mum will be wondering where I've got to.'

'I'll see you tomorrow, then.'

'Looking forward to it,' Tara said breathlessly, and then hung up.

With a contented sigh, Ryan put his phone back in its cover. He felt as excited as a five-year-old going to a birthday party, and he imagined his daughter would feel just the same when he told her.

It hadn't been as difficult as Tara thought. Her father had been busy with the accounts in the small office at one end of the back veranda when she'd broached the subject of the picnic with Jane. After her mother's initial surprise she'd actually sounded pleased about the planned outing the following day.

'Don't worry about your father's reaction. I'll deal with him. You just go out and enjoy yourself,' she'd said with a gleam in her eyes. 'It's about time you started having a life away from the farm and your work. And I like Ryan. I always have. The truth is I was sorry when you divorced.' She'd paused, reached for Tara's hand and gave it a gentle squeeze. 'You seemed so much in love.'

Tara realised she'd never really talked to her parents about the important things in her life. Of course she knew what a powerful influence her father's strong will had on his wife, but her mother's open support of her seeing Ryan came as a surprise to Tara.

'We were.'

'And still are?'

Tara blushed. She couldn't lie to her mother.

'I thought as much.'

Jane had then gone on to explain her worries about what would happen to Tara when she and Graham became too old to look after her. She revealed that Graham's injury had precipitated talk of them retiring and moving away from the farm. It was one of the uncertainties about their future Tara hadn't even considered.

'I hoped you would marry again—to someone like Ryan!' She'd paused, giving Tara a chance to let the revelation sink in. It was powerful stuff. 'But any men who showed an interest you, you pushed away or your father frightened off.'

The conversation had finished when Graham limped in, asking for a cup of tea, but Jane had said more than enough.

Marry again...to someone like Ryan.

They'd talked of retiring, of selling the farm.

The whole Fielding family dynamic was on the verge of changing.

These were the thoughts scuttling through her mind as she drove along the highway towards Keysdale. Yes, she loved Ryan. In one night he'd released her from the prison of her body and proved she could be attractive, sexy, desirable—things she'd believed she'd lost when her back had been broken and her spinal cord irreparably damaged.

And how did she feel about spending time with Ryan's daughter? Nervous? Uncertain of Ryan's expectations of her? She knew, from the brief contact she'd had with Bethany, that the child seemed to like her and was easy to get on with—not prone to tantrums or overly protective of her father. Her concerns were more about Ryan, and she had a niggling feeling the picnic might be some sort of test to see how she coped in a family scenario. Maybe she was reading too much into the situation and she should feel honoured that he wanted her to spend time with and get to know Bethany better. Yes, she *did* feel honoured, and was looking forward to the picnic.

As she pulled in to the driveway of the Riverside her reverie was interrupted—by the sight of a beaming four-year-old sitting on the step waiting for her. As soon as she saw the car Bethany leaped to her feet, and probably would have run out to meet her if her father hadn't appeared in the doorway and scooped the little girl up in his arms. Ryan's grin was wider than his daughter's.

Her worries dissipated and she wondered how she could have had doubts about Ryan's motives.

When Tara stopped the car Ryan released the squirming bundle and they both came down the path to meet her, Ryan's long stride keeping pace with Bethany's chubby-legged run.

'She's been ready since eight-thirty and must have asked me how long until you get here about a thousand times.'

'Oh, poor Ryan. And I bet you wanted the extra time in bed.'

He leaned into the window and kissed her softly on the cheek whispering, 'Only if I can share my bed with you.'

She giggled. He was flirting again and making her feel ten years younger. She glanced down at Bethany, who had begun to express her youthful impatience by pounding the passenger door with her small fists. Ryan got the message.

'I know,' he said with a laugh. 'In my dreams—for today at least.'

'Mmm… Pity.' Tara decided it was time to change the subject. 'Are you ready to go? If you are it will save getting the chair out and I can drive.'

'Yes, I have a picnic hamper, disguised as a cardboard box, and a small coolbag I borrowed from the hospital. I won't be a minute. Oh, and I'll need to strap Beth's booster seat in.'

Ten minutes later the food was packed in the luggage space next to Tara's wheelchair, Bethany was safely strapped in the back seat, and Ryan, in the front seat, was unfolding a map.

'I'm not sure where to go. There are a couple of places on the river that aren't too far away and have wheelchair-friendly walk trails.'

Tara glanced at the map and pointed to a spot about twenty kilometres south, where the river seemed to splay out into a small lake.

'Rainbow Pool,' she said without hesitation. 'It's a beautiful place—plenty of room for Bethany to run around in, an adventure trail and sheltered picnic tables.'

'Sounds ideal. Let's go.'

They turned off the highway onto a narrow sealed road that wended its way into the forest. The sun shone brightly but the tall jarrah and marri trees cast mid-morning shadows across the road. Just before they reached the picnic area the trees thinned, then opened out onto a grassed clearing running alongside the sparkling waters of a small lake that seemed to be fed by a tumble of water at the far side.

The ground was firm, flat and easy for Tara to negotiate. She'd brought her manual chair, which was more robust than the electric one; comparing the two was a bit like the difference between a mountain bike and a slick city touring cycle. Ryan unloaded the car. He carried the box and gave the coolbag and scones to Tara while Bethany skipped along beside them both, humming the theme tune of a pre-school TV show.

Tara felt happier and more relaxed than...well, she couldn't think of a time she'd been more content with life since the accident. She sighed.

'Hungry?'

She was about to say yes, she was starving, because she'd been working in the milking shed and hadn't had any breakfast, but Bethany got in first.

'I'm as hungry as a...um...hippa-pot-mus.'

'Wow, and I thought I was really hungry.' Tara chuckled. The little girl brimmed over with excitement.

'Sun or shade?' Ryan asked when they'd travelled the short distance to the picnic area.

'Has Bethany got a hat?'

There was no need to answer as Bethany pulled a floppy denim hat edged with tiny embroidered yellow flowers from her matching backpack. She placed it on her head and pleaded, 'Can we *please* sit in the sun, Daddy?'

He glanced over at Tara, who was already wearing a hat. 'And I managed to keep her still enough this morning to slather on some sunscreen. Do you mind sitting in the open?'

She shivered. There were still remnants of the early-morning chill in the air and the sunshine would be welcome.

'Yep, definitely.'

Ryan wore knee-length canvas shorts and a black tee shirt with a Bali logo on it. His baseball cap was slightly skewed, which Tara thought was cute. He looked gorgeous in his casual gear. In fact the whole package conveyed the same relaxed contentment *she* was feeling.

The area was deserted—wrong time of year, wrong time of day for crowds—but Tara imagined if more picnickers arrived they might easily assume she, Ryan and Beth were a typical family. In her dreams…

They parked next to a rough-sawn plank table and Ryan began unloading food.

'What's to eat?' Tara asked, curious to know what was in the various bags and packages.

'It's very simple. I called in to the markets yesterday afternoon.' He gave a running commentary as he unpacked each item and held them up for inspection. 'Fresh-baked bread rolls, shaved ham and salami, salad greens, some cheese, sundried tomatoes and for dessert—strawberries and fresh cream. Oh, and your mum's scones.'

By the time he'd finished Tara's mouth was watering and her stomach growled.

'Looks positively delicious.' He'd certainly remembered what she liked.

He handed her and Beth paper plates stacked high with mouthwatering food and then served himself. He settled on the broad timber bench seat with Bethany perched on his knee. They ate until they were full to overflowing, and as soon as they finished Beth was itching to explore.

'Will you come for a walk with me?' The child's question was directed at Tara.

Tara glanced at Ryan. 'Shall we pack up and then go exploring? I could do with the exercise. I didn't have time for my normal gym routine this morning.'

'Why don't you and Bethany set off for a walk? There's a bitumen track just over there. I'll pack up and follow you in five or ten minutes,' Ryan added with enthusiasm.

Could she?

Ryan trusted her with the care of his daughter, even if it was only for ten minutes.

Yes, of course she could. It wasn't as if they were perched on a cliff or next to a raging sea. It was a level sealed path meandering around a mirror-smooth lake.

'Will she be all right?' Tara looked across at Ryan and raised her eyebrows.

'You mean will Beth run into a grove of prickle bushes or climb a tree and not come down?' He tickled his daughter and she laughed hysterically. When she settled down he sat her on his knees so they were facing each other and said, quietly but firmly, 'You can go for a walk with Tara if you stay close to her all the way and don't go off the track. Do you think you can do that?'

'Yes, Daddy,' she said seriously.

'Tell me what I just asked you to do.'

'Don't go off the path and...um...hold onto Tara.' Looking over at Tara, she began to giggle. 'So she doesn't go in the prickles or climb a tree.'

Ryan seemed satisfied with her answer. She was certainly a bright child and, despite her energy, had been well behaved so far.

'She'll be fine,' he said. 'And if I haven't caught up with you in ten minutes just turn around and come back, and make sure I haven't got stuck in the prickles.'

Bethany was already at Tara's side, waiting for instructions. She reached out to hold Tara's hand—obviously the normal thing she would do when going for a walk with an adult. After Tara had demonstrated that she needed both hands to propel and steer her chair they decided on a compromise, where Beth walked on the path and stayed in Tara's sight.

A few moments later they were on their way—on a journey of discovery.

'What's that?' Bethany said as she stopped to look at a bright yellow fungus clinging tenaciously to a dead tree stump.

'It's called a fungus.'

'Fungus. Ooh, look—there's 'nother one...and 'nother.' She stopped to examine a two-metre-wide spiderweb spanning the pathway just above her head. 'Can't see the 'pider. Might be a redback. Better be careful.'

She turned, waiting for Tara's instructions.

'It's not a redback's web. They live in dark places and have a different sort of web. If you get a stick we can make a way through. A lot of spiders only come out at night.'

'Oh, so he's having a sleep and doesn't mind if we smash up his house?'

Tara was lost for words, not having a clue how to answer the not unreasonable question. She decided to use the 'change the subject' technique.

'Look over there, Bethany. Is that a little beach?'

Up ahead about five or six metres of scrub opened up to expose a sandy beach.

'I'll go and look.' Bethany began to run.

'Not too fast. Wait for me.' Tara picked up speed and reached the beach just as Bethany made another exciting discovery.'

'Come and have a look. There's tiny, tiny little fishies in the water.'

In the blink of an eye the little girl had slipped off her sandals and was wading in the shallows, ankle-deep in the water.

'No, Beth!'

But she was too late. Bethany leaned over and took a single step—which must have been enough to make the steep bank which was dangerously close to the shore crumble. The child screamed as she floundered in water at least a metre deep.

What Tara did next was a reflex reaction.

She pushed her chair hard into the soft sand and when she reached the water tipped the chair over on its side. The strength of her arms broke the fall and in an instant she was dragging herself into the water.

'I'm coming, Beth.'

She might not be able to walk but she could certainly swim.

She dragged herself into the freezing lake and grabbed the child, who was still splashing and sputtering. She clutched Beth to her side and manoeuvred awkwardly onto dry ground. As she took a moment to catch her breath she felt strong warm arms encircling both her and Beth, dragging them further up the beach. Beth gasped and then started sobbing. Ryan released his grip on Tara and hugged his shivering daughter to his chest.

'What happened? Are you all right?'

'Sorry. Sorry, Daddy,' Bethany managed between sobs. 'I—I wanted to see…' she took a deep gasping breath '…the little fishies.'

Tara's heart went out to the terrified child. She was trying to take the blame. But it was Tara's fault. *Useless, hopelessly inadequate Tara's fault*.

The old doubts came flooding back in a torrent. She could never be an effective parent. Bethany could have died because of her crippled legs, her false hopes and impossible dreams. To think she could live any kind of useful life as a wife and mother was pure fantasy. Her one blissful night with Ryan had blinded her to the reality of the rest of her life. She couldn't burden Ryan with a lifetime of looking after her. He had Bethany to care for, as well as a full-time job. It was fanciful to think he had anything left for her. Nothing had changed. He needed a wife who was complete.

She started trembling uncontrollably.

'Are you hurt anywhere?'

With his free hand Ryan began feeling for bumps, sprains and broken bones.

'I'm fine,' she said brusquely. 'Just help me into the chair and take me back.' She looked up into his bewildered eyes for a moment. Any longer was too much to bear. 'I'm so sorry… I—'

His finger resting lightly on her lips effectively silenced the flood of words that seemed to have stuck in her throat.

'No one's to blame and there's no harm done. You'll feel much better when you're warm and dry. It's been a shock, but nobody's hurt.'

He lifted her into her chair, placed Bethany on her lap, and then stripped off his tee shirt and wrapped it around them both as best he could. Then, despite Tara's protests, he pushed them all the way back to the car, sat them both in the back seat and drove back to Keysdale with the heater on full. During the trip they were silent. Even Bethany was subdued. And when they arrived at the motel unit Ryan offered only token resistance when Tara told him she wanted to go straight home.

'When can I see you again?' he asked as he wrapped the fleece jacket he'd just brought out from the motel unit around her still damp shoulders.

She reluctantly accepted his help to lift her out of the back seat and into the driver's before dealing with Beth and removing the booster seat.

Taking comfort in reclaiming some degree of control, Tara turned the key in the ignition. The longer she spent with Ryan, the harder it would be to break away.

'I think…er…I'll let you know.'

Now was not the time to try and explain the raw emotions tumbling through her mind. She needed time to put her thoughts in order, to restore a sense of reality, to formulate how to tell him there was no way a relationship could possibly work without sacrifice—the sort of painful and life-changing compromises that would tie Ryan to her in a way she wasn't prepared to accept. She wouldn't survive in a one-sided relationship, and that was what it would be. Ryan would be accepting second best—as a lover, a wife and a mother for his child. Although she'd had to adapt to some degree of dependence on her parents she felt the balance of give and take had evened out over the years. She paid her way; in fact her income had helped save the farm when it was close to bankruptcy, and now her father was out of action she was actually working hands-on.

She had little to give Ryan.

Her love wasn't enough.

Wanting with all her heart and soul to have her own child didn't qualify her to be a parent. She'd proved that this afternoon, when Ryan had entrusted her with the care of his daughter and Bethany had almost drowned. How could a woman who was reliant on a wheelchair for mobility possibly look after a totally dependent baby, an unpredictable toddler, a boisterous child? She'd made the mistake of beginning to believe in her own daydreams. With a detached eye she could see how wrong she had been to even fantasise.

And the sex!

Yes, it had been fantastic. But the novelty would wear off. Half her body didn't respond to the physical stimulation they'd both always found so arousing before the accident. Ryan had suffered enough. She didn't want to be responsible for the compromises he would have to make if they tried to heal the deep wounds of their past. She didn't have the energy or emotional fortitude to launch into a high-stakes relationship that had every chance of ending in heartbreak for both of them.

It was better it ended now.

'Goodbye, Ryan,' she said as she reversed away from him, wondering how long it would take this time to glue together the pieces of her shattered heart.

Ryan felt as if all the air had been forced out of him by one massive blow to his chest. Just when he'd thought he was making progress with Tara she'd closed herself off from him, and for no logical reason. Was she so entrenched in the predictable routine of her life that she was running scared? Did the prospect of change frighten her? Was she so tangled up in guilt about Bethany's dunking that she'd lost sight of the fact they'd been making progress in their tentative renewed relationship?

He suspected the incident with Bethany had broken Tara's spirit and eroded her confidence, but he was just as much to blame as her, letting his daughter go off with Tara alone. He should have known Beth often went off track when she got excited. If Tara hadn't been there and acted so swiftly Bethany could have drowned. But when he'd tried to explain the barrier between them had strengthened.

How could he convince her he still loved her and would do anything to win her back?

He owed her big-time, but she had left him with a look that suggested a broken heart all over again. He couldn't live with that, and had to work out a way to get through to her. Maybe he'd start by presenting her with the practical. All the things they could do to make their future viable.

Then a thought suddenly popped into his bewildered mind.

Pippa Morgan.

Tara cared deeply about her patients and especially Pippa. Maybe he could get through to her by means of tapping in to her love of medicine and devotion to her patients.

At the very least it was food for thought, and Ryan vowed he wasn't about to give up the only woman he had ever loved without a fight.

He would use any legitimate means available to win her back.

CHAPTER ELEVEN

RYAN had arranged to meet with Liam Taylor, the rheumatologist who was treating Pippa Morgan. He'd seen the young woman the previous week and her MRI scan had confirmed her right hip was so damaged by the relentless disease she'd suffered from childhood it was only a matter of time before she would be dependent on a wheelchair. If that happened it would probably be downhill from there. At nineteen, when she should be at the peak of good health, her bones would begin to crumble, her muscles waste and her fighting spirit would have to be super-strong to survive.

Surgery wasn't a cure, but it would definitely improve Pippa's quality of life. Ryan wanted to make sure that all the other options had been tried. A hip replacement was a major operation, not without possible complications, and he predicted Pippa's recovery would be slower than normal because of the disease affecting other joints.

Ryan sat in his consulting room at the end of his morning session at St Joseph's and reread the MRI report, intermittently glancing at the images on his computer screen.

The ring of his telephone broke into his reverie.

'Yes?'

'It's Dr Taylor to see you,' the receptionist informed him. 'Shall I tell him to go through?'

'Thanks, Pat, send him down to my room.'

A few moments later Liam Taylor knocked softly on his door before walking into the room. Ryan stood, shook his hand and gestured for him to sit down. Once the pleasantries were done with they got down to business.

'I can offer her pain relief and restoration of at least some of the mobility of her joint with surgery. But it won't be without some trade-offs. I wanted to check with you to make sure there were no other options for the girl.'

Ryan passed the MRI report to the rheumatologist, who studied it carefully and then looked up to meet Ryan's questioning gaze.

'You have copies of the letters I've sent to her treating GP?'

'Yes. You probably know I've started sessional work in Keysdale, and I've had several discussions with Dr Fielding about Pippa.'

Mentioning Tara made his heart lurch. She'd barely spoken to him since the picnic, despite his frequent pleas not to blame herself for Bethany's misadventure. Of course *he'd* been upset as well, but no harm had come of the incident.

She'd closed her ears and her heart to mention of anything other than work, though. It was three weeks now, and he'd almost given up on any plans he'd had to get through to her.

'Then you know she's come to the end of the line with non-surgical treatment?'

'Yes—unless there's something new. I understand she's even had a trial of an experimental drug.'

'Unfortunately I've gone as far as I can with her, and if you think you can help her with surgery, and Pippa agrees, then I'm with you all the way.'

'That's what I wanted to hear,' Ryan said with a tentative smile.

'Of course she'll need detailed anaesthetic assessment.

She's been fairly lucky so far in not developing systemic disease.'

'Like fevers, rashes, muscle involvement?'

'Right. Her disease seems to primarily affect her joints, and the most active inflammation and destruction has been in her hips.'

'If she agrees to surgery I'd want to do it here in the city.'

'Yes, of course, and I'd follow her progress.'

'I'd appreciate that.'

'Had you thought of involving her GP in the operation?'

'Pardon?'

'There've been several interesting trials involving young adults who have suffered long-term diseases like rheumatoid. Getting the patient and the family or carers as well as the GP together for regular case conferences and involving them directly in the decision-making improves the outcome of not only surgery. They also apparently respond better to other treatments like medication and physiotherapy. In fact I've tried it on a couple of my more resistant patients and there seems to be some substance in their conclusions.' He cleared his throat. 'Of course my experience is only anecdotal.'

'Sorry, I don't quite understand how the GP fits in with what you've told me.'

'The GP works actively with the surgeon and patient, including being present and ideally assisting in the operation. The couple of calls I've had from Tara Fielding suggest she cares a great deal about her young patient. It's just a way of extending the doctor-patient relationship—hopefully with some added benefits for Pippa.'

'Oh, I see.'

Ryan had shelved the idea of involving Tara in the OR at Keysdale. The way they'd been communicating lately was matter-of-fact, and usually by e-mail or telephone if it involved patients. On a more personal level their exchanges had been almost non-existent. But… It might be a way to get through to Tara—through her work and dedication to her patients.

'I'd be interested to read the studies. Could you give me details of the publications?'

The doctor smiled. 'I can do better than that. I'll send my receptionist down with photocopies this afternoon.'

They wound up the meeting and after Liam Taylor left Ryan was infused with a sense of hope not only related to a positive outcome of Pippa Morgan's surgery but also discovering a viable way to crack the seemingly impenetrable barrier Tara had erected between them.

He tapped his pen restlessly on his desk and then sighed.

He really had nothing to lose.

He was prepared to put everything into winning Tara back.

Tara scrolled down her e-mails. She'd had a busy day, and it was time to go home, but she preferred to tidy up the loose ends of her week before she left. Thankfully the list of e-mails was relatively short and she worked through them easily—until she reached the last but one.

It was from Ryan.

Even though she knew it would be work-related her heart thudded unevenly and her throat was suddenly dry. The mere thought of her ex-husband did strange things to her body she didn't quite understand. Or maybe she *did* understand. She'd tried to ignore all the signs that indicated she wasn't over him. Despite the rational part of her brain reinforcing that a future with Ryan was impossible, her bruised and battered heart didn't seem to get the message.

She took a deep breath and pressed the mouse button to open the e-mail.

It took her barely a minute to read it…twice—though she still didn't quite comprehend what he was asking.

It was about Pippa Morgan.

Right. She got the bit about the results of the MRI. She understood why he'd want to tell her about the urgent need for surgery, that a date had been set for two weeks from Saturday at St Joseph's, and that he'd organised the involvement of Liam Taylor in her post-operative recovery.

It was the last two sentences that threw her totally off balance.

I want to talk to you about the possibility of you coming up and assisting with Pippa Morgan's operation. Can we meet when you've finished consulting and I can explain?

Assisting with Pippa's operation?

How on earth did he expect her to manage that? Even if she agreed to the outlandish request it just wasn't feasible. For a start she doubted her chair would be allowed into the theatre area, let alone into an operating room. There would be too great a risk of contamination, particularly with major surgery involving bone. And if she did get into the theatre to actually *assist* would mean some sort of wheelchair modification to raise her to the level of the operating table.

Tara hadn't been in an operating theatre since her hospital residency.

Regardless of all her other objections, what if she panicked? She'd turn out to be an inconvenient liability rather than a useful addition to the surgical team. In fact she felt anxious just thinking about it.

Had Ryan lost his marbles completely?

After quickly checking the last e-mail she shut down her

computer and gathered her things in readiness for going home. What Ryan was suggesting was impractical, physically impossible and totally out of the question. And she didn't need to tell him face to face. She scribbled a note, deciding she'd do the polite though maybe the cowardly thing and leave a message with one of the receptionists to give to Ryan when he left. But as she swivelled her chair the door opened and Ryan stood in the doorway, smiling with a confidence that bordered on smugness. He obviously wasn't counting on a knock-back.

'Hi,' he said as he stepped into Tara's room. 'Did you get my e-mail?'

Tara cleared her throat, but it didn't prevent the roughness in her voice.

'Yes, just a few minutes ago. And the answer is no.' She paused and took a measured breath. 'I don't think you realise how difficult everyday tasks are for me, let alone the long drive to Perth, and getting some stranger to help me get mobile. And I doubt very much I'd be allowed anywhere near the operating theatres in a wheelchair.'

Ryan moved one of the patients' seats so it was directly opposite Tara and sat down. The intensity of his gaze unsettled her, although he was still smiling.

'I've thought of all that.'

'What do you mean?'

'I've done some research and I'm sure it can be done.' Ryan's expression suddenly changed and he looked like an excited schoolboy about to explain his way out of some way-out, non-curricular misdemeanour to an uncompromising teacher. That vulnerability she rarely saw was back, and Tara decided the least she could do was listen. In fact she was a little curious about this *research* he mentioned.

'Go on.'

'Well, the issue of getting up to Perth is easy. I'll take

you back with me after my afternoon clinic here on the Friday. If it's more convenient to use your car I'm okay with that. I'd leave my car at Liz's.' He hesitated a moment, as if he needed an extra dose of courage to continue. 'And you can stay overnight at my place.'

'But…' There were a hundred and one reasons why that wasn't a good idea. Being in the same physical space as Ryan spelled danger. And he had the effrontery to grin.

'Christine will be there to look after Beth, and I'm sure she'd be able to help you with anything you can't manage yourself. That's if you're too embarrassed to ask me to help.'

'You mean with things like showering?'

He shrugged.

'Yes, that sort of thing. My shower's a large one and could easily accommodate a shower chair and two people.'

She blushed at the thought of actually sharing a shower with Ryan.

He seemed to tune in to her thoughts.

'I'm not going to come on to you, if that's what you're worried about.' He rubbed his forehead and his face went into neutral, then he grinned again. 'Not unless you want me to.'

'I don't,' she said, a little more abruptly than she'd planned.

'And even if you did I suspect the presence of Bethany and Christine would be a passionkiller.'

He had a point, but she *didn't want to*. Did she? The thought crossed her mind that at some subliminal level maybe she did. And that was what was alarming her. As well as how, so far, Ryan had thought of everything.

'That's all very well, but I can't see any way of the hospital protocol accommodating my presence in the operating theatre.' She glanced down at her legs and succumbed to a rare moment of resentment. 'I haven't got the use of my legs. Remember?'

Tara regretted the sarcasm as soon as the words were out of her mouth. But she'd loved surgery as a student, and it seemed a little cruel that Ryan was dangling an unreachable carrot in front of her. He seemed to be undaunted by her response, though. He reached out to put his hand over hers. It was an incredibly tender gesture and, whatever Ryan's motives, she realised he knew her better than anyone. He really cared.

'No, I haven't forgotten. You know I'll never be able to forget.' He squeezed her hand. 'But I thought this might be a way to show you I can help you move forward.'

He'd touched on the aching, throbbing centre of her life. She was stagnating and had little chance of moving anywhere. The rut she was stuck in was growing deeper as time passed. Her time with Ryan—their lovemaking and the cosy domesticity they'd shared on the picnic—had opened a window to another breathtakingly amazing world that she'd naively thought was within her reach. But she'd been wrong. With Bethany's near-drowning, the window had been slammed shut.

'So tell me how you plan to make this outrageous plan of yours a reality? I know you're capable of multi-tasking, but I think you'd need a magic wand to pull this off.'

'It's not been as difficult as I'd thought. St Joseph's are quite happy to have you working in their theatres as long as first you fill out the paperwork and second you don't compromise any OR procedures and rules which might interfere with patient safety.'

'Okay, the first part is straightforward, but I can't see—'

'Just let me finish before you make any judgements. You can take your wheelchair as far as the change rooms, where one of the nurses can help you get into theatre gear.

Then you transfer into one of the hospital chairs. Before you scrub up you'll need to transfer onto a purpose-built adjustable operating stool.'

'An operating stool?' The idea of such a thing sounded fanciful to Tara. 'What on earth is that?'

'Well, it just so happens…' The pause was tantalisingly prolonged.

'Come on, you've got to explain now you've started.' Much to her annoyance, he'd captured her attention.

'There's an anaesthetist on their staff who had major back surgery a few years ago and was left with weakness in both his legs. He was so determined to get back to work after the operation he had a special seat made. I checked it out last week and got the okay for you to use it as long as Peter isn't rostered on.'

'A stool? I'd topple off if I lost my balance—'

'It has a back rest and removable arms. Mobility is controlled by a joystick and an electric motor, similar to your motorised chair.'

'Is it height-adjustable?'

'Yes, with the same kind of joystick.'

'What about a sterile operating field? I'd be scrubbed and gloved.'

'A sterile soft plastic cover is put over the stick.'

Tara was intrigued. Ryan had covered every objection she had. The prospect of getting back into the operating theatre and helping Pippa Morgan excited her and she was tempted. Ryan read her reaction in her eyes.

'I have some journal articles you might like to read that suggest there is benefit to patients with problems like Pippa's if her entire medical team is involved in major therapeutic events like surgery. Recovery is faster and results are better.'

His research and planning baffled her. She didn't know what to say.

'So you'll at least think about it?' His look was pleading, as if her saying yes meant a lot to him. He'd gone to an awful lot of trouble.

'I'll think about it.'

'Good.' Ryan's posture relaxed and he smiled. 'I need to know by the Wednesday before Pippa's op.'

'I'll think about it,' Tara repeated as she gathered up her bag and medical case and put them on her knee, hoping Ryan got the message their conversation was over. He moved out of the way as she propelled forward.

'I'll help you with your chair.'

Ten minutes ago, before their remarkable discussion, Tara probably would have been annoyed at his offer, but her mind-set had subtly changed. Just because Ryan had presented her with the possibility of not only helping her patient, but also the opportunity to do something she'd never dreamed was achievable, it didn't mean she wanted their relationship to go any further than a professional one. But she was definitely tempted by his offer.

'Thanks,' she said, and they walked together along the corridor. 'I appreciate it,' she added quietly, and was relieved Ryan didn't answer.

Before she embarked on the homeward journey Tara took a few minutes to glance at the summaries of the articles Ryan had given her.

Was helping Pippa worth letting Ryan think he could organise her career?

Maybe it was.

It certainly gave Tara something to think about.

CHAPTER TWELVE

IT HAD taken a week of agonising uncertainty for Tara to make the decision to spend the weekend with Ryan, but once she'd made up her mind there was no looking back. It was for Pippa, she kept telling herself, not for her or Ryan. Although she had some trepidation at staying the night at Ryan's house, she felt reassured Christine would be there.

And Bethany? Tara hadn't seen her since the picnic, and wondered if their relationship had changed. She'd just have to wait and find out.

To her surprise, her parents hadn't shown as much resistance as she'd expected. She thought Ryan's ongoing care and surprising understanding of what it was like for a farmer to be out of action might have softened Graham's attitude. Her mother had been all for it after she'd grilled Ryan on the phone and convinced herself he was capable of looking after her precious daughter. She said Tara deserved a break away from the farm and the opportunity to experience something she really wanted to do. She'd also assured her they could manage without her. The fact that Graham, now confident and much more mobile in his fibreglass walking cast, could do a few light chores made it easier.

The sun was low in the sky as Tara drove out of the clinic car park on Friday afternoon. Squinting against the harsh light, she took a right-hand turn towards Keysdale instead of her usual left to go home to the farm.

Her heart thudded with nerves but she wasn't about to change her mind. Going to the city to assist an orthopaedic surgeon with a major operation on one of her patients would have been routine for most doctors, but for Tara... She saw it as a turning point, a breaking away from the rigid routine of her life, and was grateful to the man who was about to make it happen.

Although she was staying with Ryan for two days, *and two nights*—she shivered at the thought—he'd promised to be the perfect host, in the role of a good friend only. He planned to take her out to dinner on Saturday night and Tara was looking forward to spending time with him.

As she pulled into the motel drive Ryan opened the front door of his unit. He must have been looking out for her. He walked down to meet her.

'Hi,' he said with a smile that set her heart dancing. 'I hope you're okay with me driving?'

'That's fine. I'm actually a bit weary. It's been a busy week.'

'For me too. I'm looking forward to an early night, so I hope you don't mind if we get some takeaway and maybe watch a DVD.'

'Sounds perfect.'

'That's if Bethany's settled for the night,' he added with a frown. 'Christine told me she's been hyped to the max today, so it's the luck of the draw whether she wears herself out or gets her second wind.' His frown deepened. 'But I guess we have to cross that bridge when we come to it.'

Tara couldn't help admiring Ryan for caring so much about his daughter's happiness and wellbeing. Despite his commitments he definitely wanted to be there for Bethany, no matter how much effort he had to put in.

He leaned into the car so she could grasp his neck while he lifted her out. He performed the task smoothly, as if he'd done it a thousand times before. Tara often resented the times when she had to relinquish her independence but today she felt comfortable and safe.

Too comfortable. Too safe!

She reminded herself she had vowed to keep a safe emotional distance from Ryan, but his physical closeness was getting in the way.

'Are you all right? You look a bit pale.'

He must have homed in on her uneasiness, but at least she wasn't blushing.

'I'm fine. As I said, it's been a long day.'

'Well, the sooner we get on the road, the better.'

Definitely—so she didn't have the opportunity to change her mind.

Tara's concerns about spending the evening with Ryan were unfounded. When they arrived at Ryan's apartment Beth was an over-excited dynamo.

After she gave Tara the grand tour of the apartment, which involved at least half an hour in the child's room examining every toy in her toybox, every item of clothing she possessed and all the other accoutrements that came with being a four-year-old girl going on fourteen, they had a quiet meal in the living room, watching Beth's favourite DVD.

'Time for bed,' Ryan announced at half past nine, which was at least two hours after her usual bedtime.

The noisy protest was as fierce as if he'd asked her to spend the night in a dark, cold dungeon full of spiders.

'No!' she announced dramatically. 'I'm not tired.'

The argument went on for a good ten minutes until Beth finally conceded to go to bed only if Tara read her a bedtime story. After two stories, a request for a drink and dealing with a bladder that seemed to be as active as its owner, she finally settled. By that time Tara had little energy left for anything more than a soothing hot shower and a comfortable bed.

'I'm totally bushed,' Tara apologised.

'What would you like to do?' Ryan said, with a face that gave nothing away of what he was thinking.

'Have a shower and go to bed.'

She might have been mistaken, but she thought she noticed the slightest twinkle in Ryan's eyes. It didn't last long, though.

'I'll get Christine to help.'

Christine had a large bedroom, with space enough for a couple of comfy chairs, a small television and a desk. Ryan had arranged for her to share the second bathroom with Tara for the weekend, which was a much more sensible arrangement than using Ryan's *en-suite*.

'No. I'm sure I can manage. It's a huge shower recess, and I see you have support rails in all the right places.' Tara suspected Ryan had had the rails installed especially for her benefit, but she wasn't about to question him on it.

'Okay, just holler if you have any problems.'

'I doubt that I will.'

Their interaction was all very civilised—as if Ryan was putting up a mate for the weekend; as if nothing more intimate had happened in the past than an enduring platonic friendship.

And that suited Tara just fine.

She managed the shower without needing help, and had no trouble transferring to the double bed. Although it took her a while to get to sleep, when she finally did she slept soundly, and was woken by a soft knock on the door. She glanced at the clock. It was just after six but already the sun was streaming through her window.

'Come in,' she said sleepily as she rearranged her pyjama top and pulled the covers up to her chin. When the door opened her reaction to seeing Ryan in boxers and a crumpled tee shirt with a steaming cup in his hand took her by surprise.

The intimacy she'd tried so hard to avoid was standing in her doorway, with a grin on his face and an aura of good times past and possibilities for the future floating around him. If he'd come across and kissed her she wouldn't have been accountable for her actions.

But he didn't. He was playing the perfect gentleman.

'I'm afraid it will have to be cereal for breakfast. Christine and Beth are still asleep, and I wanted to get to the hospital in plenty of time for you to familiarise yourself with the set-up. Make sure you're comfortable with the equipment and the OR routine.' He cleared his throat and walked over to place the cup on her bedside table. 'Though I doubt much has changed over the past ten years or so.'

'Cereal's fine.' She wanted some time alone to make sense of the *rightness*—that was the best way she could describe her feelings—of having Ryan in her bedroom at just after dawn on a Saturday morning, when she'd normally be helping with the milking. But he seemed reluctant to leave. She positioned herself a little higher in the bed and leaned over to get the cup. 'And thanks for the tea.'

'My pleasure. Is there anything else I can get you or do for you?'

'No, thanks. I'll be fine. As soon as I've finished this I'll get dressed and come through for breakfast.'

Ryan finally got the message and left her to the task of getting ready for a day working in the operating theatre, helping to give Pippa a better quality of life, working side by side with the man who had made it all possible.

She had every right to feel nervous and excited and happy all at the same time.

But she had no more time to ponder the unusual turn her life had taken. The door burst open and Bethany charged in like a rocket, all sparks and multi-colours and the joy of living that only the young were capable of exuding by the bucketload.

'I love you, Tara,' the little girl said as she flung her arms around Tara's neck and kissed her cheek. 'And I wish you could stay here all the time.'

'I love you too,' she whispered as a tear trickled down her cheek.

But any thoughts of the future with Ryan and his darling daughter were pure fantasy.

She lifted Bethany off the bed gently.

'I need to get dressed now, so why don't you help your daddy make some breakfast?'

'Ooh, yes.' Tara could almost see the cogs of Beth's young brain turning as she catapulted out of the room with almost as much energy as she'd entered.

Pippa's surgery, though complicated, went smoothly. The operation took just over three hours, but at the conclusion there was an air in the OR of a job well done, thanks to the surgical team and especially to Tara.

She'd been amazing. From the time she'd appeared in her dark blue scrubs to the moment she'd stripped off her gloves and gown and wheeled out of the theatre there'd been an incredibly positive buzz in the air.

Ryan touched her shoulder and she swung around.

'Thanks, Tara. You were great. Amazing, in fact.' He smiled and swung open the heavy theatre door.

'I should be thanking you. You're the one who went to so much trouble to organise it all,' she said as she manoeuvred through the opening. 'It went well?'

'Better than I expected. I am hopeful Pippa's new hip will last for at least twenty years.'

'And then? She'll still be a relatively young woman.' The joy in Tara's eyes dimmed for a moment.

'Unfortunately I can't predict that far ahead, but we'll just have to cross that bridge when we come to it.' Ryan stopped outside the recovery ward. 'I just want to see if Pippa's awake and tell her the good news. Then I can meet you in the staff lounge.'

'Do you want me to talk to her parents? They'll be desperate to know how things went.'

'I was going to do that after checking on Pippa—maybe we can go together.'

Tara nodded. 'I'd like that.' She hesitated a moment. 'And can I come in with you now?'

'Of course.' Ryan opened the door.

Pippa was one of two post-op patients in a room that was usually a hubbub of activity during the week. Although there were usually one or two surgeons who did elective sessions on Saturday morning, the theatres were geared mainly for emergencies on the weekend.

A nurse stood on the side of the bed, writing down her patient's obs, and the anaesthetist was at its head, monitoring the girl's breathing. They both looked up and acknowledged Ryan and Tara's presence as they entered the room. Pippa's endotracheal tube was still in place, but she was breathing spontaneously and beginning to cough, a sure sign the tube was ready to come out.

'You two did excellent work today.' The anaesthetist looked up briefly before focusing his attention on the task of removing the tube and replacing it with an oxygen mask.

'Is this going to be a regular thing? Your assistant would certainly be an asset here.'

Ryan glanced at Tara, whose cheeks had taken on a rosy pink colour. She certainly deserved the praise and had no reason to be embarrassed.

'No, I'm afraid this is a one-off,' Tara said huskily. She paused to clear her throat. 'I live and work three hours' drive away. Ryan went to the trouble of setting all this up because Pippa's a very special patient of mine.'

The anaesthetist glanced at her and smiled. 'Well, if you ever change your mind…'

Just then Pippa produced a loud gurgling cough and opened her eyes.

'You're in the recovery ward,' the nurse said, a tad louder than was necessary. 'And your wonderful doctors are here to tell you how the surgery went.'

Pippa closed her eyes briefly, before opening them again and turning her head slightly so she could see both Tara and Ryan.

'Do you want to tell her the good news?' Ryan asked softly.

Tara nodded and smiled as she positioned herself as close as she could to the bed. She reached out to grasp the young woman's hand and felt the slightest squeeze.

'It all went really well, Pippa. It will take a couple of days, but Dr Dennison tells me you'll be up and running soon.'

Ryan leaned a little closer. 'And I'll be in to see you to-morrow.'

Pippa managed the slightest smile and then closed her drowsy eyes again, signalling she'd absorbed all the information she could for the moment.

They both quietly left, and Ryan was suddenly over-whelmed by a sense of shared accomplishment, a special bond with Tara that went deeper than any professional relationship ever could.

He needed to talk to her—without the distraction of his over-exuberant daughter.

And he would do it over dinner tonight.

Ryan had informed Tara he'd booked a meal at one of his favourite restaurants, renowned for its superb food and casual atmosphere. And it was within walking distance of his apartment.

'They won't turn you away if you're wearing jeans, but I guess you'd call the dress code "smart casual",' Ryan had told her the previous week, when they'd been making the final arrangements for the weekend.

Knowing she didn't need to dress in a designer outfit was a relief, and she felt satisfied as she looked in the mirror after putting on her make-up and scooping her hair up from her neck and fixing it with a gold clasp. She certainly wouldn't win a beauty contest, she thought as she retouched her blusher and removed a speck of errant mascara, but she scrubbed up okay if you didn't look too closely at her from the waist down.

She rarely had the opportunity to go out, let alone to a city restaurant with a dangerously handsome man she was beginning to care about more than she'd planned. She kept telling herself she was looking forward to the outing, but there was a persistent niggle of anxiety in her gut she just couldn't seem to shift.

Her weekend with Ryan seemed too perfect—being fussed over by both Ryan and Christine; all the compliments on the good work she'd done in the operating theatre; being wined and dined by an attractive man; having the opportunity to spend some quality time with a delightful four-year-old who seemed to adore her. She had the ominous feeling it was all too good to be true. The reality was when Ryan dropped her home the following evening nothing would have changed. But she could see no alternative, and resolved not to let her ruminations interfere with her evening.

As she wheeled herself out of the bedroom and along the short passage to the informal living area she could hear the sounds of Christine in the kitchen, no doubt busy preparing a meal for herself and her young charge. Ryan sat with his daughter on his knee, watching television. They both looked up when they heard the bump of her chair as she stopped and put on the brakes.

Ryan's eyes were as wide as his daughter's.

'You look like a bootiful princess,' Bethany said with her usual candour.

'And I second that.' Ryan gently moved his daughter and stood up. He wore charcoal pants, a plain navy shirt and a china-blue silk tie. He looked gorgeous. He grabbed his jacket from the back of the chair and slipped it on before planting a kiss on Tara's cheek. 'In fact you look stunning,' he added as he ran the tip of his tongue along his bottom lip.

'Thank you. And you scrub up pretty well yourself.'

It was Tara's way of making light of the compliment and it apparently worked. Ryan chuckled.

'Are you ready to go, then?'

'Sure am.'

After hugs from Bethany, and a farewell wink from Christine, they set off. The restaurant was two blocks away, on the same street as Ryan's apartment, and when they arrived the place was buzzing. Ryan was on first-name terms with the head waiter and they were guided to a table in a corner with plenty of space for Tara's chair.

'Well, at least you don't have to worry about pulling out my chair,' Tara teased.

Ryan smiled without answering as he handed her the wine list.

'What would you like to drink?' he finally said.

'Just water to start, and maybe some wine with dinner. Unlike you, I have to *drive* home, and I don't want to be picked up for being out of control on a public footpath.'

He laughed as he poured chilled water into a crystal tumbler.

When the wine waiter appeared Tara didn't hear what Ryan said to him, but he came back in a few minutes with a long-necked bottle of a local boutique beer.

'I hope you don't mind?'

'No, of course not.'

Tara couldn't help noticing Ryan wasn't fully at ease. There was something on his mind. Something that was probably none of her business but that made her feel a little edgy as well.

'Is something the matter?' Tara wanted to clear the air.

Ryan paused and cleared his throat.

'Part of the reason I asked you out to dinner was that I wanted to talk to you. Over the past month you've been treating me like a leper, and we've not had a chance to talk through what's happening with us since I've been in Keysdale.' He traced lines in the condensation on his glass and then looked up with an expression that went right to the centre of Tara's heart.

'I…er…don't understand what you mean,' Tara said with her heart thudding.

'We need to talk about the accident. We were both so young, and I didn't want to hurt you and go against what you told me you really wanted, but I know now that walking out on you was the wrong thing. I should have tried harder to convince you we could survive, no matter what. I also believe you weren't telling me the truth when you said you didn't love me. I think it was just your way of ending a relationship you believed had no future.'

Ryan looked down at his drink and took a slow sip.

Tara was close to tears.

'No. Don't blame yourself. If anyone's to blame it's me. I wasn't thinking straight and I felt sorry for myself. I could only see a future abounding with problems. I knew you felt really bad about the accident, and I didn't want to fuel your guilt by having you living with me as a daily reminder of what happened. I shouldn't have sent you away, and I was kidding myself by thinking the love had gone for me.' She reached out for Ryan's hand and gave it a squeeze. 'I've always loved you and I always will.' Her voice dropped to whisper. 'And I'm sorry for the damage I've done to our relationship. I wish there was some way—'

'Maybe there is.' Ryan's eyes were bright with hope and anticipation. 'It's something I've thought a lot about over the last few weeks and I hoped I could tell you tonight.'

Tara raised her eyebrows and waited, wondering what he was about to say.

He grasped her hand with both of his, adoration shining from his eyes.

'I want to move to Keysdale.'

'But—'

'No, hear me out. It wouldn't happen overnight, but I'm sure I could secure a consultancy in Bayfield—and Rob Whelan has offered me more sessions already. It's a wonderful place for Bethany to grow up in. We could build a house together, work together. Have babies together.'

Tara was overwhelmed, but she had no doubt in her mind that Ryan was serious.

'What exactly are you saying, Ryan?' Her grip on his hand tightened.

'My darling Tara, I want a second chance. I want us to be married again.' He paused. 'And I'm certain it could work for all of us, as the family we always wanted to be.'

Tara didn't know what to say. Ryan was offering her the future she'd always dreamed of and she couldn't think of a single reason not to accept his proposal.

'Well?' he said with a grin on his face.

'Yes, Ryan. Of course I'll marry you.'

Right on cue the waiter arrived with two frosted flutes and a bottle of vintage champagne.

'How did you do that?'

He laughed, leaned across and planted a lingering kiss on her lips.

'That's my secret.'

EPILOGUE

Two and a half years later.

IT TOOK six months to build the house but, like everything else in Ryan's plans, he'd wanted it to be perfect. It had all the features to make life easy for a wheelchair-user, her husband, her stepdaughter and their new baby—and as many children as they wanted. It even had a self-contained unit for Christine under the same roof.

The rambling single-storey country home stood proudly in ten gently rolling, lightly wooded acres in the foothills about ten kilometres cast of Keysdale. There was a small paddock that was home to a gentle rust-coloured Shetland pony named Missy, an orchard of a dozen young fruit trees, and a well-tended herb garden. Today, being a very special day, a little six-year-old girl sat quietly on the veranda, gently rocking a cradle, waiting for her grandparents to arrive.

The girl looked around and smiled as the front door opened.

'I'll look after Brodie while you go and get changed,' Tara said, as Beth ran over to plant her trademark sloppy kiss on Tara's cheek.

'You look beautiful.' Bethany's smile broadened into a grin.

'Why, thank you.' She wheeled herself over to her four-month-old baby, who was sleeping peacefully. 'Your daddy just told me the same, so I guess it must be true.' She laughed as she gently ran her index finger over the baby's forehead.

She was talking to herself as Beth had already run inside.

Her mind began to wander as she settled into the rhythm of gently swinging her darling sleeping son.

So much had happened since Ryan had asked her to be his wife and the mother of his children. Her initial reaction had been one of incredulity. She'd half believed Ryan had lost touch with reality when he'd outlined his plans for their life together. He'd managed to counter every objection she'd made, though, with ideas that were not only rational and well thought out but *possible*. He'd turned what she'd thought was an impossible dream into the reality of the 'happily ever after' life she was living right now.

'Who would care for Bethany?'

'Christine's prepared to work for us for as long as we want her.'

'You want more kids. I can't—'

'Why not?'

And the living breathing evidence was lying in the cradle in front of her.

'My work?' By that time her protests had lost a little of their clout.

'If we're going to set up house in Keysdale there's no need to change anything—unless you want to. I've already approached the boards of both the Keysdale and Bayfield hospitals and they're open to the idea of setting up an operating theatre so you can assist. My guess is that you'll have other surgeons clamouring for your services.'

She now worked two days in the clinic, as well as two

sessions a week in the OR. She'd also recently embarked on part-time post-graduate studies in anaesthetics and hoped to add Diploma of Anaesthetics to her list of qualifications two years down the track.

At that moment Tara's thoughts were interrupted by a six-year-old dynamo dressed in a frothy pink dress and an aura of excitement. She burst through the front door, closely followed by her father.

'I heard a car coming. Is it Nan and Gramps?' the child said breathlessly as a vehicle pulled up in front of the house.

The baby stirred and Tara lifted him into her arms as Jane and Graham Fielding climbed out of the newly acquired four-wheel-drive they'd bought to tow their state-of-the-art caravan around Australia. Selling the farm seemed to have been one of the best things they'd done in their lives.

Jane barely stopped to hug Bethany and say hello to the adults before she had her grandson in her arms. Graham stood behind them and extended his hand.

'It's a beautiful day for a naming ceremony,' Graham said. 'Let's hope there are one or two more little ones to come.'

Tara glanced at her husband, aware of the flush of heat in her cheeks.

Ryan winked, moved over to where she sat and kissed her.

'I don't see any reason why not,' Ryan said.

* * * * *

A sneaky peek at next month...

Medical Romance™

CAPTIVATING MEDICAL DRAMA — WITH HEART

My wish list for next month's titles...

In stores from 1st June 2012:

❏ Sydney Harbour Hospital: Bella's Wishlist — Emily Forbes

& Doctor's Mile-High Fling — Tina Beckett

❏ Hers For One Night Only? — Carol Marinelli

& Unlocking the Surgeon's Heart — Jessica Matthews

❏ Marriage Miracle in Swallowbrook — Abigail Gordon

& Celebrity in Braxton Falls — Judy Campbell

Available at WHSmith, Tesco, Asda, Eason, Amazon and Apple

Just can't wait?

MILLS & BOON®
Book Club

2 Free Books!

Get your free books now at
www.millsandboon.co.uk/freebookoffer

Or fill in the form below and post it back to us

THE MILLS & BOON® BOOK CLUB™—HERE'S HOW IT WORKS: Accepting your free books places you under no obligation to buy anything. You may keep the books and return the despatch note marked 'Cancel'. If we do not hear from you, about a month later we'll send you 5 brand-new stories from the Medical™ series, including two 2-in-1 books priced at £5.49 each and a single book priced at £3.49*. There is no extra charge for post and packaging. You may cancel at any time, otherwise we will send you 5 stories a month which you may purchase or return to us—the choice is yours. *Terms and prices subject to change without notice. Offer valid in UK only. Applicants must be 18 or over. Offer expires 31st July 2012. **For full terms and conditions, please go to www.millsandboon.co.uk/freebookoffer**

Mrs/Miss/Ms/Mr (please circle)
_____

First Name
_____

Surname
_____

Address
_____

_____

Postcode
_____

E-mail
_____

Send this completed page to: Mills & Boon Book Club, Free Book Offer, FREEPOST NAT 10298, Richmond, Surrey, TW9 1BR

Find out more at
www.millsandboon.co.uk/freebookoffer

Visit us Online

0112/M2XEA/REV

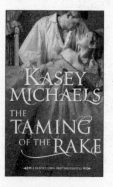
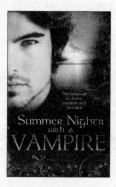
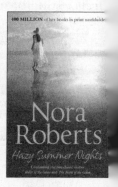